About the

Susan Meier spent most of her twenties thinking she was a job-hopper – until she began to write and realised everything that had come before was only research! One of eleven children, with twenty-four nieces and nephews and three kids of her own, Susan lives in Western Pennsylvania with her wonderful husband, Mike, her children, and two over-fed, well-cuddled cats, Sophie and Fluffy. You can visit Susan's website at susanmeier.com

Harmony Evans writes sexy, emotional contemporary love stories. She won 'Debut Author of the Year' for the Romance Slam Jam 2013 Emma Awards and was a double finalist for the 2012 *RT* Reviewers' Choice Awards. She lives in New York City. For more love stories that last a lifetime, follow @harmonyannevans

Barbara Wallace can't remember when she wasn't dreaming up love stories in her head, so writing romances for Mills & Boon is a dream come true. Happily married to her own Prince Charming, she lives in New England with a house full of empty-nest animals. Readers can catch up with Barbara through her newsletter. Sign up at barbarawallace.com

All I Want
for Christmas

SUSAN MEIER

HARMONY EVANS

BARBARA WALLACE

MILLS & BOON

First Published in Great Britain 2023
By Mills & Boon, an imprint of HarperCollins*Publishers* Ltd,
1 London Bridge Street, London, SE1 9GF

www.harpercollins.co.uk

HarperCollins*Publishers*
Macken House, 39/40 Mayor Street Upper,
Dublin 1, D01 C9W8, Ireland

ISBN: 978-0-263-32109-8

This book is produced from independently certified FSC™ paper to ensure responsible forest management.

For more information visit: www.harpercollins.co.uk/green

Printed and Bound in the UK using 100% Renewable Electricity at CPI Group (UK) Ltd, Croydon, CR0 4YY

CINDERELLA'S
BILLION-DOLLAR
CHRISTMAS

SUSAN MEIER

For Mikie.
I still miss you every day.

CHAPTER ONE

LENI LONG STARED out the big front window of the Family Diner in Mannington, Kansas, watching snow cover the sparkly gold Christmas bells hanging from the town's eight streetlights. With the breakfast rush over and the red-and-white-themed diner empty, a hush had fallen over the tiny town.

A black SUV pulled into a parking space a few feet down from the diner. A tall man in a charcoal-gray overcoat exited. His broad shoulders hunched against the snow-laced wind, but there was a strength, a power to the movement. Maybe because of his size. He had to be over six feet and was built like someone who'd spent time in the military. Snow dotted dark hair that had been cut in a sleek, sexy way that sharpened the angles of his handsome face.

A thrill ran through her. Mannington didn't have any men that gorgeous, that male, and he was heading toward the diner.

She raced behind the counter as his long strides ate up the sidewalk between his SUV and the door. It opened. He stepped inside, turning to close it behind him before he faced her.

His gaze cruised from her candy-cane-print blouse, red apron, short green skirt and red tights to her black patent leather buckle shoes.

Damn it! The first fabulous-looking man to come to Mannington in decades and she was wearing an elf suit.

Oh, well. That was life in a small town. Waitresses

dressed like elves. The cook sat outside on the back steps smoking. And her mom, the second waitress for the breakfast shift that morning, hadn't thought twice about calling to say she wouldn't be in until after ten. This was one of those mornings she needed to stay with Leni's dad, making sure he was okay because his head injury from a work accident was now causing small seizures.

Gorgeous Guy peered at the name tag on her blouse. "Leni?"

It wasn't unusual for an out-of-town customer to read her name tag and call her Leni to be friendly, but something about the way he'd said it hit her funny. As if he were disappointed.

"Yes." She smiled. "That's my name."

He ambled over to the counter. "You're the only waitress here?"

She grabbed a nearby cloth and ran it along the worn white countertop. "Yes. The other waitress is coming in later."

"How much later?"

That was a stupid question. Why would he care what time her mom came in? "She'll be here any minute now." She laughed. "But really, it's fine. I can take your order."

"Okay." He sat on one of the round red stools at the counter. "I'll have a cup of coffee."

"Sure." She turned to the pot sitting on a two-burner warmer behind her. "And you should know that it might be after ten, but the cook makes breakfast all day."

"Sorry. I had breakfast."

Drat. That was her only angle to keep him here. Now he'd drink his cup of coffee and race off—

She frowned. Unless he planned to wait for her mom?

Fears about insurance adjusters and private investigators sent by At Home Construction to spy on her dad raced through her. After two years, the company was arguing his workers' comp and questioning medical bills because they believed he could perform light-duty tasks and come back on the job.

But if this guy wanted to catch her dad working around the house to prove he was no longer disabled, he wouldn't come looking for her mother.

Would he?

No. He'd spy on her dad.

Feeling guilty for thinking the handsome stranger was a private detective, she swiped the cloth down the counter again. "Maybe you'd like a cinnamon roll?"

He laughed. "No. Thank you."

His words were kind, but precise. Leni smiled. He didn't need food and sometimes customers didn't want to talk. She would leave to him to his coffee.

She turned to walk away, but he said, "Nice town you have here."

She faced him again. "Mannington's okay."

His dark brows rose. "Only okay?"

Maybe he did want to talk? And maybe a few minutes of personal time with him would stop her from being suspicious? His brown eyes lit with a hint of amusement and this close he was so gorgeous it was fun just looking at him.

No harm in enjoying that.

"No. Mannington's a great place, but I'll be moving soon. I just finished my degree and I'm probably going to have to relocate to Topeka to get a job." She shrugged. "That's the way it is sometimes. If you want to work, you go to the big city."

"I'm from New York. My family owns a money management firm. I always knew where I'd be employed. Went through a bit of a rebellious phase, but I think everybody does, and here I am."

In Mannington, Kansas?

A guy who owned a New York City money management firm was in Mannington, Kansas, where no one had any money?

Her suspicions rose again. But at least they were talking. Maybe with a little good old-fashioned waitress chit-chat she could get him to tell her why he was here?

Especially if he was looking for her mom.

Nick Kourakis couldn't stop staring at the woman behind the counter. He'd been sent by the estate of Mark Hinton to find Elenore Long, probably the waitress who hadn't yet arrived, and instead he'd run into the most naturally beautiful woman he'd ever seen.

She had an exquisite face, a perfect figure that her goofy elf suit couldn't hide and big green eyes that shone with humor—

Until he'd asked when the other waitress would be coming in. Then she'd gotten quiet. But now that they were talking about her getting a job, things had perked up again. It didn't matter what he told her or what she told him. They'd never see each other again. That was the beauty of a conversation with a stranger. It was pointless. Exactly the diversion he needed while he waited for Elenore Long.

"So, you think you'll be moving to Topeka?"

She shrugged. "Probably."

He gestured at the candy-cane blouse. "Gonna take the elf suit?"

She laughed. "I doubt they let social workers wear them."

He loved her laugh. He loved her flowing hair. He loved that a little small talk had brought back her smile. "That's a tough job."

"I know."

"But it should be fairly easy to find work."

Her smile grew into a grin. "I know that, too."

"Well, there's just no fooling you, is there, Leni?"

She smiled again. Her full lips lifting and her green eyes sparkling.

He swore to God his heart turned over in his chest. He'd been single for so long that he couldn't remember the last time he'd had this kind of reaction to a woman. Not just an instant connection, but a welcome connection, as if the small talk he thought so pointless was a door to something—

Looking at her beautiful face, big eyes, high cheekbones, perfect nose, and lips just made for kissing, he almost suggested she search for work in New York, but that would be as pointless as a conversation about the weather. Why would he ask a beautiful woman to make such a drastic move for him, when he knew nothing would come of it?

The diner door opened and he turned. A woman in an elf suit just like Leni's walked in.

The other waitress. Most likely Elenore Long.

His eyes narrowed as he studied her. She was fifty, at least. Her chestnut hair curled around a square face and her eyes were blue. His heiress was the first of three children fathered by Mark Hinton, who'd died two weeks ago at the age of sixty. This woman was too old to be his child, even his firstborn.

He rose from his stool. "*You're* the other waitress?"

The woman began unbuttoning her coat. "Yeah."

"I think he's been waiting for you, Mom."

Nick swung to face Leni again. "Mom?"

"That's my mom. Denise Long, Mr. Owner-of-a-Money-Management-Firm. If you think we got a settlement to invest after my dad's injury, you're wrong. We can barely get the insurance company to pay his medical bills."

He fell to the round red stool again. "I'm not after your dad's money." He took a quick breath and caught Leni's gaze. "Your last name is Long?"

"Yeah."

Not taking any chances, he said, "And Leni is a nickname for something?"

He waited for confirmation but deep down he already knew the answer.

"Elenore."

He ran his fingers along his brow. "Elenore Long." He shook his head. If he hadn't been so blinded by her bedroom eyes, glorious mane of hair and sexy little body, he probably would have figured that out. "You're Elenore Long?"

She nodded. "Yes."

"Is there someplace private you and I can talk?"

She pressed her hand to her chest. "*I'm* the person you're here to see?"

"Yes."

"Why? I could barely get student loans. I don't have anything to hand over to a money management firm."

"Seriously. We have to talk someplace private." He caught her gaze. "Now."

Leni had never seen anybody's mood shift so quickly. He went from cute and flirty to serious in under a second. But that was fine since she was totally confused by him. First, he wanted to talk to her mom. Now he wanted to talk to her?

"The only people in the diner are you, me and my mom. George, the cook, is outside smoking." She glanced around. "We can just go to one of the booths in the back."

"Okay." He pointed to the last booth in the farthest corner. "We'll sit there."

He walked behind her until they reached the table. Then he slid onto the bench across from her.

"My name is Nick Kourakis. I work for a money management firm in New York City."

"So, you said. And I told you my family doesn't have any money to invest."

"I know."

His eyes darkened as he studied her. With all his attention centered on her face, she had to hold back a shudder. She had never seen a man this good-looking. But as she thought that, she noticed that his gray overcoat was stunningly made, and his white shirt and tie looked expensive. As big as he was, he wore both effortlessly, as if he was accustomed to luxury. Maybe even made for it.

She suddenly realized he wasn't gorgeous so much as he was a combination of the whole package. Expensive clothes. Sparkling clean. Handsome.

And wealthy.

Probably so rich, she couldn't even fathom the amount of money he had.

"I'm not selling anything. I'm not even here on behalf of the money management firm. I was sent here to retrieve you."

"Retrieve me?" His sultry brown eyes held her captive, sending warmth swimming through her blood, confusing her, almost hypnotizing her.

"Because I have some exciting news for you."

"Oh, yeah?" She fought the strange sensations assaulting her with sarcasm. "And what would that be?"

"First, what I have to tell you *has to* remain confidential."

Some of her equilibrium returned. "Okay."

He leaned back on the bench. "Have you ever heard of Mark Hinton?"

More of her confidence came back. Enough to put starch in her spine. "No."

"He's a billionaire…or was. We have reason to believe you are one of the people mentioned in his will."

"Oh…" Her composure took a tumble. Imagining herself getting as much as ten thousand dollars and paying off some of the bills that had accumulated since her dad's injury, she told her wishful-thinking brain to stop before she got her hopes up. "That's good. Right?"

"It could potentially be wonderful."

"Dude, wonderful to me is enough money to pay my dad's medical bills."

"It's more than that."

New thoughts scrambled around in her brain. Like buying her dad the service dog he needed because of his seizures, and not worrying about the company forcing him back to work.

But as quickly as her good thoughts set up shop, some bad thoughts came tumbling in. Adopted at eight, after a year in foster care when her biological mom gave her up, she'd always believed she was not a lucky person. The way she'd struggled for eight years just to afford her basic bachelor's degree backed that up. "What's the catch?"

"Before I say another word, I need your promise that you won't talk about this with anyone until I tell you that you can."

A laugh bubbled out. "You want me to take a vow of silence?"

"You are the first of three potential heirs to Mark Hinton's estate. A *huge* estate. You can tell your parents, but that's it. And they have to promise to keep this news to themselves. Frankly, it's a matter of *your* personal safety."

It all seemed to so preposterous that it couldn't sink in. As good as it would be to be rich, she was much too practical to believe in magic or miracles. It had to be a joke or a mistake.

When she said nothing, he sighed. "Do you have your phone?"

She pulled it out of her apron pocket.

"Search *Mark Hinton*."

She did as he said, though she mumbled, "Anybody can put up a fake website."

But her phone produced eight thousand results for Mark Hinton. Her gaze leaped to Nick's. "What is this?"

"Information on his life." He paused for a second before he added, "I was sent here by the law firm handling your dad's estate. The attorney in charge is stuck in court today. He's a friend of mine, and my family's firm manages your father's fortune, so I was picked to come in his place."

She barely heard anything after he said "your dad's estate." Her breath stumbled. "My *dad's*?"

She struggled to take it all in. Her biological mom hadn't told her anything about her father. She would always say he wasn't important, and they didn't need him. At seven, she'd known that wasn't true when her mom couldn't afford to keep her anymore.

"According to the estate lawyer, the paper trail says Mark Hinton is your father," Nick said. "But they'll be getting DNA."

She leaned back in disappointment and disbelief, her voice dull when she said, "My biological father was rich."

"One of the first multibillionaires." Nick shifted. "If you let this get out before the estate has a chance to protect you, you will be mobbed by people who want money. You'll be a target for scam artists and kidnappers. I came here not merely to tell you, but to take you to New York so the lawyer can make the process of vetting you easier for *you*."

Something Leni couldn't define or describe fluttered through her, tightening her chest, making her head spin. She looked at the eight *thousand* results to her search and saw the words *billionaire, reclusive, oil and gas prodigy* and *missing heirs*.

Her heart stopped then burst to life again with such a frantic beat she thought she'd faint. This would be more than enough money to care for her dad.

"You think this guy is my father and I'm one of these heirs?"

"The estate lawyer is fairly certain you're one of the heirs. He says the paper trail is solid. But they'll do a DNA test to confirm it."

Her voice came out as a squeak as she said, "Okay."

"For confidentiality purposes and for your safety, you have to go to New York now." He paused long enough to catch her gaze. "Will you come with me?"

Ten minutes ago, that offer probably would have scrambled her pulse. Now? The happy, flirty guy was gone. A businessman had replaced him.

She almost missed the flirty guy. But her brain had been captured by the idea that she might be wealthy enough that her parents would no longer have to worry about money.

Still, she wasn't going to New York with a man she didn't know, based solely on his word. "Give me a day?"

"The plan was to leave as soon as we told you."

She shook her head. "I want a day. Twenty-four hours to explain all this to my parents and to check you out."

"I can provide you with references—"

"No thanks. I'll find what I need on my own." She'd check every dark and moldy corner of the internet if she had to, to make sure he was for real.

There was no way she'd leave for New York with a stranger. And no way she'd get her parents' hopes up for nothing.

CHAPTER TWO

NICK KOURAKIS LEFT the diner, a mix of disappointment and confusion slowing his steps. He should have been focused on the fact that this unexpected trip was a chance to convince Leni Long to keep her dad's money with his money management firm. But Danny Manelli, attorney for the estate, didn't want him making a pitch to her. A clause in the will could give the estate trouble, and Nick could make it worse by talking about money before Danny could properly explain the clause to Leni.

Now that he had given her the basics that would get her to New York to start the process of vetting her, Nick wasn't supposed to talk about anything except the weather and football. Two things Danny was sure wouldn't accidentally tip them into talking about the estate.

That was good, sound logic. And normally Nick would be totally onboard with it. Instead, he was gobsmacked. Leni Long was the first woman he'd been overwhelmingly attracted to in a decade. But it was more than that. Something about her clicked with him. And that was so odd he couldn't shake the feeling.

Telling himself that was absurd, he walked down the sidewalk and jumped into the passenger seat of the SUV.

Behind the steering wheel, Jace MacDonald, owner of Around the World Security, said, "Where's the girl?"

"She wants a day to investigate us."

Jace shook his head, then shifted to face Nick, the gun beneath his black leather jacket visible when he turned. "It's going to be difficult to keep an eye on her here. Even for twenty-four hours." He motioned outside. "Not only are the houses and businesses spaced in such a way that an extra person sticks out like a sore thumb, but so do cars. You should have seen the people sniffing around the SUV while you were in the diner. A strange vehicle parked on a street where everybody knows everybody else's car? That's like a neon sign."

"I don't care. You heard what Danny said. That woman is worth more money than the gross national products of several small countries combined. If the wrong people find out, she'll be a target."

"Yeah, of banks that want to compete for her business." Jace snickered. "You do realize Danny's keeping you from an excellent opportunity to convince her to keep her share of the estate with you?"

Nick peeked at him. "You're not allowed to pitch your company either."

Jace raised his hands in disgust. "Got the same sermon you did."

"Then you know the problem with the will. After a few charitable bequests, Mark divides the remainder of his estate between his first child and any subsequent heirs. A good lawyer could argue that that gives Mark's first child half, with the other half split between the other two kids. Danny wants to be the one to explain it to Elenore."

Jace sniffed. "How the hell can pitching our companies' services affect that stupid clause?"

"He just wants to be sure we don't accidentally say something we shouldn't."

"That's ridiculous." Jace growled.

Nick totally understood his frustration, but he didn't want to do anything that could make trouble for Danny. "Look, you knew Mark. He was a good guy. Nine chances out of ten, he wanted that estate distributed equally among his heirs. I'm sure Danny has a plan to get all three of

Mark's kids on board with that. That's why he doesn't want us talking to her. Muddying the waters."

"Right." Jace pulled the gear shift out of Park and headed toward the interstate. "There isn't a hotel or even a bed and breakfast in this town. I'll drive you up the highway until we find one, then I have to get back here to figure out a way to hide myself and this boat of an SUV we rented so I can watch her tonight."

Nick winced. "Sorry. I couldn't talk her into leaving today."

"Not to worry. I'll deal with it. How are you going to handle the fact that she wanted time to check *you* out?" He laughed. "What's she going to find when she does a search on you?"

Nick faced the window. "Nothing."

"You're sure? The guy they call the New Wolf of Wall Street doesn't have a skeleton?"

Nick said, "No skeleton," but he lied. He'd talked his only brother into going out on a night when the roads were icy. A former Navy SEAL, he counted on himself to be one of the best drivers in unusual situations. But a combination of icy roads and other cars had bested him that night, and his only sibling had been killed.

But that was five years ago, and he didn't think the story even popped up in internet searches anymore.

"Come on. Nobody meets a guy like Hinton without a story."

"I did."

That part was true. He'd met Mark Hinton in Dubai. They'd gambled. They'd skydived. They'd talked money. Especially investment strategy. In Nick's world, there was nothing special about any of that. After Mark decided to trust Kourakis Money Management with most of his fortune, they'd had meetings on his yachts or while fishing in the Florida Keys. They drank tequila, talked about his financial goals and even about the kids who were now Mark's heirs. Though never while Mark was sober. Powerful men didn't admit weakness or failures without a nudge. Mark's nudge was alcohol. With enough tequila, Mark would talk about his kids—without mentioning their names—and Nick would nurse his regret and sorrow over his brother's death. *That* was why Mark was comfortable with Nick. Even with a thirty-year age difference, they understood each other. Understood mistakes. Understood regret.

Even now, it trickled from his subconscious to the front of his brain. He'd been too confident, cocky even. His brother hadn't wanted to go out that night. His parents hadn't wanted them to go. But he'd been so sure—

He was always so sure.

After Joe's death, he'd had to stop jet-setting, return to New York and take over the family business.

But he was still the same guy deep down inside. Instead of taking risks on the slopes or in the sky, he played with money.

And no one beat him.

Ever.

He'd gotten so good at what he did that he liked it. Until he recalled the reason why he was the "New Wolf." Even now, the grief of losing his brother sent guilt oozing through him.

He didn't understand what had happened to him in that diner that he'd forgotten Joe, forgotten his guilt and laughed with someone he barely knew. But when they returned to New York, he'd be focused again, diligent. If he was going to lose even part of the Hinton money when the estate was settled and one or two of the heirs decided to hire new money management, he'd have to find big investors to replace it.

He would not let his parents down twice.

Leni's mom only worked until two o'clock, but Leni's shift didn't end until three. Having evaded her questions about

Nick Kourakis, taking Nick's warnings seriously about the complications of people finding out she might be an heiress, Leni raced home and found her parents in the kitchen.

"Hey."

Sitting at the center island, her dad looked up from his newspaper.

Her mom glanced over from the stove. "Hey. Finally going to tell us what the guy in the overcoat wanted?"

Leni forced a smile. Denise and Jake Long had adopted her when she was in the gangly stage for a little girl. No longer an adorable infant or cute toddler, with a bit of a history of being difficult at school, most potential parents overlooked her. The Longs had given her a home, made her their daughter. Now she didn't merely know she had a biological mom out there somewhere who had given her up; she might have had a rich dad who hadn't wanted her at all.

Once again, she thanked God for her adoptive parents.

She took a seat beside her dad. "First, what I'm about to say is a secret. So, you can't tell anybody."

Her mom said, "Okay," as her dad nodded.

"The guy in the overcoat was Nick Kourakis. He owns a management firm in New York, and he told me that I might have inherited some money."

Her dad's weathered face brightened. A lifelong construction worker, he had wrinkles around his eyes that appeared when he smiled. "Well, that's great!"

Her mother gasped and walked over from the stove to hug Leni. "I'm so happy for you."

"Yeah, well, it's not assured. I have to go to New York. There will also be a DNA test to confirm my identity. Honestly, I won't quite believe all this is true until DNA says I'm an heir. So, our not mentioning this to anybody protects me from embarrassing myself if it doesn't pan out."

Part of her almost wished it wouldn't. If her biological father had been a struggling factory worker, she could have understood him not being able to take responsibility for her, but a guy who was rich and not paying child support, forcing her mom to give her up when she got sick? When it was a decision between the medicine she needed and feeding her child?

It was demeaning, insulting, infuriating.

She'd have to deal with that if Mark Hinton really was her biological father. Those feelings would all go away if he wasn't.

Her dad leaned back in his chair. "It's always good not to get your hopes up, Kitten. But maybe this family's due for some good luck?"

And that was the catch. Part of her would like to tell Nick Kourakis to take her biological dad's money and shove it. She was educated now. She had a career path. She would be fine.

But her parents wouldn't.

They'd never ask her for a dime, but she wouldn't make them ask. If she'd inherited enough money to care for her dad, she wanted it.

"Okay." She slid off her chair. "I'm going upstairs to do some investigating into everything. I'm not getting on a plane with a guy I don't know."

Her dad smiled. "That's smart, my girl."

The simple comment hit her right in the heart. She was his girl. *His* girl. Not the child of some sperm donor who'd never even checked to see if she was okay.

That was not a father.

Almost twenty-four hours from when Leni had met him, Nick Kourakis and a man she didn't recognize pulled into the driveway of the Long residence in the big, black SUV. Nick had looked up her parents' home phone number and called her the night before to say they'd be leaving at ten o'clock. He'd given her time to research him and his firm, to talk to her parents and to pack for a couple weeks in

Manhattan, but that was it. They needed to get her safely to New York.

Her breath frosty in the cold, last-day-of-November air, she hugged and kissed her short, curly-haired mom and balding dad, saying goodbye at the front door of their house, her conflicted feelings about Mark Hinton dogging her.

Nick handed Danny Manelli's business card to her parents, telling them that he was the lawyer in charge of the estate and if they had any questions, they could call him. Then he introduced her to Jace MacDonald, the guy in the black leather jacket who directed her to the back seat of the SUV. Nick got in beside her.

She frowned at the empty passenger's seat in the front.

"Jace owns Around the World Security. He'll be your bodyguard while you're in New York."

She gaped at Nick. "Bodyguard?"

Jace caught her gaze in the rearview mirror. "Trust me. If you're worth billions, you'll need one."

She huffed out a breath. "Billions?"

Nick laughed. "Yes. Mark Hinton had billions. With an *s*. Plural. As in many billions."

"I know. I researched him last night, too. It's just so hard to believe."

She shook her head and looked out the window. The guy had billions and he had left her mom so broke she'd had to put Leni into foster care.

The insult of it stiffened her spine.

Jace made a few turns and they headed north. Twenty minutes later, he pulled the SUV onto a private airstrip. When they drove up to a sleek red and silver jet, she gasped. "Holy cow."

Nick laughed. "That plane is nothing. I'm just a simple billionaire."

She knew that, too. She'd spent forty minutes the night before reading about how successful the investment arm of his family's money management firm was. What she hadn't expected was that they'd be riding in *his* plane. Not when her biological father was supposed to have so much money.

Something about that just seemed off.

She faced Nick again. "This plane is yours?"

"Yes."

He glanced over, catching her gaze, and her breath shivered.

Damn it. Now was not the time to be feeling that stupid attraction she had to him. Not only did he seem to be in charge of her, but she was too confused about her potential biological dad to add an attraction into the mix. Plus, there was something wrong with Nick using his own plane to get her. This was not the man to be attracted to.

Jace exited the SUV and came around to her door to open it. She climbed out at the same time Nick did.

Nick led her to the small stack of stairs and into the jet. She had to hold back a gasp when she stepped inside. Three small groupings of white leather seats were arranged around the large cabin. The little windows had elegant gray shades. A silver and black bar sat discreetly in a back corner. A rich red carpet covered the floor.

She took a slow, measured breath. She could not be a country bumpkin about this. She had to stay sharp.

Pretending a calm she didn't feel, she stopped by the first group of seats and slid out of her worn leather jacket.

Behind her, Nick said, "The flight's about three hours. Then, because we use an airstrip outside the city, we'll have about an hour-and-a-half limo ride."

"Limo ride?" She swallowed, picturing her blue-collar self, in her ancient leather jacket and worn jeans, getting into a limo.

He took her coat and handed it to the flight attendant who scurried to the back of the jet with it.

"Don't worry. You'll acclimate. After a day or two in

New York, you'll realize a limo's the easiest way to get around the city. Just like this jet is the most comfortable way to get from place to place."

He motioned to the rear of the cabin. "The first room you walk into back there is a kitchen. If you want a snack you just ask Marie, but she'll be serving lunch at noon. So, a snack might not be a good idea. Beyond that is an office-slash-den, complete with a pullout bed. Jace will probably go back there once we take off." He winced. "He stayed up most of the night keeping an eye on your house. He'll need the nap."

"He stayed up all night?"

"That's his job, remember?"

She did. She simply hadn't connected him being a bodyguard to him sitting in his SUV all night watching her house.

"You'll get used to it. For now, settle in. Get accustomed to the convenience that's your new lifestyle."

She couldn't fathom riding in a limo let alone owning a jet. "If I'm an heir."

"The lawyer for the estate all but said your DNA test is only a formality." He pointed to the rear of the plane. "I have some work to do, so I'll be back there if there's anything you need."

He turned to leave but she said, "Why are we in your jet instead of one of my dad's?"

Nick faced her again. "What?"

"Why are we using your jet instead of one of Mark Hinton's?"

"We're not using one of Mark's jets because we're not using anything belonging to Hinton Holdings."

"Why?"

He sighed. "We don't want to alert anyone that we might have found an heir before we confirm you."

"Because?"

This time he pulled in a long breath, obviously losing patience with her questions. "This estate is worth so much money that everyone in the world is curious about who you are. Danny devised a plan to find the heirs and keep you safe. Not using estate property is part of it. If we start using jets or houses and cars, people will know something is up and begin snooping. The longer we can keep the press and curiosity seekers at bay, the better."

She held the gaze of his dark eyes for a second, then she shook her head. She didn't think he was lying. But she did know he hadn't told her everything. Until her DNA results were back, she probably didn't have the right to push him. But she would watch him, pay attention to every word he said, because there was definitely something going on with him.

Nick breathed a sigh of relief as he headed to the seat in the back of the plane. He didn't mind her questions. They were generic enough that he could answer them. It was her nearness that threw him for a loop. He was smarter than this, more in control. His whole body shouldn't buzz just because they were standing close.

He reached the plush leather seat, but before he sat, he realized he'd forgotten his briefcase. He returned to the front and opened the overhead bin above the seat Leni had chosen.

She glanced up at him, her thick lashes blinking over her sultry green eyes, her long brown hair sort of floating around her.

"Forgot my briefcase," he explained, trying not to stumble over his words. "I kept it on the plane, thinking we'd be leaving yesterday."

She smiled in acknowledgment and his heart went from pitter-patter to a drum solo in one breath.

Stifling a groan, he headed to the rear of the cabin again, eager to return to New York to lose these crazy feelings he had around her. Part of it had to be surprise over how pretty she was. Mark Hinton wasn't even a five on a scale of one to ten, but apparently Leni's mother had been a twelve.

The other part was just plain attraction. Serious lust. Something biological that sprang up before he could control it.

So, it was wrong.

Had to be.

He didn't get out-of-control feelings and he sure as hell never let emotions rule him.

A movement in the front caught his attention and he peeked up to see Leni get out of her seat to put her purse in the overhead bin. Her head fell back as she reached up, sending all that thick, shiny hair bouncing.

This time he allowed himself an internal groan.

This was crazy.

For the first time since Danny had laid down the rules for Nick's trip to retrieve Leni, he was glad he'd been ordered to keep his distance from her. Because whatever he was feeling, he didn't want it. He had priorities, a company to run, parents to keep happy. He couldn't afford the weakness of a hellishly strong attraction.

He put his head down and went to work and didn't look up until hours later when the jet began to descend. Choosing not to go up to the overhead bin again, he secured his briefcase under his seat, fastened his seat belt and waited for the jet to slide onto the ground, relieved that he only had a little over an hour more in her company. He would leave her with Danny and never look back.

CHAPTER THREE

GIVEN THE TIME difference between Kansas and New York, it was almost three o'clock when they landed in New York. Leni had eaten a fabulous lunch, served by Marie, prepared by a chef hiding somewhere in the back. Leni hadn't seen her luggage since climbing into the SUV in Mannington, but she suspected someone had handled it. Nick had said to settle in and get comfortable with luxury...but, come on. A chef who had flown from New York to Mannington and from Mannington back to New York, just to make lunch? On a jet? For her?

It boggled the mind.

They boarded a limo and headed for the city, Leni feeling totally out of place in her worn jacket and jeans. Though Christmas decorations in shop windows, on streetlights and clinging to parking meters gave the area a familiar feel, she had never seen so many buildings in such a small place.

But she didn't mention it. She didn't want to be attracted to Nick or to mistrust him. But, unfortunately, she felt both things, and mistrust trumped attraction. She wouldn't say anything around him that she didn't have to.

When they pulled up to a building so tall that she couldn't see the top of it, Nick said, "Our first appointment... Your lawyer."

"My lawyer?"

"The lawyer for the estate."

She gasped. "I'm in jeans! You should have told me I'd

be meeting him this afternoon. I thought I was only flying here today!"

"You're fine. You're a blue-collar woman who's just been told she might be a billionaire. You don't have to put on airs."

"Lucky thing, since I hadn't given a thought to trying that."

The driver opened the back door. Nick climbed out first and extended his hand to help her exit the limo.

Light snow fell around him, and he pulled her out into it. The shiny white flakes collecting on his dark hair reminded her of seeing him getting out of the SUV and walking to the diner, huddled against the falling snow. All the feelings from the day before came tumbling back. Her attraction. Their small talk. Laughing together.

Close enough to kiss him, she fought the magnetic pull that tried to lure her in, but it was her mistrust that fluttered away. Before she'd known who he was, she'd told Nick about needing to move to Topeka and he'd told her that his family owned a money management firm and he'd had a rebellious streak.

They'd formed a connection and she felt it again, as clearly as if they were still in the diner.

She stepped back, trying to get rid of it and the fears that rushed at her when she realized where she was and why. It didn't work. All her worries tumbled out, even as the sense of connection to Nick held on.

"All I can think about is being embarrassed or scared when it's announced that I'm an heir. Doing something stupid, making a fool of myself—"

He stopped her by putting his hands on her shoulders and looking her in the eye. "You don't have anything to be embarrassed about. And as for being scared, from the couple of hours I've known you, I can tell you're strong. You can do this."

His dark eyes had sharpened with a strength that sent

a shot of attraction from her chest to her toes. This was the Nick she'd made a connection with. The nice guy. The guy she'd liked.

She had to swallow before she could say, "Okay."

He took her elbow and directed her toward the building. She swore heat from his touch seeped through her worn leather jacket and to her skin. She didn't know what it was about him that seemed to draw her in, but whatever it was, it was powerful.

A tiny part of her whispered that her feelings were right. That she could trust him. That she *should* trust him.

She really wanted to believe that, especially walking up to a building with so many floors jutting up to the sky she couldn't count them, fancy pillars carved into the exterior walls and a sophisticated medallion resting over the entry like a royal crest.

When they reached the revolving door, her knees wobbled and she was grateful for Nick's hand at her elbow. He released her when they stepped into a lobby with marble floors and red and white poinsettias scattered about. No plastic wreaths. No gaudy ornaments. No blinking lights. Just tasteful flowers. And twenty or thirty people dressed as sophisticatedly as Nick.

Her thoughts scrambled again. He only touched her when she needed help, barely spoke, had ignored her on the plane. He might be the guy from the diner, but he wasn't always nice. He had a job to do—get her to New York—and he was doing it.

She had to stop imagining good things about him.

They walked past a bank of elevators to another row hidden around a corner. These elevators had keypads and Nick had to punch in a series of numbers on the third one for the doors to open.

A man in a power suit came out of the second elevator, followed by a woman in a pencil skirt and silky blouse, visible because her fancy wool coat was unbuttoned. Like people on a mission, they bounded around the corner and off to parts unknown.

She sucked in a long breath, straightened her old jacket and smoothed her hand along the high collar of her turtleneck, hoping it looked newer than it was. Because, man, she was seriously underdressed.

When they stepped out of the elevator into an office, she didn't just think it. She knew it. A wall of glass behind the desk displayed a view of Manhattan that made her breath stutter. The buildings looked close enough to touch. And with so much glass surrounding the room she felt like she was walking on air.

A short, slender woman opened the door on the far left and peeked inside. "Hey, Nick. Could you come into my office for a second?"

Nick glanced at Leni and she forced a smile. "I'm fine. Maybe I'll go over to the window and try to see inside the office across the street."

Nick stifled a laugh, but just barely. Leni had to be the most naturally funny, most open person he'd ever met. He couldn't help comforting her when she'd admitted how afraid she was, but he'd kept his solace short and simple. Because in another ten minutes, he'd be back on that elevator, heading for his own office. His favor for his friend completed. His sanity restored.

He followed Danny's assistant, Mary Catherine, into her office. She pointed at the phone on her desk. "I have Mr. Manelli on the line."

Confusion stopped him where he was. "On the line? He was supposed to be here waiting for us."

She skirted her desk and headed for the hallway. "Why don't you let him explain?"

When she was gone, Nick picked up the receiver of the desk phone and said, "Where the hell are you?"

"Stuck in court. Remember the trial I told you I would be getting a continuance on? The reason I needed you to be the one to retrieve Elenore Long instead of me? Well, the judge didn't go for the continuance. I'm stuck here."

"Stuck there?"

"The judge thinks there's no reason to postpone a trial that won't last more than a few days. It's corporate stuff. Everybody's prepared to the max. It will take a day or two to get through it."

"Why are you telling me this?"

"Because we can't let Elenore Long sit alone in a hotel room this afternoon, tonight and all day tomorrow."

"Danny, I agreed to do this favor for you mostly because Mark was my friend and I knew how he felt about his kids' safety. But that was it."

"That was all I needed when I called you on Saturday, but through no fault of mine, things changed. That's life. You remember life? If something can go wrong, it usually does."

Understanding that a little better than Danny knew, Nick blew his breath out on a frustrated sigh. "What about Jace? He's the bodyguard. He should be with her. Not me."

"Jace had an emergency come up. He and most of his men are on their way to El Salvador."

He gaped at the phone. "El Salvador!"

"Yep. So, we're down to you. You know all the information about the identity of the heirs and potential heirs has to be kept as quiet as possible. The fewer people who know, the less chance someone will accidentally slip a name to their wife or girlfriend. Besides, you're the most closed-mouthed person I know."

"I'm not a bodyguard!"

"You don't need to be. As long as no one knows who she is, she's just another New York tourist."

"And what the hell do I do with her for the next day... or two?"

Danny's voice lifted with hope. "Anything you want. New York's a big city. As long as you stay away from talking about the estate, you could very easily entertain her for a week."

"A week!"

"Tops. I swear."

Nick squeezed his eyes shut. "You owe me."

"Big time," Danny agreed.

As his friend gave him the name of the hotel he'd booked for Leni, Nick looked through the glass separating Mary Catherine's office and Danny's. Leni stood by the wall of windows staring at the Manhattan skyline, obviously a fish out of water.

And she'd already admitted to being afraid.

He passed his hand down his face. The part of him that wanted to help her was the part he wanted to squelch, destroy, kick so far out of town he wouldn't even think about being attracted to her anymore. He'd planned on doing the eviction tonight with a bottle of scotch and four hours of work. Danny and Jace weren't the only ones with commitments.

Danny sighed. "Look, get her settled in the hotel and take her for a nice dinner."

Nick blew his breath out in exasperation. "I'm serious about this costing you one big, fat favor."

Danny laughed. "Why? Does she look like Mark?"

"No, I'm guessing she got the cocktail waitress's genes."

Danny guffawed. "That good, huh?"

Nick gazed longingly at Leni again. "Better."

"Okay. I've got to go. The judge is back from recess. And I swear I will end this trial as quickly as possible."

As Danny hung up, Nick took a long, slow breath. He didn't want to spend any more time with a woman he was already attracted to. Work was his life now. Besides, she was way too nice for him. Innocent. Sweet. He wasn't any of those. Still, he was helping Danny because Mark had been his friend. He resisted women all the time. This one would be no different.

He walked into Danny's office and straight to the private elevator. "Let's go."

Leni scrambled after him. "Where?"

"The lawyer is stuck in a trial. I'm taking you to your hotel and then to dinner."

They stepped into the elevator. "I can't go to dinner with you."

He peered at her. "You're ditching me?"

"No. I'm just not going out with someone dressed like you," she said, pointing at his black suit and charcoal-gray overcoat. "When I look like this." She motioned down the front of her jacket.

"We can buy you a dress before we go to the hotel. In fact, we can get you anything you want. There's a slush fund for vetting potential heirs. It's there to get you anything you need while you're in the city."

She gaped at him. "I'm not letting you buy me clothes." Though she almost wished she could. Her old jeans and jacket firmly announced her as someone not from Manhattan. Which made her stick out in the crowd milling about in the building lobby. The people who'd seen her walking out of the private elevator for a lawyer's office probably thought she was a petty thief.

"I can't pay you back if I'm not an heir."

"I told you, there's a slush fund. You're in New York at the estate's request. While you're here it's our responsibility to get you anything and everything you need. No paybacks. It's part of the process. We'll be putting the exact same amount of money into slush accounts for all potential heirs."

"You might have to pay for the hotel and the limo, but you're not buying me clothes."

A muscle in his jaw jumped as he motioned to the revolving door. "Fine."

She could see she'd aggravated him, but she didn't care.

She walked through the door, out into the snow and into the limo again. They took a short ride and exited the limo onto the busiest street Leni had ever seen. The jumbotron, lights and videos were the familiar backdrop of an early morning news show.

She reverently whispered. "Times Square."

Nick pointed to the right. "Your hotel is this way."

The only hotel she saw to the right was way down the street. She glanced back at the limo. "We're walking?"

"Traffic was backed up at the hotel entry. It's not far."

"Oh. Okay."

"You want to get back into the limo and wait out the line?"

Not really. Cool air massaged her warm face. The noise of Times Square and the crowded street took her attention away from Mark Hinton and money and the handsome guy walking with her who seemed to have gone from annoyed to angry. No sense poking the bear.

"Yeah. Walking's good." Shoving her hands into her jacket pockets, she peered around again. "I like seeing everything."

He pointed across the street. "My office is in that building there."

Gray brick with black slate accents. Long, thin windows. A doorman.

"Wow." She fought the question that automatically rose as she shuffled along beside him, but it bubbled out anyway. "What's it like to work here?" She gestured around her. "In all of this noise and people?"

"Our windows are soundproof."

She laughed. "Seriously? You know what I mean. You saw where I live. There are about fifteen hundred people in our entire town, and I'll bet there are three thousand on this street with us now. You can't know everybody. How do you decide who to trust?"

He peeked at her. "Reputation."

She skipped twice to catch up with his long strides. "Reputation? If you don't know someone, how do you know their reputation?"

He shrugged. "I always know somebody who knows somebody who knows them. And, if they are high enough in a corporate structure, there will be things written about them."

"Written about them?"

"In professional journals, but I do search the internet sometimes to find out things about them."

"Did you research me?"

He gave her the side-eye. "That was Danny's job."

"This Danny—the lawyer—is pretty important?"

"His firm is handling the Hinton estate. He's the boss. Any mistakes are on him."

Things began to fall in to place for Leni. Nick never lied to her, but she was beginning to understand why getting a complete answer out of him was close to impossible. *She* was the problem.

"Like mistakes you make with me?"

He stopped walking and studied her for a few seconds before he said, "Yes."

That ill-timed thrill ran through her again, and she knew why he'd stopped walking, why he was still looking at her. Their initial conversation at the diner had been flirty and fun and she wasn't a thirteen-year-old girl wondering in the boy next door liked her. She knew the signs. But he'd had to squelch those feelings. Because of the estate? Because of not wanting to make mistakes?

"You aren't allowed to get too chummy with me, are you?"

"No."

"And the reason you keep acting all stuffy is because we sort of already did make friends in the diner?"

"Yes. And that's wrong." He shook his head. "You're funny and you have a warmth about you that's very appealing. But there are things in my life that prevent me from even considering a relationship, and you could potentially be inheriting tons of money which will completely change *your* life. You shouldn't want to get involved with me any more than I want to get involved with you. Which means we shouldn't even try to get to know each other."

She'd thought the same thing herself. Except her thinking had run along the lines of not being able to trust him. And hadn't she already figured out he had secrets? Though, it did intrigue her that he'd *admit* there were things in his life that prevented him from even considering a relationship. That had to mean there was more to his backing off than keeping his professional distance. Which was good to know. A woman who had been a little girl in foster care, wishing her next set of parents would love her enough to adopt her, didn't need to be wondering why he ran hot and cold with her or why he sometimes downright ignored her. Insecurities like that ran deep and popped up when she least expected, but his explanation tamed them.

She was glad she'd asked. Knowing would keep her from worrying every time he clammed up or ignored her. "Okay."

A laugh burst from him. "Okay?"

"Yeah. Okay. See how easy that was? You told me the whole story and now I understand all the weird things you've done since you realized who I was."

"I didn't do any weird things."

She raised her left eyebrow as she gave him an "Oh, really?" expression.

"Name one."

"Well, when we met, you talked a lot. Once you found out I was the person you were looking for, you barely said anything. In the diner, you were also kind of funny."

He laughed again. "*I* was funny?"

"Not hysterical but…" She shrugged. "You know. Silly?"

"My parents would not believe you if you told them that." He turned and started walking again.

She raced to catch up with him. "Which means I have to tell them. If only because they'll get a chuckle out of it."

"You'll probably never meet them."

She sighed. He was back to being careful again. She understood, but if they were stuck together for the rest of the day and he didn't talk, their time together would be insufferably boring.

"Are we really going out for dinner tonight?"

"Yes. One thing about New York City, there are a million wonderful restaurants I can take you to."

She glanced down at her worn jeans. She did have one dress packed. She'd planned on using it for the meeting with the lawyer, though. "Just don't get too fancy."

"Maybe we *should* go look for a dress?"

"I don't take charity."

"There's an entire slush fund at your disposal. That's not charity."

"You see things your way. I see them mine."

"Look, the bottom line is I don't want any attention being called to you. Neither does Danny. Dressing to fit in is a good idea." He pointed ahead of them. "There's a shop a few blocks down. It's where I get my mom's Christmas and birthday gifts. I'm going to have Danny set up an account for you. That way, after tonight, if you feel like you want a dress or shoes or something, you can get what you want or what you feel you need while you're here. No pressure."

"You want me to shop where you get your *mom's* clothes?" She laughed. "No thanks."

He sighed. "It's a nice place. It's got things for younger people, too."

"If you expect me to shop there, it better."

"It does."

She quelled the flutter in her stomach. She longed to

look like the woman wearing the pencil skirt and silky blouse…but she also didn't have any money. Didn't have anywhere to wear something like that when she got home. Buying pretty things would be a waste. A waste of the money of a man who had hurt her. Money she didn't want—except to help her dad. She was only here on the chance she was an heir and she could help her parents. They were the ones who'd plucked her out of the system and saved her. She didn't need fancy clothes. Especially if she wasn't an heir.

"But don't get your hopes up. I'm not going shopping."

"You never know."

"I know."

"No. You don't."

She shook her head. For a guy who wasn't supposed to talk to her, he never seemed to let her get the last word.

CHAPTER FOUR

NICK TURNED TOWARD the entry of a grand hotel. Leni glanced up. A white facade was the perfect backdrop for the huge green wreath that sat above the portico. Red ornaments scattered around it glittered in the late afternoon sun.

The muscles around her heart tweaked. She was missing everything happening at home. Christmas parties, carolers, making cookies with her mom. Nick had told her to pack for two weeks and she assumed that's the longest she'd be away. She might miss the baking and extraspecial holiday tips from regular customers at the diner, along with the occasional gift, but she'd be home over a week before Christmas.

There was no point in getting homesick. Everything was under control.

She followed Nick as he walked into the lobby, marched to the reservations clerk, gave his name and got a key card. Within seconds, they were in the elevator.

He continued the silence through the ride to the tenth floor and down a quiet hall. When they stopped at a door, he opened it by scanning the key card. She stepped inside the room and gasped.

A huge window ran along the entire back wall, bringing the sights of Times Square into her room. Two red sofas sat parallel, in front of a marble fireplace with a bar off to the left. A dining table and upholstered chairs had been set up near the window.

"All this is for me?"

"Yes."

She looked around in awe. "This has got to be costing the estate a pretty penny."

"The estate has lots of pretty pennies, so don't worry about it." He glanced at his watch. "I'll be back at seven."

She nodded.

"If you need anything…and I mean *anything*, call the concierge."

"I do wish I had a book."

"I'm sure they can get you one."

With that he turned and walked out of the room, closing the door behind him.

She glanced around again. "No television." She spotted the big mirror above the fireplace, saw the remote on the mantel and laughed. "Thank goodness I watch enough house fixer-upper shows to know how they hide televisions these days."

She carefully lowered herself onto one of the two red sofas, running her hand along the smooth leather, enjoying the luxury.

Was this how she'd live if she really was rich?

Even as she thought that, the silence of her suite enveloped her. She'd hate to think that all wealthy people were lonely. But Nick was rich…a simple billionaire he'd said… and he barely spoke. Of course, she knew why he didn't want to talk to her, but he didn't even speak to his driver.

That was what had bothered her. He never even said hello to his driver, the pilot for their plane or any of the ground crew scrambling to get their luggage into the jet's belly. He walked around as if he were in his own little world.

Which was a shame. Good-looking guy like that should be the happiest man around. And with all his money, he should realize he was one of the luckiest.

She thought of her adoptive dad. How he'd worked and

scrimped and saved and barely made ends meet. Yet, he considered himself one of the luckiest people on the planet.

Nick Kourakis should be swinging-from-the-chandeliers happy and if she got the chance, maybe she would tell him that.

Nick arrived at Leni's suite at exactly seven. When she opened the door to him, he almost stepped back. His former elf wore a simple black dress with a red sweater. Her eyes had been painted with shadow and liner and mascara—but only enough to make her pretty, not overdone—and her lips were ruby red. Her long brown hair had been caught up in a twist in the back, giving her face a look of sophistication that nearly stole his breath. Black heels provided at least three inches of height and put her right at his chin. The perfect place for a woman to be.

He shook his head to clear it of that stupidity. She might be beautiful, but they'd never get to test out why coming to chin level was perfect. He would never kiss her.

That registered oddly, way deep down in his soul, in a place he hadn't acknowledged for so long the ping was a hollow, empty sound.

Calling himself foolish and exhausted, he ignored the weird feeling and said the one thing that might get her to tell him if she'd gone to the boutique after all. "You look nice."

"Nice?" She spun around once. "I look fabulous. This is the dress I'd bought for my college graduation ceremony last week. I'd brought it to wear to meet the lawyer, but I can wear it twice."

The hope that she'd shopped was replaced by another ping of acknowledgment in his soul. Her simple pleasure in the dress was fun. Almost cute enough to make him laugh.

He'd forgotten what it was like to really enjoy something ordinary. Actually, he'd forgotten what it was like to enjoy *anything*. He'd snuffed out that feeling, but one laugh from her and he remembered it, longed to feel it again.

Even though he knew he wouldn't.

He cleared his throat. "You made a good choice with the dress—and shoes."

She extended her foot and looked at her black pumps with love in her sparkling green eyes. "I know. They make me feel like I'm tall enough to talk to you without having to stretch my neck."

He'd thought they made her tall enough to kiss easily, naturally.

He really needed to get some sleep. The well-rested New Wolf of Wall Street didn't care about enjoying things, didn't compliment a woman he wasn't dating, didn't notice anybody's shoes.

But when Leni put on her worn leather jacket, he remembered her real world again. Remembered why this dress was so important to her. And told himself that no matter how tired he was, he could be nice to her.

Then she spoke. "You look pretty good yourself."

He glanced down at his black suit. "This is what I had on this morning." And the day before. It was a wonder he wasn't a wrinkled mess.

She winked and headed for the exit. "I know. You looked fabulous then, too."

His brain scrambled. Had she just flirted with him?

Realizing she was almost at the door, he had to hurry to open it before she did, confusion and fear skittering along his nerve endings. They'd talked about this. There was no point in flirting.

He opened his mouth to remind her they'd already decided they shouldn't get chummy, which in his book included flirting, but as she stepped into the hall, she casually said, "I'm starving."

His brain stopped and then started again. She'd said he looked fabulous, but he hadn't confirmed that she'd flirted with him. And the "I'm starving" comment shifted them back to normal conversational territory.

Did he really want to bring up flirting?

Especially when they'd already discussed this?

Not in a million years. "Then let's get you some food."

Outside the hotel, at a time of day when the avenue should have been dark, it was lit by hundreds of thousands of lights from jumbotrons, video advertisements, scrolling newsfeeds and storefronts. Leni looked up and down the street, her curiosity and wonder evident on her face.

Nick suddenly understood why Danny had put her in Times Square. The place was filled with tourists and her interest blended with the curiosity of the people around her. Even if she couldn't control her reactions, she didn't stand out. Half the people on the sidewalk were gawking in awe at the lights and videos and shops.

"I hope you like Italian food."

Her eyes widened. "I love it."

"Great." He motioned to his driver that they were going to walk and headed down the street to the left. "I know a wonderful place. It's low-key. A favorite hangout of visitors to the city, most of whom are going to a Broadway play."

She huddled against the cold, sinking into her jacket, but her eyes were big, taking in everything in the exciting city he barely noticed anymore.

He slowed his pace, let her enjoy the walls of advertisements on the buildings, the vendors, the Christmas shoppers, and the cacophony of sounds from people and taxis and buses.

Seeing the city through her eyes, he felt the rhythm of it. The movement of tourists and vehicles in the brisk night air, all lit by thousands of colored lights.

The crowd thinned as they drifted away from Times Square. In another block they were at the restaurant. He gestured for her to walk down the black iron steps and opened the door for her when they reached the bottom.

Warmth hit him immediately, along with the shift in noise from a busy street to a crowded bar. After a clerk checked their coats, the hostess led them to a table in the middle of the dining area. The waiter poured wine for sampling. Nick almost told him it would be fine but realized he didn't even know if Leni liked wine. Mark had been someone who drank tequila with a beer chaser. Of course, her father hadn't been around to influence her decisions.

"Is wine okay?"

"Are you kidding? Wine would be great about now."

The waiter grinned, poured two glasses and scurried away, leaving them to read the menus.

She took a slow sip of the wine and savored. "This is fabulous."

He loved the way her eyes closed as she enjoyed her sip and slowed himself down as he took another taste from his glass. It *was* fabulous. "I think you're having a fabulous night."

She snickered. "That's pretty cocky of you to say."

"It's not me. It's you. You said you looked fabulous and I looked fabulous and now the wine is fabulous."

"Sometimes fabulous really is the only word."

He shrugged, but she was right. He'd known it when he took the time to savor the wine. He might not put himself or his clothes in the fabulous category, but her in that dress, with her green eyes and red lips? She was fabulous.

"Anything you recommend?"

He glanced up and saw her studying the menu. "Any of their pasta is—" he grinned "—fabulous."

She laughed. "You *do* have a sense of humor."

"No. I just took advantage of your love of fabulous."

"Nick?"

His brain stalled at the sound of his mother's voice, but he quickly gathered his wits and rose. "Mom!"

* * *

Leni glanced up at the pretty blonde with perfect makeup, wearing a bright blue dress, standing next to an older version of Nick. *His mom and dad?*

Nick's mom hugged him. "Sweetie! What a surprise."

"And what a surprise to see you," Nick replied.

Leni had to swallow a laugh. She'd bet it was a surprise…or a shock, from the horrified expression on his face.

He glanced at her, then said, "Leni, these are my parents, Amanda and Walt. Mom, Dad, this is my *friend*, Elenore."

She knew the emphasized word was for her. He wanted her to get on board with that description of who she was.

His parents looked at her expectantly. She didn't know if she should stand or stay seated or reach across the table to shake hands, and that lack of knowledge froze her.

His father nodded to her. "Nice to meet you."

"Nice to meet you, too."

His mother grinned broadly. "*Lovely* to meet you." She pulled in a satisfied breath. "You're here for dinner?"

Nick said, "Yes." He cleared his throat before cautiously asking, "Are you here for dinner?"

"We're done." His mother turned her big blue eyes on him. "You're lucky we're on our way to a play."

From the look on Nick's face, Leni would guess he did believe that made him lucky. But he said, "Too bad. We could have eaten together."

Leni almost snorted. She didn't think his parents bought that any more than she had.

His mother's gaze slid to Leni, then back to Nick. Her expression said she was putting one and one together—her son with a woman and not really wanting to eat dinner with his parents—and coming up with a very clear two.

"So, this is a date?"

Nick's mouth fell open slightly, as if he'd had to pause

to stop the denial that automatically sprang up because he didn't know how else to explain who Leni was. He wasn't allowed to tell them the truth. Nobody was supposed to know who she was or why she was in New York. But she and Nick could be friends. All he had to do was stick with that.

Finally, he said, "I told you we're friends."

His mother laughed. "Friends could be on a date."

"Well, we're not. We're *friends*, having dinner together."

His mother turned to Leni. "He can be a real grouch sometimes."

The devil got into Leni and she smiled at his mom. "Oh, I don't know. The day we met he was actually funny."

Nick's mom's forehead scrunched. "Really? Nick was funny?"

Leni grinned. "Yes."

Amanda shook her head. "That's amazing."

Nick sighed. "Come on, Mom. I'm not that bad."

"Yes, you are." She faced Leni. "I'm hoping this means you'll be at the annual fundraiser Nick hosts for the children's wing of the hospital."

She glanced at him. "You host a fundraiser?" She wanted to say, "By yourself? Really?" But she suddenly realized that what was impossible in her world was probably commonplace in his. He'd have assistants and party planners doing the work.

"It's a thing we've always done. My dad's the one who's on the hospital board. I merely volunteer for this."

He sounded old and tired. About something he'd volunteered for...or something he'd been pressured into volunteering for?

"There's a Christmas party in the ward itself," his mother explained. "And an absolutely breathtaking ball a week later."

"Sounds nice." It sounded like a lot of work. On top of

the job of running an entire company. A company that had clients like Leni's deceased dad who had *billions* of dollars. If he'd given only half of that to Nick's firm to manage, that was a lot, lot, lot of responsibility.

His mom smiled. "I can see we're making my son uncomfortable and I don't want to ruin your dinner. But I do hope you'll come to the party and the ball."

"Yes," Nick's father said, but his eyes zoned in on her, studying her, judging her. "We would love to see you there."

No, he wouldn't. His tone said it quite clearly. But his mother was so happy to think her son was dating someone— Nick's denial had been too weak to shift her away from her hope—that guilt tweaked at Leni's conscience.

Knowing she nonetheless had to play along, she found a way to answer the question honestly without making promises. "I'd like that."

His mom smiled. "Great." She turned and headed toward the door.

Nick's parents walked through the small room packed with tables filled with diners and Nick sat down again.

Wanting to ease the tension, she said, "I told you I'd tell your parents you were funny."

"You shouldn't have. Now they're going to call tomorrow and ask a million questions."

"Look at it this way. I could have told them you flirted."

He cursed. "You are so lucky you didn't say that."

"Why? What are you going to do? Lock me in my hotel room?"

He rolled his eyes, but she could see she'd shifted his focus, and if she kept teasing him maybe he'd relax.

"Your mom sure likes the idea that you might be dating someone. Have all your other dates been shrews or has it been so long since you've dated anyone that she all but did a dance of joy?"

"It could be a combination of both."

She chortled. "My mom and dad do the same thing. Except they tried to set me up with every eligible guy on my dad's construction crew." She took a breath. The last two years had been so difficult with her dad being injured that she'd forgotten that, and the memory sent a wave of sadness through her. "But he hasn't worked in two years." She sucked in another breath. And she hadn't had a date in two years.

She was in no position to tease Nick.

The waiter arrived. They ordered. As he'd said, the food was better than anything she'd ever eaten. Preoccupied with enjoying every bite, she almost didn't notice that they didn't talk. They finished a bottle of wine and refused dessert, which meant the night was over. And she would go back to the hotel now.

Stepping out into the quiet end of the street, she let herself enjoy the city. She didn't mind returning to her room. It was cold and she had warm pajamas in her suitcase. Plus, she was tired. It had been a long day.

But with Nick silent beside her, she thought about his parents again and her guilt over deceiving them returned. His mom was expecting "Nick's friend" to show up at a hospital event when technically she was in hiding.

Because he hadn't told them the truth.

"Do you lie a lot?"

His voice jerked with surprise. "What?"

"I understand keeping your distance from people and not talking to your driver and pilots and such, but you seemed to lie really easily to your parents."

He shook his head. "I did not lie. I led them to draw their own conclusions. And what my dad ended up thinking is going to cost me a lecture because I can't tell him who you really are. But I did try to steer them away from thinking we were dating."

"Yeah, but you did it a little too late."

"I had to leave a little doubt in their minds because

we're hiding you, remember?" He sighed. "It's just better if I keep my distance."

Complete disbelief overwhelmed her. "With your parents?"

"Especially with my parents."

She glanced over at him, but he was staring straight ahead. No expression on his face. No remorse. No sadness. No sign of guilt.

"Now, see? To me that is just plain odd. After a year in foster care I was so grateful to get parents that I'd never want to be distant."

He pulled in a heavy breath. "Have you forgotten we decided it would be better if we didn't get to know each other?"

"We're not talking about ourselves. Technically, we're talking about our parents."

"That's worse. That could be construed as me trying to get your sympathy."

"Because you don't date?"

He dropped his head to his hands. "My not dating isn't reason for anyone's sympathy. This estate must be handled carefully. Danny wants to be the one who explains all this to you because there's a lot at stake."

She mumbled, "I suppose," and shut up. The beauty and noise of Times Square were enough to take her attention for the rest of the walk. Ambling through the lobby of her hotel to the elevator, she didn't expect him to talk.

But when they reached her door, the silence seemed out of place. She said the only thing that popped into her head. "I had a great time."

"What? Not a fabulous time?"

And her Nick was back. The guy she liked. They might have agreed not to get too chummy, but his "fabulous" comment was definitely flirting, at the very least teasing. Still, what would a little flirting hurt? It wasn't like stoic Nick Kourakis would fall in love with her because she teased him.

"Just not going to let me forget that, are you?"

He laughed. "No."

Their eyes met and suddenly it felt like a date. Not the weird outings she had with guys her dad found, but one of the real dates she had the first few years at university. Dates with guys who thought her pretty, made her laugh and wanted to kiss her.

Her heart sped up. What if *Nick* wanted to kiss her?

He couldn't...could he?

Why not? He'd flirted with her. And before that he'd told her she had a warmth about her that was appealing— all but admitted he liked her when he explained why their getting to know each other was a bad idea.

The silence continued as they gazed into each other's eyes. He was gorgeous, funny sometimes, and he'd taken good care of her that day.

If he did want to kiss her all he had to do was bend forward a few inches and press his lips to hers—

Her heart nearly exploded just thinking about his mouth meeting hers. She could not let her thoughts run away from her like that! She couldn't forget that Nick wasn't her friend because he didn't want to be. It would be crazy to spin fantasies about someone who'd told her up front he didn't want to get involved with her. She'd had enough rejection in her life. When she chose a romantic partner, it would be someone who didn't have secrets, someone who'd trust her and love her, just as she was.

What it felt like to kiss Nick was totally irrelevant stacked up against the truth of what she needed. She shouldn't be probing into his life or, worse, spinning fantasies about him.

She turned and swiped her key. For the first time since she heard the no-talking rule, she realized it was a wise one. "Good night."

CHAPTER FIVE

LENI WOKE THE next morning totally disoriented.

In a fancy hotel, fighting a crush on a guy with secrets, she ordered eggs and toast from room service and a pot of coffee.

When her breakfast arrived, she grabbed her cell phone and called her mom.

Her dad answered. "Hey, Kitten."

"Hey, Dad. Feeling okay?"

"Fit as a fiddle." He always said that, not wanting Leni or her mom to worry. "How's the Big Apple?"

"Huge. Except it goes up to the sky instead of spreading out."

"Oh, it spreads pretty far. Your mother's tapping my shoulder. I think she wants a turn."

Before Leni could say goodbye to her dad, her mom said, "So? What's happening?"

She told her mom about eating on the jet, riding in a limo, seeing people dressed in fancy clothes, going to the Italian restaurant and how Nick didn't want to talk about the estate because the lawyer needed to explain it all to her. He couldn't.

She bit her lower lip. "It's all kind of strange and confusing. Like I'm in a dream."

"In a way you are."

"Yeah, except I can't shake the weird feelings I have about Mark Hinton. About him having money and letting my biological mom struggle, especially when she was sick."

"Powerful men do things the rest of us don't understand."

"I suppose. But inheriting his money feels wrong…" She paused to think that through then said, "It feels sleazy."

"Sleazy?"

"It's almost like I'm so thrilled at the prospect of getting money that I'm letting him off the hook for abandoning me and my poor mom." She didn't mention that no one had seen her biological mom since she had given Leni up. Her mother knew that. When Leni was sixteen, they'd hired an investigator to look for her but never found her. They also never found a death certificate. That meant her mom had survived whatever illness she'd been fighting when she had to give up Leni. But she'd never come back for her. Hadn't even checked up on her as far as Leni knew.

That's the thing that haunted her sometimes. Her mother hadn't seemed to want her any more than her biological father had.

"But we need this money for dad. It's the worst rock and a hard place. Taking this money feels like I absolve everybody of not wanting me."

Her mom's soft sigh drifted through the phone. "Oh, Leni. Don't you remember how much your dad and I wanted you? We'd tried for years to have a child and couldn't. When the social workers put your little hand in mine, my heart melted. You brought so much joy into our lives."

She did remember. Mostly because she was eight, not a toddler, not an infant but a kid who understood what was going on. "You guys made me very happy, too."

"Because we were so grateful to get you. Your biological parents might have left you, but we were desperately happy for the privilege of raising you."

As always, her soft-spoken mother's words were like a magic balm. Still, there was something very basic about being rejected not just by a mother who didn't come looking for her after she got well, but by a guy who didn't want her at all.

And the money felt like the key. Almost as if, if she refused it, she would shake off her feelings of rejection forever. But just when she would convince herself that walking away was the right thing to do, she'd remember her sick dad and hesitate.

Would she be selling her soul, the way she viewed herself, the code of honor she didn't even realize was so strong, if she took that cash—even if it was for her dad, not herself?

Nick knocked on Leni's hotel room door that afternoon to take her for a stroll through the Metropolitan Museum of Art. Danny had called to say his trial had not ended, and when Nick asked for specifics, Danny mumbled about the length of testimony of witnesses being way over what Danny had thought they should be. But he swore the trial would finish up the next morning.

Nick had sighed and agreed to entertain Leni. Not because he felt for Danny but because he felt for *her*. She was a nice woman in a strange city, here to ascertain whether she was the heir of a huge estate, but the vetting process hadn't started because Danny wasn't available to do his job.

Nick was positive that after a morning of being cooped up, she'd be eager for even his company, but when she opened the door, she wouldn't meet his gaze.

His heart stuttered. They were right back where they were when he'd brought her to the door the night before. One minute they were practicing safe silence walking down the hall to her suite, and the next they were making flirty comments and gazing into each other's eyes. Then she'd broken the contact and run into her room.

While he'd been standing there thinking about kissing her.

What was it about being in front of a door, saying goodnight, that brought out that instinct? Or longing. What had trembled through him wasn't just a desire for a kiss. It was more. Something part of him wanted but the other part knew he couldn't have.

But she'd raced off. She'd handled the moment perfectly—getting them both off the hook.

So why wouldn't she look at him now? And why wasn't she talking? She always talked. Even when he reminded her that they shouldn't.

"Where are we going?"

Her quiet, impersonal question might be talking, but it wasn't typical Leni chitchat.

Maybe she finally realized it really was better if they didn't get to know each other? Didn't veer off into conversations that tempted him to kiss her—

"I thought I'd take you to the Metropolitan Museum."

She slid her purse strap onto her shoulder as she faced him. She wore her scruffy jacket and jeans, but the Met was filled with all kinds of people. And she looked nice. She didn't need fancy clothes to be attractive.

"That sounds great."

"I think you'll enjoy it." And they could talk as much as she wanted—about art. The Met was the best way to allow her to be chatty and use up a lot of time happily, neutrally. He was a genius for coming up with it.

Silence reigned as they rode the elevator to the lobby and walked out onto the street and into his limo.

Accustomed to her talking, the quiet enveloping them felt wrong. But he told himself not to worry. She wouldn't be able to contain herself at the Met. Plus, her not talking on the drive worked to his advantage. The questions she asked always drew him in even though he knew it was wrong. He kept falling into the feelings he'd had at the diner, the instant connection. The almost-kiss at her door the night before proved it.

She didn't say a word on the limo ride, while she climbed out of the car or even on the busy street in front of the Met. But she also didn't look around the way she normally did. She kept her eyes fixed on her old boots as they ascended the steps into the museum. Her gaze stayed lowered as they walked inside.

He hated this.

She was much too perky and sunny to keep her head down and herself quiet. But that was why he'd brought her to this enormous museum. There was plenty to talk about without once getting personal. He just had to nudge her to recognize it.

He glanced around, saw the exhibit housing the Christmas tree and smiled. That would get her talking.

He guided her to the Medieval Sculpture Hall. Her head came up slowly and she gasped at the enormous Christmas tree. "Oh, my…"

"It's a twenty-foot blue spruce." Glad he'd skimmed the information as they'd walked in, he directed her to the base of the tree where a full nativity scene was arranged beneath the lower boughs.

But her gaze stayed on the upper branches. "The angels look like they're climbing to the sky."

Proud he'd realized she wouldn't be able to resist talking about the gorgeous Christmas tree, he rocked back on his heels. "Or coming down to earth."

She stepped a few feet to the right, examining the figures scattered about the tree and shook her head. "It's the most beautiful thing I've ever seen."

He angled his head toward the door. "There's a whole building full of wonderful things. There's even an armor room. Egyptian art. Modern art. What do you like?"

Her smile returned. "I don't know. I've never been anyplace like this."

He motioned to the exit. "We have five hours to look your fill."

She headed for the door. "What happens in five hours?"

"I take you back to the hotel to get ready for dinner."

"Out?"

"Sure. If you're worried about what to wear, the account at the boutique has been set up for you. All you have to do walk in and give your name."

Her spine stiffened. "No, thank you."

"Seriously? You have access to money while you're here. Just take the limo to the boutique and use the account."

"You make it sound so easy."

"It is."

"When you have money."

Her statement was flat with a hint of bitterness, and he almost stopped walking. Locked in those few words was the reason for her unhappiness. He was certain of it. But he didn't want to be curious about her life any more than he wanted her to ask about his. He had parents to please, a brother who was gone and sorely missed, a difficult life that a good person like Leni shouldn't get dragged into.

He squelched the troublesome questions about why she might be so sad through two exhibits, but eventually he began going over everything she'd said the day before until he remembered how she'd reacted to his misleading his parents, especially her reasoning. She'd been confused by him distancing himself from his mom and dad because she'd spent a year in foster care—

That nagged at him until he couldn't stand it anymore, and his question was out before he could stop it. "Were you really in foster care?"

She turned away from a bright painting. "Yes. I was seven when my mom put me in. Eight when the Longs found me and adopted me."

Her answer brought him up short. *She'd been abandoned by her mom? In foster care for an entire year before she'd met the Longs?*

"That's tough."

"My mom couldn't keep me because she was sick. Her choice was to feed me or buy medicine." She shook her head. "My dad was a billionaire, but my mom was too broke to save herself and care for me, and she made the only choice she could. I ended up living in three different homes with three families I didn't know." She paused, caught his gaze. "It was the worst year of my life."

His heart hurt for her. There was so much sadness in that simple explanation that a longing to comfort her rose up in him.

But that was a slippery slope.

He shoved his hands into his pockets. "You know what? Let's just move along. Maybe work our way to the Egyptian exhibit."

"Okay."

The cloudiness was back in her eyes and Nick sucked in a deep breath. He'd probably been a little too abrupt changing the subject. But if he hugged her to comfort her, his brain wouldn't stop there. He'd feel her softness. Her curves. Get drawn into the strange connection he'd had in the diner, the feeling of warmth and comfort and rightness that had washed over him. He'd want things he couldn't have. Romance and connection required honesty, and he couldn't be honest with anyone, couldn't talk about his mistakes, didn't want anyone to see or know the real him.

Out of necessity, his life was nothing but business but hers could be about to change dramatically. In a very good way. And maybe he should help her realize that?

"You know, you might be surprised when you talk about the estate with the lawyer. If you're an heir, your life will change so much for the better."

She said, "You think so?" Then she peeked at him. "Is *your* life better?"

Though the question hit him right in the heart, he laughed. "Better than what?"

"The average person's?"

His little white lie was automatic. "Of course."

"Really?" She frowned. "You barely talk to your parents or your staff. I'm guessing you live alone. And the one thing you do that seems like fun—plan a ball—is probably organized by your assistant."

He scowled. "Do you always have to question everything?"

"Hey, I took a lot of psychology courses. I know what I see."

"I'm happy." In his own little way, he was. He'd built this life, this world, this persona to protect himself. And as long as he was safe, he was fine.

"No. You're not. Not even close. Take this museum," she said, motioning around them as they headed for the next exhibit. "While I'm actually looking at things, enjoying them, you're watching me. But not because you're interested in me. Because you're responsible for me and you think I'm a ticking bomb. Like any minute you expect me to explode."

"You have done some pretty weird things."

She stopped so she could stare him down. "Such as?"

"Tell my mom I'm funny."

She laughed. "Has it really been so long since you've made normal conversation that you've forgotten what it sounds like?"

"I talked to you at the diner."

"Yeah, you told me Mannington seemed like a nice town. That led me into talking about my job search. Which led you to tell me about your family business—and having a rebellious streak." She stopped, gave him a quick once-over. "Huh. I guess you do know how to hold a conversation after all."

She walked away, heading for a set of stairs. "There's an exhibit up here I really want to see. Because that's what people in museums do. They examine things. Then they discuss them. You should try it."

His footsteps echoing around him, he scrambled after her. Not to talk, though she was right. Talking about the exhibits was why he'd brought her here. But now that she'd pointed it out, he felt odd about talking. Every time he was around her, his reasoning got jumbled. His best intentions went straight to hell. His safe little world shook a bit. She didn't have the power to tear it down, but she could sure shake it.

She led him to the European paintings exhibit and honestly even if he'd wanted to talk, he wouldn't have. A reverent hush fell over them as they looked at work dating back to the thirteenth century. His breathing slowed as he studied landscapes and sunsets, blue skies and children. Knowing artists painted what they saw, he recognized he was looking at the world as it was hundreds of years ago.

"You're feeling better now, aren't you?"

He glanced at Leni. How was she so damned right all the time? "Yes."

She shrugged. "I'm really good at what I do."

And now she read minds? Answering questions he hadn't asked out loud? The woman was going to drive him insane.

Leni walked away glad she'd said her piece, but also enjoying the art. For as much as she knew the European exhibit would have a calming effect on Nick, she'd also known it would center her. She didn't want to rush her decisions about Mark Hinton's estate or jump to conclusions, and with the lawyer unavailable she had nothing but time to think about things.

She was glad Nick had brought her here. Not just for something they could discuss without consequences, but because sometimes all it took to get perspective was seeing the world through another person's eyes. Especially if that person lived in another century and their world was so different from her own.

They walked around the museum for the promised five hours, commenting on the exhibits sometimes but mostly staying silent, then Nick said it was time to go. She surreptitiously glanced at her watch. Five hours exactly.

She almost sighed. She didn't mind a person who loved precision, but he would take her to the hotel and then return to pick her up for dinner and he'd be careful about everything he said. If fun Nick did make an appearance, it would be short-lived.

It was getting old.

Just as she predicted, they stayed quiet on the ride to her hotel, and even on the walk to her room. With fun Nick nowhere to be seen, she didn't even think about a kiss good-night. But it wasn't really night. It was late afternoon. He had the entirety of their dinner that evening to sit stonily beside her. It was getting kind of insulting that he wouldn't talk because he didn't think it was appropriate for them to get to know each other.

Well, guess what? Neither did she. She had absolutely no desire to get to know grumpy Nick.

Frankly, she'd rather read a book.

She slid the key card over the lock, but as the door clicked open, she faced Nick again.

"I know you'd mentioned going out to dinner tonight, but I'm tired."

He frowned. "What?"

"I'm tired. It's what happens to people when they walk around for five hours straight. I'm going to order room service, put on my pajamas and watch some TV. Maybe I'll call that concierge guy and see if he can get me a book."

He stepped back, seeming totally confused. "Okay."

She supposed she didn't blame him. She had the whole of New York City at her disposal and she'd rather stay in. Not because she didn't want to see the city but because she didn't want to see it with a guy who didn't want to risk getting to know her.

It was weird, tiresome. Who the heck did he think he was, anyway? Did he think if he talked to her, she'd instantly fall at his feet in adoration?

She might be from a small town, but she wasn't brainless.

"I'm fine. Just in the mood for some me time. Don't worry. I'll be here tomorrow."

She entered her room feeling like herself for the first time in days. Not just because seeing the wonderful exhibits had centered her, but because she'd made a logical choice.

She didn't have to be bored with gorgeous Nick Kourakis. She could read a book.

Nick stared at her closed door. Okay. He had to admit his ego took a direct hit when she'd said she'd rather stay in and read a book than go somewhere with him. There had been a time when he was the most fun, most interesting guy on the planet. Women lined up to spend time with him. Not one of them would have preferred a book.

Walking to the limo, seeing the Christmas decorations that signaled the season of peace on earth, he stopped, glanced around. They *were* amazing.

He hadn't noticed things like Christmas decorations since Joe died. Being with Leni was opening his eyes again. Not because she was pretty, though that certainly didn't hurt. But because she was so damned transparent and honest. He knew her experience in foster care and then being raised by two loving parents played into that. Not to mention small-town living. He supposed if there were only fifteen hundred people in your entire town, life would be very different. She'd seen the good and bad side of the world, of people. Comprehended things only someone who'd gone through trouble could appreciate. And she had a degree in psychology.

Actually, she'd probably understand *him* if he told her about his situation.

Shaking his head, he started toward the door of his limo again. She'd love that. She'd already evaluated him in the museum, basically told him he was boring then refused dinner with him.

He hated that that bothered him so much.

But it did, and he wasn't sure why. He'd think it was because he didn't like being rejected. Except, this wasn't personal. They'd already decided to keep their personal feelings out of this. He only had to babysit her, entertain her, when she'd been left alone too long.

So why did her rejection skim along his nerve endings, a constant reminder that wouldn't go away?

He got into the limo and stared out the window at the lights and people on the drive to his Park Avenue penthouse. He rode the quiet elevator that opened onto his stunning open-plan home, stripped off his scarf and tossed his overcoat on the sofa to the sounds of silence. Cold, hollow silence. The same silence that greeted him every night.

She was right. New Wolf of Wall Street or not, he had become boring.

He walked past the seating arrangement, pool table and bar to the windows in the back and looked out at the city dressed for the holiday. Now that he was noticing the decorations again, he remembered how much his brother had loved Christmas, remembered their childhood Christmases. How Joe had spent months finding the right gifts for everyone, wrapped them with care and sat with bated breath while everyone opened their presents—

The cold, hollow silence morphed into sadness. He missed his brother. He'd never felt it before because the guilt was always stronger. But tonight, he missed Joe.

Missed him with the kind of ache that took ahold of his heart and squeezed until his eyes drifted closed.

He wondered what Joe would be like now, and knew they'd still be best friends. He felt the loss again. Thick and all-consuming. The weight of it on his shoulders made him pull in a long breath. In some ways, the guilt was better. Guilt pushed him to work, to not let their parents down. This sadness only hurt.

The ring of his phone burst into the quiet. He considered not answering, but knew he had to. He was his parents' only child now. If something was wrong, he had to be there.

He yanked it from his pocket, scowled at the caller ID and said, "Hello, Danny."

"Hey, Nick."

"I hope you're calling to tell me your trial ended today."

"No."

Nick sighed. He'd suspected as much, but it had been worth a shot.

"There are two more witnesses." Danny's voice wobbled in that weird way voices sometimes do when someone has something difficult to say. "We should wrap up tomorrow but if not tomorrow definitely on Friday. No one will want this thing on hold over the weekend."

"But that's not a guarantee."

"No. Sorry. Honestly, this opposing counsel has confused me at every turn. I have no idea what she's going to do next. For all I know, she might only have one question for each of the last two witnesses. But even if the trial is still going on Monday, I'll have the weekend off and I'll be able to talk to Elenore on Saturday. You'll be off the hook with her."

Relief poured through him, but he winced. Leni was one of the nicest people he'd ever met, and he was acting as if being with her was a chore.

It wasn't. Fighting his attraction to her was the chore.

He sat on the edge of the pool table. He'd told her that. Told her they shouldn't talk. Been a real jackass about reminding her of that.

All because he liked her.

Danny broke into his thoughts. "So, can you give Leni a little time out of the hotel room tomorrow?"

He'd never had a problem like this with a woman before. If he wanted someone he usually went after her. But Leni was different. She would soon be a client if she decided to keep her share of her dad's money with his management firm. And she was a nice woman who didn't deserve a broken heart from a man who only did one-night stands.

But that didn't mean he had to be a jerk. When he'd told her that they shouldn't talk, shouldn't try to get to know each other, he hadn't realized they'd be together so much. Now that he knew, he needed to shift his strategy.

And maybe he should be glad he had another day or two to make up for being an idiot.

He thought for a minute about how he'd go about doing that, then smiled.

"Yeah. I can entertain her tomorrow."

"Okay," Dany said. "Just remember not to talk about the will or the estate."

Nick laughed. The woman had called him boring. The last thing he wanted to discuss with her was a will, an estate or his job. "I can promise you the will and the estate will not come up in conversation."

He hung up the phone feeling much better. He'd taken the no-talking thing a step too far, but now that he'd figured that out, he could make it up to her.

Tomorrow he'd show her he could be a fun guy.

CHAPTER SIX

THE NEXT MORNING, the ring of her cell phone edged its way into Leni's dream about waiting tables at the Family Diner, giving out free Christmas cookies, getting big tips and saying "Merry Christmas" as she waved to customers walking out the door.

The phone rang again.

With a gasp, she sprang up, off her pillow. Confused to be out of the dream so suddenly, it took another ring before she grabbed her phone. "Hello?"

"Good morning, Leni."

Nick.

She couldn't stop the happiness at hearing his voice any more than she could stop the ripple of annoyance. She could spend 24/7 with the Nick who made her laugh, but she didn't want to spend another long, boring day with the guy who didn't want to talk.

She carefully said, "Good morning, Nick."

"Danny's stuck in his trial for another day."

And she and Nick were stuck together for another day—unless she could sway him into thinking she didn't need to be entertained? "I haven't even gotten out of bed yet. It could be a lazy day for me. It's fine that Danny's not available."

"No. It's not. It's incredibly unfair that we're keeping you in New York and not getting on with the reasons we brought you here."

Who was this guy? The Nick she knew was either funny

or grouchy. Never accommodating. "Don't worry about it. I can read a book today."

"No, your being stuck here is an imposition. So, to make up for that, I thought we'd do something really fun today."

"I'm okay with getting a book and just vegging today."

"You vegged last night. Today, I thought we'd go skating at Rockefeller Center."

Her breath hitched. She sat up a little farther on the bed. *"Rockefeller Center?"*

"It's gorgeous when it's decorated for Christmas. And they have an enormous tree."

Her entire body longed to do something physical, but more than that she loved to skate. With her busy schedule and her dad's troubles, she hadn't skated in the past two years.

Excitement filled her blood, boosted her mood, made her not care that Nick Kourakis wouldn't say a word beyond what he had to. As long as she had skates on her feet, it didn't matter.

"I love to skate."

"Good. Get your breakfast and put on something warm. I'll pick you up around ten."

"I'll be ready."

She threw aside the covers, called room service and got her shower. By the time she had herself wrapped in one of the hotel's big white robes, her breakfast had arrived. She tried not to gobble because she had until ten, but it was useless. Everything she'd done since arriving in New York had been foreign to her. Today, she would do something she loved.

In the bedroom, she pulled out two pairs of socks, her warmest jeans, a T-shirt and a sweater for over it. She applied a little lip gloss and mascara, but when it came time to do her hair, she decided against pulling it into a bun or a ponytail. She loved the feeling of her hair floating around her when she skated. She curled it but kept it down.

She returned to the sitting room just as there was a knock on the door. Opening it, she found Nick.

"Ready to skate?"

Instead of his usual suit, today he wore jeans, a thick sweater and a dark parka. With his hair just a little messed and his eyes bright, he looked young and carefree.

And happy.

If she didn't know better, she'd think he was as excited to go skating as she was.

Maybe ditching him the night before had made him realize he needed to loosen up? Maybe because he liked her?

Remembering that's exactly why he didn't want to talk to her, she stopped that wishful thinking. There was something between them. Attraction, sure. But it was more. There had been a connection that he didn't want. If she called his attention to it, he'd turn back into grumpy Nick. The guy she didn't want to be around.

On the way down in the elevator, he said, "Did you sleep well?"

"I'm finally getting accustomed to not being in my own bed."

"Good. I slept well, too."

His unexpected small talk caused her to give him the side-eye, but the elevator door opened, and he guided her outside to his limo. They seated themselves and the long car slid into traffic.

"How was your breakfast?"

She frowned. The guy who didn't want her to be chatty was chatting. Again. Still, she wouldn't be rude or, worse, call attention to it.

"I had toast and eggs. Hard to screw that up."

"That hotel is known for its restaurants." He glanced at her and smiled "Maybe we should eat there tonight?"

The smile jump-started her heart and scrambled her

pulse. She told herself to settle down because this kind of reaction was exactly what Nick didn't want.

Schooling her face into complete neutrality, she said, "Yeah. Eating at the hotel would be great."

The limo fell silent, but within a few minutes, they arrived at Rockefeller Center.

As Nick had said, the huge Christmas tree dominated the area, and she had to stifle a gasp. Lit by what looked to be millions of lights, it sat in front of the Rockefeller Center building, with a backdrop of other tall buildings. Angel statues with trumpets sat by the tree. A row of flags created a wall. At least fifty people were already on the ice.

She stepped out of the limo feeling like she was stepping into a fairy tale. "It's beautiful."

It was also a perfect day, cold but not freezing. A blue, cloudless sky smiled down on them. No wind. No snow and lots of sunshine.

"I think this is my favorite place in New York City."

No longer surprised that Nick had spoken, she sneaked a peek at him. He glanced around the space as if seeing it for the first time. She could tell from the expression on his face that he didn't intend to be a spectator. He wouldn't stand behind her watching her like a bodyguard or stalker. He wanted to be here.

But not for *her*. He was only entertaining her. If he liked this place it was because it was gorgeous and filled with fun. And she was desperate for a little fun.

Maybe he was, too?

"I can understand why it would be your favorite place. It's wonderful."

"It is."

They paid the fee, rented skates and were on the ice in what felt like seconds. With a quick push off, she skated in a big circle to get the feel of things, then eased back to him. He clearly liked this place. She liked to skate. Having something physical to do was exactly what they needed.

"Come on! Skate with me."

He stood there, looking gorgeous in his parka and jeans, but also unsure. "I haven't skated since my teens."

When he'd bring his brother.

The thought shot through Nick's brain as bright as the sun glistening off the ice. Joe had loved skating nearly as much as he'd loved Christmas.

Nick almost groaned, thinking it had been a mistake to bring Leni here—except he wanted her to have fun. Real fun. This was a place to have fun.

"You came here as a kid?"

He shrugged. "Yeah. By the time I was a teenager I was a great skater."

That made her laugh. "Conceited much?"

"It's only conceited if you talk about it all the time." Finally feeling comfortable enough on his skates to try them out, he eased his way to the far wall then back again. When he reached her, he skated a ring around her.

"Very funny."

"I keep telling you I'm not funny."

"So that was a sarcastic ring you just skated around me?"

"It was more of a proof ring." He grinned at her. The sky was blue. The world was dressed up for Christmas. And he was on skates.

For the first time in five years he felt Christmas in the air. The wonder of it swirled around him, along with a magic he didn't quite understand. Maybe because Leni was back to teasing him? Maybe because she no longer seemed quiet or careful? Maybe because she was back to her old self?

Tonight, he would nurse his remorse about his brother, but this afternoon he would not think about Joe. He would show Leni a good time and demonstrate to her that he was a fun guy in an unromantic way that would ease both of their nerves about what a jerk he'd been about not getting to know each other.

"Wanna race?"

He took off before she had a chance to answer, bobbing and weaving around other skaters. She saw a clearer path and took it, beating him to the wall.

"Ha! I win."

"You probably skated last week. So, you're on your game."

"Nope. Haven't skated in two years."

He shrugged as he made a small circle around her. "Give me another ten minutes and no one on this ice will beat me."

"How do you get through doors with that big head?"

He laughed, breathed in the air again and something inside him stilled. He'd brought her here to have fun and instead he was the one laughing.

"Race you to that wall." The second the words were out of her mouth she was skating away.

A lover of competition, he pushed off immediately and his longer legs had him beside her in seconds. "I'm going to beat you."

"Who says?" She blew past him and was at the wall before he drew three breaths.

He reached her and said, "One more time," before he shot off.

She burst after him, passed him and stood with her arms folded on her chest when he finally caught up to her.

"How do you do that?"

"What? Beat you?"

"You have short legs."

She laughed. "You have a fat coat." She caught a chunk of the material stuffed with down, but when she looked up at him to say, "It's not aerodynamically sound," they both realized she was touching him. Like a friend, sure. But they weren't friends. They barely knew each other—

Except they had that damned connection they'd made at the diner the day they met. She'd been cute and funny, and he'd been instantly smitten. They'd spent two days together and she'd made him laugh as well as made him crazy. And after Danny talked to her on Saturday, he'd only see her in his capacity as her money manager.

That didn't sit right. She was too different to like, a part of his job and a royal pain in the butt with her honesty, but the thought of never laughing with her again, casually, naturally, seemed so wrong it sent confusion rippling through him. He wanted this day, maybe *needed* this day to laugh with her, as much as she did.

She let go of her grip on his parka and jerked her hand away, but he caught it before she could put it down to her side. "Let's just do a few laps."

"Why?" Shielding her eyes from the sun with a hand nestled in bright green mitten, she said, "So, you can get your form back?"

That was as good of a reason as any. "Yeah." Was it so wrong to want to have fun with her? He hadn't had fun since Joe died and maybe that's why his subconscious had brought them here. He'd missed Joe the night before. And being here now made him remember his brother in a good way. Not the painful way that had enveloped him before Danny called.

She pulled her hand out of his, skated a circle around him. "When you were a kid, did you do tricks?"

He sniffed. "Like a trained dog?"

"Like someone imitating Olympic skaters."

She executed a perfect toe loop.

He applauded.

"Now, you do a trick."

"I didn't do tricks when I skated. I just raced."

"Raced?"

"My brother. So, I'd win, and girls would like me."

She frowned. "Your brother?"

His mention of Joe stunned him as much as it stunned her. He would have pulled back the words if he could, but they were out there now, and he wasn't sure why.

"He was only a year younger than me." He said it easily, casually, so she wouldn't make a big deal out of it, testing the words, trying to figure out why he suddenly wanted to talk about Joe. "We'd race. I'd beat him. And girls would flock after me."

She shook her head. "You have really got to do something about your ego."

She did another two toe loops and pushed off to get speed enough for an edge jump.

Nick watched her, his heart in his throat. He'd skated to get girls, but she skated for the pleasure of it and watching her was pure joy. Nothing he'd ever experienced. Something as mesmerizing as it was wonderful.

He eased over to her and took her hands, so they could skate sideways in a circle.

"This is your big trick?"

"I told you. I don't do tricks. I only skated to get girls."

She chuckled, let go of his hands and raced off. He followed her, caught her and grabbed her hand again. This time he twirled her under his arm. She spun gracefully, tilting her head back, letting her long hair fall behind her and looking like poetry on ice.

His heart swelled with longing. Of all the women in the world, why did he have to like the one he wasn't supposed to like?

She owned a big chunk of the money his company was managing. But more than that, she was one of the nicest people in the world and he was a man filled with guilt and remorse.

He didn't deserve her.

When she stopped, she said, "So tell me more about your brother."

His chest pinched. He longed to tell her about Joe. Years

had passed with him holding all this inside, and she was the one person who would understand.

Actually, that was the point. Her sweetness, her honesty made him want to open up. And he shouldn't. A man like him should let a nice girl like her alone.

"I'd rather race."

At first, she looked confused, then she smiled. "Okay." She pointed at a spot on the wall. "I'll be there two seconds before you."

He laughed and pushed off after her. He might not be the right guy for her, but that didn't mean he couldn't enjoy her company.

Just this one day.

CHAPTER SEVEN

HAVING MISSED LUNCH, they decided to have an early dinner at an Irish pub rather than at her hotel. Happy from skating, Leni glanced around excitedly as they entered. The place was dark, partially because of low lighting, but also the walls were paneled with dark wood. The floors were dark. Blinds covered the windows. Even the shiny bar was dark wood.

"It's like a hideaway."

Nick laughed. "You have a weird way of looking at things."

"Oh, I don't know. Maybe I look at things the right way and you're the one whose perception is skewed."

He shook his head as they approached the hostess. The restaurant was empty except for an older couple at a table in front and two men at the bar. The bartender, a beefy guy with dark hair and a ready smile, gave them a quick once-over and Leni suspected he was also the bouncer. She didn't miss the glance that passed between him and the hostess and she realized they were in love.

Her heart stuttered as she saw they both wore simple gold wedding bands. Without saying a word, they communicated the kind of love and commitment that anyone who looked at them would know would last a lifetime.

The hostess guided them to a little table in the back and Leni smiled her thanks before the young woman made her way back to the bar area. Leni caught the bartender's wink and the hostess's smile and her heart could have melted into a big pile of goo.

She peeked at Nick, who was engrossed in his menu, realizing he hadn't seen any of it. Two things hit her immediately. First, she was in some sort of fanciful mood because of skating. Second, a few hours of fun had changed him. He laughed easily. Held her gaze when they spoke. And suggested this lovely little bar for dinner. Like friends. Not a guy stuck with babysitting her.

They sat with their menus for only a few seconds before a waitress appeared. They both ordered a beer and she scurried away.

"See anything you like?"

She lowered her menu to the table and winced. "Just fries."

"You can't live on fries."

"So, my mother says but I've always wanted to test that theory."

"You shouldn't. You need protein, too."

She grinned devilishly. "I had protein at breakfast. This isn't a permanent rebellion. Just a little skirmish."

"I'm feeling a little skirmishy myself."

She'd already figured that out and peeked at him. "Really?"

"Yeah. You get the loaded fries. I'll get the classic margherita flatbread."

"And we can share!"

"My thought exactly."

The waitress arrived with their drafts and they ordered their appetizers. She walked away, and Leni leaned back in her chair. Fun Nick was here and better than usual. The weird connection that had popped up at the oddest times since their meeting at the diner seemed to be gone, but happy Nick was much better.

"I like it here. It's sort of like a bar back home but it's cleaner."

He laughed. "Did you go there a lot?"

"I thought I wasn't supposed to talk about my life?

You know, because it's pointless for us to get to know each other."

"Let's just say that things changed a bit. Besides, we've spent so much time together that we have to start talking about something or we'll die of boredom."

Totally onboard with that assessment, she sat up. "What do you want to know?"

He shrugged. "I don't care. Tell me about school."

"Well, scraping the money together was hard but I didn't want to be one of those people who graduated owing more money than I'd ever be able to pay back."

He smiled and nodded, and she shook her head. "Look who I'm telling. You don't understand debt."

He winced. "Sorry. I don't."

"I like that you're honest about that."

"I think you're starting to rub off on me."

She laughed. "Wouldn't that be something."

"Yeah. I just can't figure out if it's a good or bad something."

"What kinds of things are you picking up from me?"

"Your over-the-top honesty, for one."

She took a sip of beer. "That's a good thing. What else?"

"Saying things that pop into my head."

"That's all part of being honest."

He shook his head, but he also took a breath and glanced around. "It *is* comfortable in here. Reminds me of my old life."

"Old life?"

He looked down, played with his silverware. "Yeah, before I took over the family business, I traveled a lot. Went to places like this."

She might have wondered about why he seemed to be avoiding her gaze, except she'd never traveled, and she gasped excitedly. "Like Irish pubs in Ireland?"

"Exactly like that."

"Is that why you don't notice your surroundings or the

people?" She waited a beat then said, "You've been so many places that this is dull to you?"

"Not dull. But I've lived in this city my entire life. I've seen every restaurant and street. I'm kind of accustomed to it. Going to Yale was a nice change of pace."

Happiness filled her. When he was normal like this, she could just take his cheeks between her palms and kiss him. She reminded herself that she shouldn't. Not merely because grumpy Nick could make an appearance any second but because he'd warned her he didn't want a relationship. Though she could enjoy herself, she would keep her emotions under control.

"You went to Yale?" Having expected Harvard, Yale was a pleasant surprise. "Really?"

"Nothing wrong with Yale."

"No. No. Yale's a great school. So, what was your rank?"

He winced. "I was the top of my class."

She didn't doubt that for a second. "Then you went to..."

"The Navy."

Expecting him to tell her about post-grad work, she flopped back on her chair. "What?"

"By the time I was twenty-one I had had it with sitting in classrooms and writing papers. I joined the Navy, discovered the SEALs and the challenge was too hard to resist."

"The challenge?"

"I love a challenge."

"I want to save the world and you love a challenge."

He laughed at her. "You think saving the world isn't going to be a challenge?"

"I wasn't planning on making any big moves. Just saving one person at a time."

"That's nice."

"I thought for sure you were going to say that's naive."

"I've known you long enough, Leni, to realize that you probably get just about anything you set your mind to."

"My dad always said I was like a little dog with a bone." Thoughts of her dad struggling at home hurt her heart, so she said, "Tell me about being a SEAL."

"It was amazing." He caught her gaze. "Changed my life. Everyone thinks of the world through a specific set of beliefs. Going into the military shows you just how big and how troubled the world really is."

"And?"

"And?"

"Is that what made you unhappy?"

He shook his head. "Being a SEAL, being on active duty, gave me a sense of purpose. But when my time was up, I knew I'd seen things that messed up my thinking a bit. I wasn't ready to go home, but I couldn't shirk my family responsibility anymore."

She gaped at him. "Are you telling me becoming a SEAL was your *rebellious* streak?"

"Yes."

She shook her head. "And you tell me I have a skewed vision of life."

"You do. And I don't. Not really. My parents wanted me involved with the firm. Becoming a SEAL only delayed that, but it was a rebellion."

She nodded thoughtfully. "So, after the SEALs you settled down and took over the family business."

"No. After the SEALs, I was antsy and couldn't stay in one place long, so I had to figure out a way to do my duty and give myself a chance to process my time in the military. In the end, I told my parents I'd be something like a recruiter. I traveled the globe and looked for investors like your dad. After a few years of bungee jumping and skydiving with risk takers like myself, I grew the firm from being moderately successful to being one of the top firms on the planet."

She could only stare at him. She'd never in a million years have believed he'd done so much. And most of it dangerous. "Wow."

The waitress came with their food. The conversation died as they poured ketchup, cut the flatbread, asked for refills of their drafts.

She took a bite of flatbread and groaned. "Oh, this is fabulous."

"My fabulous girl is back."

Her heart skittered. He'd called her his. Even if he meant it in the most generic of ways, those words tumbling off his tongue filled her with joy. Which was ridiculous. She'd known him only a few days. And he'd very clearly warned her that he didn't think it was a good idea for them to even consider a relationship. She told her heart to settle down, but the reminder was good. Fun Nick was very hard to resist, but she had to.

They ate and laughed some more. The bar got darker, as if reflecting night falling on the street outside.

The waitress brought two more drafts. Nick talked a bit more about the jet-setting he'd done to find new clients, and she stared at him. He had to be the most interesting person she'd ever met. He knew and was friends with kings, princes, billionaires, tech geniuses.

He could have talked down to her. He could have bragged. Instead, he just talked. As if they were friends.

The power of it made her breath catch. He was better educated, more experienced, more refined, cultured, sophisticated than she could ever dream of being. And it was pretty damned hard to remind herself that she was nowhere near a match for him when her overeager heart just wanted to be with him. Even if it wasn't forever. Even if it was just for tonight.

After one more draft, they slid into their coats, walked past the busy hostess and bartender who still had time to exchange smiles and stepped onto the street. With the sun down, the brisk air had chilled even further. It seeped through her coat and made her shiver.

She slid her arm beneath Nick's and huddled next to him for warmth. "I hope the walk to the hotel isn't a long one."

He laughed. "It's not."

He tucked her hand against his chest and she all but melted. He might not mean anything by what he was doing, might not even notice what he was doing, but he was stealing her breath, changing her idea of Prince Charming and making her wish she could be the kind of woman he'd be interested in.

They walked through the hotel lobby laughing but drifted apart in the elevator.

At her door, the distance between them annoyed her. But what was she going to do? Fix his collar just so she could keep her hands on him?

"Thank you for a really great day."

"Figured I had to do something since you all but called me boring yesterday." He shook his head. "You'd rather read a book than spend another two hours with me?"

A laugh escaped. "I didn't mean it like that."

"Of course, you did." He stepped close, put his hands on her shoulders and slid them up her neck, under her hair. "You have such beautiful hair."

And him touching it sent a rain of glittery awareness from her scalp, down her spine. "Thank you. I always figured my hair was God's way of making it up to me that the first few years of my childhood were awful."

Her voice had come out soft and breathless. She didn't care. She wanted him to hear the shiver of awareness, wanted him to bend down and kiss her. She wanted their mouths to meet, their tongues to twine and the glittery sprinkles to go from a gentle rain to a torrential downpour.

"I had a good time today, too."

She smiled, giving him as much of a hint as she possibly could that he should kiss her—without embarrassing herself or ruining something about this night, this minute.

He closed his eyes and took a breath before pulling his hands away. "Thank you for today."

"You're welcome."

He could probably see the disappointment in her eyes because he'd stepped away from her. "Depending on Danny's schedule, I might see you again tomorrow."

And he didn't want to kiss her tonight if they had another day together. She understood that. Kisses were acknowledgments, invitations or endings. An acknowledgment kiss was a way of saying *I like you*. The invitation kiss said *I like you and this might go somewhere*. The ending kiss said *we had fun, I like you, but this can't go anywhere*.

He could have given her the acknowledgment kiss.

He could have given her the invitation kiss, knowing her inheritance could ease her into his world and, even if Danny was free the next day, they could see each other again on their own—if he wanted to.

The only kiss he couldn't give her was the goodbye kiss. Especially not if they had another day with him entertaining her.

No matter how much he liked her. No matter how much fun they'd had that day. No matter how right they seemed when they were together—

He didn't feel the same way about her as she felt about him. Otherwise, he would have kissed her.

She took the step back this time. She'd already realized that, though he was attracted to her, she probably wasn't his type. She wasn't a sophisticate. She hadn't been top of her class. She hadn't traveled the globe. A smart woman didn't long for a man so different from herself, a man with secrets.

And she knew he had them. She'd guessed it all along. The fact that he wouldn't tell her was a proof of sorts that what she felt pulsing between them wasn't going anywhere.

She slid her key card along the pad. "Good night."

"Good night."

In her room, she shrugged out of her jacket, tossed it on a chair and then peeled off her sweater.

She was so disappointed that her heart felt bruised. That confused her. She had accepted that she wasn't right for him—

So why did she still want that kiss?

One kiss.

It might not be good to wish for a lifetime with a guy whose world was so different than hers. But there was nothing wrong with wanting a kiss.

Was there?

Hell, no.

The guy was great, gorgeous…fun. She was allowed to want a kiss.

Tomorrow night, at her door, he wouldn't have to wonder if he'd see her again, wonder if she'd still be in his charge. No matter what happened, Danny would take over on Saturday morning.

She had one more day to get that kiss.

Then she'd go back to being a client or a customer or nothing, if she wasn't an heir. In which case, she'd be returning to Kansas and she'd never see him again—

Yeah. She wanted that kiss.

CHAPTER EIGHT

THE FOLLOWING MORNING, Leni's cell phone rang while she was eating breakfast. Seeing the ID for Waters, Waters, and Montgomery, her heart sank.

Noooo.

If that was Danny Manelli calling, his trial was over. She wouldn't see Nick that day—maybe not until the estate was settled, when she'd be his client—if she decided to keep her share of the money with him. When things would be all business.

There'd be no kiss.

Taking a breath, she told herself not to jump to conclusions, clicked the screen and said, "Hello."

"Good morning, Leni. This is Danny Manelli. You and I haven't officially met, but I'm the lawyer for the Hinton estate."

Desperate hope quivered through her. Maybe he was calling because he had something to tell her? Maybe he wanted to apologize for not being available all week? She knew there could be nothing between her and Nick, but she'd wanted that one kiss.

"I know who you are. Nick gave your card to my parents. I saw your name. But Nick has also mentioned you."

"My trial is over. This morning we can finally begin the process of me explaining a few things to you. We'll also get the DNA samples."

Her throat closed. Damn it. This *was* it. The end. She'd never see fun Nick again. From here on out he'd be the boring businessman, if she saw him at all.

She worked to keep her voice even as she said, "Okay."

"I can have a limo there in forty-five minutes. Is that enough time to get ready?"

"Sure."

She disconnected the call and immediately went to the spa-like bathroom to shower. She refused to cry. Yes, a kiss would have been wonderful. But maybe that would have made things worse? Whatever his secrets, Nick obviously couldn't give her what she needed. A real relationship. A strong relationship with no guessing, no possibility of rejection. And maybe kissing him would have drawn her in so much she might have tried for more with him when more wasn't possible?

She had to let her fantasy of a kiss go.

This was for the best.

She had herself believing that until she pulled her black dress out of the closet. Pressing it to her face, she closed her eyes. She'd worn this to the Italian restaurant. They'd had wine, great food and she'd met his parents.

She popped open her eyes again. That had been one of the best nights of her life. But she wasn't a simpleton. Lots of things separated her and Nick. Including the fact that she didn't know his secret. No matter how sweet, how funny, how kind he could be...something in his life was terribly wrong. She'd known it even before he'd mentioned it.

In her internships, she'd counseled women to stay away from men with secrets. Bad boys. Wouldn't she be foolish to fall for one herself?

When the elevator doors opened on Danny's office, her suspicions about not seeing Nick were confirmed. The tall, dark-haired man wearing a white shirt, black tie and black suit pants was the only person in the room. As she stepped out of the elevator, he rose from the big desk, extending his hand to shake hers.

"I'm Danny Manelli, Leni. It's a pleasure to meet you."

She slid out of her old, worn coat. "It's nice to finally meet you, too."

After she was seated, Danny called in a lab tech who took three DNA samples. One for his lab and two for random labs. With that out of the way, the attorney went on to explain that she was potentially one of three heirs and the estate was in the process of looking for the other two. That was all she needed to know until they confirmed she was an heir.

"But once you're confirmed, you'll have access to your share of the money."

She thought of her adoptive dad's needs and nodded.

"So, now we wait for DNA to come back before you either go home if you're not an heir, or before I set up some bank accounts for you."

"Okay." She got quiet. With four days to think all of this through and acclimate, it wasn't as overwhelming as it had been on Monday or Tuesday. Refusing her dad's money wouldn't be cutting off her nose to spite her face. Especially since her new plan was to ask for the child support her dad had never paid. But this wasn't yet the time to talk about that.

"Do you have any questions?"

"Not about the estate."

"Good." Danny relaxed against his seat as if satisfied with her reaction. "Do you have something to ask that's not about the estate?"

"Yes." She glanced up at him. "Can I go home?"

Danny shook his head. "That's tricky. Do you want to go home and risk being mobbed?"

"Why would I be mobbed? My parents and I haven't told anyone about this. As far as I can tell no one knows who I am or why I'm here. So, I'm still anonymous."

Danny tossed his pencil to his desk. "It seems iffy to me."

"It doesn't to me, and I want to go home, to talk about

this with my parents. I don't want to sleep in a bed I don't know and run around Times Square looking like a bumpkin when I'm not. In Mannington, Kansas, I'm a normal person. I want to go home."

She also didn't want to miss Nick. To walk down the street and see things that reminded her of him. Once she got home, she'd be fine. She was sure of it. The whole time they were together, she'd been smart enough to keep her wits about her. Going home would be like wiping the slate clean.

Danny studied her for a few seconds. "All right. I'll arrange it."

Nick went to his office on Friday morning and was inundated with messages and meetings. With a little persistence and focus, he was able to clear the things that only he could handle before noon. Which left him with his usual work.

When he returned from lunch, his assistant closed the door to his office, giving him total privacy. He settled himself on his big desk chair intending to buckle down, but with his brain cleared, his thoughts jumped to Leni.

Skimming his hands through her hair the night before was a terrible luxury he couldn't resist. He'd really wanted a kiss, but that was one step too far. He'd known there was a chance Danny would be free today and he wouldn't see Leni again as anything other than a financial manager. Kissing her would only confuse her—especially since he didn't want anything growing between them. Then he'd touched her hair and tripped something inside himself. Not merely a sexual attraction, their connection. The feeling that there was something between them.

But he'd already decided this. She was a wonderful person and his life was dark, bleak. He had regrets that made him moody. Work that kept him sane. He wasn't right for a fun, happy person like Leni. Not even to date.

He forced his mind to the prospectus in front of him, knocking her out of his thoughts, but before ten minutes were up, she had tiptoed into his brain again. By now she would have spoken with Danny. He knew that because Danny had told him she'd be in his office that morning, they'd do a DNA sample and he'd explain some things about the estate to her.

He didn't think she'd be overwhelmed. If anything, she probably felt like she had some answers. So, she was fine.

He took a breath, put his attention on the prospectus and managed to work twenty minutes before he wondered what she was doing that afternoon.

Not that she needed a babysitter. It was just that the city could be intimidating—

No. He'd taken her around and watched her handle herself in some pretty weird situations this week, including meeting his parents.

That made him laugh, then he groaned. He had work to do.

He focused again and he made it until four o'clock when his phone rang. Seeing Danny's name in the caller ID, he jumped on the phone.

"Hey, Danny. How did it go with Leni?"

"Really well. She's very sweet and accommodating and smart, but we have a bigger problem."

Nick sat up. "Problem?"

"I got a call from her mom. Her dad's been taken to the hospital."

His breath stopped. "What?"

"Her dad's in the hospital, but that's not the worst of it. Leni asked if she could go home. After making her promise she'd keep a low profile, I got her a flight to Topeka."

Though his heart skipped a beat out of concern for her, Nick forced himself to relax. "She'll be home where her parents need her."

"Nick, her dad's in real trouble, but her plane has already boarded so her phone is off. She's going to fly to Kansas and go home to an empty house. Her mom said she didn't even have time to leave a note."

"She won't drive home. She'll call her mom when she lands."

"Phones aren't allowed in ICU. But even on the off chance that her mom would be in the cafeteria when Leni calls her, do we want her to find out that her dad's in ICU, maybe dying—in a phone call? When she's at an airport, with no car and no idea how to get to the hospital? We can't do that to her. Someone has to meet her at the airport and tell her this."

Leni was the sweetest, nicest person in the world. Nick absolutely could not let her go through that.

He scrubbed his hand across his mouth. "If I take my jet, I can beat her commercial flight to Topeka."

"I know. That's why I called."

"Then you also know I don't have a minute to spare."

He said that as he gathered work to shove into a brief-case. If he would be in the air for three hours, he could at least get some reading done.

And not obsess about seeing her again, or worse, ac-knowledge the way his heart lifted with relief that he'd get more time with her.

Leni deplaned, happily saying buh-bye to the flight at-tendants and heading up the ramp to the gate. She raced to baggage claim, her phone in her hand as she called her mom. Again.

It wasn't a surprise that no one answered at the house, but her mom should answer her cell phone—

Nope. It went straight to voice mail, as if she had it turned off.

After a few minutes, her small bag came down the chute and rolled along the conveyor belt. Before she could grab it, someone behind her did.

She spun around to tell the man he had the wrong suitcase but found herself face-to-face with Nick.

Her heart stumbled. Crazy scenarios filled her head. Like he'd heard she'd left New York without saying goodbye and he couldn't have that.

Not letting herself give into a foolish wish, she said, "What are you doing here?"

He drew a breath. His usually serious eyes were even darker than normal. "Your dad had a problem."

It was the last thing she expected him to say and she fell back a step. "What kind of problem?"

"A major seizure. That's all I know. Your mom called Danny when she couldn't get ahold of you because you'd already boarded your flight. Danny sent me to get to you before you rented a car and drove to your empty house." He nudged his head toward the exit. "I've got a car and we can drive straight to the hospital."

She stared at him. It was the second time in a week he'd given her news that simply couldn't connect to her brain.

But this news filled her eyes with tears. "Is he all right?"

Nick solemnly shook his head. "I don't know. Let's not think the worst. Let's drive to the hospital, talk to your mom and see what's going on."

She nodded and they headed in the direction of his rental. Using GPS, they found the hospital. The information desk told them that her dad was in ICU and her mom was with him.

When they arrived on the floor, her mom came out of his room and fell into Leni's arms.

"It was the worst thing. One minute he was laughing and the next he had zoned out. I thought it was a longer-than-normal small seizure but then he started shaking and he fell to the floor. I called the ambulance immediately."

"You did the right thing," Leni said soothingly. "How is he now? Can I see him?"

"You can see him, but it took so long to get the seizure under control that he's heavily sedated and sleeping. He hasn't even moved in hours."

"I'll feel better if I see him."

Her mom nodded and turned to walk Leni into the ICU, but she noticed Nick and stopped. "I'm sorry. I didn't even see you there. Nick, right?"

"Yes. It's okay, Mrs. Long. I'm fine. I'll find a seat out here. You two go ahead."

Leni's mom nodded and guided Leni back to the ICU. In a hospital bed, with an IV and hooked up to several monitors, her dad looked awful.

Leni's mom put her arm around Leni's shoulders. "They told me that a grand mal seizure like that takes a lot out of a person and with the sedatives he could sleep through the night."

Desperate for confirmation, Leni looked at her mom. "They're sure he's okay?"

She pointed at the monitors. "That's what all those bells and whistles are for. As long as none of these alarms sound, he's fine and he's not having another seizure."

They stayed in the room and watched her dad sleep for at least a half an hour. But sitting in the plastic chair, the stress of the day caught up with Leni. She yawned.

"You should go home."

"No, I'm fine."

"You're not fine. You're tired." Her mother's head tilted. "Didn't you have a meeting with the lawyer today?"

"Yeah. He told me the bare bones about the estate. That everything had to be so hush-hush because there's tons of money and then said he couldn't tell me anything more until they got the results of the DNA test that prove I'm an heir."

"You don't seem to be upset anymore so it must have been good news."

"Yeah, mostly good." She still had the decision about

how much of this money she'd take, if any, but she wouldn't share that with her mom until her dad was home and healthy. "The thing of it is, if I am an heir, I think have to hire my own lawyer because Danny stressed that he's the lawyer for the *estate*. I know that means he's not looking out for me but for the estate.

"He also said my DNA samples had to go to the labs blind. Meaning no one could know they were for the Hinton estate. Even though Waters, Waters and Montgomery put a rush on them, no one could say when the results would be back. So I asked if I could come home." She grimaced. "I'd wanted to surprise you."

"Instead, we surprised you."

Nodding, Leni looked lovingly at her dad. What she wouldn't give for him to wake up and make a corny comment.

"Still, there's no reason for you to be here. He won't be up till morning. Go home. Get some rest."

She glanced at her mom. "Are you staying?"

"Of course. There's a pullout bed I can sleep on."

"Then I'm staying, too."

"And sleep on one of those plastic chairs in the waiting room?"

"I'm too nervous to sleep." Then she remembered Nick was with her and she sighed. "I'll send Nick to a hotel. Better yet, I'll send him back to New York. Do you have your car?"

Her mother nodded. "I followed the ambulance."

"Good. He can take his rental back to the airport and fly home."

She walked out into the waiting room and Nick bounced from his chair. "How is he?"

"Sleeping. Heavily sedated, so they think he won't wake up until morning."

"Is that good or bad?"

"Mom said the doctors told her this kind of seizure takes a lot out of a person and sleep is what he needs."

"Then that's good," he said hopefully.

She drew in a long breath. "I guess."

"Sit down."

She lowered herself to a tall-back, padded double chair big enough for two. As he sat beside her, she said, "Now that I'm here, you can go."

He looked at her incredulously. "Fly back home?"

"Or just get a hotel."

"Are you going to a hotel?"

She gazed at the door separating the ICU from the waiting room. "No. I don't think so. Mom's staying until morning. I will, too."

"Then I will, too. The chairs aren't too bad. We might even be able to get a little sleep."

"I'm too drained to argue." She leaned back, relaxing a bit. "But at three o'clock in the morning when your back aches, you might change your mind about these chairs."

He laughed. She nestled into the seat, getting more comfortable. With only the two of them in the waiting room, it got incredibly quiet when they stopped talking.

Her mind going in a million directions, she steadied her breathing to settle herself. Then she sniffed a laugh. "I remember the day I met my parents."

Nick shifted to face her. "You do?"

"Sure. I was eight by the time they got me as a foster child, so I knew exactly what was going on."

"It must have been hard."

"Being in foster care at all is hard. But it was scary too, going with another set of 'parents.' The Longs explained that they wanted to adopt me, and I was shocked."

"Why? I bet you were a cute little kid."

"Every foster home I went to, I had the ridiculous belief that these people would love me enough that they'd keep me." She met his gaze. "No one had."

"You didn't want to get your hopes up."

"But the Longs were so eager to please me that they were actually funny. After a day or two of my dad bending over backward to make me laugh or feel comfortable, I realized my forever home *was* with them. These people who always made breakfast and liked to play Yahtzee were mine forever. I decided to be the best child ever and I had a wonderful life with them."

"That's a great story."

She smiled. "I know." But the truth of where she was and what was going on washed over her and she squeezed her eyes shut. "I could not handle it if my dad died."

"He's not going to die."

"We don't know that."

Her raw fear came through in her voice and helplessness overwhelmed Nick. He leaned forward, across the double chair, and wrapped his arms around her. "We might not *know* but we can hope."

She nestled into him for comfort and he held her close. He understood her fear of having someone she loved die. He could not bear watching her go through it.

They dozed a bit, woke around three o'clock and she checked on her dad. Ten minutes later, she came back to the waiting room.

"I talked to the nurse. Everything's the same. My mom is sleeping."

Nick stretched. "That's good."

She sat on her chair again. "Yeah." This time when she settled in, she used her jacket for a blanket. Nick did the same with his big gray overcoat. They must have dozed again because the next thing Nick knew, they were cuddled against each other, his big coat covering them both in the cold December air, and light was streaming in through the big windows of the waiting room.

He just held her for a few seconds, savoring the feel of

her. He might not deserve anyone as good as she was, but if he could give her strength or courage, he would. She was a tough person, but she'd already gone through too much in her short life to have her dad die—

He couldn't fathom it. He knew how death hurt, how it ruined things, how it raced like a scourge through a family.

He took a breath to stop his runaway train of thought and when he looked down, she was gazing up at him.

"Hey."

"Hey." He couldn't protect her from this, but he would do the one thing he could do. Support her.

"We should go into Dad's room to see how he is and if my mother survived the night on that rock-hard sofa bed."

He laughed and released her, but his silent vow remained intact. He would do whatever she needed.

They walked into her dad's room to find him sitting up in bed. Her mom sat on the edge of the foot of the bed, grinning from ear to ear.

Leni raced to her father and all but threw herself into him to hug him. "Dad!"

"Hey, Kitten. Better loosen the hold."

She jerked back. "I'm sorry! Did I hurt you?"

"No. But I am a bit stiff and sore." He winced. "Weirdly stiff and sore. When I get home, I'm going to have you research seizures so I can see what this one did to me."

"Or we can just do a few tests."

The doctor standing in the doorway walked into the room. "I'm Doctor Stevens. I'm your neurologist. I've been looking at your chart and see you had a work injury."

Leni's dad nodded. "Two years ago."

"And these seizures are just manifesting now?"

"I started having small seizures a few months ago." Her dad grimaced. "That might not be true. I'm told the smaller seizures could have started long before I noticed them."

The doctor made some notes. "Let's get some tests before we make any assumptions."

He left the room and a few minutes later a nurse appeared. "I hear you're getting some tests this morning."

She looked at his wristband, asking his name, double checking. "Tests will be at least two hours." She smiled at Leni's mom. "Go get some breakfast." Without waiting for an answer, she took Leni's dad away.

Leni said, "We should do that, Mom." She glanced at Nick, silently asking for his help convincing her mom. "I know I'm starving."

"I could use something myself," Nick agreed.

But Leni's mom sighed. "I couldn't eat."

"You should eat."

She shook her head. "No. You guys go. Bring me back a cup of coffee."

Leni argued a few seconds, but eventually gave up. "If you're not going, I'm not going."

Nick said, "How about if I go find coffee and maybe some doughnuts?"

Leni sent him a grateful smile. "That'd be great."

It took him fifteen minutes to find the cafeteria but only a few seconds to realize he didn't know if Leni or her mom wanted cream or sugar for their coffee. He got a cardboard container, put three disposable cups of coffee in the slots then filled the fourth slot with creams and sugar packets. The clerk put six doughnuts into a bag, and he headed back to ICU.

He found Leni and her mom in the waiting area, seated at a round table. He passed out coffee and opened the bag of doughnuts, letting Leni and her mom choose first.

"It's all so frustrating," Leni's mom said before she took a long drink of coffee. "One minute he was fine. The next he was gone. No warning."

"That's what the service dog is for," Leni reminded her mom.

"We can't afford—" Leni's mom paused, smiled at Nick. "Sorry, don't want to air our troubles in front of you."

Nick shook his head. "Hey, no worries here. Every family has troubles."

He thought of his mom, who'd thrown herself into charity work after Joe's death, and his dad, who'd thrown himself into checking up on Nick, making sure he stayed put, making sure he made money for the family—his silent way of reminding Nick he had to make up for losing his brother.

"Besides," Leni said, taking a napkin from the stack by the coffee container, "we might not have anything to worry about financially. Even if all I take is what my father should have paid in child support, it'll be enough for Dad's medical bills."

The conversation died after that and though Nick should have wanted to ask Leni a million questions about potentially walking away from billions of dollars, he felt oddly proud of her. She had principles and guts. But she also wouldn't abandon her father.

A strange feeling tingled through him. The certainty that he should be here collided with the knowledge that being with her wasn't right. What if he gave her the wrong impression? What if he influenced her—

He almost laughed. Leni would call that notion conceited. She'd ask him how he got his head through doors.

Helping her in her time of need would not give her the wrong impression. She was level-headed and smart.

And he could handle himself, too. Yes, they'd gravitated together in the middle of the night. Yes, it had felt wonderful to hold her. But half-asleep, he'd forgotten he needed to keep his distance. Now that he was remembering, he could help her without getting close.

When Joe died, he'd forced himself through some of the worst emotions a person could feel. He could help her while protecting himself.

CHAPTER NINE

WHEN HER FATHER returned from getting his tests, the nurse suggested that they all needed to be rested when the neurologist arrived that evening to discuss the results. Leni agreed and she convinced her mom to come home with her to get a nap.

She rode in the car with her mom and Nick followed them in his rented SUV. They arrived at the Long home an hour later. Though the day was cold, the house was toasty. A batch of sugar cookies, coated in frosting and covered in red and green sprinkles, sat on the counter as if her mom had just finished making them when her dad had his seizure.

Denise removed her coat and hung it on a coatrack by the door. "Let me make lunch."

Leni gaped at her mom. "No!"

"Absolutely not," Nick agreed. "You heard what the nurse said. She wants you rested when you come back."

Denise shook her head. "I'm too keyed up to sleep."

Leni put her hands on her mom's shoulders and turned her in the direction of the bedrooms. "Go lay down anyway."

"I'll tell you what," Nick said. "You get some rest and when you wake up lunch will be ready."

Leni faced him. She might not have seen Nick's life, but she would guess he had a maid or ate out most of the time. He certainly didn't look like a guy who knew how to make lunch. "You're going to cook?"

He laughed. "I'm not a great cook but I make a mean spaghetti."

Denise half smiled. "I like spaghetti."

"Good. Go rest."

As her mom walked away, Leni studied Nick. When he wanted to be, Nick Kourakis was the nicest guy in the world. He'd picked her up at the airport, taken her to see her dad and stayed with her and her mom, not just getting coffee and doughnuts but offering moral support. And she couldn't forget how they'd moved close together in the night, snuggling together for warmth. And how he'd been studying her face when she'd awakened—

But she remembered he also hadn't kissed her at her hotel room door the night he could have. The night it would have been the perfect ending to the perfect day, he'd walked away from the chance to kiss her. And despite the way they'd cuddled together in the chilly waiting room, he'd told her Danny had called him to let him know about her dad and asked him to fly to Kansas to intercept her. His being here was Danny's idea. Gravitating together for warmth meant nothing.

"I'm not sure we have spaghetti in the house."

He shrugged. "Does Mannington have a grocery store?"

"Of course, we have a grocery store!" Realizing she'd protested too much, she winced. "A small one."

"As long as it has spaghetti, I don't care if it's the size of a minivan."

She laughed, as she re-zipped her jacket. He really knew nothing about small towns. But her mom needed support and Nick was offering it.

Because Danny had sent him.

As long as she remembered he was only here because Danny had asked, she wouldn't make too much of him being here and wouldn't get stars in her eyes.

"Let's go."

They headed outside to the SUV. Leni got in the passenger's side and Nick slid behind the steering wheel. Understanding the significance of Danny having sent him, she wouldn't lean too heavily on him. She would accept help caring for her mom. But that was it.

Apparently misinterpreting her silence, he said, "Are you worried about your father?"

Thinking about her dad and everything he might have to go through made her tired suddenly. She put her head back and closed her eyes. "No. I'm coming to terms with everything. Remembering things."

"Remembering things?"

"When he first started having seizures, I looked them up."

He laughed.

She sniffed. "You laugh, but the internet can be very effective. Especially when it says that most seizures aren't life-threatening."

Nick waited a beat then said, "His new, longer ones might be."

"I don't think so."

"You sound pretty sure of yourself."

"Not sure of myself, but sure of my dad. He's like a bull when he wants to be. It was hard seeing him weak when he was injured, but now he's back to being himself or wanting to fight whatever is going on, and to me that's half the battle."

Nick tilted his head. "Maybe… Which way is this store?"

She pointed right. He made the turn. The Moe's Market sign appeared about a block down.

He pulled the SUV into a parking space and they went inside. Leni grabbed a cart. He smiled stupidly.

"What?"

"I've never been in a store like this."

"Like what?"

He pointed toward the seven aisles of food and household products. "You think this is small. To me it's enormous."

"You mustn't have ever been in a superstore." She pushed the cart toward the fresh produce. "How deprived you've been."

He chuckled. "I think you're the first person who's ever called me deprived." He glanced around in awe. "Look at all this food. Especially the Christmas candy."

She studied the bright red, green and gold boxes of chocolates, candy canes, right beside red felt stockings. "Giving candy as a Christmas gift is very big around here." When she saw he was still staring at the boxes, she laughed. "Do you want to take a box or two home?"

He nudged his chin to the right. "Not candy, but maybe a few bags of potato chips."

She chuckled as she stopped by the lettuce. "Are you making a salad?"

"Do you want a salad?"

"We always have salad with spaghetti."

"Good to know."

Her eyes narrowed. He'd said that as if he planned on remembering it. But why? "Are you taking notes?"

"No. I just like knowing things about people for future reference."

His words slid through her. She tried not to conclude that he might be staying in her life—especially with their differences so clearly spelled out as he looked at her town's very ordinary store with wonder in his eyes. But when he was so personal, so helpful, so easy with her, the thought drifted through her brain anyway.

He casually grabbed the handle and pushed the cart up the aisle, toward the tomatoes, while Leni stood frozen by the lettuce. To her, it felt like he belonged with her. Weird as it seemed, they were good together.

She shook her head to clear it. She could *not* think like that. If Danny hadn't called him about her dad, she wouldn't have seen Nick after Thursday night—until it came time for his company to make a pitch for her to keep her Hinton inheritance in his money management firm. She couldn't fool herself into thinking he had feelings for her.

For pity's sake, they'd known each other five days. Six if she counted the current day. She'd stayed at three different foster homes *for months* and each time she'd walked in one day after school to be told to pack her bags and get ready to move on. She could still feel the sting of it. The horrible sense that she wasn't loveable. And she'd vowed she'd never let herself feel that again.

If she could be rejected after months with foster parents whom she believed liked her, six days was nothing.

Especially not a reason to set herself up for a rejection.

Where was her pride?

Where was her spunk?

She wasn't one of those women who fell for a man who wanted nothing to do with her. She was independent and in her own little small-town way, savvy.

Still, she grabbed a few bags of the potato chips he liked and met him at the end of the aisle.

"Any chance there's fresh bread here?"

She motioned to the left. "There's a bakery section down there." Then she laughed. "I'll bet some of your clients would pay to see this. I'll bet your *mom* would pay to see this."

He scowled. "I'm not helpless at doing normal things because I'm wealthy."

"Sure. Sure."

"I'm serious. I was a Navy SEAL. I know how to do things."

Confused about how being a Navy SEAL would help him make spaghetti, she tilted her head as they walked to the bakery section. "Like what?"

"Do you want to hear about the killing-a-man-with-my-bare-hands part or the how-to-survive-just-about-anywhere part?"

She stopped, gaped at him. "Did you actually do those things?"

This time he gaped at her. "What do you think being in the SEALs means? That they let me sit on a couch and watch TV while the other guys went on missions? I passed muster. I was part of missions to capture people and part of missions to rescue people."

She knew her mouth hung open, but she couldn't stop staring at him.

He put his fingers under her chin and closed her mouth. "Seriously."

"I'm sorry but it just all seems impossible." Or did it? He was a big guy. When she'd first seen him, she'd thought he had the comportment of someone in the military. And he'd told her he liked adventure...danger.

"What else did you do?"

"Classified stuff. So, don't ask."

By this time, they had all the makings of salad, spaghetti and meatballs and two jars of sauce. "I'm going to start cooking as soon as we get to your house. I want the meatballs to be ready when your mom gets up and she might only sleep an hour or so."

She nodded casually but she was in awe of him, the way she'd been when they walked out of the Irish pub. The day she'd slid her arm under his and snuggled into him as they returned to her hotel.

After ringing up the sale, Tilly Montgomery, that day's cashier, gave her a thumbs-up when Nick bent down to use his bank card. Leni shook her head, letting her know there was nothing between them.

They left the shopping cart behind after pulling out the bags of groceries. The return trip to her house was quick. In minutes, they had all of Nick's supplies on the counter.

He washed his hands. "Meatballs first. Why don't you go check on your mom while I work?"

She agreed, tiptoed down the hall, opened the door a crack and saw her mom sleeping above the covers on the four-poster bed.

In the kitchen again, she asked, "What can I do to help?"

"I cook alone," he said, his hand up to the wrist in the hamburger meat. She could see he'd added onion and some breadcrumbs.

"Are those going to be good?"

"They're going to be fabulous."

She laughed. "Stop that!"

"Why?" He caught her gaze. "I like to hear your laugh."

Her heart warmed, even though she told herself it wasn't supposed to. The smooth, sophisticated Nick was charming and almost irresistible but shift to normal Nick and they were looking at irresistible in the rearview mirror. She could have melted at his feet.

And she couldn't do that. Even if she didn't have a sick father and decisions to be made about her biological father's estate, Nick did not have those kinds of feelings for her.

She walked around the center island of the kitchen to the sugar cookies her mom had abandoned. Taking note of how many there were, she went to the cabinet to get some containers.

"I used to make people laugh all the time."

His comment came out of nowhere and she leaned around to look at him. "Oh, yeah? I thought you said you weren't funny." She pulled two big containers and one small one from the cabinet and headed back to the island.

He glanced at the cookies, his eyes narrowing as if they confused him. But he said, "I wasn't funny, per se. All my life I'd been something of a daredevil. I bungee jumped before it was wise or popular."

She snorted, as she began stacking cookies in the containers.

"I did tricks on the Jet Ski."

"Like a dog?"

"No. Like a stuntman." He shook his head. "And the reason I was pretty good with the ladies was all about having a good time."

"You're sure it's not your money and good looks?"

"I never flaunted my family's wealth."

"You don't have to. Your clothes tell the story."

"Not when I'm wearing jeans and a hoodie."

"All right. I'll give you that."

They were quiet for a second before he said, "So, you think I'm good-looking?"

Oh, she *wasn't* going to give him *that* one. The man was vain enough. "You don't?"

He chuckled. "You're not one for straight answers today."

She snapped the lid on the final container of sugar cookies. "I'm not going to feed into your vanity."

He said nothing for a second, creating the last meatball and setting it on a tray to take to the stove and the frying pan.

"I guess there was a time when I was vain."

"You guess?"

"It never crossed my mind that being lucky, showing people a good time, having some looks—" he gave her the side-eye and she laughed "—made me vain."

"So, what happened?"

He didn't reply, busy with the frying pan for the meatballs. She would have thought it was a natural pause in the conversation because he was wrapped up in his creation for lunch—which was beginning to look more like dinner—except she remembered other things he'd said. Like he'd had a brother who'd followed him around. She didn't remember seeing anything about a brother in the articles she'd read online about Kourakis Money Management. But when they were skating, he'd mentioned him.

"Was your brother in on all this fun?"

"My brother died."

His words shocked her so much, she stopped dead in her tracks.

Remembering her feelings the day before, when she'd heard about her dad, seeing him sedated, hooked up to equipment that kept him alive, her chest hollowed out, helplessness and fear rose as strong and sharp as they had been in that minute. Nick had experienced all of that and more. His brother had *died*. Her dad was alive and strong. Whatever the doctors told him had to be done, her dad would fight to do it.

Nick's brother was gone.

She watched him roll the meatballs in the pan and place them on a tray to bake. His face wasn't solemn as it had been her first few days in New York, but now that she'd heard more of his past, she could see that he didn't have secrets as much as he held something of himself back.

Whether he was afraid of another loss or simply still tired from the grief, she didn't know. But she did know that asking him about his brother had changed him back into the guy who'd taken her to New York. The business-like guy who didn't smile.

And maybe he needed a break?

"Tell me more about bungee jumping."

The expression on his face clearly said he knew she'd changed the subject and he was grateful. "It's exhilarating."

"You'd never get me to do something like that!"

"You think?" He laughed. "I never have a problem persuading people to do fun things."

Oh, she'd bet that was true. Gazing into his mischievous brown eyes, she saw the devilish guy who'd probably had his pick of adventures and his pick of women.

She sniffed a laugh. "You're such a con artist."

The last meatball on the tray and the tray in the oven, he faced her. "Not at all."

"Come on."

"I'm serious. I can tell when someone's genuinely afraid to bungee jump or skydive and I don't push."

"Right."

"I don't."

"And you never use that charm of yours on women?"

"I'm always honest. Especially with women."

When he looked at her like that, his dark eyes sincere and seductive, her chest pinched. Her breathing stuttered. Her eyes felt locked to his.

He'd been honest with her.

He put one hand on the counter beside her, so he could lean in, angling their faces inches from each other. "I don't have to be a con artist. Because I'm honest with women, they can be honest with me. Enjoy me while I enjoy them."

Oh...

The chest pinch tightened. She wasn't entirely sure she knew how to breathe.

"It always starts with a kiss…a light one…more like a brush to see if there are sparks."

Now for sure she couldn't breathe. Her entire body poised in anticipation of a kiss—the one she'd longed for—just one kiss to let her know she was more than a woman he'd babysat.

But he didn't move. Their eyes might be locked. He might have her trapped against the kitchen island, but he didn't move.

She stood frozen. Waiting. And feeling like an idiot for waiting. If he wanted to kiss her, he would.

But he didn't.

Just when she could have wiggled away from him, he bent his head and brushed his lips along hers. The sparks that flew could have set the kitchen on fire. Her nerves popped. The blood in her veins woke and exploded. Her lungs collapsed from lack of oxygen.

She expected him to pull away. After all, his demonstration was over. And she'd gotten her kiss. They could walk away now.

He did pull back a millimeter, but he paused. She opened her eyes to find herself inches away from his dark, dark gaze.

Nick knew he should pull back. God help him, he hadn't been able to resist shifting the conversation so far away from Joe that they'd never get back to it again, but the joke had been on him. The second his lips touched hers he knew he wanted more. He'd told himself that he could control any simple want but somehow that want became a need. Sharp and sensual, it wound through his blood, and after only five seconds of gazing into her eyes, he knew she felt it, too.

He leaned in again and took her mouth fully this time.

She put her hands on his cheeks and pushed off the counter, pressing herself against him. Need ricocheted through him. Her soft breasts met his chest, even as her hands kept him right where he was, as if she were afraid he would stop kissing her.

He wouldn't.

He yanked her tightly against him. He swore he could feel the frantic beating of her heart—

When that registered, he froze. He wasn't sure if her heart was beating that hard from excitement, or fear or the craziness of the whole thing, but whichever, it was wrong. She had a sick father and decisions to make about Mark Hinton's estate. She didn't need the likes of him seducing her, then dumping her. Because that's what he did. Moved on.

Leni was the kind of woman a man stayed with—

But he'd never stayed with a woman. Especially not a woman so sweet and sincere that he didn't deserve her.

He would hurt her.

He pulled away slowly, watched her eyes open and smiled at her. He could keep this uncomplicated. The past few years, he'd been a master at holding back his feelings, keeping things simple. He called on that gift.

"And that's just step one."

She licked her lips, held his gaze and whispered, "I'm not sure I'd survive step two."

Part of him yearned to believe he affected her as much as she affected him. To believe that kiss meant something. But he knew himself. He didn't make commitments. He couldn't. No woman should be saddled with a guy so riddled with guilt he buried himself in work.

Plus, like her, he wasn't sure *he'd* survive step two either. They had some powerful chemistry. But all that would do is lure her in and make it hurt worse when he left her.

He eased back, away from her. "Luckily, we don't have to worry about that."

"Yeah. Lucky." She pulled her hand through her shiny hair. "How much longer for the meatballs?"

"I usually give them a half hour."

"Okay."

She looked as confused and befuddled as he felt. They both needed a break. Leaning against the stove, he said, "Why don't you take a nap, too?"

"No. I'm fine."

"I know you are. But I have a few calls I'd like to make while I wait for the meatballs."

The relief on her face would have killed his ego if he hadn't known how much she'd enjoyed that kiss. "Maybe a rest is a good idea."

"We all want you and your mom sharp when you speak to the neurologist."

She pulled her hand through her hair one more time. "Yeah."

"Go."

She nodded and scrambled out of the kitchen.

Nick let his head fall. Holy hell. That kiss tempted him to do things that would only hurt Leni. Tempted him to believe in something he wasn't even sure he understood. When he looked at himself, his life, his regrets, he knew he had to stay away. But, oh, how he wanted her. Just one night.

If he thought he could take one night without hurting her, he would. But he couldn't. He'd seen so many glimpses into her heart that he knew how soft she was. Vulnerable, though she hid it with humor.

He had to get away and stay away.

CHAPTER TEN

LENI'S MOM WOKE about three o'clock. The meatballs were out of the oven and had been marinating in sauce. Nick put the spaghetti in a pot while Leni brought the salad out of the fridge and set the table.

When they sat down to eat, Denise said, "This is nice."

Glad her mom looked awake and normal, Leni reached for the salad bowl. "Did you have a good rest, Mom?"

"Yes." She laughed. "I must have needed it. If you don't mind, after we eat, I'd like to get a shower and go directly to the hospital."

Nick said, "Whatever you want."

Leni winced. "I'm sorry—" She carefully peeked at Nick. They hadn't really made eye contact since that kiss, but she knew why. The touch of their lips had been electric. Something neither one of them had expected. That led to the bigger kiss, the better kiss, the *real* kiss. It was a demonstration gone off the rails and they both knew it. "—I never gave you the chance to shower."

"I didn't bring anything to change into. I had to race to my jet to beat you to Topeka." He laughed. "I'm getting accustomed to wearing the same clothes for two days when I'm around you."

Denise looked horrified. "She's not trouble, is she?"

"No. She's very easy to get along with."

Leni's heart stumbled. Nick wouldn't look at her when he said it, but his ears got red.

He liked her.

He'd said it before, a couple different ways. And that

kiss more or less proved it. But they'd only known each other six days. If she wasn't an heir, she'd be returning to Mannington, never to see Nick Kourakis again.

She'd gotten her kiss. The one kiss she wanted. She should be content with that.

Except—

Nobody had ever kissed her like that, and she was about damned certain no one ever would again. It seemed wrong, absolutely positively wrong, to walk away without at least exploring that.

But he didn't want to. He'd warned her off. Still, he'd warned her off before they'd gotten to know each other. Now that she'd had a few glimpses into his life, she was willing to guess that his aloofness had something to do with the loss of his brother.

What if she could help him through that?

What if fate had brought them together because whatever they felt, it was strong enough to ease him out of his mourning and back to life again?

It was risky.

But she couldn't leave him stranded in the limbo he seemed to live. She'd seen him sullen and quiet in New York and happy here in Mannington. There was a connection. She knew it.

The question was, did she want to risk rejection and heartbreak for a man she'd known six days?

They finished eating. Denise left the kitchen to shower. When she was ready to go, they climbed into Nick's SUV and headed for the hospital.

It was dark when they reached it. The moon rose over the buildings and the trees around it. Christmas decorations at nurses' stations, over doorways and in windows went unnoticed as they walked through the corridors to the ICU.

They waited an hour for the doctor, but Leni gratefully

used the time to tease her dad and watch her mom relax degree by degree the more her dad teased and chatted.

The neurologist arrived with two younger men, one of them rolling a cart with a computer. He explained that there was scarring in her dad's brain, in a very good place. Which sounded like an oxymoron until he said, "It's a good place because we can remove it."

Her mom's eyes widened. "You're saying brain surgery?"

"Yes. And as with any surgery there are risks, especially when we enter the brain. But we're confident that once the scarring that's been building since his injury is removed, his seizures will disappear."

They asked the neurologist a million questions. Nick leaned against the windowsill, listening, adding a comment or question here and there.

Leni took it all in. But in the end, she felt the surgery had too much promise to ignore.

Except she wouldn't want it done in Kansas unless the best neurosurgeon in the world worked there. To hire the best neurosurgeon in the world, she'd need money.

And she might have money. Tons of it. If Mark Hinton was her biological dad.

The weirdness of it almost did her in. She wouldn't have the wonderful father she had now if her biological father had wanted her. But he hadn't wanted her, so she didn't want him either. Except she needed him to save the father she wouldn't have had if he hadn't abandoned her. The logic scrambled her brain.

They stayed with her dad after the neurologist left, discussing pros and cons, but when visiting hours were over, they went home.

Exhausted, talked out, Denise went to her room.

Nick faced Leni. "Are you okay?"

"Yeah, I'm fine. I just have a lot of thinking to do and

need time on the computer researching everything that doctor said."

Nick laughed. "You like to research."

"Smart people do." She took a breath. "I'm going to be looking for the best neurosurgeon on the planet. Someone who's done this surgery hundreds of times."

"Makes sense."

She caught Nick's gaze. "To employ him, I'm going to need tons of money."

He studied her for a second. "You need your inheritance."

"Yes."

"You don't seem very happy about it."

She sucked in a breath. "It's weird. To help the father who raised me, I have to accept the help of the man who abandoned me."

"Did you ever stop to think that this would be what Mark would want to do?"

She sniffed a laugh. "What?"

"Mark wasn't a bad guy. He was an overworked, very paranoid, fearful guy. He didn't abandon you as much as he counted on your mom to take care of you. I'll bet he hadn't even known your mother was in trouble."

"He never checked on us."

"He barely got himself to work some days. The only time he was happy and felt safe was fishing in the middle of the ocean. Hundreds of thousands of people depended on him for jobs. He knew the pressure of that."

"So much that he didn't have time for one little girl."

"Don't think of it like that. Think of the stress, the pressure."

She pressed her lips together.

"Leni, your father had very few happy days. You love life. I'll bet after your experience in foster care, it wasn't easy for you to get to that place emotionally. But the Longs helped you. They made you the person you are today.

Don't throw away your happiness over this. Take a deep breath, be glad for the money to save your father and forgive Mark. Otherwise this will ruin your life."

There was so much wisdom in what Nick said that she let it sink in. Especially since she almost felt herself forgiving Mark Hinton for abandoning her. Not only had his stepping aside resulted in her having the best parents in the world, but also his gift of money would save her dad. How could she stay angry with him after that?

A strange warmth filled her soul, a lightness, as if she'd done the right thing.

"I get it."

"It's difficult that your dad has to have the surgery, but I don't think you'll be sorry you're opting into the estate."

"I hope you're right."

"I am. Don't use my screwed-up life to judge what it's like to be wealthy. I had everything at my disposal as a child and I had choices about things like where I went to school, joining the Navy, even jet-setting after leaving the SEALs. I had the most amazing life."

"That's true."

"Had it not been for my brother dying, my life would have stayed very, very good and I'd probably be on a beach somewhere now."

She searched his eyes. He was telling her everything would turn out okay and she appreciated that. But there was more, a bigger story in his eyes, sadness over his brother's death. She simply didn't know how to get to it. Or even if she should try.

"You wouldn't have come home for Christmas?"

"I would have been home Christmas morning. I always made it in time for gift exchange with my family. But the big picture is I had a life I loved. I worked, just not in a conventional way. I wouldn't have been stuck in my office all day or doing Danny's bidding when he couldn't get out of a trial."

"Then you wouldn't have met me."

He looked away. "Yes, and how blissful it would have been not to know that I was a vain guy who lied to his parents."

She laughed. Every time the conversation became about him, he deflected. But she understood that. It was part of why she couldn't get to his sadness. He didn't want her to.

Before she could say anything, he pushed away from the counter. "Anyhow, if you don't need me, I'm going to leave you to your research. I've got some work I have to do, too."

"Okay. Give me a second to fix up the guest room."

He caught her arm as she turned to scamper away. "I said that wrong. I'm going back to the airport to hop in my jet, and work through the flight home."

"Oh."

Her brain stalled. Why would he want to leave? It was late. He was clearly tired. He shouldn't drive an hour to an airstrip and spend even more hours in the air before he got home. Of course, he did have a bedroom in his jet. And he'd given a week of his busy life to entertain her. He really could be behind in his work.

She opted to stay positive. He was a busy guy. He had to get back to his job. The man had kissed her like a guy so smitten he couldn't help himself. And he'd taken the time to help her see she needed to forgive Mark Hinton. Whatever was between them, it was growing.

His leaving had nothing to do with her and she would respect his choice.

"I can't thank you enough for your help."

"It was my pleasure. But it's time for me to get home."

"Okay. Sounds good."

Within minutes he was leaving, outside her parents' house, ready to climb into his rented SUV. She stood beside the vehicle door, handing him a plastic container of homemade Christmas cookies, not quite sure what to say or do.

In her heart of hearts, she hoped he'd catch her shoulders and lean down to kiss her goodbye. No preliminary kidding around this time. She wanted the invitation kiss. The one that said *I like you. There might be something here worth exploring.*

She wanted *that* kiss.

But he didn't catch her shoulders and lean in to touch his lips to hers. He looked at the container of cookies with the weirdest expression, as if no one had ever done anything nice for him, his lips kicking into a crooked smile.

"Are these the iced sugar cookies I saw on the counter?"

She stuffed her cold hands into the pockets of her old coat. "Yep."

"They looked wonderful."

"I saw you eyeing them."

He shook his head. "You don't miss anything."

She said, "No. I don't," hoping he realized she was telling him that she knew what was going on between them wasn't simple or easy. She was a small-town girl with the most basic of educations. He'd traveled the world, served in the military, had been raised in luxury. It probably wasn't wise for them to start a romance.

But after that kiss, how could they not?

He opened the SUV door, tucked the cookies on the passenger seat and turned to her.

"I probably won't see you until after Danny gets the DNA results."

Hope tingled through her. He could have easily gotten into the vehicle when he put the cookies inside. Instead here he was, only a few inches away from her. Close enough to touch. Close enough for him to kiss her.

"I need to be here anyway."

"Okay." He paused a few seconds, gave her a weak

smile, then slid behind the steering wheel. "See you in a couple of days."

He wasn't going to kiss her. He wasn't going to go in for seconds, after that amazing kiss?

He'd said the kiss had been a demonstration, and the first part might have been. But the second part had been real. She *knew* it.

She took a step back. "Yeah. See you then."

He closed the door and drove off. She stood shivering in the driveway, watching his taillights disappear in the darkness, vibrating with feelings she didn't understand. It had been the best two days and the worst two days. She'd forgiven her biological father because like it or not, his money would save her adoptive father. A father she loved.

But something else had happened. With that kiss, Nick admitted that he liked her, and driving away as he had, he'd admitted he wasn't going to do anything about it.

Rejection spiked. Sharp, miserable, edged with darkness.

She closed her eyes, telling herself not to be foolish. Today was Saturday. She'd met Nick the Monday before. They'd only known each other six days. She was foolish to be upset or even concerned that he hadn't kissed her again.

She took a breath, fighting the feeling of not being good enough, knowing why her mind had gone in that direction. She might have forgiven Mark Hinton for not wanting her, but that didn't mean her biological parents' rejections hadn't left a mark.

She needed to get over that, too. But a sense of unworthiness ran deep, and she had no idea how to let it go. Wash it away. Send it off into the universe.

But she would figure it out. She had to. She'd accepted her dad's money. She'd felt that lightness in her soul. Moving on was the right thing to do.

Now she just had to figure out how.

* * *

Her father came home from the hospital the next morning. He'd gotten some new meds and appeared to be totally back to being himself. After twenty-four hours of Leni and her mother watching him like two hawks, she'd returned to work at the diner. She *might* be inheriting tons of money, but they didn't have it now and they had bills to pay. And there was also the chance she wasn't an heir. Everyone was so sure Mark Hinton was her father. She had niggling doubts.

After the lunch rush and before the dinner rush, George went to the back steps to smoke and Leni found herself alone in the diner again. As she had been the day Nick arrived.

Longing swept through her. She let herself feel it but didn't get carried away. The confusion and emotions of potentially inheriting billions of dollars and her dad's illness could have made her crazy. She knew to control her feelings, her reactions. She'd done it before, when in foster care. She'd call on that discipline again.

The pocket of her apron buzzed, and she pulled out her cell phone. Seeing Waters, Waters and Montgomery in the caller ID, she had to sit.

This was it.

"Hello, Danny."

"And hello to you, Miss Leni Long…confirmed child of Mark Hinton."

Her breathing stopped. "Mark Hinton really was my dad?"

"Three DNA samples don't lie."

"Oh, my gosh." The truth of it rattled through her, not finding footing because she wasn't sure what it all meant. How her life would change. But Danny was right. DNA didn't lie. And though she hadn't been a hundred percent certain she wanted Mark Hinton to be her dad, she had made her peace with that, too.

Something *Nick* had encouraged *her* to do.

She told herself to stop thinking about him. They were good together. Sort of. At least she thought so. But right now, she had more important things to figure out.

Danny's voice brought her back to the present. "So, I'll need you in New York again to run through a few things. The estate can't be distributed until all the heirs are found, but with this proof you have access to your share of the money."

Meaning, she could get her dad the best neurosurgeon in the world.

Her heart sped up. That was her priority.

"When do you want me?"

"Tomorrow?"

"So, I'd fly out today?"

"Or I can arrange for Nick to come and get you."

No. The time for depending on Nick was over. She wanted to be smart Leni. The foster child who'd adapted to her surroundings, studied, put herself through university. So, he could stop thinking of her as a responsibility and start seeing her as…a friend, for now. The other stuff, the romantic stuff, would blossom if it was meant to be. But she wouldn't push or even think about it. It was time to put her best foot forward.

"I can fly commercial." She laughed. "Actually, I'll make my own reservations."

Danny said, "Okay. The estate will reimburse you. Since you wouldn't get here until this evening flying today, make the arrangements for early tomorrow morning and reservations at the hotel where you'd been staying. When you get to New York, you can come right to the office and we can get down to business."

"Thanks."

"You're welcome. And, Leni." He paused. "Congratulations. Your life is about to change in the best possible ways."

She said, "Thanks," but the doubts she'd been fighting all along flooded her brain again. She was a blue-collar woman entering a diamond-necklace world. And maybe that was another thing she needed to change? Nick only knew her as needy Leni. In her worn coat and scruffy jeans. With the sick dad.

But she wasn't needy anymore. She had billions of dollars at her disposal. She could start looking for a neurosurgeon and maybe get some new clothes, so she didn't always feel out of place.

It was time to step into her new life.

When they disconnected the call, she searched online for her hotel, called the number and made reservations. When that part of the call was complete, she asked for the concierge and within seconds he said, "Can I help you?"

"Yes. You probably don't remember me, but I stayed at your hotel last week." She winced at how stupid she sounded and pulled in a breath. "I'm going to be there again this week. Nick Kourakis told me that if I needed anything or needed to *find* anything in New York, you were the one to ask."

"Absolutely. How can I assist you?"

"I need some clothes. Really *nice* clothes. Good clothes. Clothes that scream *money*."

He laughed and gave her the names of three shops near the hotel, eased her fears about looking like a grandma when one of them was the boutique Nick had suggested, and wished her a good day.

She immediately looked up the three stores and smiled. He really did know his job. All three offered private consultations and Leni made appointments for the following afternoon. She wasn't going to play this by ear. Her life was changing, and she couldn't pretend it wasn't.

She would more than step into her world. She would take control.

CHAPTER ELEVEN

LENI HAD BOOKED the earliest morning flight, but with the time difference she arrived in New York City after eleven o'clock. She got to Danny's building around noon, and she had her appointment at the first shop at two. She didn't have to rush.

She accepted the three no-limit credit cards Danny gave her and the checkbook with accompanying bank card. He explained there were three heirs, but there was wording in the will that might result in her only getting one quarter rather than one third of her dad's estate—still, billions of dollars.

She told him she couldn't understand why anybody would fight about that and Danny had laughed. Then he slid into a conversation about security. She would be getting a limo with a driver.

That part concerned her, but she kept it to herself. She was an heir now. There would be plenty of things about this life that would be different. She had decided not merely to accept that but to take control. Today was the day all that started.

With her briefing complete, she took off for her appointments at the stores. Her new driver—parked at the building entrance and waiting for her—drove to the address Leni gave him, a small shop on an out-of-the-way street.

She pushed open the etched-glass door and walked into a sea of merchandise showcased in a room with black woodwork, white walls, upside-down fishbowl light fixtures and bronze tin ceilings.

Leni held back a *Wow*.

"Can I help you?"

"Yes. I have an appointment at two."

The clerk smiled and pointed to a set of steps that had been painted black. "Upstairs. Third floor. With Iris."

On her way to find Iris, she noticed the first floor was filled with bohemian clothes. Things she could see herself wearing in her downtime. The second floor was filled with what she considered work clothes. Pants, soft sweaters, pencil skirts, shiny blouses and dresses. All of them beautiful.

She didn't see a person until she reached the top of the third flight of stairs. Two women and a man stood in a semicircle in front of three full-length mirrors. Except for two chairs near the mirrors, the room was empty.

"Elenore?" Dressed in a black sheath and pearls, the older woman walked over and took her hands before kissing both of her cheeks.

"You must be Iris." Leni pulled back, ignoring the cheek kisses which she thought a bit much, and examining the black sheath and pearls. Lovely and obviously expensive, but not quite the image she wanted to project.

"It's such a pleasure to have you at our store."

Okay. She knew the woman had no idea she was one of the Hinton heirs but apparently making an appointment came with certain assumptions. "I'm glad to be here."

"What are you looking for?" Iris asked. "Casual, business or formal?"

Leni said, "All of them."

Iris smiled and faced the young man and thirty-something woman in jeans standing next to her. "Bill, Mandy, let's start with casual clothes and work our way to formal."

When Iris and her team left, Leni glanced around the room. Though another person might consider a shopping trip oodles of fun, she was on a mission. She had to look like she belonged in her new world. And, yeah, buying a ton of clothes probably was going to be fun.

A few minutes later, Iris and her employees each brought an armload of jeans, shirts and sweaters. Leni instantly fell in love with a white silk blouse and pumpkin-colored wool pants, a green sweater and artificially aged jeans, with high-heel ankle booties. Still, not everything they brought was her style, so she went out to the floor and waded through racks of jeans and pants, dresses, skirts and blouses and matching jewelry.

That's when the joy of it hit her. She could have anything she wanted. It was both exciting and humbling, and in some ways confusing.

But Iris was always beside her, talking about fit and tailoring. Bill and Mandy went ahead of her, pulling things they recommended. Now that they had seen a bit of her taste in clothes, Bill had an eye for casual wear that screamed big money while still being comfortable and Mandy knew the colors Leni looked best in.

Just when she thought she was done and wouldn't even have to go to the other two stores, Iris said, "Now, let's talk formal wear."

"I don't plan on going anywhere formal."

Iris chuckled. "This is New York City, darling. You won't be going out to dinner on a Friday in anything less than a cocktail dress. And if you're staying through the holiday, you'll also be going to a Christmas ball or two."

Mandy scrambled over, carrying two gowns. One green velvet, which Leni knew would make her eyes look amazing. The other a red flowing thing that caused Leni's heart to chug to a stop. Bill brought an armload of shorter dresses, half of which sparkled.

She remembered Nick's mom mentioning a Christmas ball and a Christmas party at the children's ward for the hospital. She'd said she'd attend, so if she got an official invitation, she intended to be ready.

She tried on the shorter dresses and the green velvet, saving the red one for last. Everything worked. The soft, supple fabrics cruised along her skin like a lover's caress. Bill and Mandy pinned the waistlines of three of the cocktail dresses to perfect their fit.

Iris stood on the sidelines approving everything.

When they were done and Leni was back in her old jeans and worn T-shirt, she handed Iris one of the no-limit credit cards.

Though Leni waited nervously, the card was approved in seconds. Iris returned it to her, and she glanced at it. It didn't look any different than her own Mastercard, but it worked a hundred times better.

Walking to her limo, she cancelled her other two appointments and had her driver take her to the hotel where she'd reserved a suite, the same one where she'd stayed on her last trip. Less than an hour later, her purchases began arriving with bellboy after bellboy rolling carts of bags and boxes into her room.

She wanted to laugh—who wouldn't?—but the reality of having so much stuff stopped her cold. First off, she thought about buying luggage, so she could take it all home—then she realized she probably wouldn't wear a lot of these clothes in Mannington. Maybe the jeans. And the really cute boots. But most of this "stuff" she would wear in only New York. Danny had mentioned her serving on the board of one or more of her dad's companies and she liked the idea.

Really liked it.

She would see firsthand how businesses were run, have a part in the decision making, make sure employees were paid decently and no one harassed an injured employee the way her dad had been harassed.

She felt the reality of her new life clicking in. She

wasn't just a woman who was getting billions of dollars. She had responsibilities. Choices. Options. Power.

And she'd probably have to be in New York as much as she was in Mannington. So maybe she needed to get a condo? She couldn't move all these fabulous clothes to and from Mannington. It simply made more sense to have a home here. She'd spent her teen years thinking she'd be a social worker in Topeka, but with the newly inherited fortune, she could see herself doing so much more for her community.

That's when she knew she needed to sit, breathe. She called room service for tea and curled up on the red sofa, letting everything sink in, going over her quick decisions, making sure she wasn't reacting when she should be planning.

Feeling out of sorts, Nick left work early. Today had been the day when Leni met with Danny to discuss specifics. He told himself he didn't care. He told himself the Hinton money wasn't any of his business until the estate was settled and the time came to discuss where the heirs would put their money.

Entering his condo, he ignored the silence that greeted him, but after having been with chatty Leni for days, through some tough things, but also some fun things like skating and the Irish pub, the quiet of his home was deafening.

He tossed his briefcase to the sofa. But as he turned, he saw the little plastic container of cookies on his dining room table.

Christmas cookies. Homemade. Not cookies his mom had ordered from the exclusive bakery in Long Island. Not cookies made by her friend who'd studied pastry in Paris.

Just plain, iced sugar cookies with sprinkles.

He walked over, opened the container and took a

cookie. He bit into it and the soft, buttery confection melted in his mouth.

He groaned. He couldn't remember ever eating a cookie this good. He also couldn't remember the last time anybody had done something so simple, so thoughtful. Six cookies in a little plastic container had almost done him in. As she'd put it into his hand, he'd nearly melted.

He'd nearly kissed her again.

Which was wrong.

He shook his head, went into his bedroom to change into jeans and went to his kitchen to order takeout—

But he remembered that Leni had been through a difficult weekend with her dad in the hospital. Monday, Danny had called and told her she was an heir. This morning she'd flown to New York and had a meeting with Danny.

Her head was probably spinning.

He'd bet it was.

And she had no one in New York to talk to.

Concern for her filled him. But as much as he wanted to help her, he couldn't really ask her to dinner. That was too date-like.

He looked at the cookies. So full of Christmas cheer. The spirit of it filled him. Peace on earth. Being kind to each other. Helping each other—

He slid his phone from his jeans pocket. He hit her number in the contacts section and within seconds her phone was ringing.

"Hey."

Sounding totally surprised, she said, "Hey. What's up?"

"I know you had a busy day with Danny but—" Feeling like a sixteen-year-old asking for a date, he had to remind himself that he was calling for her. He wanted to hear how her dad was, but he also knew she was probably overwhelmed about the estate and would need to talk. If he had to stretch a truth to find a way to give her that time, so be it.

"I was thinking about going Christmas shopping tonight. For my mom," he clarified, to make the story work. "Since you made fun of the boutique, I thought maybe you'd like to come with me and help me find a more hip store."

"I'd love to."

"Good. I'll be at your hotel in ten minutes. Is that enough time?"

"Sure."

"And then maybe we could get a bite."

"Okay."

"Okay. My limo will be outside your hotel in ten."

He hung up feeling better. Infinitely better. But only because he liked her enough that he wanted to be sure she was okay. Not because it was a date, or anything close. He just wanted to be sure she had someone to talk to.

Leni disconnected the call and stared at the phone, but only for a few seconds. Nick's offer might have confused her but she didn't have time to wonder if this was a date. She had to change into one of her new pairs of jeans, a cashmere sweater and the hottest-of-hot black leather jacket.

Riding down the elevator to the lobby, she told herself this wasn't anything special. He needed help shopping and, after today, she felt like a shopping pro. She was a perfect choice to help him.

It was all good.

She stepped out of the lobby onto the street and into the falling snow. Though Nick stood by the door of his limo, she tipped her face up, let herself enjoy the soft wet snow and Christmas spirit that shuffled through the air around her. Christmas in New York City might feel different than at home—shinier and more expensive—but it was still Christmas.

As she reached the door, she said, "Hey! Thanks for

asking me to help you shop. The hotel really was starting to close in on me."

"You're welcome." He winced. "But I had an ulterior motive. And more than help with finding my mom a Christmas gift. I wanted to hear about your dad."

She slid into the limo and Nick followed her. "He's fine. Really good. New meds are keeping everything stable, but after a few hours of hunting for the world's best neurosurgeon, I realized I was out of my league and contacted his neurologist. He and I are now on a quest for the best neurosurgeon on the planet."

Nick sighed. "That's really good."

"It is. So, what are you thinking about getting your mom?"

He shook his head. "No idea. I just know that you dissing my favorite shop sent a shot of panic through me. If my mother hasn't liked my gifts all these years, I've failed."

She laughed as the limo pulled out into traffic. "Failed?"

"My brother used to buy the best gifts."

Her heart stilled at his mention of his brother, but she casually said, "Oh, yeah?"

"Yes. He'd find the cashmere sweater in that year's 'hot' color, when I didn't even know years had hot colors."

"Oh, they do. One year it's pink. The next year it's olive."

He peeked at her. "And you know this?"

"Of course, I know this. I might not live in New York, but I don't live under a rock." She pulled out her phone, searched *hot color.* "And speaking of living under rocks. I'm thinking I might need a place in New York."

His eyebrows rose. "Really."

"Yeah. I bought a bunch of clothes today." She stopped long enough to roll her eyes. "I mean a *bunch.* And I realized I wouldn't wear half of them in Mannington, and would only need them for board meetings for Mark Hinton's…" She paused and amended that to, "my dad's companies."

* * *

Nick heard the change in her voice. She really had begun to accept that Mark Hinton was her dad.

When he said, "I'm glad," he wasn't just talking about being glad that she'd be attending board meetings. He was glad she seemed to be adjusting to who she really was.

He'd also noticed the black leather jacket, the trendy jeans, the new boots and her own cashmere sweater. "You look good."

She looked *great*. She looked like someone stepping into her future, becoming herself.

"Thanks. Anyway, when I realized I shouldn't lug all this stuff to Mannington where I probably wouldn't wear it anyway, I thought about getting my own place."

She truly was moving into her role. Nick couldn't have been any prouder and he knew Mark would have been, too.

"I think it's a good idea."

"Yes. I'm sure Mark had a condo here, but Danny reminded me we don't want to use my dad's condos or houses or jets and alert the media that I've been found, so I thought, hey, I have billions of dollars at my disposal. I don't need to stay in a hotel."

He smiled, warmth filling him. She was so cute and so smart. "No. You don't."

"So, tomorrow I may call a real estate agent and start looking."

"I know a person or two. I could make a call. I'll tell them you are a friend from the Midwest and ask for discretion."

She peeked over at him. "And you'll get it?"

Making eye contact took the warmth that always filled him when she was around and turned it to the kind of heat that would be nothing but trouble for them. So, he glanced away. "The price you'll pay for a condo will result in a hefty commission. Remember how I told you about not kissing and telling?"

She nodded, but her face turned red. Reminding her of the kiss had been a bad idea. Not just for her. She might be embarrassed but the heat already in his system turned to molten lava.

He sucked in a quiet breath, hoping she didn't notice. "Well, it works the same for real estate agents. Wealthy people need discretion. Real estate agents provide it to get their return business. And their friends' business. Discretion is like currency to them."

She nodded and pulled her phone from her jacket pocket. "I got my things today from this great boutique. And they had a top that I'm positive your mother would like." She hit her screen a few times, then displayed the address.

Glad she got both their minds off that kiss, Nick texted it to his driver and in five minutes they were standing in front of the etched-glass door.

Snow fell around them. Leni's face glowed in the light of a streetlamp as they walked to the door. "I might get something for my mom, too."

"I thought you said this wasn't a mom store."

"It isn't." She led the way to the door. "My mom's very youthful. Your mom's a trendsetter."

He laughed, especially when he realized there was a difference. Leni really was rubbing off on him.

They walked into the shop and Nick noticed Christmas music playing softly in the background. Tinsel edged the front counter. A ring of poinsettias almost hid the cash register.

"Leni! You're back!"

"Here to Christmas shop, Mandy," Leni happily said.

Nick wasn't surprised Leni remembered the clerk's name or that the clerk remembered Leni's. She'd probably spent a hundred thousand dollars that afternoon.

"Looking for a sweater for my mom and something like a kimono for his."

Nick frowned. "Kimono?"

"Something long and luxurious. Almost a duster," Leni clarified, talking to the clerk. "I want her to be able to wear it with jeans when she's shopping and look like queen of the world."

An older woman came down the stairs talking. "I have just the thing."

"Hey, Iris!"

"Hey, Leni. Who's your friend?"

"Nick. His mom is New York high society. I want to put her in an outfit that will make her feel funky and cool."

Iris laughed. "For when she lunches with her friends, so she looks like the hip one?"

"Exactly."

Nick had no idea what a kimono was, but apparently it was a good choice because Leni didn't merely gasp when Iris led them to one in the back, she touched it reverently.

"Silk," Iris said.

"It's perfect."

Nick studied it. Pale blue like his mom's eyes, it didn't look like something she might wear, but it did look like something Joe would have bought her.

"I like it," he ventured uncertainly.

Iris said, "Are you sure?"

"I've just never bought my mother something that I haven't already seen her in."

"You mean something similar?" Leni said.

"Yes."

Sliding her hand beneath his arm and nestling against him, she laughed. "Well, she will love this."

After a quick squeeze, Leni headed for three rows of sweaters and chose four for her mother. Nick stood behind her, not quite uncomfortable because shopping with a purpose almost felt okay.

Actually, watching Leni ponder sweaters for her mom gave him a boost. He knew Denise would love them, but he also knew her mom needed them. Seeing the joy on Leni's face at being able to buy things for her mother filled him with that indescribable feeling again. The feeling he had when she savored the wine. The feeling he had when she gave him Christmas cookies.

When they stepped out into the street, into falling snow with Christmas lights and tinsel billowing in the wind, he recognized it. This was the feeling he'd had as a child, the breathless wish for a toy or a video game he wasn't even sure his parents knew existed, the childish wonder of a holiday made for parties and presents. A day his dad didn't work or talk about work. His mom beamed over roast turkey and pie. And he and his brother couldn't sleep for anticipation.

And he didn't want to lose it.

He wanted this feeling to last forever.

If Leni was the reason why he felt it, he wasn't letting her go yet.

"How about another trip to the Irish pub?"

Her eyes widened. "Absolutely."

He opened the limo door for her and she slid inside. In a few minutes, they were climbing out again and heading for the little bar.

Celtic Christmas music poured out as he yanked on the door to let her enter first. In the few days that had passed, the place had been decked out with lights and tinsel.

"Now it really looks like the bar back home."

He laughed as the hostess said, "Good evening."

"Good evening. There are just two of us."

She smiled. "Right this way."

They walked back to the same table they'd had the last time they were there, and Nick wondered if it was a coincidence or if she remembered them.

He didn't say anything as they sat, but he recalled that day after skating. How much fun they'd had. How Leni had cuddled against him in the cold on the walk back to her hotel.

Feelings buffeted him, nudging him to take some time to think this through, but he ignored them in favor of keeping the wonderful mood they'd created.

He made her laugh over hamburgers and fries and encouraged her to have a third draft when she would have stopped at two.

"Today's the day your world changed. In a way, we're celebrating."

"I certainly spent enough money."

He smiled. "And you don't even have to care." He called for the waitress to bring the check. He gave her a credit card and she returned it with the receipt.

After he'd signed, he and Leni rose and slid into their coats. But out on the street, when his limo driver opened their door, he hesitated.

"Feel like walking?"

Her head tilted and she smiled, as if she remembered the last time they'd made this walk. "Yeah." She tucked her arm under his as he signaled for the driver that they would be walking.

Their feet made imprints in the snow that had fallen while they ate. Cold air filled his nostrils and horns beeped around them, but somehow it added to the magic. Everyone seemed to be laughing and chatting, carrying packages, talking about holiday plans.

Two blocks never went by so quickly.

They stomped the snow off their shoes and entered the lobby of her hotel. Though he considered letting her walk to her room herself, he got a weird, uncomfortable feeling about the day.

She, Danny, Mary Catherine, Jace and Nick himself should be the only five people who knew she was an heir. But administrative assistants and clerks saw papers all the time. People passing office doors heard things they shouldn't.

Leni was a small, soft, big-eyed girl from the Midwest, and though he was sure she could care for herself in normal situations, nothing about this situation was normal.

He motioned to the elevator and she headed there. An older couple joined them on the ride to her floor, so they didn't say anything. But as they ambled to her suite door, he remembered walking into the diner the first time he'd seen her. The elf suit. Their small talk. That wash of instant connection.

If he let himself, he could drift back to those few minutes. He could see her smile. He could feel his heart tumble when their eyes met.

Need spiked, sharp and sweet, along with something simple and reverent. He had never felt like that. And the pull of it was so strong his fingers tingled with the need to touch her, to tell her he was crazy about her—

But that wasn't right. She was on the brink of a whole new life. And even if she wasn't, she deserved so much more than him. Somebody so much better. Somebody special.

Still, he didn't even try to stop himself when instinct had him bending to brush his lips across hers. Quickly. Just a taste. He couldn't have her, but one little goodnight kiss didn't hurt.

She blinked at him.

He could almost hear her saying *Wow*, even though she didn't utter a word. He saw the intensity in her eyes and wished for thirty seconds he was a better man.

But he wasn't.

He knew who he was.

Not a liar. Not really a con man. Just somebody with the gift of persuasion. He could kiss her a million times, maybe even get her into bed. He could give her the best Christmas she'd ever had.

And then what?

What happened when she discovered he was responsible for his brother's death? That he wasn't lily white or even dingy gray? His soul was black from narcissism and selfishness that had led to losing his best friend.

Then what?

He'd become who he was: a solitary, stoic workaholic because he didn't want to hurt anybody else, but he also didn't care to feel the pain of that kind of rejection.

He would not take that risk.

CHAPTER TWELVE

LENI WAS ON her way to Danny's office the next morning to talk about when and how she'd get on the boards of some of her dad's companies, when her phone buzzed. Looking at the caller ID, she saw Nick's name and her heart perked up. He'd kissed her again the night before. Not the deep, romantic kiss he'd given her in her mother's kitchen. But a nice, normal goodnight kiss.

In some ways, that one had been more powerful. Filled with the happiness of their evening together, that kiss and been exactly what it should have been. Soft and sweet.

Still, she wasn't going to be a lovesick puppy about this. She would be cool and sophisticated. She answered her phone with a very casual, "Hey, Nick."

"Hey. I got a call from my mom this morning. She reminded me about the party in the children's ward that was supposed to be Friday afternoon. It's been moved up to tomorrow because we're in for a blizzard on Friday. I know it's short notice, but she'd love for you to be there."

She'd love, not *he'd* love.

She closed her eyes, telling herself it was idiotic to make that kind of distinction. The point was, they were getting more time together. More time to get to know each other. More time to figure out what was happening between them.

Striving to sound normal, she said, "Okay. I can be there. I only have a meeting with Danny, then my afternoon is free."

"Have your driver bring you to the hospital around

one-thirty. Party starts at two o'clock, but if you get there a little early, I can show you around."

Her pulse kicked up. Just as he'd told her to come outside to his limo the day before, didn't come up to her hotel room to pick her up, he wasn't going to fetch her for the party either.

As if he were deliberately making the distinction that this wasn't a date.

She stopped that thought, too. They'd never get anywhere if she was so picky about everything. For all she knew, this was how dates happened in New York. Or maybe among rich people. Because everybody had a limo, nobody had to fetch anybody.

"Okay."

"Okay."

She hung up the phone, shaking her head, reminding herself she couldn't nitpick Nick's behavior. She had to roll with at least some things.

With the fundraiser only a day away, she could have gone shopping. But that seemed weird when she'd spent oodles of money the day before. Surely something in the eight tons of clothes she'd bought would be good enough.

In her suite, after her meeting with Danny, she looked up more information about the fundraiser and tons of articles popped onto her screen. She was only interested in seeing how people dressed, but then she saw a picture taken six years before—further back than she'd gone in her search of Kourakis Money Management the day she'd met Nick. The photo was of Nick and his parents and another man. The caption gave their names and the other man was Joe Kourakis.

His brother.

She stared at the picture. Nick looked like a kid. A bad kid. The kind of kid who stole cars for fun and broke the hearts of starry-eyed socialites. His brother didn't look old enough to be out of high school, but he was listed as CEO of Kourakis Money Management. Their mom's head was tilted back as she laughed. Even their dad was smiling.

She squeezed her eyes shut, thinking about how that little family had changed, reminded again that something about Nick's brother's death haunted him.

The temptation rose to ask him about his brother when she saw him the next day, but she couldn't bring up something so emotional at a public event and she also thought it wasn't right to ask. Nick should tell her. She should let him broach the subject.

Forcing her mind off that, she reminded herself she needed to figure out what to wear the next day. She shifted her focus to pictures of the women attending the function. Sheaths and sweaters, an occasional pantsuit. A picture of Nick's mom grinning over the success of the function. Her heart hurt for Amanda Kourakis.

But for Nick, too. He'd said his life would have been very different if his brother hadn't died. Now she saw how.

The next day, Nick arrived at the children's ward at one o'clock. His mother was already there, firing orders at the caterer and the three people sprucing up the ward's existing decorations. She had a photographer, of course. Her public relations firm would send a press release chronicling the event, complete with pictures. Kids would be kept in their rooms so the food, cookies, decorations and brightly wrapped gifts would all be a surprise when they stepped into the activities room.

When he hugged his mom, she said, "You're here early."

"I got antsy."

"Antsy?"

"Yeah. I was in my office, preoccupied with being here…" Picturing Leni in a new dress, trying to guess how she'd wear her hair, even though he knew that was wrong. "I was wondering how things were going and I figured I should just come down." So, he'd stop thinking about Leni and get his mind on the fundraiser.

"Well, I'm glad you're here!" She gave him another quick squeeze. "Why don't you walk around, take a look at things, make sure I'm not missing anything?"

He laughed. "You're not missing anything. You're too thorough. But I wouldn't mind sneaking a peek at what we have to eat."

He walked away, and his mom called, "You can look, but no picking! I want every tray to be perfect."

He glanced at the food and gifts, all beautifully displayed, and eventually found his way to the office of the director. She gave him a rundown of things that had happened in the ward in the past few months, purchases and the ward's wish list, which he tucked into his pocket as something to discuss with Leni. She had the kind of money that would allow her to be a benefactor. Talking to her about potential donations, responsibilities she might want to pick up, would get their relationship back on track. He shouldn't have kissed her the night they'd shopped, mostly because the sweet kiss had rocked him as much as the sexy one had.

Still, it wasn't himself he was worried about. It was Leni. He hadn't wanted to give her the wrong impression. But the kiss was an easy, natural goodbye kiss. Nothing to get excited about. So today he'd be cool. And she'd be cool, and they'd be fine.

But when he noticed it was one-thirty, his gaze drifted to the elevator. When she finally stepped out at almost a quarter till two, his breath stalled. Not because he was relieved that she'd come, but because she looked amazing.

She wore black high-heel boots and a green dress that exaggerated her eye color, with a black wool coat draped over her arm. Her hair had been left down to curl along her back and swirl around her when she moved. A man in a sedate suit stood beside her, but Nick recognized him as one of Jace's employees. Someone he could dismiss.

He walked over and, unable to stop himself, caught both of her hands. "You are stunning."

Leni's heart stuttered. She told it to stop, but how could she be neutral when he looked at her like that?

She laughed. "This is what a little money can do."

He laughed and addressed Chuck, the driver Jace had assigned to her. "I think we're good here."

Leni frowned. "Good?"

"Sure. Everybody here is in the same tax bracket. Jace has security at all the entrances and exits." He smiled at Chuck. "No sense in overkill."

Chuck stepped into the elevator and Leni faced Nick. "So, what's going to happen here?"

"First, my mom will give a little speech about the good work the hospital does, then kids sit on Santa's lap and get gifts. Then there's a light lunch."

Her heart warmed. This was exactly the kind of charity she was looking for to share her wealth, but businessman Nick seemed to be back. She'd thought they'd ditched him days ago. But here he was again.

She glanced around, searching to see if there was an obvious way to bring fun Nick back. But she remembered the picture of this event from six years ago. The shot of his laughing mom, smiling dad and handsome younger brother—with bad boy Nick, who even though he looked totally out of place, had been here supporting the children's wing.

Obviously, this charity, this event, had been a family thing. Now it seemed like only Nick and his mom were involved.

She would be kind, especially to businessman Nick. "Sounds good."

He motioned to the left and said, "Let me take your coat," as a man in a black suit approached them. Leni handed the coat to Nick and he handed it to the guy in the black suit.

Nick's mom walked over. She took Leni's hands, leaned in, kissed her cheeks and said, "Thank you for coming."

Leni's heart broke a bit. Knowing what she knew now about Amanda losing a child and how it had changed her family, her life, she could have hugged her forever. "It's my pleasure."

"My son told me you are now a client of the firm."

She had to give points to Nick for that one. Though he'd given his mother a good explanation for her presence in their lives, he hadn't told her Leni was a Hinton heir.

"Yes. It's official."

"Well, that's wonderful." Amanda peeked at her watch. "I've gotta run. It's time for my greeting. We have to start the program exactly at two o'clock or the thing will run too long and I'm sure everyone has dinner plans."

Leni smiled and nodded as Amanda bustled away. The short talk she gave was both heartrending and upbeat. Leni applauded with everyone else.

Nick motioned for her to walk down the hall. "Let's go to the activity room and watch the kids open gifts."

Leni and Nick followed his mom and stopped beside Santa, who told the kids to form a line.

Leni's heart shattered. There were children in casts and on crutches. Kids with shaved heads. Little children in wheelchairs.

As if reading her mind, Nick leaned in and whispered, "Most of these kids will be home for Christmas."

"Really?"

"Yes. Medicine is so different now. We're seeing more and more kids recover and go on to lead normal lives."

"That's fabulous."

"And something your dad was a part of."

She laughed. "Why, Nick Kourakis, are you trying to get into my pocketbook?"

He grinned at her. "You didn't bring a pocketbook."

"Well, it looks like I should have."

He laughed merrily. Her heart perked up and she was having a little trouble controlling it. How could she not like him more and more with each passing minute? Seeing the picture of his family before his brother died, she realized how difficult it must be for him. Not just because he was mourning, but because it was clear his family had suffered the kind of loss from which some families don't recover.

How could she not long to see him as happy as he had been six years ago?

Santa arrived, and she stood with Nick, enjoying the kids as they hopped on Santa's lap and gave their Christmas lists.

The wishes of the kids ran the gamut of silly and normal to sentimental and wonderful. One little girl wanted her grandmother to get a washer, so she didn't have to go to the Laundromat. From the corner of her eye, Leni watched Nick type her name into his phone.

She smiled at him and he smiled at her. That rush of adrenaline that she'd felt the first time she'd seen him raced through her. After last night's kiss and today's easy conversations, she didn't even try to stop it. He was a great-looking guy, who clearly loved these kids and his mom. He was good at his job. And thoughtful enough to fly to Kansas to help her and her mom through the worst day of their lives—even as he was clearly still struggling with his own loss.

There was no way in hell she could stop herself from falling in love with this man. If the situation ended with him not feeling the same way about her, she was going to end up with the biggest broken heart in recorded history. But today she just couldn't stop herself from letting go and letting herself feel everything her heart wanted to feel for him.

CHAPTER THIRTEEN

NICK SAW IT. She'd given him *that* smile, and he'd felt the same thing he'd felt the first time he saw her. Smitten.

He reminded himself that he didn't deserve her. But that didn't mean he couldn't fall for her. How could he not when she was light and simple, easy to be with? And real. So wonderfully real in a world that was filled with money and power and posturing.

Still, he'd have to be careful. He might long for the feelings she inspired in him. Might even want to indulge them if only in his own heart. But he couldn't really act on them.

So, he let her limo take her home and resisted the urge to call her that night. The next morning, despite the snow, he made it to the meeting Danny had set up for him to explain details of Mark Hinton's estate to her. Show her slides of houses, give her lists of companies and things like yachts and Jet Skis.

He hadn't expected he'd be needed this soon, but Danny had explained that Leni was smart and adjusting to everything quickly. The more information they could get out of the way before they found the next heir, the better.

She wore a pink sweater and jeans with boots made for snow and he smiled to himself about her practicality. Something he didn't see a lot of in his world.

When Danny suggested lunch, he bowed out, blaming work and got into the elevator which returned him to the lobby. His phone rang before he could get outside, and he paused to take the call. As he stood talking to one of his managers, the elevator to Danny's office opened again and Leni walked out.

Alone.

He squeezed his eyes shut. He had no idea why she hadn't taken Danny up on is offer of lunch, but watching her walk through the lobby, out the revolving door into the hellacious winter storm, his heart stuttered. All the same, he told himself to give her time. She'd easily make friends. She'd easily fit in. She just needed time.

His chest tightened when he thought about how quickly and how easily she'd also find dates. With her looks and down-home charm, men would flock to her. He pulled in a breath to loosen his chest but went back to his call.

Watching her fall in love with someone else would be part of his penance.

Leni took her limo back to her hotel and busied herself searching real estate listings on the internet and trying to decide which of the three real estate agents Nick had recommended she'd choose to help her.

Eventually, she chose an agent and contacted her by email. Saturday morning, the agent called her and Sunday afternoon, they met at the coffee shop across the street from her hotel to talk about what she needed. Using her phone, the agent pulled up six potential condos and Leni chose three to see the following day. And the agent left.

Bored at three o'clock in the afternoon on a lazy Sunday, she nearly called Nick. But she hesitated. Friday, Saturday and now Sunday had gone by without a word from him except a very professional overview of her dad's holdings at Danny's office.

Did she really want to be the one to call?

She got a second latte, settled in on one of the stools at the counter and used her phone to research Mark Hinton again. Really curious about him now that she was hearing how he lived, how much he had and how alone he was. He could have had anything he wanted—except friends. Extrapolating from things Nick and Danny had said in their meeting, she realized he hadn't trusted anyone.

She scrolled through three of the websites dedicated to him, including one where people tried to guess his whereabouts. She shook her head with wonder. Didn't people have anything better to do?

"Hey."

She glanced up to see a youngish woman, maybe twenty-four, smiling at her. "Mind if I sit here?"

Leni shifted over a bit on her stool, as if she needed to make room for her, then told herself not to be silly. "Sure. I just need one chair," she added, making fun of herself for the way she'd shifted over to make room.

The young woman laughed and tucked a strand of her long black hair behind her ear. "I'm Sandy Wojack."

"I'm Leni." She stopped a bubble of panic that formed in her chest. If Mannington had a coffee shop, people would sit with other people all the time. If they hadn't been introduced, they'd introduce themselves.

But she was an heir of a multibillion-dollar estate. And in the thirteen days since Nick had found her in Mannington, nine of which she'd spent in New York City, no one had introduced themselves to her. No one had come up to her.

Of course, she hadn't been out much.

"I saw you with the real estate agent and was trying to overhear the addresses of the condos you were looking at."

Leni stiffened. Nobody in Mannington would admit to eavesdropping like that. "Oh."

"Real estate is so tight here, right?"

She had no idea. "Absolutely."

"I was hoping I could get a lead from your agent." She laughed. "But you're buying out of my price range."

And that felt downright weird. Nobody talked money with a stranger. At least, no one from Mannington did.

She reached to pick up her phone to gather her things and leave, and realized it was side-by-side with Sandy Wojack's phone. Not where she had put it…at least eighteen inches away from her.

Fear washed through her. Wasn't that how people cloned phones?

Hell if she knew!

"How did this get here?"

Sandy blinked innocently.

And Leni felt like an idiot. Sort of. She slid her phone into her expensive designer purse, lifted her even more expensive coat from the back of her stool and let her ridiculously expensive black boots carry her outside.

For the love of all that was holy, she might as well be wearing a sign that she had more money than she knew what to do with.

She raced back to the hotel, jumped inside her room and leaned against the closed door, her heart pounding. Not sure if she was panicking for nothing or if she'd just been identified, she sucked in a breath, raced to her hotel room phone and dialed Nick's number.

"I think I'm in trouble."

His voice hardened. "What kind of trouble?"

She told him the story of Sandy Wojack, and after he cursed, she burst into tears. "I don't know why I'm crying, except that it all felt really wrong, really odd." She took a breath. *"Invasive."*

"I'm coming over. Call Danny, tell him what you told me and then call room service and get us a really good bottle of scotch."

By the time Nick made it to her hotel room, she'd called Danny and had also taken a quick shower. The whole damned encounter had felt wrong and though the shower didn't ease her apprehensions, the warmth of it eased her nerves some.

Nick entered carrying Chinese food. "You're okay?"

"Yes. And I'm sorry. I feel really stupid for crying. Danny's not okay, though. He's going to look up cloning phones to see if she could have done that and he's calling his media contacts."

"He'll figure this out." He held up the bag of Chinese food. "Hungry?"

"Starving."

"Good. Is Danny calling back?"

"If he finds anything."

"Okay, we'll eat Chinese food, find a movie on pay-per-view and wait for his call."

Having him in the room made her feel safer somehow and that's when she began feeling foolish. Someone had sat down beside her at a coffee shop and started talking real estate. There was no sin in that. Yes, her phone had been moved and the girl—Sandy Wojack—had seen the condos she would be looking at—

Damn. Even trying to make it sound innocent, it was bad.

"I'm not going to be able to buy any of the condos I saw today."

"Not if we find out Sandy Wojack is a reporter." He winced. "Or that she sold your story to a reporter."

"Damn."

"You'll know to be more careful the next time."

"I will." She picked up the container of fried rice and slid some onto a paper plate provided by the Chinese restaurant. By the time she had a whole plate of wonderful-smelling goodies, Nick had the remote in his hands, searching for movies.

They watched a comedy for forty minutes, alternately eating and chatting, but as the reality of what had happened with Sandy Wojack sunk in, her stomach soured.

"I know this."

Nick peeked over. "You know what?"

"How much my dad had. And even how money makes people a little crazy."

"It's going to be fine."

"No. It's not." Just as her instincts told her she and Nick were falling in love, her instincts were telling her Sandy Wojack was a bad person. And her instincts were never wrong.

The chime of Leni's hotel room phone burst into the room and she and Nick exchanged a glance. He picked it up and said, "Hello?"

"It's Danny."

"It's Danny, Leni."

Leni let out her breath. "Put it on speaker."

Nick clicked the speaker button and said, "Hey, Danny, you're on speaker with me and Leni. What did you find out?"

"That Sandy Wojack's already tried to sell her story to three papers."

Leni squeezed her eyes shut.

Nick said, "How'd she figure it out?"

"She didn't. She was watching Leni because her clothes were expensive, and she was considering a seven-million-dollar condo. When the real estate agent left, she saw Leni reading about Mark Hinton on her phone." Danny took a breath. "She secretly took a few pictures of you before she sat down to talk to you. The woman must be a professional con artist or something because she told two of the papers she had the spyware to clone your phone."

Nick sat back on the red sofa. "Then she knows everybody involved and all of our phone numbers."

Leni shook her head and walked over to the wall of windows, looking out at Times Square.

Danny said, "Yes and no. Leni didn't text much. Her mom. A few friends. So, all Sandy really has is information about Leni's friends in Mannington and your number and my number. As well as the hotel number."

"Then she's not staying here tonight."

"No. She can't."

"She can stay with me."

For that Leni turned. "No."

She would not stay overnight with him. She wouldn't risk tumbling into bed because she was scared and helpless and overemotional. "There are hundreds of hotels in this city. Pick one."

Danny said, "How about if we pick one closer to my office, Leni?"

"That would be great."

"Call your real estate agent and cancel those showings tomorrow."

"Yes," Nick agreed. "I gave you three names. We'll move on to the next one."

Leni pulled in a breath. "Okay."

"Give me ten minutes," Danny said. "I'll have you in a hotel so secure even Nick will have to check in with your bodyguards."

"Okay."

CHAPTER FOURTEEN

THE UPROAR THE next day was beyond Nick's wildest dreams. He couldn't imagine what Leni was feeling. Her picture graced the front page of several newspapers, including national newspapers. The New York City television news programs showed the crowd of reporters outside the entrance to her Times Square hotel.

Danny had gotten her a new phone and when she called her mother with the new number, she'd had to explain that she'd been discovered and things were about to get weird. Hearing that, Nick had called Jace and Jace had dispatched two people to Kansas to protect her parents.

Nick watched it all with a huge hole in his heart for Leni. When noon hit, and her stomach growled, he got the strangest idea.

"What do you say we go out for dinner?"

She turned to him, her green eyes as big as two plates. "Are you kidding? Go out in that?"

She pointed at the window and he shrugged. "You can wear big sunglasses."

"In a restaurant?"

"You won't need them in the restaurant."

"Yeah, well, I thought I was safe in a coffee shop, too."

"You'll be safe. We'll go somewhere no one will know or care who you are."

"Mars?"

"Paris."

She gaped at him. "Paris?"

"Why not? It could be fun." He gave her a coaxing smile. "More fun than sitting in a hotel room."

He could tell from the look on her face that she couldn't argue that.

"Okay. Should I pack?"

"For an overnight trip."

She headed for the bedroom of her new suite where everything was shades of brown and gray with big blue throw pillows on the sofa and chairs.

While she dressed, Nick ordered sandwiches from room service, then he called his pilot. They ate lunch while the pilot prepped for the flight. Before they left, she asked for a few minutes in her bedroom. When she came out, she was wearing her old jacket, white turtleneck and jeans.

"That Sandy woman said she'd gotten curious about me because of how expensive my clothes were."

Her voice held a sadness that broke his heart.

She shrugged. "This outfit kept people away from me for a whole week. I like to wear it."

"Sure."

They rode down in the elevator and got into her limo. She barely said anything on the drive to the airstrip. When they stepped into the plane, Jace's two men followed them.

"This is weird."

Nick shrugged out of his parka. "Not really. Things will eventually calm down. Like your dad, you may find places to stay where no one cares who you are. Like Idaho."

Taking a seat, she laughed. "I don't think they'll care in Mannington."

"Really? No one will extort money or threaten your future kids?"

"I don't think so."

Sitting beside her, he smiled at her naivete.

"I like Mannington. I trust the people in Mannington, and I've been giving this whole money thing some thought. I've decided that since I can't live out my dream of being a social worker, I should find something to do to satisfy that need. At first when I was talking to Danny, I'd thought being on the boards of my dad's companies would work, but now I don't think that's a good idea. I don't want to be the face of a multibillion-dollar fortune."

"So?"

"I've decided to fix my town."

He chuckled. "How do you fix a town?"

"First, I'd invest in all the businesses. You know, to kind of beef them up. Like new chairs and booths in the diner. A new oven for the bakery across the street because they're always complaining theirs is too small."

"Makes sense."

"Then I'd find a way to bring work to the town."

"Ah…so people don't have to move to Topeka to find work."

"Exactly. I don't think I'm trying to buy everybody's love because they already like me. But I do believe they will see that having me around will have its benefits."

He considered her idea—knowing that wouldn't even put a dent in the Hinton fortune—and finally said, "I like all your plans and I hope you won't be disappointed."

"I won't be."

He cut her a look. "You sound so sure."

"And you sound so cynical."

He laughed. "That's my old Leni."

"There is no old Leni or new Leni or nice Leni or sharp Leni. I am always going to be myself."

Relief whispered through him. Not because he was glad she would remain herself, but because she was back to being feisty. "That I believe."

"Good."

"Okay. Can I make a few suggestions for your plan?"

She gave him a confused look, but said, "Sure."

"Beef up your police department and fire companies."

Her face brightened as she thought that through. "That makes sense."

"Bring in a clinic. Staff it with enough doctors that it can be open at least sixteen hours a day."

"I like it. It means more jobs."

"True. But it's also a safety issue. You'll have a doctor available when you need one."

The reality of why she'd need that hit her and she sighed. "Yeah."

"Speaking of safety. How is your dad?"

"He's good. He and mom went online and looked up the doctors and hospitals his neurologist and I found for him. He has appointments with three neurosurgeons."

"Three?"

"The guy is looking at brain surgery. We want all the opinions we can get."

"Good idea."

They went back to discussing Mannington and Leni's ideas to make it cleaner, nicer, safer, with more jobs, but eventually her sleepless night took its toll and she drifted off. The peaceful expression on her face took his breath away. The longing to stay with her forever rippled through him.

But that was wrong. She deserved so much more.

Especially since she had a plan that made her feel safe. She hadn't said that was why she intended to spruce up her town, bring it life, but he knew that was at least part of it. She felt safe there, among people she knew. Still, if he accidentally let himself think of her being in his life, happiness filled him. The happiness of having her at his side, the male pride that she loved *him*. But he only let himself think like that for a second because it was wrong and when he remembered that, misery filled him.

He might not have been happy before he'd met her but at least he'd found purpose in growing the family business, living up to his dad's expectations. Now all that felt empty.

He didn't care. Empty. Not empty. It didn't matter. That was his life. All the life he deserved.

He called Marie who hustled to the front of the plane. He whispered, "Could you get us a blanket?"

She nodded and raced off, returning with a thick white wool blanket. He placed it over Leni, then yawned himself. It had been a long, miserable twenty-four hours. He reached over and took a section of the blanket to cover himself and within minutes was asleep.

Nick woke after three hours, but Leni didn't stir until they landed. Though it was seven o'clock at night in New York, it was two o'clock in the morning in France. And it was cold.

When the plane stopped completely, he signaled for Marie to take their blanket and bring their coats. "I'm sorry to tell you that it's a little chilly in France in December."

She blinked up at him. "I have my coat. It's not like we were planning on going to the beach."

"But we could. If you wanted to, we could simply tack a few days onto the trip and head for an island where it's warm enough to wear a bikini."

She chuckled. "Right. That's funny."

"No. That's your life now." But he saw what he was doing. Sadness and longing had him subtly trying to convince her to go somewhere they could be together. Somewhere her safety and his past wouldn't be an issue.

"And maybe that should be part of this trip. Maybe you should look around and realize you can go anywhere you want. Live anywhere you want."

She took a breath.

He told himself not to argue his case, but his mouth didn't listen. "I'm serious. You can be an island girl."

"I know. But I like my plan about Mannington."

He had to admit he did, too. And having her consider an island was just his stupid selfishness. He wanted her.

He wanted to be with her, but not as himself. He wanted to hide or run and forget everything.

But that was even more wrong than trying to persuade Leni to give up her life, her friends, her parents for him.

She had responsibilities now.

He rose from his seat, took their coats from Marie and helped Leni into hers. They deplaned into the dead of night.

"I'm guessing there's a time difference."

He winced. "Yeah, I added the seven hours travel time to noon in New York and figured we'd get here for dinner. But in all the confusion I forgot the time difference."

She took a deep breath of the frosty air and glanced around as they walked to a waiting limo. "I see that."

"In a few hours we can have breakfast. Yummy pastry and rich dark coffee."

She laughed. "Sounds great."

He winced. "But then we have to get home."

"Really?"

"I also forgot the charity ball on Friday."

She gasped. "For the children's ward."

"Yes."

"Your mom wanted me to go to that."

"I'd like you to go to that."

The peace and quiet of the French countryside must have worked its magic because she smiled her Leni smile. "Then I'll go."

The drive from the airstrip was long but when they got close to Paris, Leni could see the lights of the Eiffel Tower and the trip suddenly felt real.

She was in *France*. She really could go anywhere she wanted. Do anything she wanted. As long as she could protect herself.

Because it was so late, Nick checked them into a gorgeous hotel. She expected them to go to separate rooms, but he opened the door on a suite.

"I know you're fine. I know you're safe," he said as they entered the room, bellman on their heels. "But I'll just feel better if you're within yelling distance."

Her mouth went dry. She knew he'd put a blanket over her while she was sleeping, then crawled under with her. The extreme circumstances they were battling were definitely bringing out his protective instincts...but what if they were bringing out more than that? Sharing a room... Would they be sharing a bed?

She thought back to their kiss and even though she knew they'd be an explosive combination, she didn't want to end up in bed because he was afraid. She wanted more kisses. She wanted him to woo her.

It was stupid to be such a romantic. But she was. She always had been and Nick was, too. He'd hinted at it right before he'd kissed her the first time in her mom's kitchen.

"Anyway," Nick said, glancing around the room that was soft shades of yellow with white sofas and chairs and bowls of white roses on every flat surface. "Those two doors are to the bedrooms. You can pick the one you want."

Disappointment and relief collided and flooded her. But disappointment won. He hadn't even thought of sleeping with her.

Which could be considered gallant.

Or prove that he didn't have the same feelings for her as she had for him—

Then why the blanket? Why share the blanket? She knew damned well there had to be more than one blanket on that plane.

She shook her head to clear it of the idiocy. She was tired. "It doesn't matter which room." She pointed to the one on the left. "I'll take that one. I still need some sleep."

"And when you wake up, I know the perfect café for breakfast."

She smiled and nodded, went into the room and face-planted onto the thick white comforter covering the big bed.

Soon she wouldn't have to worry about reporters or charlatans following her around. This situation itself was going to drive her crazy.

He made good on his promise of a café the next morning. Though it was cold, they sat outside drinking rich black coffee and eating pastries with names like cream puff, croissant, madeleine, macaron. With her wearing her old coat, they walked to the Eiffel Tower, along the Seine and then they had to go home.

But the trip had refreshed her. She'd put on new jeans when she dressed that morning and one of her beautiful soft sweaters. But she'd also slid into her old jacket so that when they reached her New York City hotel and she got out of Nick's limo, she looked like an average tourist. Her bodyguards discreetly walked ten feet in front of her and at least ten behind. She didn't look at them. She didn't draw any attention to them or herself. She simply got into the elevator with the first one, climbed to the floor of her new hotel room and walked down the hall.

When she entered her room, the oddest sense filled her.

She hadn't been afraid in Paris and, damn it, she refused to be afraid now. This kind of sneaking around, pretending to be just an average person, walking into a hotel room while discreetly surrounded by bodyguards wasn't her.

She was stronger than this. Smarter than this. More easygoing than this. That's how she intended to behave from now on.

Nick checked on Leni over the next few days, but he didn't go to see her. He was already too tempted to do something that wasn't right, to change her mind about where she lived and how she lived. His selfishness was back and if he got too close, he'd want more and persuade her to give him more.

Because that's what he did best, persuade people to see things his way. The night his brother died he'd persuaded Joe to go out when he didn't want to. If he'd listened to Joe, his brother might still be alive now.

He couldn't forget that.

On Friday, he arrived at the ball early enough to ease his mother's fears about whether everything looked perfect. As opening time approached, he stood with his parents in an informal receiving line where they could welcome guests. He tried to tell himself he wasn't watching for Leni but when she appeared at the back of the line his heart stumbled.

Every time she walked into a room, she stole his breath, but tonight he wasn't sure he'd get it back. Her red gown clung to her breasts and tiny waist but belled out with layer after layer of soft, shiny red fabric. Her shoes must have had five-inch heels because she was taller than he'd ever seen her.

He laughed remembering the first time she'd worn high heels around him, thinking she was tall enough to kiss, and his heart twisted.

He'd never met anybody like her. Normal and fun, but tonight she looked like royalty. Her head high. Her smile real. Her face breathtaking.

As she inched her way toward him, he thanked his lucky stars that he'd already worked all this out in his head and wouldn't make a move on her. Then he realized something that stopped his heart.

This would be their last night together for weeks. Soon, she'd be leaving for Mannington for Christmas. She wouldn't return until she had to. He'd endure a quiet Christmas at his parents' where everybody thought about Joe but no one said a word. He'd feel it. He'd feel their anger and their loss. Then he'd go to work and avoid talking to anyone for weeks.

By the time she came back to New York, they'd both be so different they might not really like each other. Or, worse, their paths might only cross when Danny called them both into his office.

She finally reached his parents. His mother hugged her. His *father* hugged her. Probably because he now knew she was one of the three Hinton heirs.

Leni shifted away from his parents, and Nick held his breath. This was his last night with Leni as Leni. Their last night of being two people so attracted to each other they experienced an almost irresistible pull.

He didn't know how it would end, but suddenly he knew he couldn't let this opportunity pass.

Her eyes had been painted with green shadows that gave her a mystical air. Her hair was pulled up into something that looked like a ponytail of curls that cascaded to her shoulders. Her red dress sparkled as if someone had hidden glitter in the fabric that hugged her curves.

He took her hands. "You are stunning."

"Thanks. You don't look so bad yourself."

He glanced down at his tuxedo, then laughed. "I guess men are lucky. We don't have to figure out colors or styles. We just have to look good in black."

"Well, you are amazing in black."

Her heart could attest to that from the jump in her pulse when she saw him. Good God. Could a man be any sexier? From his height to his shiny hair to the way he held himself as if he'd been born in a tux.

He made being rich look really, really easy.

He caught her elbow and turned her toward the ballroom. "Why don't we get a glass of champagne?"

She motioned to the receiving line. "Don't you have duties?"

He shrugged. "I think I'm done."

Because he wanted to be with her? After days of a phone call or two to be sure she was okay, he wanted to be with her? Maybe just for one drink?

Probably. She wouldn't make a big deal of it. Wouldn't let her aching heart get too excited. He might look at her with longing in his eyes, but since Paris he'd treated her like a friend.

So, she smiled at him the way she would a friend. "I'd like a drink."

They walked into the room that had been filling with people. White poinsettias acted as centerpieces on tables covered in crisp white linen. But red and green accent lights added some whimsy, making the room festive. A string quartet played softly in a far corner.

Nick took two flutes of champagne from a passing waiter and handed one to her. "Merry Christmas."

She would have thought it odd that someone was wishing her Merry Christmas a week before the actual event. But that afternoon she'd been shopping for her parents, being told Merry Christmas by some very happy clerks.

They touched their glasses together with a soft clink and she took a sip of the most perfect champagne she'd ever tasted. She closed her eyes in ecstasy.

"So good."

He laughed. "I love that you close your eyes to savor."

And she loved that he used the word *love* because right now, in this moment, he wasn't looking at her like a friend. His gaze had softened and his smooth voice was velvety seduction.

Maybe he'd missed her? Maybe he'd decided to stop fighting?

He introduced her to a few friends and business associates who were extremely curious about her but too polite to ask the questions she could see shimmering in their eyes. She made conversation about their jobs and families and everyone eagerly joined in. She might not have been born to money, but she did know people, how to be kind and polite. That was her and she'd already decided she wasn't losing herself.

As Nick swept her away from the last group, he laughed. "You're getting really good at this."

"I just decided to stay myself." She caught his gaze. "This is me. I'm not letting a bunch of crazy curiosity seekers ruin my life."

His head tilted as he studied her. "You're really okay?"

"I'm really okay."

"I knew you would be. I knew you'd figure it out."

For him, she would figure out anything. But she suspected in his own way, he probably knew that too, so she only smiled.

When it came time for dinner, he led her to his family's table where his father rose as Nick seated her.

Extremely glad for the online videos she'd found on etiquette, she took her seat, sending Nick a smile of thanks as he sat on the seat next to her.

She suddenly felt like Cinderella. Not at her first ball—the one where she'd lost her shoe. But the next ball. The one after the Prince had found her and told her he loved her. The one where he showed her off.

Because that's what this felt like. Nick had introduced her to friends and business associates and now she was dining with his parents, like part of their circle. It was heady fun, but there was a deeper message. She fit. And he liked that she fit. He liked *her* and he was done fighting it.

After dinner, they listened to a few speeches of thanks to volunteers and benefactors of the children's ward of the hospital, then the band began to play. She and Nick danced to the first few songs. Then his friends began asking her to dance. Nick would let her dance with three friends, then he'd rescue her, and they'd dance again.

She swore she really was Cinderella.

The night passed in a blur of champagne and laughter. Giggling on their way to the street and their limos, Nick stopped them in front of hers.

"This was so great. You made a usually dull event tons of fun."

And champagne had made *her* tipsy enough that she flattened her hands against his chest, feeling the smooth silk of his white shirt.

She looked up into his shiny dark eyes. "I think we're a good team."

"I think we are, too. So, I was thinking maybe we'd both take your limo." He caught her gaze. "Say yes, because I already told my driver to go home."

Her chest tightened and breathing became difficult, the way it had the first time he kissed her. She knew this was it. He wasn't just going to kiss her again. He was coming home with her.

She worked not to sound nervous when she said, "Sure."

The driver opened her limo door and they slid inside. The door closed, cocooning them in a dark, silent world.

The limo pulled into traffic, but neither one of them said anything. Glad for the short trip, she stemmed her nervousness as Nick helped her out of the limo and led her to her suite.

The second the door closed behind them, he pulled her to face him. His head descended slowly, and she held his gaze, keeping her eyes open until the very last second. She wanted to see everything, every emotion that flickered in his dark, dark orbs. She wanted to remember everything on the night of the first time they'd make love.

CHAPTER FIFTEEN

EVERYTHING SUDDENLY FELT right in Nick's world. As he brushed his lips across Leni's, the sense of rightness morphed into pure pleasure. She tasted like champagne and happiness. Everything he wanted in this minute. Everything he needed to remember her by.

Because he would not sleep with her. It didn't matter that their luxurious kiss rolled through him like thunder or that his heartbeat pounded in anticipation of touching her. He would only take this so far.

He unbuttoned the silk jacket that matched her gown, knowing only thin fabric would separate his palm from her skin, but reminding himself that had to be enough. He wouldn't hurt her. He wouldn't edge his way into her world. He only wanted this taste.

So, he kissed her, her mouth eager beneath his desperate one. There was something hot and mysterious between them. There had been from the first second their eyes locked. Tonight, it rose like thick smoke from a raging fire.

A voice deep inside him told him this was it. Real love that offered peace and contentment. Maybe even a second chance. And he should grab it.

Another voice, the stronger voice, reminded him he didn't deserve it, but more than that *she* deserved better.

Still, he smoothed his hand along the silk of her bodice, knowing taut skin lie beneath. Temptation spiked, but his conscience tweaked again. He ached for this and he knew why. He wasn't looking for redemption that wasn't his to find. But a new start suddenly loomed on the horizon because everything about her was fresh and original. Unique. Wonderful. She would make his life an open door. He'd never want anyone else. Anything else.

But that was the point. He couldn't walk away from his life. He had commitments. Sins that couldn't be forgiven. A life that would drag her down.

Only a true sinner would drag someone like her into his private hell.

He pulled away from her. "I think I'd better get going."

Her gaze connected with his. "Why not stay?"

Her voice was soft, innocent. His walls yearned to crumble. Need tore through him.

Which was why he stepped back. He wouldn't hurt her, but he couldn't tell her that because he didn't want to get into a debate about his reasoning. He wasn't sure he'd win. So, he fudged a bit.

"It's late. I had a long day."

She walked her fingers up the buttons of his shirt. "I wouldn't make you do all the work."

He couldn't help it. He laughed. But he wouldn't let himself forget who he was and why he had to let her go.

He brushed a light kiss across her lips. "You're nuts."

"But I think that's why you like me."

He turned toward the door of her suite. "Yeah. You're probably right." He kept it light, simple, so she wouldn't spend the night wondering what she'd done wrong. But in that second, he vowed he would never see her again unless it was in his office or Danny's.

Leni woke the next morning dreamy happy. She yawned and stretched and could have stayed in bed all day, except she wanted to see Nick. It was Saturday, but that didn't guarantee he wasn't working.

The night before had been perfect. Though Nick had laughed when she'd said he liked her because she was a little crazy, she knew that was true. She'd sensed all along that he needed more happiness—maybe more craziness—in his life. Now he saw it, too.

The most amazing idea hit her. She threw back the covers, climbed out of bed, ordered coffee and toast from room service, then called the concierge.

"I need to find a small Christmas tree and decorations."

He told her she could order a tree and have it delivered, then directed her to two nearby places where she could get sparkly ornaments, some tinsel and lights. He again suggested she could have them delivered too but she wanted to be the one delivering them.

After a quick shower, she called Jace and asked him for Nick's address. When he asked why, she told him about the Christmas tree and, though he hesitated, he told her the driver knew the address.

Two hours later, she had a small tree in her limo trunk, two bags of simple ornaments and happiness in her heart. She and her bodyguard walked into the lobby. The doorman's eyebrows rose.

"I guess I have to be buzzed up to Mr. Kourakis's condo."

His eyebrows rose even higher. "Mr. Kourakis?"

"Yes."

He hesitated a second, but said, "Let me call him."

He called, gave Leni's name and after a wince, he hung up the phone. "He's on his way out for the day, but he'll see you."

That struck her oddly. Still, Nick had always been a difficult man. She knew he'd want to see her. He might not like surprises, but he did like kissing her and she liked kissing him. And whether he wanted to admit it, he needed a Christmas tree.

Nick waited by the elevator for Leni. When the door opened, she walked out holding two bags, with a bodyguard behind her carrying a three-foot Christmas tree. He nearly laughed.

But he couldn't. He'd given her the wrong impression the night before and now he had to fix it.

She set the bags down and slipped out of her coat. "I came here to spice up your condo, give you some Christmas cheer."

After instructing the bodyguard to set the tree, already in a small tree stand, on the table by the window, he dismissed him.

When the elevator door closed behind him, Nick folded his arms across his chest. "How do you know I didn't already have a tree?"

She laughed, rose to her tiptoes and brushed a quick kiss across his lips. "Lucky guess."

Something soft and warm floated through him when she kissed him. He longed to grab and savor it, but he couldn't. Leaving her the night before had been the hardest thing he'd ever done and now he'd have to say goodbye again.

Except this time, she had to understand this was the end of anything romantic between them.

She took the two bags of ornaments to the table, removed the boxes and put a bright red ball on one of the tiny limbs.

"Look, Leni. I think you and I have to talk."

"Talk while I decorate. Any chance you have coffee?"

"I can make you a cup, but… Listen." He nearly lost the struggle inside him. She looked so perfect in his home. And one by one, as the brightly colored balls filled the small tree, the spirit of Christmas, the memories of happier days and what the week before Christmas was supposed to feel like, filled him.

He reminded himself that he didn't want to hurt her, walked over, took the ornament from her hand and led her to the sofa.

She sat, but he didn't sit beside her. He lowered himself to the chair across from her, put his elbows on his knees and took a breath. He was going to have to tell her the truth. He didn't know why he hadn't realized that all along, but he saw it now.

"I'm not the nice guy you think I am."

"Yes, you are."

"No. See? That's what's wrong here. You have this vision of me being a nice guy that's not true. If I take what you're offering, I'm going to hurt you."

"I don't think so."

He leaned forward a bit more. "You know my brother died. What you don't know is that he died because of me. My father is angry. After five years, my mother is still confused about how we're supposed to go on without him. But we all know it's my fault he died. I all but dragged him out in an ice storm. I was home from my gallivanting and wanted to have some fun."

He pulled in a harsh breath, ran his hands down his face. "I see everything from that night in slow motion in my head. Him trying to talk sense into me. Me telling him I was a Navy SEAL. I'd done things that would amaze him. I could certainly drive in a little ice. My parents angry because they didn't want us to go out. But I kept insisting and, in the end, I won. The roads were worse than anything I'd ever seen. But I got it in my head that this was like a mission and I needed to do it."

Memories of that night froze his chest, filled him with self-loathing.

"The few cars on the road were slipping and sliding but I was okay. Then I lost control and I couldn't even tell you how many cars I hit or how many hit me. I banged my head and blacked out and when I came to, paramedics were shouting about Joe. I looked over and he was so still. So quiet."

He stopped. He couldn't level his breathing, as those

minutes came back full force. Paramedics scrambling. Firemen shouting. The fear that his brother was dead racing through him like a wildfire.

"You think you killed your brother?"

"I know I killed my brother. The accident might not have been my fault but going out was. Both of my parents warned me. Joe argued. My dad got mad." He shrugged. "I wouldn't listen. Now I have parents who look at me and see the guy who killed their son. It's all I can do to handle the burden of that.

"Losing my brother drained something from my soul. My family is never going to get over this because we can't blame fate. We can't come to terms with it because, when we try, all we have is the fact that I pushed when I shouldn't have. You're a good person. Too good for that kind of life. Too good for me."

"Nick…"

He rose from his chair. "No. Don't you get it? It's been five years and we can't move on. You do not know what it's like to look at your parents and realize you took away their good son. The son who stepped up to run the family business, when I refused to settle down and globe-trotted like the world owed me fun. He's the one who bought the best Christmas gifts and took Mom and Dad to brunch once a month. You don't know what it's like to have to try to be everything my brother would have been to make up for cockiness, arrogance." He shook his head and fell to his seat again. "You don't know what it's like to come home at night with that day's pressure morphing into the next day's stress, sprinkled with guilt and the grief of *my* loss. While everyone feels sorry for my parents. No one remembers I lost a brother, too."

"Oh, Nick…"

She rose and knelt in front of him, but he gently nudged her back, so he could stand, then help her stand.

"I won't drag you into that. But more than that, I know I don't have the mental energy to be the kind of man you deserve."

Leni nodded, the whole story swirling around in her head as she desperately worked to understand him. All along she'd known something was wrong. All along she'd known it somehow connected to his brother. But she'd never taken in the signs. She'd ploughed ahead, believing that something as strong as what stirred between them would conquer anything.

But she heard the pained resignation in his voice. He'd killed his brother. He was bruised and broken. And he was correct. That was the kind of emotional wound a family only got over with courage and work.

He'd been telling her that all along, pushing away all along and she hadn't listened.

She was an idiot.

No, she was the seven-year-old foster child, desperate for parents to love her, who always wished and hoped and saw things that weren't there because she so desperately wanted love. Wanted everyone to be happy. Wanted the world to work the way it should.

And she'd always ended up hurt. First, her dad didn't step up to help her sick mom. Then her mom dropped her off and never looked back. Three families had her as a foster kid and all three asked for her to be moved on to another home.

Not only did she know what it was like to be the star in a drama that was totally out of her control, she knew there were some things that didn't work out. Just as there were some wounds an outsider couldn't heal.

She slid her coat from the back of a chair, where Nick had laid it, but glanced back at the tree. She'd had such good intentions and worried that leaving it behind would only bring back bad memories for him, but in the end she decided to leave it.

Maybe it was time he faced some things. Maybe the tree would push him to do that?

Maybe then he'd realize they should be together...

In her head, she cursed herself for her wishful thinking. She was always like this. Hopeful. Positive. But the world wasn't always a positive place and not all answers were easy. She knew that. She had a mom who had abandoned her. A father who hadn't wanted her at all. She'd been *lucky* the Longs had found her.

Not everybody was so lucky. Not everybody's life worked out.

And she had no right to interfere. Despite her education and her longing to help him, she couldn't.

Horrible sadness rose in her. A combination of the grief she felt rolling from him in waves and her own grief for him.

As the elevator door closed behind her, sorrow for Nick rose in her. He should be the happiest guy on the face of the earth. Instead, he might actually be the most broken.

Tired, worn down, angry with herself for pushing Nick, Leni removed her coat in her suite, called Jace and told him she wanted to go home. Back to Mannington.

She almost called her mom to pick her up at the private airstrip, but she decided to rent a car instead. Her brand-new bank card was like a little miracle worker. She never had to ask the price of anything. She gave the card number to the clerk on the phone and she got anything she wanted.

Tonight, she wanted an SUV delivered to the airstrip to get her through the Kansas snow and home.

Home.

That's where she needed to be. That's where she was who she was supposed to be. Not some New York socialite who got herself involved in things that were over her head, things she couldn't fix. Kansas was where she belonged.

Evening arrived as she drove the hour to her parents' house. She pulled the big SUV into the driveway, grabbed one of the three suitcases with her new clothes in them and headed inside.

Opening the door, she called, "I'm home!"

Wearing an apron, her mom peeked out of the kitchen. "Leni! What are you doing here? We thought you weren't coming until Christmas Eve."

Not about to tell her mom she'd fallen in love with Nick and forced him to relive the worst night of his life as he told her he didn't want what she wanted, she fibbed just a little bit.

"I was sitting in my room and I thought, 'I should be making cookies right now,' and here I am."

"Because you want to bake cookies?"

"Because I do whatever I want now."

Her dad came up behind her mom. "Don't let that go to your head, Kitten."

Oh, she wouldn't. She'd learned her lesson with Nick Kourakis. He'd given her every sign, every hint, that his family was in real emotional trouble and she'd missed it.

She thought of Nick casually mentioning his brother when they were skating but not being able to elaborate and her eyes drifted shut. He'd been so wonderful. Every time she'd had a problem like her dad's hospitalization or when Sandy Wojack told the world she was an heir, he'd been there.

She'd genuinely believed he loved her because everything he did for her was so natural, so honest, as if it had come right from his heart.

But he was the one who'd been in real pain and though she'd seen it she hadn't realized the depth of it and she'd pushed him.

Remorse shivered through her, hurting her to her core.

She took a breath. Reminded herself that she couldn't do anything about what had happened between them and that she'd be careful from here on out, wouldn't barge ahead, would pay closer attention to people, the way she'd been taught at university.

She shrugged out of the big parka she'd bought on her spending spree and hung it on a hook by the door, then rubbed her hands together. If it killed her, she would be happy. She would not let her parents see how upset she was.

"So? What are we making?"

"The cutout cookies that you like so much."

The same cookies she'd given Nick the weekend her dad had been in the hospital.

She fought the urge to weep. He'd always been there when she needed him, and she'd missed the signs that he needed her more.

"We'll ice them," her dad said proudly. "Then decorate. Maybe with sprinkles."

Her dad's happiness being able to do such a simple thing like make cutout cookies made her laugh. She breathed again. Told herself this was where she needed to be until she sorted out everything in her head. But what was there to sort? Money hadn't bought Nick's family happiness. Her love hadn't healed Nick. Her pushing had hurt him.

Her mom made two big bowls of batter which they refrigerated while she and her dad played a quick game of Yahtzee. When the dough had chilled, she reached for the first bowl of batter.

"Oh, sweetie, get an apron." Her mom motioned toward Leni's pink cashmere sweater. "You don't want to ruin that."

"Why? I can always buy another." The words came out choppy, mixed with tears and confusion.

Having money was such an odd thing. So much good, but so much bad.

"Kitten?"

The tears spilled over. "I found out some things today that broke my heart. Especially since I made things worse."

Her dad put his arm around her. "What? What happened?"

"Nick and I seemed to be getting involved romantically." She sniffed. "He always pulled back and I decided to push, and he told me that his brother died in an accident and he'd been driving and he's not over it. Neither are his parents. But I pushed, and he had to tell me, and I knew I'd done nothing but bring back bad memories."

Her parents exchanged a glance. Her mom said, "You didn't know."

"I realize that." She rubbed her hands down her face. "But I keep getting these odd, disjointed memories of us having fun and being happy and I feel like I missed something. Like there was something I should have done."

"Oh, honey." Her mom sat her down at one of the kitchen stools. "You always wanted to change the world. But there are things you can't fix."

"Not even with money," her dad quietly said. "But that doesn't mean you stop trying."

Her dad's words comforted her. Especially when she remembered her plans for Mannington. Jobs. Money for the diner, grocery store and bakery. A bigger police force. A clinic.

Calm flitted through her and took root. Keeping busy was exactly what she needed to do.

That and stay away from Nick. She'd really thought that whatever hummed between them was good. But all it seemed to do was remind him of what he couldn't have.

Her heart broke for him, but it broke for herself, too. She loved him and she'd hurt him.

Nick left the half-decorated tree exactly as it was on his dining room table. Every morning it mocked him. Every night it made him wish he could just walk over and hang the rest of the ornaments like a normal person.

By Wednesday, he couldn't go to work.

Thursday, he couldn't get out of bed.

Friday, he got up, made coffee and stared out the window at Central Park. None of the tricks he used to force himself back to life after his brother died were working. He was hungry. He was tired. But he was too broken to care.

The sound of his elevator doors opening turned him from the window. "Dad?"

"I heard you weren't at work."

Oh, God. Just what he didn't need: a lecture from his father. "I think I had a touch of the flu." Leni asking him if he lied to his parents a lot popped into his head and he didn't know whether to laugh or cry. He *missed* her. He felt that more than the grief and remorse over losing his brother, and then that brought new pain. New self-loathing. He had no right not to miss his brother. To push him aside. To forget him.

His dad strolled into the living area. "Your mother was sort of hoping you were holed up with that Long girl."

The preposterousness of his dad's statement made him hiss out a breath. "What?"

"You like her."

He did. So much. Too much. He walked from the window to the sofa. His sweatpants baggy after days of not eating. "What difference does it make?"

"It makes a lot of difference." His dad sat on the sofa. "You mother thought Leni was helping you get beyond some of your grief."

"I'll never get beyond this."

His dad's face grew solemn, so sad Nick couldn't remember ever seeing that expression before. "You have to get beyond this."

Nick sat on the chair he'd sat on to tell Leni to leave.

To explain why he couldn't love her. He tried to say something but nothing came out.

"You liked Leni, right?"

He groaned internally at having this conversation with the father who pushed him and yelled at him, but he was dutiful now. So, he didn't argue.

"Of course, I did."

"Your mother thinks she was nature's way of nudging you to finally get beyond all this."

He sniffed. "My mother thinks a lot."

"Yeah, well, I took the job in the beginning. I forced you to work. I pushed you and yelled at you and made you get up every day and go to the office and have a purpose."

Nick stilled. "You didn't boss me around because you were angry with me?"

"No! I didn't want you to sink into a depression so far we'd lose you. Do you think I wanted to force you to work? I knew how hard Joe's death was on you. I *knew* you blamed yourself. Suffered in silence. And I knew if we let you go on like that, you'd never recover."

Thinking back on those days, seeing them in a new light, brought tears to his eyes. Everything was so confused. "I'm not exactly recovered now."

"Actually, son, I think that's what's nagging at you. You *are* recovering. You want to move on. But part of you won't let you. Holding onto the guilt is your penance."

Nick took a breath. "Oh, yeah?"

"Your mom and I went to therapy. Not for us. To figure out how to help you. That was our therapist's conclusion. Your guilt is how you think you make amends. But all you're doing is losing your life, too. Your mom and I don't want to lose both of our sons. Now that we finally see this light of hope, we're not letting it pass." His dad rose. "I won't push. Neither will your mom. This has to be up to you. But you like her. Maybe even love her. And it's time. We miss Joe, but we miss you, too." He paused, put a hand on Nick's shoulder. "We want you back. The real you."

The real him? The happy-go-lucky guy who only wanted fun was gone.

And though his dad might think he wanted the old Nick back, Nick wasn't that guy anymore.

He didn't want to be. He liked who he was now.

Leni would tell him that was vain.

He laughed. Then sniffed as the elevator doors closed on his dad. Setting aside his grief was too much. Too, too much.

He thought of skating with Leni. He remembered how he'd thought of Joe in a good way and how he'd been able to think about him without dwelling on it.

He thought of the Irish pub, telling her about his real self and having her nestle against him as they walked back to her hotel.

He thought about kissing her, being drawn in, always thinking about a future with her because that's what he'd been fighting. The knowledge that he wanted more with her.

He'd sent her off in the worst possible time of year in the worst possible way. He'd ruined her Christmas with his bluntness.

But he also might have ruined his one chance with her. She was a smart woman. He'd told her to move on and she'd probably listened.

He rubbed his hands down his face. His horrible life collided with the possibility of a new one. Strength he never realized he had punched its way up from his soul.

He missed Leni with an ache that gave spark and breath to the new yearnings struggling for life. His life.

His dad was right. He had to move on.

But could he?

And if he did, would Leni even want him anymore?

* * *

It took far too long for Nick to get from New York to Mannington. And when he got there, he froze. The Long house
was dark. Still, he knocked. But no one answered.

It flitted through his mind that her dad might have had
a seizure, but their network was too strong. She'd have
called Danny and Danny would have called him.

So maybe they were at Christmas Eve services?

Suddenly a light came on in what Nick knew to be the
kitchen, so he knocked again.

With her parents on their way to bed, Leni finished the
last chapter of her book and almost turned out her light
but there was a knock at her door.

Emotionally and physically exhausted, she walked to
the kitchen to turn on the light, then into the living room
where she opened door to find Nick.

Her chest tightened and hope rose, but she reminded
herself of everything he'd told her. She'd pushed him into
admitting the worst secret anyone could have and he'd explained that was why he didn't want a relationship.

She'd done enough damage to this man. She wouldn't
do anymore. So, she smiled politely and said, "What are
you doing here? Did something happen with the estate?"

"No. I'm visiting you."

Her heart hurt just looking at him. His eyes were tired
as if he hadn't slept in days. His chin and cheeks had at
least three days' growth of beard. Now that she knew the
extent of his grief, his pain, everything inside her hurt
for him.

"Can I come in?"

"Sure. I'm sorry! I should have let you in right away."
She wouldn't be so foolish as to believe he'd come here
because he loved her. The things he'd told her were too
deep to be dismissed in a few days. But maybe he'd come

to talk. They'd always been able to talk. And maybe she *could* help him?

He stepped inside and shrugged out of his parka, which she hung on a hook by the door. "I missed you."

That broke her heart. She wanted it to mean a thousand different things, but knew it was merely proof she'd insinuated herself into his life. "I missed you, too."

She motioned for him to sit on the chair and she sat on the sofa across from him.

"I had a long talk with my dad. My parents would like me to fall in love with you."

She would have laughed at the second part of his confession, but the first part threw her. "You had a long talk with your dad?"

"He told me he'd pushed me after Joe died because he knew my grief and guilt were too much to handle. That if he hadn't given me a purpose with running the family business, I might not have ever recovered."

She pictured his gruff dad saying that, then realized she might have interpreted his dad all wrong. What she saw as gruffness might have been his desperate way of keeping Nick from crumbling.

"He's probably right."

Nick leaned forward, his elbows on his knees, his hands clasped. "They've watched me take the blame for Joe these past five years, wondering if I'd ever get beyond it."

"Oh." How sad for them. How sad for Nick.

"Then you came into the picture and they said I changed."

"You had." She'd seen him changing, loved that he could be so fun with her.

"Their thought is that you nudged me back into the real world because I really liked you."

Her heart stuttered. "What do you think?"

He met her gaze. "That they were right."

"So, all the pushing I did wasn't bad?"

"You didn't push."

"I wasn't the desperate foster kid once again looking for love?"

"First of all, you have love. Your parents adore you. But, second, we were drawn together. From the second our eyes met the first time, I felt it. You are the perfect woman for me. You make me laugh. You make me think. You got me out of my condo more than I'd been out in five years. And you pick good Christmas gifts. My mother loved that kimono thing. We did our Christmas this afternoon, so I could come here to see you."

A small laugh escaped. She didn't see the grief and pain that had been on his face the day he'd told her about his brother. Everything felt washed clean.

He sat back, ran his hands down his face. "I hope I didn't ruin what we had. My life was a mess. But I'm ready to move on. Though I'll never forget what happened, never forget Joe, he wouldn't want me to live the way I have been."

"From the things you'd said, he sounded like a good brother."

He shook his head. "He was."

They were quiet for a minute. Leni took a breath. She felt a nudge. An odd sensation that someone was telling her it was her move. That he'd dwelled enough on the past and she was the one helping him move into the future. "Want a cookie?"

He laughed. "The iced ones?"

"Made them myself with my dad and mom."

She led him into the kitchen. Pulled milk from the refrigerator and a container of cookies from the cupboard. Before she could open either, Nick caught her by the waist and spun her around.

He pressed his lips to hers, kissing her long and deep and she melted into him.

When he finally broke the kiss, he said, "I think I love you."

She slapped his arm playfully. "You goof. I know I love you."

"Even though you have more money than me now?"

She pretended to ponder that. "We'll see how it goes." Then she bounced to her tiptoes and kissed him this time.

"You know I expect you to woo me."

"Does anybody really woo anybody anymore?"

"I don't know. I don't care. But I want wine and roses, to be taken to dinner…"

"And trips to France?"

Her eyes widened. "Yes! More trips to France."

He kissed her again, not desperately, as he had before, but with a simple longing that matched the beating of her own heart, the buildup of hope that she wouldn't be alone anymore.

They really were a good pair. The best pair. Because they both understood that life wasn't always easy, but they could handle it.

Together.

EPILOGUE

As usual on Christmas Eve night, snow fell on Mannington, Kansas. One year after their first Christmas together, Nick and Leni left the totally remodeled Family Diner, which they now owned and which they paid George handsomely to manage. The old Christmas bells that typically hung from the streetlights had been cleaned up and repainted. Red ribbons graced the parking meters. The storefronts for the bakery, coffee shop, auto mechanic and grocery had been renovated. All the sidewalks had been repaved.

Wearing a black leather jacket and to-die-for black boots with jeans and a new white turtleneck sweater, Leni took a long drink of air. "Do you think your mom will like what we got her for Christmas?"

"I'm not exactly sure how you had time to shop when you were arranging to move one of Hinton Industries' manufacturing plants here."

"I had a little help from a special Santa."

Nick laughed. "I'm glad you figured out how to get help." He glanced at her. "It's been a busy year for you."

"And you."

"Yeah, but I didn't become wealthy overnight, meet a new brother and sister, go through a complicated surgery with my adoptive dad and singlehandedly become the redevelopment authority for one very happy small town."

She grinned. Becoming a Hinton heir had been one surprise after another. Fixing up her small town, making it somewhere everybody loved to live, had been the obvious thing to do. But finding real love with Nick, finding a partner, had made it all like a great adventure.

"It was a fabulous year."

As always when she said the word *fabulous*, they exchanged a glance and laughed.

"Now, you have to plan a wedding."

She took in a deep drink of air. "Is this a proposal?"

"Yes." He laughed. "Finally." He pulled a ring box from his jacket pocket, paused in the street and got down on one knee. "Leni Long, will you do me the honor of being my wife, my life partner, person destined to spend most of our money?"

Though she had been expecting the proposal, tears filled her eyes. "Yes."

He got up and kissed her. As always, her heart warmed, then her limbs warmed, then heat filled her. Somedays she couldn't believe this man loved her. Other days, she couldn't believe she'd managed so many years without him.

They broke the kiss and smiled at each other. Looking at her beautiful ring, she said, "Where should we get married?"

"Well, your dad loves the Key West house."

She pondered that, gazing around at the new storefronts as they walked through the snow on their way to the house they'd built as their home base. His New York penthouse was empty more than it was occupied these days.

Friends said hello and waved as they walked by. Snow sparkled in the glow of the streetlights. The sound of the choir rippled out from the well-lit church where Christmas Eve services were being held.

This was and always would be her home.

She stopped Nick. "I think I'd like to get married here."

He glanced around. "Here?"

"On Christmas Eve."

"Christmas Eve?"

"And I'd like to invite the whole town."

He gaped at her. "That's fifteen *hundred* people."

"I know!" She laughed merrily. "But we can afford it."

He shook his head, but when he looked around, he saw what she saw. Not merely a group of houses and businesses, but friends who sometimes felt like family. He saw hope. He saw the future.

He slid his arm across Leni's shoulders and began walking again. "I suppose you're going to want to build a hall big enough for fifteen hundred people to celebrate."

"And maybe expand the church."

He threw his head back and laughed. The minute Leni had entered his world, he'd gotten his life back.

As for his love of adventure? He had more than a feeling this woman was about to take him on the ride of his life.

* * * * *

WINNING HER
HOLIDAY LOVE

HARMONY EVANS

Chapter 1

Mariella cast an eye toward a clock on the wall as she waited for Terrence Jones, the owner of the Beach Bottom Gift Shop, to return from running an errand. She leaned her elbow on the counter and jabbed at a stuffed Santa with her manicured fingernail.

She had been in the midst of shopping for some gag gifts for the office holiday party when he asked her to mind the store. She'd almost said no but the twenty-five percent discount he offered had appealed to her thrifty nature, and would help her win points with her boss.

A former police detective and notorious flirt, Terrence had gotten tired of the rough streets of South Side Chicago and had retired to Bay Point where he peddled trinkets to tourists and residents. Glancing around, she had to give the man some credit. October had just rolled into November and the small shop was already decorated and stocked for the holidays. Terrence had no taste, but at least he had a ton of inventory. She didn't mind doing him a favor but hoped he would hurry back.

Josh, her son, had the day off from school due to a teacher's conference, so she'd taken one, too. Shopping with him always left her with a headache. Getting it done in the early afternoon would help her avoid ruining her entire evening.

Her only child was a senior in high school, a soccer fanatic and a trend follower. Like most teenagers, he always wanted to be seen in the latest styles. The past few months had been rough for Josh, so she tried to do whatever she could to make things easier.

At least the store is empty.

A little unusual, she supposed, for midday during a workweek in downtown Bay Point. As a single mother, she'd learned to be thankful for any time alone, however brief, and wherever it occurred. The downside was she tended to dwell too much on the past.

Mariella reached up and massaged away the tension settling at the back of her neck. However long it took Terrence to get back, she was going to make the best of the situation.

Just like she'd done with Josh.

Raising a son without a father was hard, but she had no choice. Jamaal passed away when Josh was just three years old. He was the love of her life, and although they'd married young, Mariella never regretted it.

At the reading of his will, she'd been shocked to learn he'd inherited a small home on the outskirts of town from his late paternal grandmother. It was the only thing Jamaal had ever owned, and he'd kept it a secret from her. His lawyer told her that he'd dreamed of someday living in it, but sadly, never got the chance.

Three years ago, when Josh was fourteen, they'd moved from East Los Angeles to Bay Point. She wanted a better life for her son, who was starting to hang around the wrong crowd at school.

The small, friendly community welcomed them with open arms. She and her son felt safe, and Josh had thrived in his new school, despite what he felt was "a ton of homework." Although he missed his friends, he quickly made new ones.

After a few months she landed a position as executive assistant to the mayor. The pay was decent and her boss, Gregory Langston, was revered. His family was one of the most powerful in town, and he'd achieved more at his young age than most men did in a lifetime.

At the age of twenty-six, Gregory had become the youngest and the first African-American mayor in Bay Point. Now at age thirty-two, he was well into his second term, happily married to Vanessa, owner of Blooms in Paradise, a local floral shop, and a proud parent of a two-year-old girl.

Due to his efforts, and many others', Bay Point was slowly changing, from boarded-up shops and minimal dining choices to a thriving Northern California tourist destination. New stores, restaurants and housing were popping up everywhere, breathing new life into the old town.

Though she was grateful for her job, it wasn't as challenging anymore. She'd recently finished her bachelor's degree in economics, with a minor in public policy, and desired a role where she could really make a difference.

She balanced her chin on the heel of her palm. Her future had never been so uncertain. She was thirty-four years old and a widow on the brink of being an empty-nester. If a more suitable job opportunity didn't open up in Bay Point, there would be little reason to stay. The mere thought of starting over in a new place made her feel ill.

Being alone didn't necessarily scare her. Though she'd gone out with a few men, the experiences did not go well.

Her child had always been her first priority, and would continue to be even when he was out of the house. Still she couldn't deny that she missed being in a relationship.

Night after restless night she wrestled with her negative thoughts and pent-up desires. Flipping the pillow over to the cold side never helped. Perhaps a man by her side would.

Forcing a smile, and desperate for something to do, she walked over to the back corner of the store. Terrence stored his cleaning supplies in a small cabinet behind a couple of squat, fake palm trees with thick trunks wound with strands of red and green lights.

She rooted around for a dust cloth, and heard the front door creak open. The glass rattled as it closed. Turning, she stayed crouched down, out of sight.

Terrence didn't believe in security cameras, and claimed all he needed were those two palm trees. He'd caught a couple of shoplifters by hiding behind them. She did have a full view of the store, and the customer who had just walked in. She held her breath, recognizing him immediately from the posters that hung in her son's room.

Sam Kelly.

He was one of Josh's favorite professional European soccer players, though her mind blanked on the name of his team. Wherever he was from, he was a long way from home.

Though she was confident he couldn't see her behind the fake foliage, she tucked herself in and against the wall. Her yoga practice, which kept her body toned and limber, was paying off.

"Hello? Anybody here?"

Mariella's heart started to race, like it was doing backflips in reverse, and she couldn't speak. Sam's voice had a dignified, majestic quality to it, classy with an edge of curiosity.

Whoa. This is better than any discount. It wasn't every day she got to spy on a gorgeous man with a British accent.

When nobody answered, he shrugged and began to browse around, hands clasped behind his back.

She'd never scrutinized Sam's glossy image hanging on her son's wall. But now that the sports star was here, right before her eyes, she couldn't help herself.

Sam's toffee-colored skin had the burnished, healthy tinge of someone who spent a lot of time outdoors. She didn't know his age, but surmised he was in his early thirties. He was of above-average height, with the lean, muscular build expected of a professional athlete.

Though it was rude not to make her presence known right away, she wanted to play the voyeur, if only for a moment.

His canary-yellow T-shirt had a slight sheen to it, with a blue coat of arms logo. The black athletic shorts he wore were loose around his muscular thighs, just skimming his knees. The expensive sneakers on his feet, black with gold stripes, were the same ones Josh had begged her to purchase for weeks.

Suddenly, her eyes began to water, and a tickling sensation in her nose followed. She sneezed, just once, quietly as she could manage.

He whirled around. "Who's there?"

She emerged from the palm trees. "May I help you?"

Sam's deep brown eyes glided over her body, drawing pulses of head-to-toe heat, and gleamed a little brighter under the fluorescent lights.

He folded his arms across his chest. "You can tell me what the devil you were doing hiding behind that palm tree."

Being a really awful spy, she thought. The truth embarrassed her, so she decided to make light of the situation and held up two fingers, both shaking slightly. "Actually, it was two palm trees."

A car honked outside, and she nearly jumped out of her skin. Sam acted cool, as if he hadn't heard it. He was probably used to distractions, like thousands of people cheering for him in the stadiums.

"I apologize, but remain confused."

He bowed before her, a gesture that seemed destined for a royal court. It charmed her as much as his posh accent. She wanted to run to the window to see if there was a carriage outside, but suspected there would only be a limousine.

"I was looking for a dust cloth," she explained.

"Behind one, I mean, two palm trees?"

Mariella nodded, despite his dubious tone.

A smile flecked at the corners of his mouth. "What an odd place to keep cleaning supplies."

He shrugged, and then ran a hand over his close-cropped black hair. "Anyway, I'm looking for a holiday gift. Can you help me?"

She let out a breath of relief, thankful he'd changed subjects. "Of course, Mr. Kelly."

"Wait a minute. How do you know my name?"

He took a step toward her, his eyes cautious and his tone guarded.

"My son talks about you all the time. He loves soccer."

She left out any mention of the poster, and that she sometimes watched European soccer on television with Josh. The latter only because she rarely paid attention to the game, preferring to use the time to read a book or shop online.

"Nice to know I have a fan in this town. I was getting a bit worried."

He smiled, more in wonder than in ease, and she couldn't take her eyes off him.

"You're the first person to recognize me."

"Really? Do I get a prize?"

She blushed, not meaning to sound coy or flirtatious, but she was a little surprised at his statement.

Bay Point had begun to rebuild its prior reputation as a destination for celebrities, so it wasn't so unusual he was here. Many of the townspeople were movie and TV buffs. It wasn't inconceivable that some wouldn't be aware of popular sports stars, especially those from overseas.

Sam began to sort through a rack of beach towels. A look of amused horror on his face, he held up one emblazoned with pink and green pineapples.

"I don't know. That depends."

Hope rose within her, but she paused to ensure she answered him with an even tone. "On what?"

"On whether you're a fan of mine, too."

She held back a smile. Was he simply being pretentious? Flirting with her? It was difficult to tell. His overall politeness and good looks could cover a multitude of sins or internal thoughts.

She opened her arms wide.

"I don't know. You just got here."

A smile tipped from his lips right into her heart.

"What's your name?"

She steadied her gaze on his, wondering if she should tell him. If he was just passing through town, she would never see him again.

Sam nudged her elbow playfully as if he sensed her reluctance. "It's only fair, since you already know mine."

"My name is Mariella."

He repeated her name, in a lower voice than before, bringing his accent to a whole new level of sexy. It was as if he was savoring it in his mouth, and an unexpected spark of electricity looped through her body.

"Very pretty."

A knot formed in her throat at his compliment, even though she wasn't sure if he was referring to her name or her looks.

"Thank you," she managed. "Now that we've got the introductions out of the way, I can help you find what you need."

He glanced about the store, in the haphazard way men do when they are overwhelmed by the task of shopping.

"I'm looking for a gift to send back to England."

"For a special girl?"

"Yes. My mum."

His leaned-in, *gotcha*-grin made her cheeks blaze. *Maybe he's single*, she thought, and maybe she should just mind her own business.

"Oh? How sweet." She took a step back, and crashed into a rack of orange bikinis.

Her face heated when one dropped on the floor. She crouched down to pick it up and got an eyeful of Sam's muscular thighs. She was naturally clumsy, so pretending to struggle with the hanger to get a closer look was easy. When she stood, she felt his eyes on her shoulder as she replaced the merchandise to its proper spot.

"Is it her birthday?" she asked, a little light-headed.

She mulled over a rack of maxi dresses emblazoned with colorful beach umbrellas, thinking that might be a nice gift. Considering she lived in Great Britain, which she heard had a lot of rain, she might appreciate a real umbrella instead. Unfortunately, Terrence didn't sell those, so she moved on to a table filled with petrified sea life.

"No. Mum is just a little upset I'm in the States. I need something really nice so she'll know I'm safe, alive and healthy."

Sam picked up a green bejeweled starfish, and shook

his head in disgust. "By the way, the more tasteful and expensive it is, the more it will keep her off my back."

Mariella worried her lip, concerned that due to Terrence's gaudy inventory, she wouldn't be able to help Sam find the perfect gift.

"In that case, I'm not sure if this is the store for you. We cater to tourists who want a special memento of their visit to Bay Point. We may not have what you need."

"I'm sure you have everything I need."

His warm smile and upbeat tone made her almost believe he was talking about her, not something to buy, and reinvigorated her confidence.

"I'm sure I can help you find something." She motioned for him to follow her. "Is she picky?"

"Does the queen live in Buckingham Palace?"

His tone held a note of annoyance, much like Josh's did whenever he felt she was being too overbearing.

Mariella laughed in familiar kinship with the woman, if only because they were both moms of males. She also sensed there was a deeper conflict between Sam and his mother, and suspected his gift would do little to relieve it. How many times had she thought that buying Josh just one more video game would erase the subtle tension between them?

"There are no castles in Bay Point, and while we do have some tacky tourist shops, I can assure you this is a lovely town."

"I'm sure it is, but I'm not here for a visit. I'm the new boys' head soccer coach at the high school. I'm taking over for Coach Lander."

Mariella stopped, her hand poised over a plastic paperweight in the shape of a whale, and blinked in disbelief. News traveled fast in Bay Point and she was surprised she hadn't heard of his arrival.

"I know Coach Lander had a heart attack just before school started in September. Lots of parents were wondering who was going to replace him, but as far as we knew, the administration was still looking."

She handed the object to him, and his smile turned tentative. Somehow she knew it wasn't the whale's fault.

He shrugged and set it back on the display table. "I'm your man, but only until Coach Lander is ready to return full-time. The press release goes out tomorrow."

Though she sensed Sam's discomfort, she couldn't deny her own excitement that he was going to be a temporary resident of Bay Point. Her fingers played with the ends of her hair, and when she caught him looking at her, she stopped.

"My son Josh will be thrilled. He's a forward on the team. Our last name is Vency."

Sam gave her a matter-of-fact nod. "Sounds familiar. Coach mentioned a few kids I should be aware of this season. Your son was on the list."

"How kind." Mariella's heart burst with pride that in the next beat constricted into worry. "I should let you know that Josh did have a bicycle accident this summer, but he's doing okay now."

Sam frowned, and she wondered if she should have mentioned Josh's injury at all. "Was he badly hurt?"

"Yes." She swallowed hard, remembering the aftermath of his accident. "He was on his way home from visiting a friend, and a car sideswiped him. Thankfully, he was wearing a helmet. Still, he landed on his knee."

Sam's eyes crinkled as if he'd just imagined the scene. "Ouch."

Mariella nodded. "He's healed up and his doctor cleared him to play sports, with the caveat that he goes to physical therapy for at least another month."

Recovery over the summer was slow, but only because Josh refused to do his exercises on a consistent basis as instructed by his therapist. Hounding only annoyed him, and frustrated her.

"I'm glad. Coach told me Josh always does his best to put the ball into the net, and he's the key to a winning season this year. He's still going to try out for the team, right?"

Mariella tucked a strand of hair behind her ear. "I'm not sure. It's really up to him."

His amiable smile chased her worry away, but then her fear of Josh playing soccer ratcheted up again, in spite of his handsome, courteous coach. Soccer was a grueling and intense sport, and even though he'd suffered only minor injuries over the past three seasons, that didn't mean he wouldn't get hurt worse.

Still, there was a chance he wouldn't play at all. Ever since the accident, Josh had been sullen and withdrawn. Whenever she mentioned the tryouts or playing soccer again, he changed the subject, or didn't answer her at all. Though he continued to watch soccer on television, she was concerned he'd lost his drive to participate on his former team.

She'd spoken to his doctor about her concerns, and he assured her that things would get better once he got back on the field. Maybe Sam would be able to reinvigorate his enthusiasm and help put her own fears to rest—for good.

"If he doesn't show up, I just may have to recruit you," Sam warned.

Though he probably wasn't serious, the slow grin on his face scored major points with her heart.

"I can run, but I can't kick a ball at all and my aim is terrible," she protested, playing along.

"It's easy. I'll teach you someday."

Whether he was serious or not, a smattering of tingles

flirted through her body and caught her off guard. She tried to laugh them away.

"Thanks. But why don't we find your mother a gift first?"

Mariella wanted to know more about Sam Kelly, but didn't dare ask. He was here, but not to stay, and it was naive to think that what she felt for him now was anything but idle fascination. She wasn't the type to get stars in her eyes, and vowed to keep her senses in check.

That lasted about thirty seconds, and she found herself appraising him again as they weaved their way through the display tables. His upper torso reminded her of a sculpture; the bold angles of his muscles were apparent despite the unfortunate presence of his shirt.

She stood as close as she dared, and the mild waft of musky cologne emanating from his skin drove her crazy. She wanted to snuggle against him and just inhale him first. Other things could come later, she thought wickedly.

Over the next twenty minutes she showed him various items, each of which he dismissed as tacky or cheap, and she silently agreed with his opinions. Despite Sam's sports star status and gorgeous looks, she found herself growing more at ease in his presence. He seemed to be a genuinely nice person, and who wouldn't like a guy who wanted to reassure his mom with the perfect gift?

After perusing every table and display, they ended up near the fake palm trees. She was about to give up when her eye caught sight of a large snow globe. It was perched on the lowest shelf on the wall, very close to where she'd been hiding.

Mariella reached past him, and her arm briefly rubbed against his side. She felt the hairs on her arms stand up as she stooped down to grab it.

She stood and held the snow globe in front of her to examine it more closely. The clear glass bloated the angles of Sam's facial features outward, as if he was standing in front of a fun-house mirror, and she fought back a grin.

"What's so funny?" he asked.

Mariella smiled, surprised he'd noticed her reaction, and rapped on the globe lightly with her knuckles. "I can't believe it's not plastic, like nearly everything else in this store."

He reached for it, but she held it away from him. It was about the size of a grapefruit, and when she flipped it around, the snow inside began to drift over the scene.

The effect was quite charming, and despite the air-conditioning blasting overhead, made her feel warm inside.

"The mountains and the little town below them remind me of Christmas."

As she handed it to him, his fingers grazed hers, and she shivered involuntarily.

"Cold?" he asked, his gaze rimmed with concern.

Mariella shook her head, and rubbed her hands across her upper arms, wishing it were his touch instead. He watched her closely, and by the gleam in his eyes, there was no doubt in her mind he felt something, too.

He held the snow globe up. "I didn't see any mountains on the drive from the airport, so I gather this is not Bay Point?"

"Lord, no. It never snows here," she laughed. "Those are probably supposed to be the Sierra Nevada Mountains, which are north from here. Great skiing, if you're into that sort of thing."

Sam's laughter filled the room, but there was a harsh edge to it, too. "I can injure myself just fine on the soccer field, thank you very much."

"So what do you think?" she asked after he handed it back to her.

"The snow and the mountains will remind my mum of the French Alps. It's perfect. I'll take it." He added a quick wink as if they were partners in crime. "Plus, she knows I hate skiing."

When they got to the counter, Sam held up his phone. "Can I pay with this?"

Mariella shook her head as she rang up his item on the old-fashioned cash register. "As you can see, Terrence isn't that technically advanced."

"You know how to work that thing?"

"A dying talent, I know." She giggled. "When I first moved to Bay Point, I worked here for a few months until I found a full-time job."

Sam slid a bill across the glass. "Okay, this should cover it."

She stared, openmouthed, at it. "Um. We don't take this currency, but we do take credit cards."

Sam palmed his forehead. "I'm sorry. I do have American money."

He thumbed through the cash in his wallet, and handed her a twenty-dollar US bill.

Mariella handed him the correct change, but when she tried to give him the fifty-pound note back, he nudged her hand away and winked.

"Keep it, so I don't accidentally try to use it again and embarrass myself. I'm new in town and want to protect my reputation."

Staring hard at the bill, she wondered if she should accept it and if she did, what it would mean. Possessing something of Sam's made him all the more real in her heart, and that might not be a good thing. But when she looked into his eyes, she could tell right away he was being genuine.

"Thank you, Sam."

She reached under the counter where her purse was

stored and slipped the bill into her wallet, hoping she wasn't making a royal mistake.

"Are you homesick?"

He paused before answering. "Not really. I'm used to traveling and being on the road. This is one of the rare times in my life where I'll be staying put in one place. At least until the soccer season ends."

Their eyes met and held, sending another ray of hope through her mind. It was hard to focus on him while the meaning of his words spun through her brain.

Sam wasn't leaving tomorrow, or the next day, but someday he *would* leave. As far as romance, she had to discard any hint of possibility and keep her heart firmly rooted in reality.

"Shall I gift wrap this for you?"

"Yes, please."

Mariella handed him a pen and a gift tag. While he was writing, she folded a small white cardboard box and gave the inside a generous padding of bubble wrap. After securing the snow globe in white tissue paper, she placed it in the box and taped it shut. Glossy silver wrapping paper and a red bow were the finishing touches.

"Beautifully done, thank you." He slid the tag into an envelope, and she watched as he licked it. "But I'm afraid I've changed my mind."

"What's wrong?" She hitched in a breath and stared at the box, wondering what could have happened.

He placed the envelope on the counter. "I don't think my mother will like this gift after all."

Her eyes snapped to his face. "Why not?"

"I think you'll appreciate it more."

A smile started at the corners of her mouth, even though she was thoroughly confused. She tried to give him the box, but he lifted it away and set it back on the counter.

Her voice trembled. "I don't understand."

"I saw how your eyes lit up when you were looking at the snow globe." He touched her hand and a hot blush slid over her face. "I want you to have it."

He picked up the box and gave it to her, and even though she felt a bit silly, she took it.

"But what about your mom?"

"Is there an antiques store in town?"

She wedged the box under her arm. "Yes, just make a right at the corner and go down a couple blocks. You can't miss it."

"Thanks. I'm sure I'll find something there. Mum loves anything older than her. And since she's perpetually thirty-five, that gives me a lot of leeway."

Sam turned, but seemed reluctant to leave. "I'll let you know what I find the next time I see you."

She smiled, throwing reality aside to ride the seesaw of hope inside her. "Yes. At tryouts."

He backpedaled down the store's center aisle, keeping his eyes on hers the entire way.

"Is that a promise?"

Mariella didn't dare speak, so she nodded, her head moving up and down, seemingly in slow motion. She was glad only the top half of her body was visible behind the counter, as Sam reached behind him to grasp the doorknob. Otherwise, he would have seen her knees almost knocking together as she stared at his muscular frame.

She gave him a little wave as he walked out the door. When he was gone, her gaze morphed back into focus even as her brain tried to capture the spellbound way he'd looked at her as if he was trying to remember something about her.

She opened the envelope and read the card aloud.

"Thank you for helping me to forget."

The words, written in neat cursive, and signed with his first name only, intrigued and saddened her at the same time.

Forget about what, she wondered. *And why?*

Mariella set the box down below the counter, next to her purse. While stowing the card alongside the British pound in her wallet, she felt fortunate for their chance meeting and her heart began to beat more rapidly, as if affirming her feelings were true.

She realized she'd received a third gift from Sam Kelly, though he didn't know he was the one responsible. Simply by being in his presence, the ice of loneliness encrusted around her heart had begun to thaw.

He'd made her forget, too.

Sam stepped outside, closed the door to the shop and squinted. The sun seemed to shine brighter here in California, like it had something to prove to the entire world. Or maybe it was because he'd just met a beautiful woman.

Right now he was glad to be standing on a street corner in Bay Point, rather than in his lonely flat in the south of London. Though a cold shower would be immensely helpful right about now. He'd been hard almost the entire time he was in the store.

He resisted the urge to turn back to look through the window to see if Mariella was watching him. Instead, Sam looked down and exhaled a sigh of relief.

His long soccer shirt and baggy shorts had done their job and hidden his physical reaction to Mariella. As soon as he'd laid his eyes on her, it had sprung to new life.

She wasn't a classic beauty, but had high cheekbones and perfectly arched brows. Thankfully, she didn't possess the haughty cater-to-me manner he'd experienced with many attractive women. Her nut-brown face was clear, smooth, appearing supple to the touch, if he had dared to reach out. Now he wished with every fiber of his being that he had.

Like most men, his lower half acted independently, giving uninvited props to his visual mind and vivid imagination. The sudden and achingly raw desire for her had surprised him.

After a deep, steadying breath, he started to walk in the direction of the antiques store. Out of Mariella's realm, his body began to settle down. Later on, when he was alone, he knew he'd have to contend with images of making love to her.

Sam had broken two of his own unwritten rules for dealing with the opposite sex. First, not to get so enamored with a woman that he lost his senses. Second, never, ever give presents.

Both had happened today, but only one thing would keep him in check. Mariella was the mother of one of his team members, so dating her was out of the question. In fact, it was a stipulation of his contract. And right now he had no desire to travel thousands of miles home. He'd only arrived a few days ago.

His weather app displayed a temperature of sixty-five, yet the sun cresting overhead made it feel much warmer. The heat seemed to radiate from within his body outward, like the longing he'd had for Mariella whenever she got too close.

I wouldn't have minded getting closer.

He sighed again, looked up and shaded his eyes.

Sam heard that it never rained in Southern California, and he hoped the same was true here in the northern region of the state.

He'd come to Bay Point to escape the dreariness of London, and for a lot of other reasons, too, none of which included finding love. Opportunities for sex, on the other hand, seemed to find him, no matter where he was.

Not sure if that was because he was famous or just too damn lucky. He stopped walking, shrugged and kept going. Not really caring.

Except for one woman.

Mariella's interest in him was cool at first. Her guarded actions made it easy to believe she didn't know him. But even before he told her his name, he'd seen the spark in her eyes, when she peeked her head out from behind those ridiculous palm trees.

Their mutual attraction seemed to be as much of a surprise to her as it was to him. As the moments between them went on, it spiraled outward in intensity, like ripples on a pond. The fact that she didn't throw herself at him like so many women did had turned him on even more, though he wished she had.

It became increasingly hard to think straight without seeing her, and wanting her, in his arms. And he knew he was sunk, a rock to her depths.

Every time Mariella moved, it took everything in his power to hold back his steps, to not go to her side right away, and see what she wanted to show him. If he appeared to be a snob, he certainly didn't mean it, even though he did think the merchandise was disposable.

He chuckled to himself, knowing his mother would have called what he felt in his gut a stomachache. Mariella's interest in him? Mere female curiosity.

His mother was very practical, and had neither patience, nor time, for romance. It was a badge of honor that she'd not seen one episode of *Downton Abbey*, although she did say once that she cried when Princess Diana and Prince Charles divorced.

He'd never thought he was the romantic type, either,

and was still puzzled why he'd decided to give Mariella the snow globe. Maybe it was to stop the feelings he didn't understand that made him rock-hard. Thoughts that could only get him into trouble.

At first he thought she'd be angry with him. She'd taken the trouble to wrap the gift so expertly. Would she have taken that much care if she knew it was for herself?

Mixed in with an abject shock was also a grand sense that what he'd done had pleased her.

Her green eyes, set a little too close to her nose, had lit up, but not the same as before. Rimmed with the darkest, longest lashes he'd ever seen, her eyes had shone like gentle beacons, guiding him somewhere he'd never been before. If he dove into their depths, what would he find? What would she?

Pushing his thoughts aside, he continued on Ocean Avenue, Bay Point's version of Main Street. With its copper streetlamps, the blue-green patina reminiscent of the ocean, and the cracked, sand-dusted sidewalks, the little town had undeniable signs of stubborn longevity. He passed Bay Point Bed-and-Breakfast, his temporary lodging, owned by Maisie Barnell. She was a nice woman, if not a little nosy, who loved to carry on a conversation. For hours on end, it seemed. The sooner he found a more suitable place to live, the happier he'd be.

On his way to the antiques shop, he peeked into storefronts and caught a bit of shade now and again under their colorful cloth awnings. Many of the merchants were taking advantage of the weather to begin their holiday decorating. He dodged ladders draped with strings of lights and boxes of pine boughs and wreaths.

Sometimes he forgot to walk in the practiced manner that helped hide his slight limp, although the residual pain from his injuries was gone for the time being. His mind seemed stuck on Mariella, like a bolt stripped of its grooves, and though he knew it was wrong, he couldn't wait to see her again.

He thought of how her cowl-necked ivory blouse, the fabric sheer enough to trick the eye, hinted at the fullness of her breasts. Tonight he'd be dreaming about the way her navy skirt clung to the curves of her torso, and wake up wishing he was kissing her head to toe.

But it was her smile that had struck him the most. It was worth the stress of shopping, an activity that he despised, made worse because it was a gift for his mother.

When he'd hinted to Mariella that he would recruit her for his team, her full mouth had drawn together in a lush bow of shock, but almost immediately after, the right corner of her lip had smarted, as if she was intrigued, though it could have been a nervous tic.

The silent respect she appeared to have toward him, and what was underneath her reserved and cautious nature just waiting to be discovered, excited him, too. He didn't readily understand his feelings, but for the time being, he accepted them at face value.

Mariella was a woman he could chase, if he decided to, rather than someone chasing him, as per usual.

Was she single?

She wore no ring, but that didn't mean she didn't have a husband, boyfriend or lover. A band of gold or a glittery diamond only meant as much as two people ascribed to it. He'd never knowingly broken up a relationship, but he did believe in fate.

It was a shame she was off-limits.

Sam found the antiques shop, but it was closed. There was an Apartment For Rent sign in the window. After putting the number into his phone, he walked on until he reached a small café. He ignored the signs hawking peppermint lattes and bought an iced tea with lemon. The drink was refreshing, but did not cool his yearning for Mariella.

After he was done, he double-backed toward the inn. He had an early evening meeting with his assistant coaches that should help him focus on what was important.

A man in a pink-and-tan Hawaiian shirt hurried toward him down the narrow sidewalk, carrying a paper sack. Sam stepped aside to let him pass, but the guy nearly collided into him anyway.

The old Sam would have gotten upset at the man's rudeness; not enough to say anything mean, however, the incident alone would have pricked at him all day.

But ever since his devastating injury, he tried not to get too upset or angry anymore, especially over things in life he couldn't control. His mind was too busy, trying to reason, trying to process all the possible outcomes for his future. Like whether he would ever return to pro soccer, or even the United Kingdom, for that matter.

The *what-ifs*.

The *what-now*.

Everything in his life had changed, including him.

While he'd failed to find an appropriate gift for his mother, he might have found the perfect woman. Sam smiled with the realization that his time in the United States, however brief, could prove to be interesting and satisfying.

He knew better than anyone that there were always multiple ways to a goal.

Chapter 2

"Josh! Come on! We've got to go now or we'll be late!"

"I told you," Josh yelled back. "I don't want to go!"

He had just turned seventeen in September and his voice sounded as deep as a man's. But in Mariella's heart, he was still her little boy.

His father was six foot two, but Josh rang out at five foot eight inches, and he was still growing.

His upper body was compact and ripped with muscles. There was a full-length mirror in the mudroom, which she'd installed so she could double-check her appearance before she went outside. Sometimes she caught him looking at his reflection and she hoped he liked what he saw. He was such a handsome young man.

Josh was also a gifted athlete, and his greatest strength lay in his legs. His speed and grace on the field had helped the Bay Point Titans become one of the best high school soccer teams in the NorCal region.

She leaned against the stair railing and took out a cloth-covered band from the back pocket of her running shorts. Gathering up her long, black hair into a neat ponytail, she tapped her foot on the bare wood floor and considered her options.

Going upstairs to continue the conversation would likely result in an argument. Lord knows there were plenty of those recently. But allowing Josh to continue to stew in self-pity was not going to help him get out of the funk he'd been in since the accident.

No matter his age, she would never stop worrying that he would get hurt. She also wouldn't allow him to quit the team out of self-pity. If he didn't show up at tryouts that was essentially what he was doing.

Her heart blossomed with renewed hope that getting him back on the soccer field where he belonged would help make everything right again.

Especially between us.

They'd been so close, prior to moving to Bay Point. For a long time, Josh was angry with her for taking him away from his friends, some of which he'd known since kindergarten. Though he'd eventually settled in and made plenty of new ones, he never let her forget how much he missed his "real" home.

Wearily, Mariella started to climb the narrow stairs, which always felt like Mt. Everest whenever she had to try to get Josh out of his room. To take her mind off the conflict that lay ahead, she ran her fingertips lightly against the mauve wallpaper, original to the Colonial-style house. It was worn, but the silk-like texture still felt luxurious.

She could have replaced it, and a lot of other things in the house by now, but something always stopped her. Redecorating was time-consuming and expensive, but it also meant setting down permanent roots.

She'd learned a long time ago to look for the beauty in life, which she often found in the oddest of places. It was easier than trying to understand life itself, and required no real commitment on her part.

Soon, though, it would be time to decorate for the holidays, something she did enjoy doing, and she made a mental note to have Josh start bringing all the holiday decorations down from the attic.

They usually went back home to South Central LA to visit her parents for Thanksgiving. Before they left, Mariella would have the tree and everything else up, so that when she got back, she could just enjoy the holidays.

She took a deep breath before stepping into Josh's room, and held back a frown. He was playing computer games as usual. Headset over his ears, palm over his mouse, he wore an old Bay Point Titans T-shirt and shorts. A good sign. At least he was thinking about going to tryouts.

The blinds were shut, but the windows were open and a mild breeze blew in fresh air, overriding the subtle odor of dirty socks, corn chips and wet towels.

Mariella pursed her lips in mild annoyance. A few slats were broken on one of the blinds. She'd warned Josh to be careful raising and lowering them. They, too, were original to the house, and were fragile due to age.

It was obvious he hadn't listened to her, but she decided to let it go. The argument wasn't worth it. The house she'd inherited had already proven to be a money trap and she made another mental note. Add blinds to the list of things in the house needing to be repaired, besides their relationship.

Mariella turned the wand, allowing the morning sunlight to stream into the room. The warm rays spreading over her face helped wash away her irritation.

Josh turned in his chair and lifted his arm over his eyes. "What did you do that for?"

"To see if you would melt," she replied with a smile.

"Ha-ha." His arm thumped back against his desk and he didn't bother to look up at her.

As Mariella stepped toward him, her foot nudged an empty water bottle. She picked it up and wedged it under her armpit.

"What's not funny is the fact if we don't leave soon you will miss your opportunity to play soccer this year."

"So?" he muttered, eyes focused on the screen.

"So…it's your senior year," Mariella responded sternly, ignoring his insolent tone. "This is your last chance to letter in the sport, which as you know, looks—"

"Great on my college applications and could help me get a scholarship," he replied impatiently. "I know, Mom. You've told me this a million times."

She snapped her fingers. "Then if you know, let's get going."

Josh fiddled with his headset and Mariella hoped their conversation wasn't being broadcast throughout the internet.

"I told you before. I don't ever want to play soccer again. And even if I did, I can't. Not like before. Not with my knee."

His voice cracked a little, and her heart broke a little more for the pain he'd suffered over the past several months.

Mariella softened. "I understand you're—" she stopped herself from using the word *afraid* "—concerned, but the doctor cleared you for sports. Though it may feel uncomfortable at first, you're okay to play."

His lips trembled, but he still refused to look at her and continued to focus his attention on some sort of military-looking game. From her brief glance at the screen, it had everything she hated—guns, blood and gore.

"I don't care. Besides, Coach Lander isn't even going to be there."

"No, but Sam Kelly is, remember? You were so excited when I first told you he was stepping in to coach the team. What happened?"

Josh jerked his chin toward her, his tone abrasive. "I still think he's cool, all right? At least the administration didn't replace him with some chump who doesn't know anything. Or worse, a parent."

"Good deal. No chumps, no parents. You'll be fine."

"No, I won't," he insisted. "Coach Kelly is a pro player, so he'll probably want me to be perfect. He'll want everyone on the team to be as good a player as he is."

"I'm sure he just wants you to try your best."

"With this knee?" he snorted, returning his attention to the computer.

She put her hand on his shoulder, which he promptly shrugged off. "You're cleared medically, Josh. And you're still taking physical therapy, so if there is any soreness after practices, we can get it taken care of right away."

His hand paused over the mouse, and she could almost see his brain whirring.

"If I go, will you puh-leeze lay off me?"

Mariella hesitated. She didn't want him to try out to get her off his back. She wanted him to go because he wanted to play soccer, but she had to start somewhere.

"Maybe. But only because you said please."

He rolled his eyes, and Mariella held in a sigh of relief as he slipped on and laced up his soccer cleats.

When Josh stood, she exhaled and gave him a hug.

"Do me a favor. Don't give up before you even get on the field."

He broke away quickly, and she blinked back the start of tears. She tried not to let it bug her when he resisted her affection, but it did.

"I won't have to even bother trying. The coach will take one look at me and give up for me."

She set her lips in a firm line. *He better not.*

The thought of anyone not doing right by her son made her temples pulse with anger and the beginnings of a headache sprout.

She was concerned about Josh. He continued to blame himself for the bike accident, even though it wasn't his fault. Worse, he never wanted to talk about his feelings; instead, his behavior and attitude spoke for him.

Would things have been different if his father were alive? It was a question always in the back of her mind.

With her heart in her throat, Mariella followed her son as he walked slowly down the stairs.

On the way to the high school, Mariella racked her brain trying to think of something to say that wouldn't upset Josh. The drive was short, but the silence between them made the time drag, and knots formed in her stomach.

Seeing Sam again made her both nervous and excited. Since the article about his new position dropped in the *Bay Point Courier*, the whole town was abuzz. The town had a colorful history as a secret hideaway for movie stars, but this was the first time a well-known sports figure had made his way to its sandy shore. And he hailed from London, no less, home of kings, queens and princesses.

She wondered if the man had had any privacy since.

Mariella stole a glance at Josh. He seemed lost in thought, and likely hoped he wouldn't have to talk at all. As soon as she parked, he grabbed a water bottle and his gear, and with an emotionless "see ya," strode off.

At least he said goodbye, she thought, watching him slowly half jog, half walk toward the field.

He's going to be okay, she told herself for what seemed like the millionth time. *And so will I.*

She reached the bleachers, sat down and scanned the field.

Sam hadn't arrived yet, so she eyed the track surrounding the perimeter, aiming to get in the miles she'd missed in the morning. One of the elementary schools was in dire need of a new playground, but there were no funds in the local budget, so she was working with the board of education to write the application for a state grant. She'd volunteered her skills and time, hoping the experience would help further her career.

Mariella stood, turned and put one foot on the bleacher and began to retie the laces of her worn running shoes.

Suddenly, she looked up and cringed at the metallic twang caused by two children bounding down the stairs, and at the sight of Leslie Watkins trailing behind them. Her son, Dante, was one of Bay Point High School's star athletes, and she let everyone in town know it.

She was thinking so hard about Josh and Sam she hadn't seen Leslie, a woman who made it a point to be noticed by everything and everyone.

"I'm so glad tryouts are being held in the morning," Leslie called out, waving her manicured hand in front of her face.

Mariella took her time tying her shoelaces, and then looked up, stifling her annoyance. Conversations with Leslie simply started, without a hello and often without any context, and ended without a goodbye.

"Agreed. It's only ten a.m. and I'm sweltering."

Leslie got down to the bottom step and pushed her sunglasses on top of her head.

"You're going to run in this weather?"

Mariella ignored the dumbfounded look on Leslie's face.

Her metabolism was slow, and seemed to decrease every year with age. It was hard work maintaining her curves.

She grinned and patted her flat tummy. "Have to work off a giant lemon bar I ate at Ruby's this morning."

Leslie narrowed her eyes, and Mariella guessed it was her weak attempt to show understanding. "That shop has a lot of us hitting the gym, me included."

Mariella found that hard to believe. Leslie was model-tall and as thin as a birch stick, with the bitchy personality and spray tan to match.

"I guess no one can resist them, even you," Mariella replied as she vowed inwardly to avoid any sweets. That morning's indulgence would have to be the last one for a while. She was starting to train for a half marathon, her first, and it was time to push her body beyond its current limit and control her desires.

Leslie cupped her hands around her mouth. "Matt! Jamie! Don't go any farther than the playground," she yelled, and then turned back to Mariella. "Normally we would stay and watch, but today I'm very, very busy."

"Don't let me keep you," Mariella said lightly, eager to get rid of the woman. She didn't know how long the try-outs would take and she wanted to get her run in.

Plus, she already saw Leslie plenty. She was PTA president and Mariella was vice president, and both were very active in the school.

She grabbed hold of her right ankle, pulling her calf back toward her buttocks to stretch her hamstring. She hoped Leslie would take the hint, but instead she shaded her eyes and prattled on.

"Dante looks good out there, doesn't he?"

"Yes. Both of our boys have grown so quickly. I can't believe they're seniors!"

Mariella spotted Josh kicking a ball toward the white-netted goal. From a distance, he looked as though he couldn't care less if he made it in or not, while Dante was moving so fast his blond crew cut flashed in the sunlight as he passed the ball from one player to another.

Leslie folded her arms and sighed. "Dante turned eighteen earlier this month. We wanted to celebrate in Hawaii, but as usual, we had to postpone until the end of soccer season."

"Oh, really?" she responded, trying to sound interested though she couldn't care less.

Mariella recalled that for Josh's birthday they spent the day at the beach and then went to his favorite restaurant. She couldn't afford Waikiki, and most of her savings was going to his college fund, but at least he hadn't spent all day in his room.

Leslie slipped her sunglasses back over her eyes. In the haze of her dark lenses, Mariella could almost feel a verbal jab coming on, like a nasty cold.

"You look so young to have a teenage son," Leslie said, her tone riddled with vague condescension. "I've been meaning to ask you. What's your secret?"

Mariella clenched her toes in her sneakers, uneasy about the question, even though she'd been asked it by nosy people throughout Josh's life. It was nobody's business then, and it sure as hell wasn't Leslie's business now.

One didn't have to peer close to see the crow's feet at the edges of Leslie's eyes, and Mariella felt blessed to have the type of skin that aged well.

She pasted on a smile and tapped the brim of her baseball cap. "I stay out of the sun."

"In California? Good luck!" Leslie said with a burst of laughter, followed by a dramatic sigh. "Well, I guess the Big Island is still fabulous in March."

Mariella fought the urge to roll her eyes at Leslie's aggrieved tone. At the low sound of sporadic clapping, she lifted her chin and held back a frown as she watched Josh half run, half limp away from the goal.

Leslie followed her gaze. "Are you sure he's ready to play so soon after the accident?" Her voice was almost a whisper as if she was afraid Josh could somehow overhear.

Despite a firm assurance from the doctor, it was the same question Mariella wrestled with day after day, night after night. But she wasn't about to reveal her worries and woes to Leslie.

She forced a smile, as she had so many times in the past few months, in spite of the pain of seeing her son combat his injury.

She had to help him triumph.

"Dr. Hamilton gave him the all-clear."

Leslie lifted her thin nose into the air. "Just because he's the father of the mayor's wife, doesn't mean you have to believe everything the man says. You should get a second opinion."

About to put her Mama Bear gloves on, Mariella bit back a sharp retort that could have had tongues wagging in Bay Point for weeks.

"Josh is fine, Leslie. But thanks for inquiring."

"If you say so," she replied.

She jogged in place, wishing Leslie would just go away, but the woman flashed a conspiratorial grin.

"But I'll tell you who definitely *is* fine...the new soccer coach," she blurted. "If we gals have to suffer in the stands, at least we've got some eye candy this season."

There was no way Mariella was going to tell her she'd already met Sam several days earlier, so she feigned ignorance.

"Oh, yes, I read an article about him in the newspaper."

Leslie waved her comment away. "I knew about him for weeks."

"How did you find out before everyone else?"

She frowned as if she couldn't believe she was asked the question.

"Don't worry about it, Mariella. Unlike that old coot Maisie, I have access to real, legitimate information that matters. Like hot new arrivals to our little town."

Maisie was the unofficial matriarch of Bay Point. People sought her out and told her things because they trusted her to listen. As far as Mariella knew, she always used her information to help, not hurt. She wasn't an "old coot;" she was a valued member of the community.

Mariella's fingers shook with anger as she adjusted the band on her upper arm that held her smartphone.

Maisie was driving home from the grocery store when she witnessed Josh's bike accident and called 911. She also organized meals with her church group and had them delivered to Mariella's home. She would never forget what Maisie had done for her and Josh, and hoped to someday repay the favor.

"I had no idea who he really was," Leslie continued as if Mariella wasn't even there. "I really don't pay attention to the sport." She licked her lips. "But now that I know what he looks like, I sure wish I had."

"Hot new arrivals?" Mariella repeated. She cocked a brow and kicked at a few pebbles with the toe of her right shoe. "Don't forget, you're married to one of the most successful men in town."

"Yes, but that doesn't mean a girl can't look."

Leslie fanned her hand in front of her face. "And, honey, when I look at Sam, mine eyes have seen the glory!"

Mariella held back a smile, watching Leslie act like an

overgrown teenager, and was determined to keep the gaga factor in check.

"We've already had some private conversations," she confided in a tone meant to incite curiosity, but Mariella refused to bite.

Leslie winked as if sharing a secret. "Here comes the man himself, and because I'm your friend, I'll let you have a turn."

She walked away, without saying goodbye, of course.

"You are not my friend," Mariella muttered when she was out of hearing distance. But she wouldn't want her for an enemy, either.

She slid her sunglasses on and turned her attention to Sam. Clad in dark blue shorts and a Titans polo shirt, he could have been a model for a men's fashion magazine. The only clue he was a coach was the whistle hanging around his neck.

He looked good far away, but she knew—and apparently, Leslie did also—he looked even better close up. She shook the thought from her head and watched him approach. He didn't appear to be in too much of a hurry to get to her.

But as she continued to study him, she noticed that while his gait was confident, he did favor his left leg every once in a while. It was as if there was a hiccup in his step.

Growing impatient to see him, she decided to meet him halfway. No use in him thinking that she was an overblown diva like Leslie. Besides, she told herself as she jogged toward the middle of the field, her feet were itching to run away all her stress. About five feet away from him, out of breath, sweat trickling down her spine, with her legs about to collapse in a heap on the ground, she stopped in her tracks. Not because she was out of shape. She wasn't.

It was the way he was looking at her. Even though he

had dark sunglasses on, she could feel a haze of desire emanating from him, and this time, she wasn't afraid.

The sight of Mariella...was a wonder. Better than the first time, yet still as powerful, like an unexpected punch in the gut. A sudden fishhook of attraction made breathing a little harder. The hair on his arms stood up even as he told himself to chill out.

What the hell was wrong with him?

Sam stopped for a few seconds, rolled his shoulders back and continued to walk to her, ignoring the slivers of pain darting through his left leg.

Her body appeared more athletic than he'd first noticed at the shop, probably because it was hidden under her office clothes. He thought about her being nestled against him, and cords of his back muscles furrowed and pulsed.

Today she wore black, body-hugging nylon jogging pants that ended at the ankle, orange-and-black running shoes, a tight fitting camisole top and a baseball cap.

Somehow, he managed to speak.

"Hello, Mariella. It's nice to see you again."

He loved the way her name rolled off his tongue.

He refused to call her Ms. or Mrs. Vency. She could correct him, if she chose. Somehow, he kept his hands planted against his sides, instead of reaching for her trim, little waist.

How easy it would have been to bring her body close to curve against his. If they were alone, and if it wasn't for that darn contract.

Her skin gleamed in the hot sun, making his stomach quiver in an outlandish way, like he was on a roller coaster, click-clacking up a hill, not knowing what was on the other side.

Sam wasn't afraid of heights. *God, no.* He wasn't afraid of anything, except what this woman could mean to him.

He couldn't keep his eyes off her.

Dark sunglasses, the perfect cover. He could have been staring somewhere past her head, centering his attention on some imaginary dot in the distance, instead of the small circle of diamonds that hung on a thin gold chain just above the notch of her cleavage. He wondered who had given her such a sexy necklace.

His curiosity was like an itch he couldn't scratch, much like his need for her. He figured he'd better get used to it. Hoping she couldn't see his desire, and at the same time, wishing she could feel with her own hands how much he wanted her.

"I'm glad you showed up. Now, let me see. What position should I give you?"

His statement was unabridged flirtation, but no one was around. No one could hear. He hadn't even played one game yet, and he was in danger of breaking his contract already.

Sam waited as she crossed her arms, anticipating her reaction. He didn't expect amusement.

"I told you before that I'd make you lose. I told you I'm terrible at sports."

"And I told you I would teach you."

He smiled, hoping to dazzle her, but the look on her face was anything but. It was almost as if he'd gone over the line, and her deep frown was his penalty.

"I'm not important, Coach. But my son is. All I care about is whether or not Josh makes the team."

Sam's heart fell at the slight hardness in her voice. The fact that she'd addressed him so formally didn't escape his attention, either.

He sighed inwardly, and wasn't going to bother to flirt

with her again. Maybe he'd read her wrong. It was clear from her tone he'd better stop while he was ahead, even though he didn't get nearly as far as he wanted to.

"If he works hard, I don't see why not. Tryouts will give me a good perspective."

"I've always thought tryouts were so unnecessary. Why can't those who played last season automatically be considered for the next?"

Now it was his turn to cross his arms, like a boss.

"It's to make sure that the position each guy had last season is still the right one for him, the one he wants to play, and is good for the entire team."

She rubbed her hands together. "I don't know if you've noticed, but Josh…" Her voice trailed off. "Limps a little sometimes. As I mentioned the other day, he was involved in a bike accident and his left knee was injured."

He glanced back over one shoulder. The faces of his players were hard to see, their arms and legs blurred, little meteors of movement across the field.

"Which one is your son?"

Mariella laughed. "I'm sorry. I forgot you've never seen him in person. Josh is the one in the sky-blue shorts, and the Bay Point Titans team shirt, of course."

He turned back. "No, I hadn't noticed his limp. But then again, most of the players just arrived, and I haven't had a chance to evaluate anyone yet."

She sucked in a breath. "You won't hold it against him, will you?"

He ran a thumb across his bottom lip, pausing a beat when he saw Mariella was watching him, looking doubtful.

"Not exactly."

She folded her arms tightly against her chest. "What do you mean, *not exactly*? His doctor cleared him for sports. Surely you'll take into consideration his—"

He held up a hand. "I treat everyone the same. Everyone gets the chance to succeed, or fail."

It was what he wanted for himself, if he ever returned to pro soccer. He didn't want his teammates feeling pity for him, making things easy. If he wasn't ready to put one hundred and fifty percent effort into every game, like he had for almost ten years, then he wasn't fit to be on the team, let alone playing a sport that demanded so much from him.

Mariella pursed her lips, reminding him of how kissable they looked. "I can respect that, just as long as Josh isn't on the bench all season."

"That's up to him. I can't guarantee that he won't be on the bench. After all, it is the only place to sit on the field," he said, trying to lighten the mood. "But if he tries his best, and shows commitment to the team, he'll do fine."

Mariella frowned. "All I'm asking is for you to give my son a fair shot."

"A fair shot?" he repeated. "A second ago you were practically begging for me to go easy on him."

The ponytail on top of her head waved back and forth like a snake.

"I don't want that. Not really. I'm just worried about him, that's all."

He took a chance and put his hand on her shoulder. Touched her just long enough and light enough to verify her skin was as warm and silky-smooth as he'd imagined. Best of all, she let him.

Sam lowered his voice. "I'll take care of him," he assured her, reluctantly pulling his hand away. "No worry lines on that beautiful face, okay?"

The edge of a smile appeared on her lips. "When will you be making your decision?"

"Sometime this week. We've got a game next Saturday, and I'll need his final paperwork before he can play."

"Just send it home with Josh and I'll make sure to sign it."

Mariella started to jog away, but he touched her arm again. She turned around, hands on her hips.

"If he's hurting, he should tell me. I know what it's like."

She looked at him, her eyes softening, but she didn't ask what he meant, didn't ply him with questions.

Smart woman. No wonder he liked her.

Chapter 3

Mariella pulled the stopper and stepped out of the claw-foot tub. She watched the water swirl down the drain and hoped it would take her thoughts of Sam with it.

Seeing him at tryouts confirmed one thing in her mind. The man was either dangerous to her stable life, or the antidote for it.

She was drying off when the doorbell rang. Quickly, she hung up her towel and wrapped herself in her white terry-cloth robe.

Josh had called a little over an hour ago to tell her he was going to have dinner with friends after soccer practice. Maybe he'd changed his mind and decided to hang out with his mom instead, or more likely, his computer.

She tossed a rueful glance back at the vanity, where her homemade carrot and honey mask, and a stack of unread magazines, beckoned to her. Both would have to wait. Her son needed her.

"Josh, did you forget your keys again?" she shouted, padding downstairs in her bare feet.

She peeked through the curtain, and instantly wanted to melt face-first into the door. Instead, she unlocked and opened it wide.

She braced her shoulder against the jamb. "I didn't know coaches made house calls."

Sam had a way of making his standard uniform of long black shorts and a gold-and-blue Bay Point Titans T-shirt look naturally elegant. No whistle hung around his neck, but that was okay, because she was whistling at him in her mind. His skin was darker than when she'd seen him last. The long days spent in the sun made the hair on his arms and legs more obvious.

"And I didn't know you were home. I was looking for Josh. Is he here?"

The smile he gave her was better than the most luxurious bubble bath. It slid around, under and through her, and made her tremble. But the tenor of his voice seemed overly professional, as if he wanted no misinterpretation, and that threw her off guard.

She clutched the top of her robe in her fist. "Oh. Josh told me he was going out with friends after practice."

His eyes passed over her face, then midchest to her hands. "May I come in, anyway?"

She hesitated, remembering the heat that coursed through her body just being near him in the store, and then on the soccer field. Now he was on her front steps, where it would be so easy to throw her arms around his neck, her legs around his hips. Instead, she dropped her hands and waved him inside.

He bowed slightly before entering, and her mouth twitched at his formality. Maybe she could curtsy her way into his heart, she mused as he followed her into the small living room.

"Sorry for the mess in here. As you can see, I'm getting ready to decorate for the holidays."

Two small easy chairs were laden with old magazines and newspapers Mariella had found in the attic during the weekend, including back issues of the *Bay Point Courier*. She was fascinated by the history of the little town, but hadn't read any of them yet.

Most of the weekend was spent digging through the boxes that held all of her decorations. There were sets of ceramic snowmen and snowwomen, Mr. and Mrs. Claus, poseable elves made of green felt, and colorful wooden nutcrackers in various sizes.

Sam weaved around the towers of boxes and joined her. "No problem. I take it you love Christmas?"

"Everything but the credit card bill afterward."

The only other seating option available in the room was an antique love seat. She preferred more modern designs, and was slowly selling everything she didn't like, except this one. It was so small she had no choice but to sit nice and close to Sam.

They sat down on the edge and swiveled toward each other. Their knees bumped, causing the flap of her robe to peel back. Part of her lower left thigh was exposed and she felt a kiss of cold air on her skin.

Mariella considered smoothing the fabric back in place, but didn't want to call attention to something he may not have even noticed. How easy it would be to slip her robe from her shoulders, or allow him to do the honor. He'd notice then. He'd notice everything about her.

"This is cozy."

Mariella smiled. "Henry Wexler calls it a settee. Did you ever get a chance to go into his store?"

"I did. I bought a beautiful antique silver tea set. Mum collects them and hates tea. Go figure." Sam shrugged. "Even better. I'm renting Wexler's upstairs apartment."

She raised a brow. "Oh, I didn't know he owned the entire building."

"Yes. Lucky for me, he had a vacancy, and it's completely furnished. I moved in last weekend."

Mariella didn't have to ask where he lived before. The day after she met him at the store, Maisie was visiting the mayor, and on her way out, she told her that Sam was staying with her. If she hadn't personally met Sam, she would have pressed the woman for more details about him. But since she had, she felt an odd sense of loyalty he really hadn't earned yet.

"I'm glad you're getting settled in. Now, I'm not sure why you are here, but can whatever you have to say wait until I go change into some real clothes?"

"What if I say I like you now, just as you are?"

Her nipples tightened at the sexy lilt of his accent, and when she squirmed in place, they rubbed against the thick fabric of her robe. She wondered what he would do if he could see how his voice affected her, and what it would be like to hear it every day.

Leaning back against the armrest, she looked him straight in the eye. Her robe opened slightly in the middle, revealing the curve of her breast. She left it alone, not caring if he noticed, daring him to stare.

"Let's cut to the chase. Why are you here, Sam?"

Sam folded his hands across his chest, like he wasn't sure what to do or say next, and his eyes slid shut. When he opened them, they were troubled.

"I'm concerned about Josh. He wasn't at practice today."

"What?" Mariella straightened with alarm. "He just called me."

His sympathetic look did not ease her anxiety. She was overjoyed when Josh was accepted to the team in the same position he'd played last season. To learn he wasn't fulfilling his obligations was distressing.

"I'm not saying he didn't. I'm just telling you he didn't call from the field."

"I don't understand. Is this the first practice he's missed?"

Mariella rubbed her hand against her forehead, embarrassed and stressed at the same time. Did raising a teenage son ever get easier?

Sam nodded. "Yes, but he's been distracted at the others. Is everything okay here at home?"

She bristled openly. "What are you saying? Are you accusing me—?"

"Calm down. I just want to help."

He tried to touch her arm, but she inched away, ready with a sharp, practiced retort. "We don't need your help, Sam."

Hurt flashed in his eyes, but her deep indignation refused to acknowledge it. Though he probably meant well, she hated when anyone insinuated that she couldn't handle her own kid.

"Everything's fine." She made a measured effort to soften her tone. "I'm sorry Josh ditched practice. That's not like him at all, but I wonder where he is?"

Sam took his time answering, and she wondered if he thought she was overreacting.

"Probably hanging with friends, just like he told you, so I wouldn't worry. The good news is that he's playing well."

She sighed with relief, even though inside she was only mildly reassured. "I'm glad to hear. By the way, I never got a chance to thank you for admitting him to the team."

Sam shrugged, like he knew all along Josh would make it.

Mariella had hoped that because of her son's injuries, Sam would take it easy on him. On the flip side, she also wanted Sam to treat him equally and fairly. She'd learned the hard way that coddling could be damaging her son's self-esteem, and she blamed herself for their strained relationship.

"He earned it. But remember only he'll know if his playing is affected by his injuries."

Mariella inclined her head toward Sam, knowing he was right. She could only pray that Josh would speak up if he was having problems.

"Do you think that's why he is having trouble focusing?"

"It's possible. If he can identify the issues he's having, I can help him make some adjustments. It's better than just not coming to practice."

Mariella put her hand on her chest, suddenly pained that her son could be running away from his problems, rather than facing them head-on.

"Thanks. I'll tell him, after I ground him for the rest of his life for lying to me," she said with a wry grin.

She rarely punished Josh, which she'd come to realize was part of the problem. Still, a long talk was in order when he came home.

"Glad I could help, but I have another concern I want to speak to you about."

A tickle of worry rose in her stomach as his eyes perused her face. "About Josh?"

He shook his head. "No, the soccer field. It's playable, but in terrible condition. I was wondering if you or any of the other parents had noticed it."

"I did," she affirmed. "But I haven't heard any complaints from the other parents. Did you ask Coach Lander about it?"

"Yes. He felt bad he wasn't around this summer to manage things so the proper maintenance could have been done."

She chuckled softly, but meant no offense. "The guy

does baby it as if it was his own lawn. What are you going to do?"

"We can use sod in some places to fill in the ruts and holes, and lessen the chance for injury. But that's only a temporary fix. What the school really needs is a brand-new field. If the decision was up to me, I would recommend they upgrade to artificial turf."

Mariella raised a brow. "You mean the kind they use for pro football?"

He gave her a slow nod. "And the kind I've played on my entire career. I was thinking about talking to the athletic director about my concerns. Since I'm only a temporary employee, do you think that's out of line?"

"No, not at all. I think that's a great idea." She tapped her index finger on her chin. "Maybe there's a way I can help."

"Really?" Sam leaned forward, sending a pleasant whiff of his cologne her way. "I'm all ears."

She crossed her legs. "I'm the vice president of the Bay Point High Parent-Teacher Association. We help raise money to fill the gap where budgets fall short and advocate for our children within the school system. Do you have an organization like the PTA in the United Kingdom?"

"Maybe. I went to a boarding school, where it was every kid for himself."

She smiled. "I'm not promising anything, but I'll talk to the principal. You handle the athletic director."

Sam gave her a teasing grin. "And maybe we can meet in the middle?"

"We'll see," she replied. Excited about the prospect of teaming up with Sam, it was difficult to keep her voice and emotions on an even keel.

"Thanks. Looks like you and I are going to see a lot more of each other. I've missed you."

Warmth spread through her body, even though he was probably just being polite. After all, everyone on the team would benefit from a new field.

"You did? Why?"

He gave her a sheepish smile. "I'd hoped to see you on the sidelines during our practice sessions."

"Josh gets embarrassed if I hang around too much."

"My mother did that all the time. I used to hate it, but deep down, I knew she couldn't help it. A hen protecting her chick."

"Are you her only son?"

His face turned grim. "Her only child, period. And she never lets me forget it. What about you?"

"My mother and father are still together, and I have one brother. They live in East Los Angeles. I grew up there."

He pursed his lips. "Oh? So you *are* like me. A stranger in a foreign land."

She laughed. "Moving from LA to Bay Point was definitely culture shock. But I like it here, and I hope you do, too."

"I'm liking it more and more."

Though his words seemed fraught with meaning, she was too afraid of disappointment to probe them further. *At least in person*, she thought, knowing she would analyze them later.

"Too bad you're only here for a while."

Her subtle yet hopeful hint, cloaked in a steady voice, was quickly shot down.

"Like I said before, when the high school soccer season ends, I'll be moving on."

She hitched her shoulders back. "Oh? Where to?"

He shrugged, but there was a look of assurance in his eyes. "Not sure. Maybe back home. Maybe somewhere else in the States."

She heard his words, loud and clear, though somehow they still managed to prick her heart. Her only recompense was that Sam's tone seemed less resolute, though it still had the edge of someone who could not stay in one place for too long.

A few nights ago she'd finally given in to the temptation and did a search on Sam on the internet. She knew from her son that he was a popular player, but she didn't know just how much.

It was shocking to learn he had suffered an injury to his left leg. It had sidelined him from soccer, though perhaps not permanently, as per the London gossip blogs. She'd also found plenty of articles about his playboy antics.

Mariella had little interest in being just another point on his scoreboard, but she was unashamed that on many sleepless nights, she toyed with the idea. Flirtation, she reasoned, as long as it was out of sight and hearing from her child, was harmless. No chance of a broken heart.

Sam snapped his fingers. "There's one thing I'm missing from Josh. The medical release forms. He never turned them in."

"Thank goodness I keep a copy of everything. I'll be right back."

She left the room and went into her office. It was in the back of her home, next to the kitchen, and looked out onto her garden. The forms were filed away in a two-pocket folder where she kept all important school paperwork.

Back in the living room, she found Sam standing near the fireplace. It had a stone front and mahogany mantel, and was one of her favorite places in the house. She set the document on the coffee table and went to join him there.

He picked up a picture of her and Josh in a silver frame. She was hugging him tightly, and he was smiling.

"You two look adorable. I can tell how much you love each other. How old was he?"

Her eyes smarted with sudden tears, and she turned away and pretended to cough so he wouldn't see.

It took only seconds to compose herself. "About five, and don't ask how old I was," she warned.

"I wouldn't dare." He put the photo back on the mantel. "We British have been known to be polite, reserved and very private. You never know what we are thinking."

She opened her mouth, wanting to ask him what he thought of her. Was she just another soccer mom to him or could she be something more?

"Fine, old construction. Reminds me of home," he said with a knock on the wood. "Does it ever get chilly enough in California to light this thing?"

"In the wintertime, the nights can get cool. You'll see."

"Maybe someday, if I get too cold and you get too cold, I can come over and light it for you. We could sit in front of the fire."

"And do what?" she blurted. "Talk about soccer?"

Without waiting for an answer, she hurried back to the coffee table. In the rush, she brushed against a stack of old magazines. They tumbled onto the table, sending Josh's medical forms to the floor.

"I should have stapled them together," she muttered.

"Let me help," Sam offered.

Mariella barely heard him she was so frustrated with herself as she knelt down. Chin to her chest, robe tucked between her legs, she set about picking up the mess.

He knelt down next to her. "You want to know what I would talk about?"

She looked up at him and shook her head.

"How beautiful you are."

Her hand paused at his words, heat wafting over her

face. It had been a while since she'd heard them from a man as handsome and accomplished as Sam. But could she believe him?

Since their brief time alone on the soccer field, her mind was in a haze. Thoughts of Sam crept up often throughout the day, and nights were preoccupied with fantasies that would likely never come true.

Sometimes she felt like her dating life was over, so his compliments were a great boost to her ego. But what good were they, if nothing could ever happen between them?

What did he stand to gain from giving her compliments, especially since he did not plan on staying in town? By the time spring rolled around, he would be on a plane, back to wherever.

She dropped her chin back to her chest, confused and barely able to look at him, and went back to picking up the papers.

"Is that what you think, or is that what you know?"

Sam stopped her hand and she lifted her face to his.

"It's what I see."

Mariella held her breath as he touched the middle of her bottom lip with his finger, let it trail down her chin, then along her jaw.

"It's what I wish I could feel, more than what I'm doing right now."

His caress didn't go any farther than the tip of her ear-lobe, yet she felt it all the way down to her loins.

Mariella didn't know where Josh was, but he could walk in the house at any time. It forced her from the tenderness of the moment back to reality.

She shied away from his touch and whispered, "You don't mean that. I know how you are."

"You do? How?"

Her eyes met his. "I know what I've read."

He dropped his hand into his lap. "Ah. My past has followed me, courtesy of the internet."

"Photos don't lie."

Sam waved her comment away with both hands. "Photos and stories can be doctored. Funny, you struck me as the type of woman who wouldn't read that trash."

She lifted her chin, even though his tone made her feel slightly ashamed. "I didn't want to read it."

"Then why did you?"

She handed him the forms, which he promptly rolled up and stuck under his arm. "I was curious about you."

He stood. "Ever hear of asking someone outright?"

Mariella refused his outstretched hand as she got to her feet, knowing that if she grabbed onto it, she might never let go.

"I couldn't. I don't even know you."

"Exactly."

He clipped out the word, and there was a sharper edge to his accent she didn't like. His whole demeanor changed. An invisible wall was put up that hadn't been there before, and Mariella knew that it was her fault.

Sam backed into the hallway. "Tell Josh if he misses another practice, without a medical excuse, he's off the team. No exceptions."

He was out the door before she could ask any questions. Mariella hurried to the living room curtains and as she watched him drive away, she realized she'd forgotten to tell him about the barbecue she hosted every year for the team on the night before their first game. Worse, she'd also likely destroyed her chances of ever getting to know the real Sam Kelly.

On his way home, Sam spotted Josh walking on the side of the road, backpack slung over his shoulders, about a mile from downtown Bay Point. Head down, hands shoved in his front pockets.

Even from a distance, the boy appeared troubled.

Though he hardly knew Josh, concern arrowed its way through him, and as he got closer he honked his horn.

Josh didn't look up. Whether that was because of the headphones over his ears, or he recognized Sam's car, he didn't know.

Traffic was light, and when it was safe, he turned on the silver SUV's hazard lights, and made an awkward U-turn. He wasn't sure if he'd ever get used to the steering wheel being on the left side of the car, as opposed to the right as it was in the UK.

When he was on the other side of the road, he rolled down the passenger-side window and slowed the vehicle to a crawl.

"Hey, Josh! Get in!"

The boy looked over, eyes widening as recognition dawned.

"Coach? What are you doing here?"

"Looking for you. Hop in. I'll give you a ride home."

He shifted his backpack uneasily and kept walking as Sam rolled alongside, but stopped moments later.

Sam braked hard and looked into the rearview mirror at the same time. He breathed a sigh of relief to see there were no cars behind him. He reached over and pushed the door open.

"Geez, Coach. Watch it!"

He didn't look scared, just shocked.

"Sorry," Sam muttered as he looked into the rearview mirror. Several cars were slowing down behind him, so he rolled down his window and waved them on.

"Get in, will you? We're holding up traffic."

"I don't need a ride. I live just up the road."

Josh glanced both ways, as if contemplating his next course of action.

"I know where you live. Get in anyway."

Sam swallowed a groan when Josh hesitated again.

He'd only been coaching for a week, and he'd already learned how overly sensitive teenagers could be. Sometimes just changing his tone of voice made a world of difference in how they reacted to his instructions and guidance.

"I just want to talk to you," he said, hoping he sounded more reassuring.

Josh shrugged his shoulders, got in the car and slammed the door shut.

Sam exhaled a breath of relief and checked the rearview mirror once more. The road was clear of traffic, and he merged onto it.

"When you didn't show up today, I went to your house."

Josh slumped down in his seat. "My mom knows I wasn't at practice, too?"

Sam nodded, and turned off the hazard lights.

"Ah, man." He leaned his head back and groaned. "That also means she knows I lied to her."

"Right again, mate." He paused a beat. "So, do you want to tell me why you skipped out on your obligations today?"

Josh looked down at his hands and mumbled, "I don't know. I just didn't feel like going to practice."

He glanced over. "Take those headphones off, please. I have something important to say."

When they were in Josh's lap, Sam continued. "You want to be part of this team, you have to come to practice, no matter what. Is that clear?"

He wanted to cringe at the parental tone of his voice, and would rather be barking out ways to improve a kid's soccer skills than sternly admonishing bad teenage habits.

"My leg hurt today."

Josh's voice was low, and from the tone of it, Sam could tell the words probably hurt more.

"I told you if it got bad, you could sit on the bench."

"But I'm afraid if I do, you'll bench me for good!" Josh accused.

Sam knew from experience how difficult it was to admit pain, but he couldn't let Josh use that as an excuse.

"The only way that will happen is if you stop showing up, and you stop trying on the field."

He braked for a red light and turned his head. "You think I don't know what it's like to have an injury? To be afraid of the pain?"

"I'm *not* afraid," Josh interrupted.

The light turned over to green and Sam continued as if he hadn't heard.

"But that's no reason to stop playing the game you love. Your doctor felt you were physically ready. Now you just have to work on being mentally ready, too."

"I told you I'm not afraid." He gave an exasperated huff and turned away, brooding.

Sam figured he was either trying to take it all in, or dreaming up more excuses. Lately, with his own injury, he was adept at doing the latter.

"I'm sorry for being a loser today."

Sam shot Josh a hard glance, but he was still facing the window. "I don't coach losers. If aspects of your playing are different because of the injury, identify it and I can help you," he added. "As I stated, I've been there. I know what it's like."

"So if you're all recovered, why did you quit the pros?"

Sam pulled up to the curb beside Mariella's home. "I'm *mostly* recovered. I still do physical therapy, too," he clarified, nudging Josh's arm playfully. "And I didn't quit. I just took some time off to coach you rotten bunch of blokes."

"Thanks, Coach." Josh smiled shyly. "For the ride, and for the advice."

He draped his wrist over the steering wheel. "You're welcome. Now, what are you going to tell your mom?"

"The truth," Josh said without any hesitation.

"Great answer." Sam nodded. "See you tomorrow."

When Josh was safely inside, Sam drove downtown.

All the holiday decorations were up and the little town looked like it had been transported back to the time of Charles Dickens, without the snow. The streetlamps were wrapped with pine boughs and white lights. Each one of the "frosted" windows had a vintage holiday scene and he'd heard this was the first year all the stores were leased and open for business.

He was surprised to see so many people out and about on a weeknight. Couples arm in arm and families with kids browsing the shops, which were open late for holiday shopping. The old-fashioned carousel, smack dab in the middle of the square, was whirling slowly, lights twinkling merrily. With his window rolled down, he could hear the carnival-like strains of Christmas music and he smiled.

In general, he was pleased with his temporary home. Bay Point was charming and had more restaurants than he'd expected, though it could use a few more pubs. The people were friendly, sometimes overly so, but they seemed to mean him no harm. The beautiful beaches and temperate weather made him forget to be homesick for London and the career he'd left behind.

As he steered his SUV around the back of the building, he wondered if he would run into his landlord, Henry Wexler, the owner of Relics and Rarities. Short and squat, Wexler's rounded belly was always the first to show around a corner, and it swung like a pendulum whenever he moved.

He was shocked to learn his mother already knew the

man. They'd met at an antiques show in London, and had kept in touch over the years. She utilized Wexler's extensive contacts to add to her collection of English porcelain, and from what his mother told him, he was always glad to assist. It made him wonder if the apartment vacancy hadn't been prearranged.

Sam shook his head again, as he did after he'd ended that particular call with his mother. Just when he thought he knew everything about the woman who had borne him, he realized he didn't know anything at all. Except that she would love the tea set he'd sent to her.

He grabbed his duffel bag and climbed the stairs to his place. Compared to his tiny apartment in Bay Point, his flat on Farnborough Close, Brent, a borough of London, was a palace. Still, it suited him. Though he had plenty of money, he preferred to live in comfort, not over-the-top glitz.

He just hoped he wouldn't regret his decision to come over to the States and take this job in the first place.

His publicist told Sam that coaching in the United States was a great way to build his name on this side of the pond. Soccer was rapidly growing in popularity here, with professional teams sprouting up in several major cities. The sport, called football everywhere else except the US, had a worldwide appreciative fan base that bordered on mania.

His mother tried to guilt him out of it, by claiming he could heal up in London just as well as he could in California. He knew she would have been perfectly happy if he'd stayed in England, feeling sorry for himself.

Sam never claimed to be a self-aware kind of guy. He fully admitted to himself on a daily basis that he didn't know what he wanted, except to get away.

Brent, the town where he was born, was home to the legendary Wembley Stadium, the home of English football, and a place dear to his heart. He'd played on its famous pitch too many times to count. But his pride, his ego, not even the hordes of admiring females, could persuade him to stay.

He slung open the refrigerator and grabbed a light beer, cringing as he popped the cap off. The sound always brought him back to the day when his injury happened.

They were up a point and he'd been defending the team's hold on the ball. So intense was his focus, he didn't notice when another midfielder from the opposing team came after him at top speed and tried to steal it from him, until it was too late.

The crack of bone against bone.

The *pop* that filled his ears, and the instantaneous, gut-wrenching pain that faded his consciousness.

Emergency surgery was performed. Afterward, he awoke and learned he'd torn the anterior cruciate ligament, or ACL, on his left knee and bought himself an instant vacation. His career had come to a grinding halt and all his opponent got was a red penalty card. That they'd also won the game was the final, bruising blow.

Tears sprang to his eyes at the memory. He blamed it on sudden grogginess as vigorously as he pondered what would become of his fame.

All eyes had been watching Sam on the field that day. As soon as he hit the green pitch, knee twisted crazily to the side, the crowd began to root for him to get up.

To the average fan, soccer was something to watch and while away the hours of a day. To fantasize about being in the same cleats as a favorite pro player, dodging your opponent, trying to make the almighty goal, all the way to the bank.

But to him, soccer was his entire life and was for a long time. He'd been kicking that ball since he was six years old; had been playing professionally for ten. Now, at thirty-two, he may have to make other choices. Decisions he didn't even want to think about.

Sometimes life just wasn't fair.

"Go, Sammy! Get back in the game," he muttered to himself, but not even close to the vehemence of his so-called fans that day. Back in Brent, he'd never wondered if they really cared about him, or if they cared about the game more.

He took a slug of beer and voted the latter. He was entertainment, a fantasy figure, and nothing more.

Sam finished off the beer, rinsed the bottle out and threw it in the recycling bin. He'd dismissed an earlier call from his mother. Now, as he did his nightly regimen of crunches on the floor, he debated calling her back.

Though he loved his mother, she was a bit overbearing. His dad, who loved watching him play professional soccer, died ten years ago. He knew she was lonely since his passing, but that didn't give her the right to try to run his life from afar.

One reason he'd taken the coaching gig was to prove he could teach soccer to someone else. So far, he seemed to be doing okay, and was actually enjoying it. Expectations were high, from the kids to the athletic director to the parents, but he kept his attitude positive. What mattered most was that he was still involved in the game that he loved so much. This little side gig gave him an opportunity to explore a second career, if he decided not to return to professional soccer.

Or if his injury decided it for him.

Sam felt his phone vibrate in his pocket and he slid it on.

"You're up late. Did you get my gift?"

"Yes. I loved it."

"Excellent. Henry helped me pick it out. Otherwise, I probably would have chosen something tacky."

"Yes, Henry does have great taste. You, on the other hand, often do not. I was pleasantly surprised."

Sam grinned. "I can always count on you to be forthright, Mother. Anyway, what's up?"

"When are you coming back home?"

He knew, by the tone of her voice, that she had settled back into her favorite floral easy chair, and expected a prompt answer. The one *she* wanted to hear. Unfortunately, he couldn't give it to her.

"I'm not sure when or if I'll be back," he hedged. "I'm here until March at least."

She sighed heavily. "Are you at least coming home for Christmas? I want you to help me decorate."

During the holidays especially, his mother was more needy, and anxious to spend as much time with him as she could. The only reason she probably didn't follow him from country to country during the soccer season, which in Europe was most of the year, was because it would be too taxing for her.

Buying antiques was expensive therapy, but at least it kept her out of his hair.

"Probably not, Mum. I'll probably stay in Bay Point for Christmas," he replied, refusing to confirm his whereabouts so far in advance. "At least the paparazzi aren't following my every move here."

"That's all part of being a star," his mother urged.

"Sometimes I think you like it more than I do," he grumbled.

"What mother in the free world doesn't want her child to be popular?" she harped with a disgusted snort.

He rolled up into a sitting position. "I don't know. Fame sometimes feels fake to me."

"Why should it? You've earned every flash, every bit of ink, real and virtual."

"I never wanted it," he insisted, steadying his elbow on his good knee.

"That's what makes it so perfect," she reasoned, and then paused for a long moment. "Haven't I given you everything you've ever wanted?"

He heard her sniffling back tears. Though he didn't know if they were genuine or for show, his voice softened.

"Yes, of course you have, Mum."

"Then why not give me something I want. Come back home to Brent where you belong. You can go back to playing soccer. Or you can just relax until you figure out what you want to do."

"I don't know. I'm not ready to decide yet."

"Are they even paying you?"

He rolled his eyes at the question.

"We worked out an arrangement."

"How much?" she demanded.

He held the phone away from his ear, thumb poised over the end call button.

"Don't make me be rude, Mother."

His mother had provided everything necessary for a child to survive: food, clothing, shelter. His father, an investment banker, worked a lot of hours to afford the expensive roof over their heads, and the jewels on his wife's fingers. She'd loved him and been his rock when his father was too busy with his business affairs.

He hated when she treated him as if he was still a teenager, and recalled when he'd made the mistake of telling her how much he was earning as a bagger at the local grocery store. She'd gone up to the shopkeeper and demanded he give her son a raise, and the man ended up firing him.

She huffed out a breath in a way that made him even angrier. "It can't be nearly as much as you could make playing pro soccer."

Sam got up and paced the living room. He knew he'd reached a point in the conversation that would make it a struggle to keep his voice calm.

"Of course it's not, but I don't need any more money. What I need is—"

Mariella.

Her name popped into his head, when normally he would have told his mother he needed to be left alone.

Before she could argue with him further, he told her he was tired and hung up.

Afterward, Sam cleaned his apartment. He was the only man he knew who cleaned for relaxation. It didn't hold a candle to great sex, but that wasn't an option right now.

For most of his dating years, he'd been with women who had not been worth the effort or the risk to be a better man.

Too often, he would drown his sorrows in the arms of a woman he didn't really want, at least for more than a night. A woman he knew he would never, and couldn't ever, love for a lifetime.

When he was in his early twenties, he'd started to care deeply for a woman. It ended the day she sold the story about their relationship to the London gossip magazines. Her betrayal hurt him to the core, and now he was very wary of trusting any woman, especially when there was an instant attraction.

He didn't know when he realized he needed the love of a woman who could see past his so-called fame, into the person he was inside. Maybe it was when he was laid up in a hospital bed for a month, when the steady stream of visitors dried up, and so did his coverage in the newspapers. He'd had plenty of time to think, to review what had occurred in his life up until then, and he learned he was still very much a secret to himself.

For so long, he'd been focused on life "outward"—

success, money and prestige. There was still so much about him he needed to discover, and he didn't want to go at it alone.

He retreated to his bedroom and separated his dirty clothes into piles by color. His apartment did not have a washer and dryer. There was a laundromat close by that had pick-up and drop-off service; all he had to do was place the call. He dreaded doing his own laundry, so he appreciated the amenity.

Around eleven, he hopped into the shower. Despite the fact that he'd been out of Mariella's presence for several hours, he couldn't shake the longing he felt for her. It was as if she were right in front of him, and he grabbed his penis, imagining her watching him as he stroked and stroked.

He saw her naked before him, the hot water coursing between her breasts and sliding down both of their bodies. Her eyes trained on his fist moving faster and faster as he watched her hands stroke between her spread legs.

It wasn't long until he was limp, energy spent, panting with his forehead against tile. Mariella evaporated in his mind as the water ran cool down his back, ending his fantasy.

Later in bed the sheets were cold, scratchy and unwelcoming. Sam thought how nice it would be to have Mariella beside him, wrapped in his arms. Then he counted the months he had remaining in Bay Point.

With a sad sigh, he decided his fantasies were safer for both of them, plumped his pillow and fell asleep.

Chapter 4

Sam blew his whistle hard. He threw his hands up high into the air as if it could rid him of the intense frustration he was feeling.

"C'mon, guys! What's the matter with you?" His players stopped in their tracks. None of them was where he'd instructed them to be on the field.

"Huddle up," he shouted.

When they all assembled in front of him, he dropped his whistle against his team polo shirt and gave them his sternest look.

"Have you guys forgotten? Tomorrow is our first game!"

The Titans were playing against the Bulldogs. In the past, the Bulldogs had been one of the worst teams in the district. Sam knew better than to trust they would fare the same this season. Underdog teams had nowhere to go but up.

Dante scoffed, and puffed out his chest. "We beat them last year, and the year before, with our hands tied behind our backs."

Sam crossed his arms against Dante's know-it-all attitude. Even though he was one of his best players, he wasn't going to allow Dante to circumvent his authority.

"Don't count the Bulldogs out yet. I went and watched a scrimmage match a couple of days ago, and they've got a couple of new juniors who are blazing down the field." He waved his clipboard in the air. "A lot more than I can say for most of you today."

Some of the boys grumbled aloud in response. Others stabbed at the dirt with the toes of their cleats, actions that also rankled his nerves. Most, however, appeared to be listening to him.

Sam stuck his clipboard under his arm and slammed his fist down onto his open palm. His words may have been harsh, but he wasn't about to sugarcoat the facts.

"Winning doesn't happen with a click of a button. It requires constant diligent improvement on the part of each member of this team so we can all perform at the highest level at all times."

He wiped the sweat from his palms on his black shorts. "Let's try that formation again," he barked, clapping his hands together to get their attention. "And put some life in it."

Josh stepped forward out of the pack, uniform shirt sticking to his chest. "We can do it, Coach." He glanced back at his teammates. "Right, guys?"

All of them were nodding, except for Dante.

Sam raised an eyebrow, pleased it was Josh who was encouraging the rest of the team. Maybe it was because he wanted to be selected as team captain, an honor bestowed on a deserving senior who showed the most leadership potential.

"I'm counting on it," Sam said with deliberate gruffness. "Watch those ruts!"

He warned them daily to be careful, but also didn't want

the condition of the field to drastically affect the way each one of them played.

The boys ran off, and when they were in place, he blew his whistle. This time around, they had more energy, and Josh even scored the winning goal for his scrimmage team.

Sam, pacing the sidelines, instructed them to drill the formation a few more times, until practice was over.

"Great job, Josh!" Mariella yelled out.

He whirled around, being careful of his bad knee, and saw her standing a few feet behind him. She was struggling to hold on to two bulging grocery bags.

"Let me help you with those," he called out.

The cautious smile he got back was worth the interruption.

Without waiting for an answer, he took the bags from her and set both on a nearby bench.

"Thanks." She whooshed out a breath. "Those were heavy."

"What are you doing here?"

He hoped he didn't sound like he didn't want her around. Quite the opposite. He'd missed her.

It was the first time seeing her since he'd stormed out of her home. He'd wanted to call her and tell her he was sorry, but he also knew it was always better to apologize in person.

"Tim's mother called and said she couldn't bring the snacks today."

He frowned as he watched her shake what he assumed was a cramp out of her hands.

"I hope it isn't anything serious."

"She told me she had to go pick up her youngest from school. Not sure of the reason, and it's really none of my business. I was next on the list, so here I am."

"I'm glad to see you. I'm sorry about our conversation. It ended badly."

Her eyes gleamed with surprise, and she glanced around briefly.

"Did you miss me?" Her voice was almost a whisper.

Sam didn't want to ask if she'd been avoiding him, but if she thought staying away from him could make him want her any less, she was wrong. He fought the urge to touch her cheek, and instead held the clipboard at his waist.

"I haven't seen you anywhere but in my mind in over a week."

He wanted to tell her he wished she were in that white robe she'd worn, teasing him with her slim, brown, bare legs.

Without moving his head, he took his time reviewing her long-sleeve, light yellow button-down shirt and a navy skirt with a sweater tied around her shoulders. Today her attire was all business, and she wore it to perfection.

"Then I accept your apology." She smiled, and seemed not to notice his open perusal of her. His dark sunglasses worked their magic once again.

"I work full-time, so I can't attend too many practices, but most parents don't, right?"

He nodded. "Dante's mother is here for almost all of them, but I gather that's because she doesn't have anything else to do."

"Except gossip," Mariella giggled.

Sam wasn't even going to touch that one. He pointed to her fuchsia-and-blue footwear. "Love the sneakers."

"Thanks. I changed out of my pumps in the car. My heels would have sunk in this dirt."

"You're very wise. I would mention you look very pretty today, but I don't want to be accused of flirting."

"I won't tell if you won't," she teased and then turned to dig into the grocery bags.

The straightness of her back flowed into a bottom so

round it made him go stiff. With a low groan, he planted the clipboard in front of his waist again.

"Hmm…could be dangerous, pretty lady."

She turned, glanced at him over her shoulder and smiled, seeming not to notice his predicament. He waited a minute until it was safe to put the clipboard down on the bench. Then he helped her set out prepackaged cheese and crackers, a variety of yogurts and fruit. Another parent had already dropped off a cooler stocked with Gatorade and waters.

When they were done, Sam stepped back a few paces to appraise their work, and Mariella.

"The guys will appreciate these snacks. They've been pretty sluggish all afternoon, until your son stepped up and gave them a pep talk."

"Really? Josh did? I'm surprised. He's usually not that encouraging to himself, let alone others. You must be a good influence on him."

She folded her arms over her chest, and he batted away thoughts of his hands there instead.

"Now who's flirting with whom?" His heart dug a new well of hope when she returned his sardonic smile.

Sam turned his back to the field, creating what he hoped was a wall of temporary privacy for the two of them.

"I really am sorry the way our conversation ended the last time we were together."

She put her hands on her hips and took a step toward him, almost close enough for him to feel the heat from her body.

"I will only forgive you if you promise to behave yourself going forward."

He leaned in close enough to smell the sweet rose-scented spice of her perfume. "That's a promise I'm not sure I can keep."

Her mouth parted and before Sam could give in to the strong urge to kiss her, he turned away. His whole body ached with need, and the sooner he got away from Mariella, the sooner he could get back to focusing on what was most important.

Preparing for the team's first game.

He lifted his whistle to his lips, and felt Mariella's hand on his arm. He turned and searched her eyes.

"What is it? Practice is nearly over, and I have to give the guys some final feedback."

"This won't take long. I have good news. I spoke to the principal a couple of days ago, and received an email from him today."

She clasped her hands together, and her eyes lit up with excitement. "He wants to set up a meeting with you, me, Leslie, and Brian Putnam, your boss, to discuss."

"Why Leslie?" he asked, still holding on to the whistle.

"She's the president of the PTA. Remember?"

He let the whistle slack against his chest. "Oh, yeah. No wonder she's been hanging around, spying on me."

Mariella shook her head. "I don't think so. She probably thinks you're cute."

He shrugged, knowing he couldn't care less what Leslie thought about him. He only cared about Mariella, although a lot of good it was doing him.

"Anyway, that *is* great news. Thanks for helping to kickstart this project. I'll help in any way I can."

"No problem," Mariella said. "We can talk about it more tonight."

Sam scratched his head in confusion. "Tonight?"

"The potluck barbecue at my house," Mariella replied. "Didn't Josh tell you?"

He rocked back and forth on his heels, not quite believing his good fortune. Since it would have been inappropriate to ask her out on a date, he'd been hoping for an opportunity to spend some time with her. Now he would just have to find a way to talk to her alone.

"I heard some discussion about it, but I didn't know I was invited."

"Of course you are. I have it for the team every year. In fact, you're the guest of honor."

"Then I wouldn't miss it for the world."

Mariella smoothed her dress and took one last look in the mirror. On impulse, she swirled around once more, admiring the garment's deep purple hue. It was one of her favorite colors to wear in autumn and winter.

Her excitement grew as her fingers traced the white piping along the scoop neckline, which also trimmed the bell-capped sleeves and hem, and played nicely with her nut-brown skin.

Although she could have worn jeans and a T-shirt, as host of the event, she always dressed up.

Her mother taught her to look beautiful for herself first, instead of for a man. She'd never understood that concept until she moved to Bay Point, where she knew no one, and was so focused on parenting her child she'd relinquished dating.

"Men come and go," her mother used to say as she braided Mariella's long black hair, "but we women must go on."

Unfortunately, her mother, who believed in "mind over matter," never agreed with her decision to move, while her dad knew that sometimes a change in environment was best, and helped pay for her moving expenses.

There were so many times Mariella thought her mother was right. That she had made a mistake in moving to Bay Point. But for Josh's sake, she'd made the best of the situation. Landing the job at the mayor's office, getting her degree, making new friends. Now it was time to put a renewed focus on her.

She dabbed some of her favorite perfume behind her ears, and didn't feel at all guilty for wanting and needing to look good tonight.

For herself, but also for Sam.

When he'd visited her home, she'd outwardly rejected his flirting, though inwardly she'd loved the attention. Seeing him again that afternoon made her realize that perhaps she'd been too hasty. She was tired of putting aside her needs, her desires, but she still had to be discreet.

Mariella brushed her hair out in long strokes, and sighed at her reflection in the mirror. She almost wished she were a teenager again, doodling hearts in notebooks, unconcerned about what people would say, or think, or do.

Whether he deserved it or not, Sam had a reputation as a playboy, and in some respects that was immensely freeing.

She didn't have to worry about him committing to her, because his track record indicated he wouldn't. So she was off the hook, too. She just needed to decide in her mind that she could handle having a little fun, without the labels, the love or the commitment.

Mariella shut the door to her bedroom and went downstairs. Her guests would be arriving soon and she wanted to double-check that everything was ready.

She'd hosted the barbecue for both the boys' and girls' junior varsity and varsity soccer teams for the past three years, offering up her home and her yard, both of which were quite large, for a few hours. It helped ingratiate her and Josh into the Bay Point community, particularly the soccer moms.

It was also her belief that the event helped her win her bid to be vice president of the PTA, a role she really enjoyed. Being involved in the organization kept her close to key staff at the school, apprised of many upcoming changes and allowed her to feel she had a purpose in Josh's education, besides being a worrywart.

The gathering was potluck, so that kept her costs down. She supplied the beverages, plates, utensils and paper products. The soccer team always cleaned up, as best a group of teenagers could, she mused to herself.

Some parents stayed for the event, but some did not. Most of the single parents chose to drop off their dishes and pick their kids up later. She was never offended, and could certainly empathize with the need to have some alone time.

Mariella ventured outside. Her backyard was extensive, and bordered by native California perennial wildflowers. The grass was green and lush, watered by an underground irrigation system.

"How does it look?" Josh asked.

He'd covered the ten folding tables she'd borrowed from the school with gold vinyl tablecloths. There were sprigs of fresh purple and red mums in small bud vases on every one, and the potluck table had all the plates and utensils neatly placed on one end.

She appraised her son's long shorts and T-shirt emblazoned with the logo of one of his favorite basketball teams. He'd recently started taking greater care of his appearance, and she was proud of him for it.

"Everything looks great, and so do you," she replied and gave him an awkward sideways hug. "The last thing I need you to do is to check that we have a nice mixture of beverages in the coolers."

"Sure, Mom."

He lumbered off, his limp barely visible now.

To her relief, he'd even started doing his physical therapy exercises on a regular basis, and without being asked.

She didn't know what was the motivating factor in Josh's life, but she was sure Sam had something to do with it. He'd had a positive influence on her, why not her son?

Since Josh's father had died, Mariella always felt he needed a strong male role model. Her own father had tried, but when they moved to Bay Point, he and her mom only visited about six times in three years.

A slight breeze lifted the ends of her hair as she picked up and moved the folding chairs into small clusters to encourage conversation. The weather was unseasonably warm for November. She straightened a stack of light-weight, cotton throw blankets, which she'd placed in a large wicker basket. They were there for the taking in case any of her guests got chilly as the night wore on.

Mariella glanced over at the hedges surrounding the house. They were strung with multicolored Christmas lights, providing a festive glow. She'd thought of every-thing, down to the sign on the front door directing guests to the backyard, except how hard it would be to hide her attraction to Sam.

In the spirit of the season, she'd simply have to be nice, not naughty, she thought with a decided jerk of her chin.

The first to arrive to the potluck was Emily Stego and her mother.

Emily played goalie on the varsity girls' team, and was also Josh's first crush. She was probably the reason why he was paying so much attention to his clothes and hair. Mariella sincerely hoped Josh would work up the courage to ask Emily out on a date.

"One last soiree," Emily's mother commented.

Mariella led the way to the potluck table. She'd forgot-ten the woman's name, and was too embarrassed to ask.

"Yes, since this is Josh's senior year, someone else will have to take over hosting these next year."

Emily's mom set down a macaroni casserole. "Your house is perfect for the occasion."

"Thank you, but I'm sure a suitable replacement can be found," she replied, smiling.

"The beverages are in the coolers over there under the trees, if you'd care for a soda or water."

More guests arrived, including the assistant coaches and their families. Mariella excused herself to go and greet them.

In a short time, the main entrée table was laden with a variety of foods, including some very appetizing vegetarian options.

She was organizing the desserts on a separate table when she heard a chorus of shouts, and then a rousing, though off-key, rendition of the Bay Point High School anthem.

She turned, and as Sam rounded the corner of her house, the boys and girls in the backyard erupted into applause. The parents and coaches quickly joined in and so did she.

"It's the man of the hour!" she called out.

There were a few "hear, hears" from the adults in the crowd, and Sam bowed in response.

Mariella couldn't help but notice how handsome he looked in tailored blue pants and a white polo shirt that stretched along his chest and biceps.

Leslie accompanied him, her arm looped through his. Her husband was nowhere in sight. She felt a pang of jealousy, and was disgusted by it, but there it was.

She reached for the square glass pan of brownies he held in his hands, and smiled. "Hello, Mr. Guest of Honor. You didn't have to bake."

Leslie beat her to it, and claimed the brownie pan.

"He didn't bake these. They're mine. All Sam needs to do is win games."

Sam stepped out of the realm of both women and motioned for his team to gather around him.

"And we will, right, team?"

With hoots and hollers, the boys agreed. The girls and their coaches joined in the mini pep rally, too.

Throughout the evening, everyone clamored around Sam. She noticed he barely had an opportunity to eat, so she fixed him a plate, wedged through the crowd and brought it over to him.

"We can't win if our coach starves to death."

He took the plate from her and her heart raced at the huge smile on his face. She knew it was meant just for her.

"I'm fine, Ms. Vency. Thank you."

She left and floated from group to group, making sure her guests had what they needed, all the while trying to keep her eyes from tracking Sam.

Emily's mom was gone and Josh was at Emily's side. It was sweet to see them talking, their heads bent toward each other, and she wished she could talk to Sam in the same manner. As the festivities wound to a close, she put out some plastic containers so people could take home leftovers, and then headed back inside to the kitchen.

She filled one side of her sink with clean, soapy water. Not wanting her guests to take a dirty dish back home, she always offered to wash their empty casserole pans.

Sam peeked his head in the door. "Need some help?"

She nodded, more out of shock he was there than actually needing his assistance.

"I'll take that as a yes."

His eyes widened at the stack of casserole dishes, and he grabbed a sponge from the front edge of the double-bowled sink.

"Plus, I owe you for feeding me."

She looked at him askance, and when she inhaled the scent of his musky cologne, knew that if she got any closer it would be very tough not to be naughty.

"Are you sure you're up to this? You're a popular guy. You have to keep your strength up to sign all those autographs."

"I'd rather be here, with you, scraping grease off pans."

Mariella grinned and waved a soapy hand in front of her face, in tandem with her heart fluttering in her chest.

"How romantic."

Both of her hands were submerged, and she watched in fascination as his left hand sank into the clean water. It tangled with hers, massaging her knuckles gently.

"I haven't even gotten started."

She hitched in a breath and stared outside, and saw members of the soccer team cleaning up. It only made Sam's movements and the sensations she was experiencing as he stroked her fingers under the water more intimate.

Mariella turned to look at him, her heart beating even more wildly now. "Sam, don't."

She jerked her chin toward the window. "Someone could come in and see."

He removed his hands slowly, and then flicked some suds toward her. "You're no fun."

"I am, too," she protested, despite his good-natured tone. "Under the right conditions."

"And doing dishes together isn't one of them?"

She laughed. "Usually not."

"I bet I can persuade you." He leaned his right hip against the sink, stuck his hand inside the water and began to massage her hands again.

"I'm only doing this because the water is clean."

She laughed, stared into his eyes and quickly looked away in case anyone outside glanced over at the window.

"I'm glad you have some standards."

"I do. And you beat them all."

Her face heated, and he started to work his way to her wrist, and then up her arm.

Suddenly, she heard the sound of the kitchen door opening. It was Leslie, a disconcerting smirk on her face.

Had she seen?

Sam jerked his hands out of the sink and grabbed a nearby dishtowel. She grabbed a casserole dish and plunged it deep into the water. When little bits of brownie floated to the surface, she realized the dish belonged to Leslie.

Leslie looked at the two of them, and Mariella could practically see the wheels of the gossip machine that lived in her brain turning.

"Hey, some of the parents are looking for you," she said, addressing Sam. "They want to say goodbye."

"Go on, Sam," Mariella urged. "I can get these."

When Sam was gone, Leslie stepped into Sam's place, but did not offer to help.

"He's a nice guy, isn't he?" she asked.

Mariella shrugged. "Of course. Anyone can see that."

"You, more than anyone."

The bright pink headband she wore in her blond hair suddenly annoyed Mariella, almost as much as her line of questioning.

"What do you mean by that, Leslie?"

"He's single. You're single."

She turned on the faucet and rinsed the dish clean.

"So are a lot of people in Bay Point. What are you getting at?"

"Just be careful, Mariella. People see, and people talk. You don't want Sam to lose his coaching position because of inappropriate behavior, do you?"

She dried Leslie's baking dish and handed it to her.

"Don't worry about me, Leslie. I can take care of myself."

Chapter 5

Thirty minutes later the soccer players who remained helped load the folding tables into her car to be returned to the school on Monday, before leaving with their parents.

Josh decided to walk Emily home, and she and Sam waved goodbye to them from the top of the driveway.

Mariella went to the backyard, and smiled when he followed her. She grabbed a blanket from the basket and wrapped it around her shoulders. It was more a gesture of habit, rather than actually being cold.

Even though they hadn't done anything wrong, after the unsettling conversation with Leslie, her nerves were still on edge.

Mariella shivered, her body still humming with pleasure from Sam's touch. There was no reason for him to stay with her any longer, yet she was glad he didn't leave.

"Thanks for a great event."

"We had great weather, and I think everyone enjoyed themselves. That's all I can ask for."

"I stayed behind because I wanted to talk to you about Josh."

She hugged the blanket around her and frowned.

"What's the problem now? I thought you said today his playing had improved."

"It has, so much so that he is among those I'm considering for team captain."

She clapped her hands together, relieved. "He will be so excited if he's chosen."

Sam nodded. "I'm really happy with not only his performance, but also his leadership."

"Just don't push him too much. That's my job."

Her voice grew soft with regret. "Sometimes I feel like I expect too much from him. I'm being too overprotective, aren't I?"

He closed the gap between them and huddled the blanket more neatly around her shoulders.

"You're just being a mom. I wouldn't expect any less."

It wasn't the most romantic thing to say, but when Sam's forehead grazed hers, and idled there, she knew he wanted to kiss her. It was a tense crackle of an invite, tempting her to place her hands around his neck and make the first move.

She knew she should push him away, but she couldn't.

Leslie's warning, which in retrospect felt more like a subtle threat, waved a white flag in the back of her mind.

To quibble about its meaning would be to take herself out of the moment, but making the wrong choice could have lasting impact.

Then why did the wrong thing feel so right?

Face-to-face now, his gray eyes were ruminative and his brow furrowed as if he was thinking of the potential consequences, too. She couldn't read his mind, but she could feel the heat between them, threatening to ignite.

This was what she'd hoped for. A gorgeous man, his lips mere inches away, her body craving more.

She let the blanket fall to the ground.

There was a tangible sense that she should let go of herself and fall into him, but still she hesitated. Frozen in place, but melting underneath.

She brought her hand up to his face, likely smooth in the morning, rough stubble now in the night. His intake of breath was slight, like the breeze before a windstorm. In the moonlight, his eyes, blunt under the influence of desire, searched hers.

Closing her eyes, she felt his warm breath on her skin. His lips brushed hers, drawing in a searing pleasure in the pit of her stomach, and her toes to their tips.

Sam grasped her arms at her sides, and she stood frozen in place, kissing him back. Her desiring him, him wanting her, was like trying to wade out of quicksand. It was futile. Slowly, they would get sucked in and plunge into its depths.

But at least they'd have fun on the way down.

Suddenly, his phone buzzed against her upper thigh.

"Damn," he muttered. "I have to go."

"It's okay, Sam. I understand."

She thought it was odd he didn't check his phone to see who it was. Whoever it was, he or she was more important than being with her.

Sam reached for her hand and tried to bring it up to his lips, but she slipped away. The chaste kiss on the cheek he gave her before he left only heightened the sense that something had been lost, that she'd been cheated out of much-needed intimacy.

Back in the kitchen Mariella finished cleaning the rest of the dishes while waiting for Josh to return home.

The interruption was an unwanted wake-up call. A time

to step off, step back and face facts. She was treading on some very dangerous ground, and she wasn't the only one who could get hurt.

Sam turned off his phone, something he now wished he'd done prior to the party. He pulled out of Mariella's driveway, hating to leave her. Ever since they met, he'd known it would be a challenge to keep his attraction under wraps.

Tonight was no different.

God, he'd wanted to smash his lips on hers, make her a part of him and kiss her like she'd never been kissed before. He'd been so turned on, touching and massaging her hands in the soapy water, he'd nearly gone out of his mind.

At a red light, he closed his eyes briefly and saw again the disappointment on Mariella's face before he walked away.

She'd *wanted* him to kiss her, and keep on kissing her, perhaps for the rest of the night. They had shared a short but passionate kiss that was pleasurable for them both. Still, he didn't want to hurt her, and by the look in her eyes tonight, that was exactly what he did. She probably would never let him near her again.

Sam eased off the brake and continued on his way home, not at all eager to get to his quiet, lonely apartment.

Having traveled all over the world, Sam never wanted to settle down in one place or with one woman. He'd come to realize Mariella could change his mind, and that scared him. If anyone could move past his wealth, his fame and see he was really just a simple guy at heart, it would be her.

He wanted her, and for more than one night. The interruptions, first by Leslie, then by technology, should have deterred his lust, but they didn't.

Her beauty and sensual curves were a wonderful bonus.

Every time he saw her he was reminded of how tempting she was, but those weren't the main things that attracted him to her.

Mariella was down-to-earth, and he had a hunch she would be loyal to him, unlike some of the other women he'd allowed himself to be close to.

He licked his lips, but the taste of her was gone and he wasn't sure when he'd get the chance to kiss her again. The team's first game was tomorrow and he'd be incredibly busy for the next several weeks.

If she wants to see me, I'll make the time.

Sam rolled down his window and smiled warily. It felt good to make some sort of decision about their relationship, even if they were in the very early stages.

Breathing in the salt-scented air, he bypassed his apartment and decided to go to the beach for a while before going home. The sound of the waves would calm him down, so maybe he could get a good night's sleep.

He rubbed his stomach, remembering how Mariella had brought him a plate of food. The barbecue was more fun than he'd thought. The parents were friendly and welcoming, and he'd enjoyed sharing stories about his career as a pro player. Nobody asked for his autograph, or pressed him about when he'd be back playing full-time. For a few hours it was easy to forget he'd once been in the public eye.

It was a nice feeling. Being a normal guy, instead of a famous one. He'd grown tired of always being on guard. One wrong word, one date with the wrong woman, and heaven forbid, a mistake on the field, brought on a firestorm of media attention. In some cases, the stuff said about him was so outrageously untrue, he could have sued for libel.

In the last two months of his pro career, he had been so frustrated he just wanted the season to end.

"Be careful what you wish for," he muttered as he pulled into the beach parking lot.

Though he knew it was impossible, sometimes he wondered if he'd brought his injury upon himself. Maybe he'd wanted change so much, forces in the universe had worked to bring his life to a complete halt. Or perhaps he'd just had a run of bad luck.

Whatever the cause, it had led him to Bay Point, and Mariella. Meeting her was making him rethink his whole outlook on everything.

Sam selected a spot away from other vehicles and turned off the ignition. Though it was dark outside, it would be easy enough to walk down to the beach, kick off his shoes and dig his toes into the sand. But he decided to stay in his car. He powered on his phone and it rang almost immediately.

"Tell my mother the answer is no."

Niles, his sports agent, laughed. "Is that why you didn't pick up before? You know I can't do that. Nobody can."

Sam blew out a breath as his frustration came galloping back. "I have. Hundreds of times."

"And has she listened?"

"Never."

Niles chuckled again, and Sam wondered where he was this time. The short-statured man with a pudgy stomach and salt-and-pepper comb-over loved to travel to expensive locales where he could don his beloved Madras shorts, have a fruity cocktail and make deals for his clients.

"It's not just her, it's everyone in the country. Haven't you been reading the papers?"

Sam stared out his window at the waves, wishing he could dive in and disappear.

"Thankfully, I haven't seen those papers in the States. And I hate reading papers online."

"So do I, so I'll keep it brief," Niles replied begrudgingly. "I'm getting emails from fans around the world. I need you back on the field."

"No, you need an assistant." Sam smirked.

"Quite so." Niles laughed. "But he or she would never make me the kind of money I stand to make with you."

Sam could imagine Niles chewing on the end of one of the Cuban cigars he preferred, but never smoked.

"And nobody could stand being with you."

When Niles began to protest, Sam cut in. "Your words, not mine. Remember?"

"I just prefer to work alone. That's not wrong."

"Nor is me being tired of hearing how disappointed everyone is that I'm not playing for Valor anymore."

"You owe it to your fans!" Niles insisted.

Sam pinched the bridge of his nose to stem off the headache beginning to surface.

Just because he was famous didn't mean he was required to explain every decision. It wasn't the constant travel or the soccer groupies that seemed to follow him everywhere. He simply wanted a break. Time just for him, for reflection and for figuring out what he really wanted out of life.

"I don't owe anybody anything."

"You're sounding a bit like Scrooge, my friend."

"Bah humbug," Sam grumped in agreement.

"Listen to me, Sam. I'm concerned about your welfare. Guys as competitive and as talented as you are don't have an easy time transitioning out of the pros."

"I kind of had a little help, Niles. Care of three little letters. A-C-L. Remember?"

"You've got that beat. Are you seeing the physical therapist I told you about? And did you ever find a gym in that godforsaken town? It's important that you stay in shape."

Sam couldn't help but smile. Niles was obsessed with making money, but at least he made his clients feel cared about as he filled his own coffers.

"The therapist is great, I joined the gym the other day and by the way, I kind of like Bay Point."

Mariella had a lot to do with it, but that was none of his agent's business.

"I'm going to pretend I didn't hear you say that." Niles sounded aghast. "How is the coaching job?"

"It's fine. It's different than playing, for sure, but I like being able to run things my way."

"Taking some cues from your former coach?"

Leo Minor, apparently named for the lesser lion constellation, was prone to yelling and screaming to get his way. No guy wanted to be a victim of his very loud roar.

Sam grunted. "If I did, most of my team would probably quit."

"Regardless of his methods, he knew how to win."

"Be a good agent and wish me good luck. We have our first game tomorrow."

"I'm raising my cocktail in your honor," Niles replied. "I hope you're successful, but not too successful. I'm expecting you back in Brent in a few months."

"I'm not promising anything, Niles."

"Just promise me you'll look at some of the offers I emailed your way this morning," he begged.

"It's Saturday already for you. Go back to sleep."

Sam ended the call and tossed the phone onto the passenger seat, not caring if Niles was offended by his abruptness. But he felt even guiltier about leaving Mariella for a conversation that had only made him angry, and for putting soccer first, when in that passionate moment, that hadn't been necessary.

When he'd been recovering in the hospital, he'd begun

to realize how much of his life he'd lived on autopilot. Since childhood, he had been programmed to compete and to win, at all costs.

Now, unable to play at the same level he had before, his belief in himself had been crushed. He had to find something else, or someone else, to believe in.

Soccer just wasn't enough anymore.

He started the SUV and backed out of the empty lot.

Maybe it wasn't fair to either of them, and maybe it wasn't right, but he had to see Mariella again.

Tonight.

Leftovers are evil, Mariella thought as she made space for one more plastic container in the refrigerator. Most of her guests ignored her plea to take them home, probably figuring Josh would eat them.

They were right.

As soon as he returned from Emily's house, he had a snack before going upstairs. If he didn't consume the rest of the food by the end of the day tomorrow, into the trash it would go.

After washing her hands, she set the teakettle on the stove and turned on the gas. Then she unwrapped a piece of cake she'd managed to snag before it was all gone and placed it on the kitchen table. Since she was denied the sweetness of a longer kiss from Sam, she was going to enjoy every bite.

A gentle breeze rustled the yellow café curtains that hung at the window above the sink. She stood nearby and wondered if she'd ever wash another dish without thinking about Sam, or get an answer to the question that was on a constant loop in her mind.

Who had called him and what was so important he had to leave right away?

An insistent knock on the back door startled her. The teakettle whistled annoyingly at the same time. On tiptoe and on edge, she leaned over the sink, parted the curtains and looked out.

Sam! What was he doing back here?

Mariella rushed to the stove, turned off the kettle, and then walked calmly to the door and opened it.

He stood just outside the illuminating radius of the porch light, so his expression was unreadable. Though Mariella was excited to see him, she could only manage a tight smile.

"I didn't expect to see you until tomorrow, at the game."

"Can I come in?" he asked, with his hands behind his back. "I promise this won't take long."

She nodded and stepped back so Sam could close the door. When they got into the kitchen, he appeared troubled.

"I have a confession to make."

At his words, she put her hand on her chest, expecting the worst.

"What is it?"

He kept his eyes on hers, and his gaze was so penetrating and kind, she relaxed even though she didn't know what he was going to say.

"I missed you, and this time I couldn't go to sleep without letting you know it."

"You mean you've missed me before?"

Her innocent tone belied the torrent of warmth rushing through her veins. When he nodded, she dropped her hand to her hip and fought back a wide smile.

"You could have called."

He took a step toward her, reached out a hand and stroked her hair. "No, I had to say it in person. And more important, I wanted to apologize for leaving so suddenly."

Mariella resisted the urge to lean into his touch, not sure what he wanted from her.

"Is everything okay? Do you want to talk about it?"

"I do, but I'm not sure you will like what I have to say."

Her heart fell, and she backed away from him, glad she'd decided to be cautious.

"Why don't you let me be the judge? Would you care for some tea? The kettle is already hot."

He nodded and she walked over to the small cupboard that held all her teas. Her hand shook as she put one Orange Blossom tea bag each in two mugs, poured the water and brought them to the table. Sam declined her offer of sugar, honey or milk.

"I like my tea plain, too."

Mariella sat down next to him and dipped her tea bag back and forth in the water, before setting it on the saucer she'd placed on the table earlier.

Sam did the same, and when he was done, he took a tentative sip. "Delicious. Did you know in Great Britain, there's a science to making tea?"

Mariella gave him a wry glance. "It's just hot water and a tea bag. What's so scientific about it?"

"I'll teach you sometime. Believe me, you'll notice the difference in taste."

She took a sip, wondering about his motives. "You're going to teach me soccer and how to make tea the British way? Sounds like you're planning to stick around."

"Would you like it if I did?" he asked, touching her hand.

She set her mug on the table, cupped her palms around it and didn't look at him.

"I don't know how to answer that, Sam."

"How about the truth?"

He gently lifted her hands into his and Mariella began to tremble.

"I don't know. It's too soon to say, and I don't understand why you are asking me."

"Maybe I'm just looking for a reason to stay in Bay Point. You can be that reason."

Mariella felt her heart fill with hope, but she still had to be careful. If he wanted the truth from her, she deserved the same.

"Who called you on the phone tonight?"

Sam sat back, and her hands slipped from his. The night breeze came through the window, almost extinguishing the red peppermint-scented candle on the table. Though he didn't seem shocked by her question, he watched the flame flicker before answering.

"My agent. He and my mother are both pressuring me to return home, right after the season ends."

She faced him and raised a brow. "Do they realize the season is just beginning?"

"They believe in planning for the future."

His grim smile noted he wasn't happy about the intrusion.

"And your agent?"

"Niles just wants my money."

She leaned over and blew out the candle, wishing his mother and his agent would both go *poof.*

"And you don't want to go back?"

"I'm not sure. It's too early to tell." He paused as if measuring his words. "You see, I came here for the wrong reasons, and now I want to stay for the right ones."

Mariella's ears perked up. Was it because of the injury to his knee? In her view, the aftereffects were barely noticeable. He hadn't limped at all during the barbecue. Or was it something else?

Not sure she wanted to know the answer, she pushed her mug away, and the contents slopped over the rim. She grabbed a rag from the sink, mopped up the spill and remained at the counter when she was done.

"How will you know?" She bit her lip as he got up and joined her.

Sam tapped his forehead to hers, and she held her breath as he looked deeply into her eyes.

"It's all going to depend on you."

"Me?"

"On whether you'll let me kiss you again. This time, with no interruptions."

He traced her hairline with one finger, and his nearness made her shiver with anticipation.

"No interruptions?"

He shook his head and cupped her face in his hands as if he was handling something exquisite and fine.

"Ever since we met, I haven't been able to stop thinking about you, and I don't know what to do about it."

His voice sounded tortured, and sent a tingle down her spine.

"You didn't have to come back here tonight," she whispered. "But I'm glad you did."

Sam pulled her close and she leaned her head against the warm, hard ridge of his collarbone. She could feel the solid length of his desire against her belly, and her knees went weak.

"Maybe if I kiss you, just once more, for good luck, I can walk out of here and we can just be friends."

Mariella lifted her chin. "Why don't you try it and see?" she challenged, looking deeply into his eyes.

Sam touched his nose to hers, and she felt prickles of pleasure as the tip of his tongue darted into the hollows at the edges of her mouth.

She pursed her lips, and as he licked the delicate bow in the middle, she opened them and sucked in his tongue.

Little by little, she took his flesh into hers, enjoying his groan of delight as she wrapped her arms around his neck, and tasted hot, unrelenting need.

He backed her up against the counter and broke the kiss, burying his head deep into her neck, licking her there into submission. His tongue lapped at her skin, slow and sensuous, and she swore she could feel every one of his taste buds on her skin.

Mariella mewed low and curled into him, tilting her pelvis forward, trying to get as close as possible to the hard bulge pressing against her.

The breeze blew through the kitchen, cooling the wet skin of her neck, and she leaned away, shivering. He opened his eyes briefly, and then captured her lips again.

She pulled him closer, resisting the urge to roll her abdomen back and forth against him. Doing so would put her over the boiling point, yet doing nothing made her head swoon with desire.

Let him know you want him.

With a low moan, she cleaved her mouth to his with no shame. Her mind whirled away any fear as their embrace deepened.

Let him know so he'll never forget.

They kissed for a long moment, and then she broke contact. She leaned her elbows back on the counter and opened her eyes. There was a thin veil of sweat on his forehead as Sam stepped forward, ensuring there were no gaps between their bodies.

"Where are you going?" he muttered thickly.

"Well, Coach Kelly," she murmured, looping her hands around his neck. "What's the verdict?"

"First, kissing is one thing I don't have to teach you."

Mariella smiled and nuzzled his bottom lip with the tip of her nose. "And the second?"

"I want to kiss you more."

She laughed and he brought his lips back down to hers, but she dodged the kiss, and sank her mouth into the side of his neck.

Mariella inhaled his scent, mild soap with hints of smoke from the barbecue. Without warning, her tongue darted out from her mouth to taste his skin, and she felt his stomach cave in. To know she could shock him, could control him somehow, gave her a boost of pleasure in her loins.

"Woman, you don't know what you're doing to me," he groaned.

He lifted one hand to her right breast, making her mouth water. The fabric of her dress and her silk bra underneath were thin, and her nipple puckered to life at his touch.

Sam whistled low. "But I can feel what I'm doing to you, baby."

Breathing hard, he flicked his thumb over the large, tight nub. Her arms went slack at her sides and she gasped when he pinched it and held on for a few seconds. He tugged her nipple gently toward him as if he wanted to see if it would puncture right through her clothes.

Mariella traced the tight cords of his neck with her nose, disoriented with pleasure, as he cupped and lifted both of her breasts in his hands. Drawing a tortuous circle on each nipple with the pads of his thumbs, she became conscious of the dampness between her legs.

It was clear he meant to drive her crazy. She licked at his mouth, taking great care at stroking his lips with her tongue. Laying her cheek against his, she brought her hands around to his back and began to massage the thick muscles there. She felt his body relax into hers, and his low grunts echoed into her ear.

This is madness, she thought, as he kissed her again, even more urgently than before. And she tried to keep up with his heart-pounding, pent-up passion. Her body alert to the hardness of his, she clung to him as their tongues competed for purchase within each other's mouths. Through the haze of their kisses, she suddenly pushed him away.

"Hey, what's wr—?" Sam asked, eyes glazed over.

She shook her head wildly, turned toward the window and pulled at the front of her dress, hoping that was enough to force her nipples back to a normal state.

Before she was…before they were…

"Mom, I'm hungry. Are there any leftovers?"

Caught.

Mariella heard her son's approach before he even stepped into the room. As he did, he let out a small gasp of surprise and Sam whirled around.

"Coach, what are you doing here?"

She turned on the faucet and washed her hands. "He forgot his phone here earlier, so he came back to get it."

Sam glanced over, picking up her implied cue, and pulled his phone from his right pants pocket. "Got it now. See you both at the game tomorrow."

"See ya, Coach!" Josh said before heading straight to the refrigerator.

Mariella waited until Sam left, and then locked the kitchen door. Leaning against it, she exhaled and thanked God for two things: leftovers and the squeaky third step on the staircase.

Chapter 6

Mariella leaned back against the headrest as she waited for Josh, debating whether to shut off the holiday music on the radio.

When he was younger, they'd always sung Christmas carols together, mostly when driving back home to visit her parents. The practice continued even when he became a teenager. It seemed to be the one time of year where he let down his inhibitions.

The bike accident had changed him, and made him more wary and cautious of everything, including being himself.

She couldn't blame him for feeling that way. A serious accident could change one's perspective of the world. It was like having a broken heart, and trying to make sense of what happened, even as you were healing from it.

A little Bing Crosby could help, she mused. The radio station was playing the crooner's greatest hits, so she let it stay on. Maybe the music would encourage Josh to try on a more festive mood.

He was upset with her because he wanted to go with friends to the game, but she'd insisted on driving him. It was their tradition, she told him, and besides, this was his last "first" game of high school soccer. He could celebrate with his buddies afterward, while she tried to figure out how to remove Sam Kelly from her mind.

Or how to get him into her bed. That was far more interesting.

She shivered and decided against opening the window, as the weather had turned chilly. Early-evening temperatures were forecasted to dip down into the low fifties, perfect weather for a soccer game.

To beat the chill, Mariella had chosen a red turtleneck, topped with a cream angora vest, skinny black jeans and her favorite black ankle boots. She couldn't wait for Sam to see her outfit, although she knew he'd probably be totally focused on the game.

As he should, she thought, covering a yawn. He shouldn't be obsessing over almost getting caught in the heat of passion with the mother of one of his team members.

She thought about it enough for them both. With surprisingly little regret.

Sam awakened illicit, hidden desires she didn't know she was still capable of feeling. Most of her previous dates had never gotten that far because she wasn't that attracted to them. The ones that did ended badly, mostly due to the grief she felt over her husband's untimely death.

Lust was fast and fleeting, and much easier to justify, but Mariella often wondered if true love was worth it. The deeper past hurts were, the more pain an individual could potentially inflict on a tender heart. As a widow, Mariella knew loving someone didn't rule out the fact that one day you would still be alone.

She turned her head and looked out the window. Even if it was possible, she believed pursuing a relationship with Sam right now was the wrong move. The next few months would be stressful enough without trying to parse out her feelings for Sam. The college application process, plus her PTA duties, would take up her limited free time.

Her son was growing up, becoming a man. Maybe he could handle it if she had a relationship with his coach, but she didn't dare take a chance.

Josh got into the car and shoved in his bag. Mariella jumped in her seat, so lost in thought, she didn't even hear him open the door.

"A little warning next time, please! You scared me half to death." She started the ignition and backed out.

"Wake up, Mom. The first game hasn't even started."

He smirked, but his mood seemed brighter as if he'd forgotten about their earlier argument.

"I've never fallen asleep at any of your games."

She gripped the steering wheel with both hands. His excitement was palpable and she didn't want to ruin it. She wasn't going to ask if he was nervous; she had that one covered, too.

"Then how come you never know what's going on?"

She smiled at his good-natured ribbing. "I know enough to know when you win or lose, don't I? I'm there to support you. I don't need to completely understand every aspect of the game."

He ran his hands over his uniform shirt, straightened his shorts over his thighs and then pulled at his gold soccer socks.

"If Dad was alive, I bet he would know everything about soccer."

She didn't know why he was bringing up his father now, but his words made her heart hurt. A strand of hair had loosened from her casual updo, and she tucked it back into place to distract herself from the pain.

"I'm sorry, Josh," she said, glancing over quickly.

"Forget about it," he replied in a clipped tone. "It doesn't matter."

But she knew it did, and there was nothing she could do about it. By not dating because of a few sour experiences, she'd backed herself into a lonely corner, and denied Josh the chance to have a stepfather. It wasn't fair to him.

"Why don't you ever talk about Dad?"

Mariella sighed and turned off the radio. Bing Crosby couldn't get her out of this one.

"I guess because I'm afraid if I talk about him, you'll be sad."

Josh rolled his eyes. "Mom, I can handle it."

The years without Jamaal hadn't wiped away the memories of her first love.

"We married young. He enjoyed football, so I bet he would have felt the same about soccer, too. It just wasn't as popular back then. He was smart and kind and just a wonderful guy."

Josh frowned. "I don't remember him at all."

"You were only three when he died." She reached over and squeezed his hand. "Your dad would be so proud of you now. I just know he would be."

But Josh wasn't listening. Instead, he was pointing at the windshield. "Mom, here's the school."

Mariella had been so engrossed in the conversation she'd almost driven by it. She made a quick right turn and parked the car as close to the field as possible. From her space, she could see the bleachers were already three-quarters full with people waiting for the pregame show by the school's marching band.

"Good luck! I love you."

But Josh had already grabbed his bag and slammed the door. The harsh sound was a bookend to the conversation, and a painful fact.

Nothing she could ever say or do would ever make up for the hole in her son's heart, or the time missed with his father. It was something she would have to live with for the rest of her life, and so would he.

Sam stared openmouthed at the red numbers on the scoreboard, and then at the boy who was at fault. Josh had made a stupid mistake that had cost the team the home opener.

His other players hadn't done their best, either. He wanted to rage and scream with frustration, but he knew he couldn't do that to a bunch of emotionally sensitive kids, even though they sometimes acted like spoiled brats.

He shook his head, knowing if he took a time machine back to his teenage years, he'd probably acted the same way.

The pit in his stomach seemed to widen by the second as the sense of defeat settled in. Losing was never easy, and he'd expected it to feel the same as when he was playing pro.

But it didn't.

It felt worse, and as coach he knew he had to take some, or maybe even all, of the blame.

Sam glanced back at the bleachers. He'd spotted Mariella as soon as she arrived. She'd been happy and smiling, and he remembered the twinge of pleasure in his gut when she'd waved to him.

Now her hands covered her mouth in shock as the other parents glared at her with angry looks on their faces. They were likely the ones who tried to do his job from the stands, who railed against him, too. He felt a strange sort of solidarity with Mariella, even as he wondered what the hell had happened to her son.

The opposing team was cheering, high-fiving and celebrating their win while his players stood around no doubt wishing they could slink off the field.

The referee blew a whistle, bringing the Titans coach and players out of their funk.

Both teams hustled to form a line in the middle of the field, and then proceeded to slap hands hung low, in a show of sportsmanship no one on his team was feeling, including him.

But that was how the game was played. You won, you lost and you played the next one.

Sam blew his whistle. "Huddle up on the sidelines!"

When everyone had assembled and formed a misshapen circle, he took a deep breath and spoke, trying to portray a sense of confidence he really didn't feel.

"Team, this was a tough loss for all of us. But the only thing we can do is to learn from it and move on. And that's exactly what we're going to do."

"I'm sorry, Coach," Josh choked out, sounding as if he was holding back tears. "I don't know what happened out there."

"I know what happened. You lost us the game, you numb-nut!" Dante shouted. "If you had passed the ball to me, instead of trying to take the shot yourself and be the hero, we would have won. Instead, you're a loser."

"Stop it, Dante," Sam said sharply. "We're all losers today. We win as a team and we lose as a team."

He pointed at his players with his clipboard, making eye contact with each one.

"Each one of you has something you can improve on, and believe me, I'll be dissecting everyone's performance in this game like a Thanksgiving turkey."

Dante shook off the arms of his teammates and stood in front of Josh with his fists clenched.

"You're wrong, Coach. I'm not a loser. Not like this guy," Dante shrieked, poking Josh in the chest. "He doesn't even deserve to be on the team."

"Get out of my face, man!" Josh warned through clenched teeth. "Get out of my face!"

"Josh!"

Sam turned his head and saw Mariella cupping her hands over her mouth and screaming.

"Josh, don't!"

He turned back just in time to see Dante push Josh to the ground. Josh quickly rebounded and took a swing at his teammate. Like his goal, the punch missed, but that seemed to anger Dante even more.

Sam wedged himself between them. "Hey! Break it up!"

Despite his efforts, a second punch connected, and Sam heard cartilage crunch. Blood spurted from Josh's nose.

The two boys stepped around him and kept swinging at each other.

Sam couldn't believe this was happening.

When he was playing pro, fights in the stands among fans were commonplace, sometimes turning into dangerous melees. But on the field, no matter how he and his teammates felt about each other, they never would have dared to take a swing. They respected and supported each other. Besides, if they didn't, their coach would have had their balls in a sling.

"Break it up, I said!"

He grabbed them by their sweaty collars and pushed them onto the bench, one at each end.

"Take a seat, and learn to love it. You'll both be here for the next game. Maybe two."

Soon Dante was surrounded by a semicircle of friends.

Josh, on the other hand, was alone, his nose bleeding heavily.

Sam felt a twinge of pain in his heart for the kid. Someone should have been supporting him, but it looked like most of them had taken Dante's side, while the others looked like they just wanted to run away.

In his white button-down shirt and black dress pants, he felt more like a principal than a coach and he cursed inwardly. With one lousy loss and a lame fight, the dynamics of his team were broken. He would fix it, no matter what it took, but wished there were a playbook for coaching teenagers.

He flipped his gold paisley tie over his shoulder before stooping to examine Josh's injuries. He was bent over and looked like he was about to puke.

"Can we get some help over here?"

A medic, who had been in the process of packing up, grabbed his treatment bag and rushed over.

"Who's hurt?"

Sam got out of his way. "Um…the kid with the blood?"

"I know." The guy laughed. "I was just trying to lighten the mood."

Sam scowled, in no mood for jokes, and was about to tell the man just that when Mariella rushed over.

She knelt at her son's side, but turned back and spoke to Sam. "Oh, my God. I saw him getting hit. Is his nose broken?"

"I—I don't know," he stuttered, not liking the anger he saw in her eyes.

The medic wrapped a towel around an ice pack and gave it to Josh. "It doesn't appear to be, but I advise an X-ray just to be sure."

Josh lifted his head and snuffled. "Mom, chill out. I'm okay."

Leslie swooped in, and Sam was reminded of a vulture

circling the dead. He didn't remember seeing her in the stands, but he'd heard another mom saying that the woman rarely paid attention to the action on the field, preferring to people-watch and gossip instead.

"Dante, how about you? Are you okay?"

Mariella turned and glared over her shoulder at Leslie. "Of course he is," she said in a curt tone. "My son is the one who's hurt, or didn't you notice all the blood?"

Leslie folded her arms across her Titans T-shirt. "It was pretty clear from the stands that it was your son's fault."

Mariella stood up and the two women began to argue. It was clear from their rising voices that things could escalate even further if he didn't step in, once again.

He waved his hands in the air. "Time out, ladies. I've already had to break up one fight. I don't want to have to break up another."

Leslie flashed a quick smile. "I don't know about her, but you won't have any trouble with me, Coach. Can I collect my son now? My husband is waiting for me at home."

Sam nodded and wondered why the man hadn't shown up at the game. In fact, he'd never even met him.

More parents arrived to pick up their children, and from the looks on their faces, they weren't happy with him, either.

He backpedaled a few steps and clapped his hands to get the attention of his team.

"Everyone is excused except Josh, for obvious reasons. I'll email you guys a link to the footage of the game tomorrow morning. At practice on Monday, we'll talk about what happened and how we can *all* improve our game."

It didn't take long for everyone to gather their things and leave. He was surprised no other parent chewed his ear out, but he supposed he'd have a few emails waiting for him when he got home.

Mariella walked over to him. "Coach, can I talk to you?"

He raised an eyebrow at her professional tone. After what they'd shared last night, he'd expected something a little warmer.

With a sigh, he followed Mariella downfield, out of earshot of Josh and the medic, who, although he was annoying, had managed to stop the bleeding.

She whirled around. "Why did you let this happen?"

"What are you talking about?" Sam stepped in close, to further ensure nobody could hear them.

"I saw Dante push Josh first, and you did nothing to interfere."

"Josh got in his face, too," he added.

Her mouth dropped open. "It sounds like you're blaming him. This wasn't his fault. It's yours."

He raised his palms to stop her verbal assault, even though he knew she was right. "Everything happened so quickly. I stopped it as soon as I could."

"Not soon enough," she said, spitting out the words. "Now my son possibly has a broken nose. He's been through enough pain, Sam."

He tried to touch her elbow, but she pulled away.

"Leave me alone. I have to take Josh to the emergency room."

Mariella stalked away, and then without looking back, she and the medic helped her son off the field.

Watching them go, he realized that due to the fight, there was no way he could make Josh team captain, and Dante was no longer an option, either.

"That's going to go over well with the PTA moms," he muttered.

Sam walked back to the bench and his knee started to throb. He grimaced as he hefted his equipment bag over his shoulder. Somehow, he'd figure out a way to get back into Mariella's good graces. Turns out his old coach wasn't the only one who could put his balls in a sling.

Josh pressed the ice pack against his nose and snuffled. "I ruined everything."

His voice sounded like it was swathed in cotton, but the dejection in his tone hurt Mariella the most. It made her wish she could turn back time.

"Only your shirt," she joked. "I'll have to deploy my superhuman laundry skills to clean that thing."

"Mom!" he moaned, splaying his legs across the kitchen floor.

"I'm just kidding," she said, skirting around them. "You didn't ruin everything, Josh. You only made a mistake."

He leaned his head on his arm. "Doesn't matter. Everyone hates me."

Mariella rubbed her hands over her eyes, wishing she could just lie down, but not daring to yawn because she knew Josh would take offense. She needed coffee, strength and Sam, but right now she had none of those.

They had waited for over an hour in the emergency room at Bay Point Community Hospital before being seen by a doctor. Telling the intake coordinator she worked for the mayor had not gotten her any special consideration or preferential treatment. In fact, she wondered if it had lengthened her wait instead.

"Josh, eat."

A slice of pizza lay on his plate. He pushed it away. "I'm not hungry. I couldn't taste it anyway."

The X-rays had revealed his nose was intact. He would have some pain for several days and would be practically living with an ice pack on his nose for the next few hours.

"At least it's not broken," she reminded him.

Josh picked up the nose brace that would protect him while he was practicing and waved it in her face.

"You really expect me to wear this thing?"

"Yes," she said firmly. "Just think of it as battle gear."

"Battle is right." He snorted and then squinted in pain. "When I see Dante, I'm going to—"

She slapped her hand on the table so hard the salt and pepper shakers tipped over.

"You aren't going to do anything."

He slumped farther down in his chair. "If I had my old crew, they'd have my back. They'd do something."

The group of boys Josh grew up with was part of the reason why she moved. As they got older, many of them had gotten involved in petty crimes, and she didn't want Josh to fall in line with them.

"You've got *me*, Josh. You don't need them."

She knew the statement was futile, but she said the words anyway.

"Don't tell me what or who I need. We never should have moved here!"

He ran out of the room and up the stairs, making all the stairs creak with his stomping, not just the third one.

Mariella sank down into one of the kitchen chairs, her exhaustion complete. She started to reach for a piece of pizza, and then buried her face in her hands. Her stomach in knots, she wasn't hungry, either, and always felt this way after an argument with Josh.

Her son was crushed that he'd cost his team the game, and the nose injury just made things worse. She didn't think he would quit, but she didn't rule it out, either.

It would sure make things easier for her if he did.

She'd never have to see Sam again.

Sam sat in his SUV, across the street from Mariella's house, debating whether to get out and knock on the front door. This time he was certain he wouldn't get a warm welcome.

He swore silently. The twinkling lights on the manicured hedges reminded him of last night, when he'd first kissed Mariella. He didn't believe in letting arguments fester, but it was too late to apologize now.

He crooked his elbow against the door. So why was he here? He wasn't the kind of man to make a fool of himself for a woman. Or at least he didn't used to be.

The lights went out in the living room, and then a few minutes later one light went on in what he assumed was a bedroom upstairs. She was going to bed and he'd missed his opportunity, though she probably wouldn't forgive him anyway.

As he drove away, he wondered if Josh would be at practice on Monday, or if Mariella would force him to quit the team because of him. The season had gotten off to a rocky start, and if he couldn't see Mariella, at the very least on the sidelines, this was going to be the longest four months of his life.

Chapter 7

Mariella clicked the alarm on her car and took a deep breath, grateful to be out in the fresh air instead of in the office. She'd left work a few hours early to attend a meeting with the principal and athletic director about the condition of the soccer field.

Leslie had texted her earlier in the day. Mariella didn't ask, nor did she care, why she couldn't be at the meeting.

Whenever she thought about how the woman had blamed Josh for the altercation between their two sons, she seethed inside. The less she had to interact with Leslie, the better, though with the number of PTA events planned for the rest of the school year, she couldn't avoid her forever.

She headed toward the school entrance, ignoring the butterflies fluttering in the pit of her stomach. When she got there, she pressed a button by the door, gave her name and waited to be buzzed in.

Sam would be at the meeting, too. She hadn't seen or

heard from him since the first game, and there was another one that night. She'd hoped he would contact her and try to smooth things over, but he hadn't and that hurt more deeply than she'd expected.

Despite her feelings, she knew how to keep it civil. In her official capacity as PTA vice president, she supported his idea for artificial turf. Not for him, she vowed, but for Josh and the rest of the kids on the team, and those who would play after them.

It was just hard to stop hoping he could be more to her than just her son's soccer coach.

Mariella's nose wrinkled at the clean but strong scent of industrial bleach in the hallways. The churning in her stomach worsened with every step.

She reached the school office and the secretary led her down a hall to the conference room. Her breath caught in her throat when she saw Sam already there, waiting. The principal and athletic director had not arrived.

Sam stood as she entered the room, but she refused to meet his eyes. She felt like royalty when he pulled out the chair next to his, even though she figured he was just being polite again. He waited until she sat down, then followed suit. They declined the secretary's offer of something to drink, and she left the room.

Mariella stared at the white wall in front of her. Out of the corner of her eye, Sam seemed uncomfortable. He tugged at the collar of his Titans sweatshirt.

"The mayor let you out early, huh?"

"When Gregory found out about the meeting, he was all for it," she replied without a smile.

"Thank you for coming," Sam said quietly. "Leslie isn't here and I wasn't sure you were going to show up."

"It's my duty as PTA vice president."

He gave her a mock salute. "Is that the only reason you're here?"

She shot him a look. "Yes. Shouldn't it be?"

"I don't know. I only hoped that—"

"What?"

"That you wanted to see me, too."

She crossed her arms in a show of defiance.

"Do you think I've missed you?"

"My ego wants to say yes, but my heart isn't sure. Except for one thing," he added.

"What's that?"

The little smile on Sam's lips threatened to melt her defenses.

"That I've definitely missed you."

He reached a hand under the table and stroked her knee. "You look beautiful today."

Defenses melted.

She touched the lapel of her custom-made gray pantsuit, paired with a silk, sleeveless ivory tank. She'd spent a small fortune on the garment in Beverly Hills, so she only wore it for interviews or important meetings.

She batted his fingers away. "Shh. I hear voices."

Seconds later Principal Desmond Taylor, followed by Brian Putnam, the athletic director, entered the room.

They all shook hands, and the two men settled into their seats.

"Before we get started," Principal Taylor said, "I'd like to express my thanks to you, Sam, for traveling all the way from London to coach the boys' soccer team this season."

"It was an honor to be invited," Sam said. His regal voice sounded humble. "Five regular season game wins so far and only one loss shows just how talented the boys are."

Principal Taylor adjusted his navy blue tie and cleared

his throat. "We also appreciate the fact you took the position with no pay."

He turned to Mariella. "As a member of the PTA board, you are aware how budget-strapped we are. Because of Sam's generosity, the only cost to us is the rent on his apartment."

"Sam's experience and expertise are invaluable," Brian added. "He's taken a load of worry off my shoulders."

She heard through the grapevine that Brian had separated from his wife over the summer. He'd found her in bed with another man and was now even more consumed with his job than ever before.

Mariella nodded, and shot a quick smile at Sam.

"My son, Josh, has already learned so much from Coach Kelly. I do want to apologize for his involvement in the altercation after the first game."

"I appreciate that, and would expect the same from Leslie," Brian said. "Will she be joining us today?"

Mariella shook her head. "She declined the meeting."

"That's too bad."

Sam folded his hands on the table. "If you recall, Josh and Dante sat the bench during the second game, and I believe they learned a valuable lesson. Sportsmanship before, during and after a game is crucial to a winning team. Titans are supportive of each other, no matter what."

Principal Taylor smiled in agreement and then glanced at the clock on the wall. "Let's get started because I know Coach has a three-thirty start time for practice."

"Thank you." Sam cleared his throat. "Although I'll only be here a few months, I feel it's important to let you know the concerns I have about the soccer field."

"We keep it mowed and fertilized, don't we, Brian?"

"Yes," Sam interrupted, acknowledging Brian's nod.

"But there are ruts and bumps from years of abuse. It's simply not safe."

"He's right," Brian said. "Coach Lander took the lead on making sure the field was well cared for, but since his illness, the conditions have declined. I also pulled a report on the monies we've spent on maintaining the current field over the past three years."

He passed out copies to the group. "As you can see, costs have been growing exponentially. Currently, we don't have enough money in the budget to give the lawn appropriate care."

Mariella traced one of the graphs with her finger. "Hmm…costs go up even as conditions continue to deteriorate. Why is that?"

"I had another landscaper, a friend of mine, evaluate the field as a favor to me," Brian said. "His conclusion is that the drought conditions we've experienced over the past few years in our area have damaged the soil. Reseeding, season after season, has rarely worked and is a waste of money."

Sam jumped in, addressing Principal Taylor. "An uneven field can cause undue stress on the body, and even cause serious injury. It's like a ticking time bomb just waiting to go off." He handed the report back to his boss. "I recommend we replace the existing field with artificial turf as soon as possible."

"I agree with Coach," Brian said. "It's only a matter of time before someone gets hurt."

"What's all this going to cost?" Principal Taylor asked, staring hard at the two men.

Sam furrowed his brow. "I'm not sure, as I've only played on these fields for most of my professional career. I've never been involved in the transition over from grass to turf."

The principal steepled his fingers. "But I assume you'd

know what to look for in terms of quality? Good turf versus bad turf?"

"Of course." Sam nodded. "I'd be happy to help evaluate samples and choose a vendor."

"I can call other athletic directors and soccer coaches I know in the region and get recommendations," Brian offered. "This won't be a difficult task."

Principal Taylor leaned back in his chair and huffed out a breath. "But paying for it will be. We cannot ask taxpayers to do more than they are already."

"I did some research this weekend," Mariella piped in, and three heads swung toward hers. "There are grants available for this type of work. Once we select the vendor, I'd be happy to help write up our application."

"Oh? I didn't know you did that kind of work, Mariella," Principal Taylor said.

She fought the urge to roll her eyes, not believing he hadn't heard about her recent efforts for the betterment of Bay Point.

"So far, I've written two grant proposals for the city. You know the new steps going down to the beach over at Xebec Crossing? It was paid for by a grant I wrote, and I also worked on one for a new playground."

"You're hired!" the principal called out and everyone laughed.

"The PTA can help with fund-raising, too, to help defray the costs," she added.

They discussed a few more details as a group before adjourning a few minutes earlier than expected. After they all said goodbye, the athletic director and the principal stayed in the conference room for another meeting.

Mariella was silent until she and Sam were outside the school entrance.

"Good meeting, wasn't it? Sounds like you're going to get what you wanted."

"Not everything I want," he said. "I'll walk you to your car."

"You don't have to, Sam," she demurred. "I don't want you to be late."

"Start walking," he said, smiling, "and I won't be."

They moved toward the parking lot. She clasped her hands behind her back and glanced over at him. "I meant what I said back there. Josh loves soccer, but he seems to love it even more now that you are here."

He shrugged. "I'm not used to being a coach, and I'm still learning the best ways to deal with the kids and their parents. Both can be very temperamental."

Mariella smiled encouragingly. "You're doing fine, and like the principal said, everyone appreciates you."

"What about you? How do you feel about me?"

She looked straight ahead, her throat tightening. "I like you, just like any other parent would."

"That's not what I meant. How do you *feel* about me?"

"I don't know, Sam," she replied, bowing her head.

He stopped short just before they reached her vehicle. "Why don't we meet off the field and figure it out together?"

She turned toward him, wanting so badly for him to kiss her, but they were still on school property.

"Where and when?"

"I'll text you the details later tonight."

Mariella leaned against her car in disbelief. Sam Kelly had just asked her out on a date.

Sometimes it pays to eavesdrop.

Sam spread a thick blanket on the warm sand at Coquina Cove, and set a picnic basket on top.

As soon as he'd heard about the so-called private spot on Bay Point Beach from conversations at Ruby's Tasty Pastries, the local coffee shop, he knew he had to experience it himself.

Glancing up at the sky, he smiled. It was just after 8:00 p.m., and the sun was already half-set, with hues of red and orange mixing with the dark blue of twilight.

Perfect for seduction.

He had a sensual image of Mariella in his mind that was part of his fantasies for weeks. Knowing she would be in his arms soon made him throb with desire.

Since there was no address, he'd texted Mariella directions and the GPS coordinates. Even with that information, he'd had a little trouble locating the hideaway. Since she was a local, he hoped she'd have better luck, even though she said she'd never been to the cove before.

He peeked into the basket, borrowed from Maisie Barnell. The woman hadn't outright asked, but he could tell she wanted to know about the lucky lady at the picnic table. While he wouldn't fess up a name, he did tell her she was a Bay Pointer, to which Maisie enthusiastically applauded.

Sam could still feel the imprint of Maisie's wet kiss on his cheek. A thank-you for helping her with her mission to see all the single ladies in Bay Point married in her lifetime. A lofty goal, he thought, that some folks would even call crazy.

He didn't have the heart to tell Maisie that marriage wasn't on his mind, especially since his stay in Bay Point would be brief. Something told him the woman wouldn't have believed him anyway.

Though he didn't think his attitude was unusual, as he got older, being married seemed to be a must-have milestone. His mother griped he'd long since passed it.

His phone buzzed and he saw a text from Mariella,

letting him know she'd arrived. Access to the beach cove was gained by walking down a rocky path hidden among a dense grouping of trees. He made his way up easily, and took her hand to escort her.

Midway down, he became impatient and swept her up in his arms. Her white linen miniskirt flipped up briefly, almost exposing her underwear. He was pleased she'd dressed up for the occasion, but hoped she did it more for herself than for him.

"What do you think you're doing?" she demanded with a giggle, smoothing her skirt back down. "I can walk down on my own."

She looped her arms around his neck and nestled against him. He sighed inwardly at the feel of her warm bare legs against his arm.

"Yes, and the sun will have set by the time you get there," he breathed, already getting a hard-on.

"It's steep," she said innocently. "I was being cautious."

"And I'm just being gallant," he said, nudging her closer. "Besides, this will make up for me not picking you up at your door."

"I didn't want Josh to see you."

"I understand." He gave her a peck on the forehead. "You want me to be a secret. Your secret."

He stopped walking, leaned down and gave her long, slow kiss. When he lifted his lips, she gazed into his eyes.

"Is that so wrong?"

"Only when I want to shout to the world how beautiful you are."

The sound of Mariella's laugh rang in his ear. "Put me down, Sam."

"At your service, sweetheart."

Sam set her down with a gallant bow, admiring her red-painted toes and red leather sandals.

"Allow me to give you a tour of our dining facilities tonight." He spread his arms wide. "We have a gorgeous sunset, a warm blanket, LED candles and champagne."

She laughed and tucked her legs under her. "No turkey or pumpkin pie? It is almost Thanksgiving, you know."

He waggled his eyebrows and patted his flat belly.

"And ruin my figure? I have fruit and cheese instead."

After joining Mariella, he reached into the basket to get the food. "Any plans for the holiday?"

She took the wrap off a small bowl of grapes. "We're heading down to my parents' house in East Los Angeles. What about you?"

"I'm going to Cozumel to visit a former teammate of mine," he replied, snagging a piece of cheese from another plate. "He's living there with his wife and teaching soccer to underprivileged children."

Sam filled two plastic flutes with champagne while she took off her red leather sandals.

"So what are we celebrating?"

He raised his glass. "You. Me. The fact you're still talking to me."

"I know," she teased and took a sip. "Mmm…very bubbly."

He took a large swallow of his drink and his eyes grew serious. "After what happened at the first game, I really thought I'd never see Josh or you again."

"I admit I was really angry. But when we both calmed down, I realized how hard he's worked and how much he loves the game."

Sam nodded. "He's a talented kid. I'm just sorry I couldn't name him team captain. When I announced who it was today, he didn't seem too upset."

She put her hand on his knee. "You helped him get past his injury. That's what is most important. Did he tell you he's going to his last physical therapy appointment on Friday?"

"No, but that's terrific news."

"He has you to thank for it."

Sam finished his champagne. He lifted her hand and kissed her knuckles. "I'm sure his mother had more to do with it than me."

"Thanks. Being a single parent is hard. I've given up a lot for my son."

He nodded and drew her into his arms. "I can only imagine. Tonight is your night off. Don't think about anything."

"Hmm. You're making it too easy." She bit into a piece of cheese. "This is delicious."

Sam nuzzled his nose against her ear, enjoying the smell of her perfume.

"One other thing bothered me about that first game."

"What's that?"

"My good luck kiss didn't work," she pouted.

"Since we have another game tomorrow night, I guess we'll have to try again, won't we?"

Her good luck kiss may not have worked for that particular game, but since their time together, he'd thought of nothing else.

The fact that they'd almost been caught made it all the more exciting. If Josh had not interrupted them, he would have made love to her right there in her kitchen. On the counter, or on the floor, it didn't matter to him. He suspected that in the heat of the moment, she felt the same.

On Coquina Cove, tucked away against the cliff and shielded by its rocky overhang, they were safe from roving eyes. The location was remote and romantic, and there were no houses around as far as he could tell. But the possibility they might get caught only increased his desire for her.

"I have a confession of my own to make. I've wanted you since I saw you on the soccer field."

She finished her champagne and handed him the empty glass.

"I thought it was that day in the gift shop. Didn't my palm trees turn you on?"

"No. It was those tight little jogging pants you wore that drove me crazy." He trailed a finger down her cheek. "Or maybe it was you running around the track, always in sight, but out of reach, during the tryouts. I could barely concentrate on what I was doing. And then that night in your kitchen."

"Your accent was the deciding factor for me."

"Oh, really? Not my looks or my money?"

"No, just your voice," she teased.

His skin flushed hot when her eyes traveled up and down his body. "But I'm sure there are other parts of you that will turn me on, too."

There it was. The invitation he'd been waiting for, and needed to hear.

Sam smiled and held in a breath of relief. Her boldness seemed sincere, but he needed to ensure there was no misunderstanding on his part. He couldn't bear the thought of hurting her.

His feelings for this woman were growing complex, and would take time to sort through. Right now he just wanted to love her with his body, and worry about his heart later.

"Mariella. Are you sure?"

"Is this your British politeness at work?"

"No, I care about you. I want you to be comfortable with me, with us. I don't want you to re—"

She sat up, pressed two fingers against his lips. The tears in her eyes moved him to the core of his being.

"Shh… I won't regret this. Just kiss me, Sam, until I can't feel anything but you."

He gazed at her, giving her one last chance to push him away, but she leaned in close to him. It was dark now, and the candles made her skin glow even more beautifully.

Knotting his hand in the back of her long hair, he crushed her lips to his. There was nothing demure about the way she accepted his tongue in her mouth. She opened up as if she was starving and he was her sweet nectar, her only source of nutrients.

Her lips, so plump and eager, never departed from his as she cradled her arms possessively around his neck and pulled him closer while their kisses flourished and bloomed.

She murmured low in her throat while he tried to satiate her with warm, wet kisses that tumbled over and over. Mariella clasped his head between her hands, sucked on his bottom lip until he groaned, and he knew this time she needed more.

Laughing, she broke away, breathing heavily, and got up on her knees.

He lay down on the blanket and clasped his hands behind his head. He watched, fascinated, as her fingers slowly worked the pearl-like buttons on her red cashmere sweater. The garment slipped easily from her shoulders, revealing a red lacy bra.

Her belly, exposed and flat, served as an altar to her firm breasts, larger than he'd even imagined, as she bent over him. He remembered feeling them over her clothes in her kitchen, and his mouth began to water.

Unable to restrain himself, he propped himself up on one elbow and stole a quick lick. The fabric was rough, and her nipple bounced against his tongue, and before he could grab onto it with his mouth, she pushed him back down.

"Oh, baby, why?" he protested.

Giggling, she gave him no answer as she unsnapped the front of her bra, releasing her breasts to him. He gasped at the sight of her dark nipples, and even darker areolas, and then licked his lips. His hard-on grew in his black jeans, and he caught her eyes appraising the bulge.

She straddled him and undid the buttons of his black button-down shirt, her breasts swaying in the air above him. He hurriedly shrugged out of his shirt and tossed it to the side, then ran his hands over her curves while she moved her hips suggestively over his jeans.

He sucked in a breath as she kissed his bare skin, from his chest to the waistband of his jeans, nipples grazing a hot trail all the way to his belt buckle. With a hard swallow, he got rid of it and then his jeans and underwear, kicking them aside, too.

She let out a coo of delight as his penis sprang free, but before she could touch him, he hiked up her skirt and put his hands on her thighs. Moving higher, he touched her between her legs. Her underwear felt as lacy as her bra, but more important, the fabric was wet with her desire for him.

"Get rid of these," he grunted, and he folded his hands back behind his head to watch her strip.

Mariella shimmied out of her skirt and her underwear, and he let out a slow whistle. The wedge of hair between her legs was black and thick and wiry, just the way he liked it.

He took her hand and tugged her forward until she collapsed on him, straddling his abdomen once more.

She leaned back against his raised knees and Sam took his time exploring between her thighs. His fingers slipped easily through her silky moistness, until she threw her head back and moaned so deeply it made him tremble.

After retrieving a condom from his jeans and slipping it on, he laid her onto her back. Eyes glazed over, she reached for him hungrily. He gripped her pubic hair lightly and spread her wet flesh with his fingers, tickling her softness.

Mariella tried to touch herself, but he batted her hand away. So biting her lower lip, she spread her legs wider, teasing him with an open view. Licking his lips, he got in between her and leaned back on his haunches. She was glorious. He grabbed her hips and bent his head, wanting to taste her so badly, but knew he wouldn't be able to contain his need for her.

With a groan, Sam lurched over her, bracing his hands on either side of her head and penetrated her. He gritted his teeth and almost came instantly. She was as tight as a virgin, and her internal muscles locked onto his throbbing penis, boosting his pleasure.

As he moved inside her, Mariella's mouth pursed with pleasure and she dug her heels into the blanket. He caught one of her nipples between his lips and sucked slowly, leisurely, not willing to let go of one hardened tip for the other, even though he was sure it was just as tasty.

Before long he weakened and began to massage her other breast. She cried out as he propelled himself inside her deeper, but just as slowly, so she could feel each and every inch of him.

She thrashed her head so he caught it gently between his hands, her words unintelligible as she bucked her hips to meet his, daring him to thrust even deeper.

Releasing her hard, soaking-wet nipple, he laid his full weight upon her. Her breasts rubbed against him as they moved together. After a while he slowed down and stroked the hair away from her face. Tenderly, he kissed her neck, not quite believing he was here with this beautiful woman, who was about to be totally his.

She massaged the small of his back with the heel of her palm, a gesture that was unusual, but one he found incredibly erotic. Her feet slid up and down the backs of his legs in rhythm with his movements. With her head sandwiched lightly between his forearms, she whispered his name with every single plunge, as if she was claiming him.

Sam covered her mouth with his lips and increased his speed. Flesh slapped against flesh, the sound mixing with the waves crashing against the shore. It was a sound only for them, and he moved even faster, loving the music they were making.

Suddenly, he tore his lips away. His eyes roamed the starless sky.

Nearly overcome by the white-hot pleasure searing them both, his body stilled and he wasn't sure he could go on. He gulped in the salt-scented air, but it wasn't enough.

He wanted her.

She leaned up and kissed his chin, and he stared down at her, marveling that she was so beautifully his. He wanted to freeze his place deep inside her as he desperately tried to hold on to the last of his senses.

"Don't move, Mariella," he commanded. "I'm so close."

A bead of his sweat dropped down and trickled between her breasts. Without thinking, he licked it away and the tenuous hold he'd had disappeared.

"Me, too, Sam."

Her voice was husky. With the sexy way she lifted her hips, encouraging him to go on, he was willing to risk everything for her.

Deeper and deeper, he thrust himself into her until there seemed to be no end to the bold sensuality of her hands. Her nails sank into his skin, but he felt no pain, only that she needed him as much as he needed her. Faster and faster he moved until she began to writhe with torrid wails of pleasure he knew he would never forget.

Hot tears came to his eyes. With a loud gasp, he stilled and let go in spurts of heat. There was no time to consider the shock of his emotions, because as he cradled Mariella's face between his palms, he discovered she was crying, too.

Chapter 8

Mariella drove into the parking lot at the back of Relics and Rarities and pulled next to Sam's SUV. The large vehicle towered over her small hatchback, giving her the privacy she needed to do some last-minute primping.

Tonight was the first time she would be visiting Sam's apartment. They'd avoided meeting there because they didn't want to attract the attention of Mr. Wexler. But Sam had texted her earlier that the coast was clear, so they made a date.

She pulled out her compact, checked her reflection and liked what she saw there.

The past four weeks were some of the happiest ones in her entire life. Her feelings for Sam were evident in the glow of her cheeks and the spark in her eyes. He'd opened doors of her sexuality that had her body craving him day and night. More important, he'd opened her heart.

I'm in love.

But within her joy, sadness lurked.

Waiting to see him was the hardest part.

It seemed like she was *always* waiting.

Tonight was the last time she would see him alone for a few weeks. He planned on traveling back to London for the Christmas holiday.

A lump rose in her throat. He hadn't even left and she already missed him. Deep down, she admitted it was hard to accept her feelings for Sam because it meant one day soon, she would have to let him go.

"I'm being selfish," she said before closing her compact and tossing it back in her bag.

It was the truth, but she couldn't help it. She wanted Sam to stay in Bay Point and with her forever. And she bet if she asked every one of his team members, they would agree.

The Titans were having their best season in years. They'd won every game, except the home opener. But win or lose, each one was like a nail in her heart because as soon as the season was over, Sam would leave Bay Point and return to England permanently.

After every game she wanted to rush from the bleachers into his arms and give him a kiss of congratulations, but she had to wait until she could sneak away and see him.

Mariella dealt with the separation as best she could, and always sat in the same place on the bleachers so she'd be easy to pick out in the crowd.

He'd give her a nod and a slow tilt of a smile he'd saved just for her. The heat of his gaze would reach all the way up to the stands. When he turned back to the field, she could hardly breathe, let alone concentrate on the game.

Did he draw strength from those moments? She did, and knowing he wanted her made the waiting worth it.

With Sam in her life, she had even more confidence that she could do anything, be anything. Though he couldn't be her partner in public, she claimed him as her partner in her heart.

They never really talked about his eventual departure and she wondered why. Keeping quiet wouldn't make the truth go away. Maybe he was just as anxious about it as she.

Keeping their relationship a secret was difficult, too. She'd dreamed about making love under her Christmas tree and in her own bedroom, but that was impossible. They'd been back to the cove a few times, but stopped for fear of getting caught.

On date nights she told Josh she had a PTA meeting or was having dinner with friends. He would barely look up from his homework or computer. Lately, instead of gaming, he spent his time finalizing his college applications. He seemed glad to have some time to himself, but it didn't make lying to her son any easier.

Still, Mariella refused to feel guilty.

Every second spent with Sam was precious. Their time together was short, only a few more months, and she wanted to treasure every second of it.

They talked and texted as often as they could. Her day job and freelance grant-writing projects kept her busy enough so she wouldn't constantly obsess about him. In the past few weeks, she'd had several more meetings with Leslie and other members of the PTA regarding the new turf for the field. Several fund-raisers were being planned throughout the school year to raise monies not covered by the grant.

The danger of a damaged soccer field brought Josh's injury to her mind, as well as Sam's, and she knew she had to bring that project to a close as quickly as possible. She didn't want either of them to get reinjured.

Even as they got closer, Sam would never talk about how his injury happened. All he would say was he was still rehabbing, so she stopped asking. His knee was the only place on his body he didn't allow her to touch or kiss.

In general, he kept the details about his life in England to himself. One night he'd told her he found it difficult to trust women, based on his celebrity status and failed relationships. He asked for patience…and time.

Mariella choked out a harsh laugh. She got out her brush and stroked it quickly through her hair. Didn't he realize they didn't have any time? Maybe in his mind, their relationship was nothing more than a short-term fantasy.

A text from Sam popped up on her phone.

What are you waiting for?

She glanced up and saw him waving at her from his kitchen window. Smiling, she waved back, hurried out of the car and up the stairs.

He opened the door right away. "Something wrong with my outfit?"

Her eyes widened at the innocent smile on his face, which would be seared in her mind forever, not to mention his attire.

She burst out laughing and walked inside. After kicking the door closed behind her, she tossed her bag on the couch.

"You're wearing an apron?"

And it was one of the gaudiest ones she'd ever seen. Blueberries and cherries stuck in the middle of pine boughs splashed on a hot pink background, topped off with a white lace ruffled hem.

"I told you I was cooking tonight," he replied without batting an eye to her outburst.

Mariella molded her palms to his heavily muscled chest. "Where'd you get it?"

He winked and turned around. "Beach Bottom Gift Shop, where else?"

She gasped at the sight of his bare buttocks. *Was the man trying to drive her into a frenzy?*

"I should have known," Mariella groaned.

With a wicked grin, she lifted the hem up playfully for a peek. "I don't think it's meant to be worn like this."

"A culinary artiste like *moi* can't be distracted by clothes," he blustered.

His fake French accent sounded even funnier cloaked behind his British one.

"I must be free to move around."

"And free to love," she laughed, looping her arms around his neck. The slip of the L-word wasn't intentional, but she left it there to see what he would do.

Sam raised a brow. "Love?"

She nodded, her heart hammering in her chest as he paused a beat to gaze into her eyes.

"But dinner is almost ready," he protested mildly. "I made Jambalaya Gumbo."

Mariella peeked around Sam's shoulder. From where she was standing in the living room, she could see the kitchen, and the bedroom beyond.

She nestled her head against his chest and inhaled his masculine scent. The only thing she was hungry for was him.

"The food smells good, but you smell better. How about we cook up something ourselves? Then I can really show you how much I appreciate your artistry."

He locked the door, and then licked the deep vee of her neckline.

"Do you like my dress? It's black lace on top, black leather on the bottom. I bought it special for you."

Sam slipped his hands under her dress. "I do, but I'd rather see it on the floor."

His name caught in her throat as he suddenly cupped her bare ass. She had some surprises, too.

"Hmm," he said in a sexy tone. "Great minds think alike."

She squirmed with delight as he alternately squeezed and massaged her bare curves. Under the apron, his manhood poked and rolled against the leather. She resisted the urge to grab onto it and never let go.

"Then what are we waiting for?"

Sam ridged his teeth against the most sensitive spot on her neck until she moaned. Suddenly, he lifted her up and she clamped her legs around his hips. His penis landed between her legs, hot and long and throbbing.

He walked them both into the kitchen, and after pausing to turn off the stove, headed straight into the bedroom.

The wrought iron bed appeared to be an antique, and the room was so small it was wedged against the single window. The curtains were drawn and the only light came from the kitchen.

He tossed her down on the bed and slipped off her heels. The springs squeaked noisily as he laid his warm body on hers.

She folded her arms around his waist and started to untie his apron. "Let me help you take this silly thing off."

He reached behind and brought her arms to rest above her head, pinning them together with his one hand.

"No. This first," he whispered.

Mariella stiffened as his hot tongue dove into her mouth. Though he'd caught her by surprise with his need, soon her toes curled into the thin blanket and she was writhing beneath him.

She spread her legs, planted her heels into the blanket and dueled back, determined to prove she wanted him more. Her fingers grabbed onto the rails of the bed, wrists still bound by one of his hands.

It was the taste of him she couldn't get enough of and she stroked her tongue inside his mouth until they were both out of breath.

Sam released her wrists and stood. He lit two votive candles on the night table.

Mariella turned her face and stared, eyes wide, her fingers clinging loosely to the bed rails. His hard-on was as huge as the grin on his face.

She still had her dress on, but wished she didn't. She wanted him immediately.

"Ready to do the honors?"

He put his hands behind his head and gave a little shimmy, but his penis barely moved under the tent of his outlandish apron.

Mariella covered her face and laughed out loud at his antics. "I thought you'd never ask."

She sat up and moved slowly to the edge of the bed. Facing Sam, she parted her legs and put her feet on the worn wooden floor.

He'd joined in her laughter, but when he stared into her eyes, he knew things were about to get serious.

"Come here," she instructed.

Licking her lips, she felt exposed and raunchy as he moved toward her. The blanket felt cool and rough on her bare privates.

When he was mere inches from her face, she raised a hand and he stopped. She felt herself go wet at the pleasure waiting for her just beneath the whimsical cotton.

With a tip of one finger, she lifted the fabric, peeked underneath and wriggled slowly on the bed in anticipation.

He was harder than she'd ever seen. A long, dark slab of flesh with a hint of pink at the top. And it was all hers.

As if drawing aside a curtain, Mariella used the back of her hand to push the apron aside and over him. She watched, in fascination, a tiny drop of liquid emerge, glistening at the tip.

"Oh, my," she cooed. "Somebody's hungry."

His Adam's apple bobbed in his throat as she ran her hands up and down his back, taking her time to feel the corded muscles underneath.

"Starved," he rasped. "Take this damn thing off me."

Sam put one knee on the bed, and the mattress sank there with his weight. The one that was injured he put between her legs.

His hairy legs tickled her, and holding back a grin, she covered him up again.

"Not so fast."

Sam lifted his chin and groaned in frustration until she ducked her head under the apron. His deep sigh matched hers as she inhaled his clean, musky scent.

Under the cloak of the apron, she'd created a hot and secret place to pleasure him. His penis throbbed against her cheek as she slowly slid it against her flesh. He grunted as she sucked in his engorged length.

She grabbed onto his ass for leverage, closed her eyes and swirled her tongue around him. Once, and then a few times more.

His muscles tensed and he uncovered her head. The candles flickered, but didn't go out as he untied and threw the apron on the floor.

"I want to watch you. Loving me."

Sam's words rocked her to the core, but she could only nod. When she did, he pushed himself into her mouth a little deeper. Moaning, she accepted him and he threaded his hands into her hair.

"Baby," he breathed, elongating the word.

She tilted her eyes up and knew she had Sam under her complete control.

As she sucked and licked him, taking her time, the curtains billowed out. The briny scent of the Pacific filled the room, reminding her of Coquina Cove, where their love affair had started.

And she never wanted it to end.

He was heavy in her mouth, and her heart was thick with emotion as she tantalized him. Running her tongue and lips along his darkly veined flesh meant she was branding him as her own, even if he didn't realize it.

Mouth full with him, Mariella tentatively wriggled against his knee. She wanted to burst when her open, wet flesh made contact with a tight ridge of scars. Sam licked his lips in approval as she pleasured herself, too.

He also didn't mind when she cupped his testicles in one hand, gently manipulating them. It was the first time she'd done that, and he bucked forth, almost choking her.

She opened her mouth so she wouldn't hurt him, and he withdrew halfway before she pounced on him again.

With her every stroke, she could feel him restraining himself like a caged tiger. Her mouth felt bruised and wonderful, her nose heady with the scent of his raw desire.

"Mariella," he groaned when she took him between her lips again.

The urgency, the speed, the depth.

She held on. She controlled it all.

"Oh, God."

A guttural shout, and he gripped his hands around her face. Releasing his seed in her mouth, her head and his manhood moved as one. She held on, her arousal growing, and greedily sucked and swallowed, until he was spent.

Then she collapsed back onto the bed, the force of his climax flowing through her body. The breeze slid over her hot, swollen mouth. She slipped her dress up and over her head. Lifting her heels, she perched them on the edge of the mattress and waited quietly.

She cringed at the pop of Sam's knee as he knelt slowly on the floor in front of her, and hoped the pain in his knee wasn't bad.

He said nothing at first, but she felt his hands trembling as he began to massage her thighs.

She gasped and widened her eyes. To keep her arousal at bay, she tried to concentrate on the patterns the candle flames made on the ceiling in the dark room. But it seemed the harder she tried, the more aware she became of the way Sam was touching her.

"You're so beautiful, Mariella. My honeyed goddess."

His voice was hushed, almost in awe.

His face was close, his breath, hot waves.

And when his tongue swirled into her, it was reverent.

She arched her back from the mattress, and slowly down again to the center of his world, to his sweet tongue and gentle kisses.

Oh, how I love this man.

Mariella closed her eyes and succumbed to his ardor.

"No way we're done yet, baby."

His voice vibrated against her wet flesh, turning her on even more. She craned her head up to watch him, and when she did, he cupped her breasts.

Caressed her nipples.

One finger flicked them button-hard.

All while his tongue kept moving...darting...seeking.

He was watching her dissolve, driving her mad.

She laid her head back onto the bed. Now she was under his control, bucking her hips as he played with her, blotting away everything in her mind but him.

He moved and kissed the insides of her thighs, paying

close attention to the area where they curved down to her ass, tickling her with his lips to distraction.

"Sam, don't stop," she begged, craning her head up once more. "Go back. Love me again there, p-please."

The stark desire in his eyes brought another wave of emotion, threatening to take her places she wasn't sure he wanted to go. She wanted him to love her with his deepest self. Would that ever be possible?

He lowered his head, and she sank back down and squeezed her eyes shut. But even then she wasn't ready when he focused the tip of his tongue on her most sensitive part.

Mariella caught his head between her thighs and screeched out a moan, which soon became catlike and echoed through the room.

They were sounds she'd never made before.

A strange and primal ecstasy in their ears.

She grabbed at his hair, panting hard and at the brink. Sam gave her one final lick and wrested his head from the viselike grip of her legs.

Their bodies were slick with perspiration as he scrambled on top of her. His weight felt heavenly, possessing her. Immediately, Mariella clamped her legs around his waist, not wanting to be apart from him for a second.

Sam thrust once, his engorged thickness filling her up. He retreated almost completely and seconds later, impaled her again. And again.

"Mariella."

A short, satisfied gasp from his lips made her call out his name in ragged breaths, teased out by his ever-increasing pace.

She bit the side of his neck in shock at the force of her orgasm as they came together, moved fluidly together. His stubble scratched her jaw, and she licked his skin, tasting salt.

Mariella waited until he was snoring lightly before whispering in his ears, "I love you, Sam," hoping her words would somehow float through his dreams to nestle in his heart.

Hours later, after making love again and entwined in each other's arms, Sam struggled to stay awake. He stroked Mariella's long hair, tangled and messy around her shoulders. One lock was half-twisted around her left nipple, now softened.

He licked his lips. He knew how to make it hard again.

He also knew if he touched her again, he might never let her go home.

Sam cracked open one eye, spied the clock on the night table and sighed in frustration. It was ten o'clock. His woman had to leave very soon, and he knew she would be hurt if he fell asleep again.

His woman.

The words sounded nice tumbling around in his brain. He'd much rather Mariella stay with him, in his bed, all night, every night. But that was impossible.

Every night? He whispered the words to himself, not quite believing them. It was rare when he wanted a woman to stay with him more than a few hours, let alone all night.

I guess there's a first time for everything.

Losing sleep wouldn't be the only hazard to making love to Mariella every night. It would lift the barriers to getting emotionally close to her. He snuggled her tighter to him, knowing he was already halfway there now.

His chest heaved with anxiety. On second thought, maybe it was a blessing she had a kid.

Determined to keep both of their hearts safe from future hurt, he slid his arm away from her and swung his legs over the bed. He debated whether to ask her to join him in the shower.

"Sam, can I ask you something?"

He sucked in a breath. "Hmm?"

"How can you possibly leave me after what we just shared together?"

He turned around and stared into her eyes. "I'm leaving you? I think it's the other way around, honey, but you and I both know that's the way it has to be."

"You know what I mean," she said softly.

Yes, he knew and he didn't want to think about it.

He stood to face her and put two fingers on her lips. "Shh. Let's not ruin a wonderful evening by talking about this now."

"Why not?" She sat up and folded her arms, and he heard the impatience in her voice. "I'm tired of pretending that you going back to England isn't the elephant in the room. Don't you want to stay in America and be with me?"

Sam sat back onto the bed, his emotions mixed. For the first time in his life, he was falling in love with a woman and he didn't know what to do.

"It's not that simple."

Mariella reached for his hands, but her touch only worsened his anxiety.

"It is," she insisted. "Just. Stay."

He slipped away, leaned over and gave her a soft kiss.

"You don't understand the pressure I'm under right now. I can't just make a split-second decision. There are a lot of factors in play, including the fact that I'm just not sure I'm ready to give up on my professional soccer career yet."

"You wouldn't be giving up. You'd be doing something different."

Sam huffed out a breath. "But that's the problem. To

quit what I've worked so long to achieve...for good? To coach high school soccer permanently?"

"You act like it's been torture," she accused.

"It hasn't, and you know it," Sam said, reeling his surly tone back in. "I'm really enjoying it. The kids are playing better than ever. Best of all, we're winning."

She nuzzled her nose against his chin. "It's a testament to your coaching ability."

He felt a rush at her compliment, knowing she meant every word. Still, he didn't want her to get her hopes up.

"Maybe, but I'm not sure I've achieved all I have to accomplish in the pros."

Sam knew it was difficult for most people to fathom. There were many who dreamed of being in professional sports, not realizing the drive, effort and sheer determination it took to get there and stay there. His doctor had told him he could go back to playing pro next year, if he so desired.

He took her hand in his. "Can't we just enjoy what we have now, without worrying about tomorrow?"

Mariella sighed. "You're not giving me much of a choice, are you?"

"No, but I'll give you a lot more loving, if you'll let me." He brushed her hair away from her shoulders and trailed a finger down her chin.

"Stay a little longer, Mariella. Please? I promise I'll be the best Christmas present ever."

When Mariella smiled and took him back in her arms, Sam thought it was a fair compromise.

But even he couldn't have predicted that when she straddled his hips, took him inside her and rocked their bodies until both of their heads were banging against the headboard, that the cries of desperation would be his.

Chapter 9

The doors to the gym were thrown open wide, and teens eager for the Bay Point High Winter Dance were already trickling inside. The music was lively, a mix of Christmas music and pop tunes to get everyone in the mood for a good time.

Mariella tapped her toe in time with the music. She was in charge of one of the punch tables, and was busy arranging plastic cups in neat rows of ten. Every so often, she glanced up, hoping to see Sam.

Chaperones were expected to dress formally, and she was happy to oblige. She twisted a little so the skirt of her off-white, sleeveless, tea-length dress wrapped around her legs. In the spirit of the season, she'd pinned a large rhinestone snowflake brooch on one side.

Her ballet flats were cream-colored satin and they were so cute she found herself looking down at her feet more often than she probably should have.

More kids started to arrive so she carefully filled the cups with lemonade, trying not to spill any on the white linen tablecloths. They were on loan from Maisie Barnell, and she wanted to keep them as clean as possible.

Just as she finished, Sam walked in the door in a black tuxedo and polished black wingtip shoes.

All eyes, including hers, were on him.

He made a beeline for her table, pulling at his white starched collar. "Damn this tux. Did you ever think you'd be reliving the horrors of a high school dance?"

"Oh, it's not so bad." Mariella lowered her voice. "At least we're together."

He nodded, and his eyes roamed over her dress. The knowledge he knew every inch of her body made her quiver with desire. She still got chills thinking about the time they spent together in his apartment.

Mariella didn't know when there would be another night like that, but she was grateful just to be in Sam's presence.

Tomorrow he was returning to England to celebrate the holidays with his mother. When she asked him to chaperone the dance at the last minute, he accepted.

Strands of red and green streamers crisscrossed the gym ceiling, mimicking a glittery sky. Beautiful red and pink poinsettias, provided by Vanessa Langston, the mayor's wife, were clustered about the room and at the corners of each refreshment table.

The balsam fir trees trimmed in red and white lights with gold ribbons, donated by the city, were the prettiest decorations of all.

Mariella was proud of the efforts of her fellow PTA moms and other volunteers. She'd even been able to stomach spending time with Leslie, listening to her rattle off all the gifts she was expecting from her husband. Mariella suspected she bought them all for herself and just wrote his name on the tag, but didn't dare say that.

It was the holidays after all. Everyone had a right to indulge in a little make-believe.

She finished pouring the punch and stowed the empty containers under the table. "Let the madness begin."

"I think we both need a good luck kiss."

He touched her hand and she promptly snatched it away.

"Sam, have you lost your mind? We can't. Not here."

Mariella was grateful for the music blaring out over the deejay's speakers, which covered their conversation.

"Then I'll have to satisfy my hunger for you with a cookie."

He took one from the tray on the next table over before she could stop him.

"You're impossible," she scolded.

He took another bite and leaned over the table. "And you love me because of it."

She crossed her arms and glanced up into twinkling eyes, not sure how to respond. She hadn't told him how she felt, not directly. Had he heard her whispered devotions in his ear that night in his apartment? If so, how did that make him feel?

Shouts of laughter interrupted her thoughts and she saw that the gym was almost full. She waved at Josh, who had just arrived. He'd finally gotten the courage to ask Emily to accompany him to the dance.

Mariella shooed Sam away and he took his place near the doors.

Josh sauntered over to the table, with Emily holding on to one arm. The young woman wore her hair in a cute pixie style. Her brown eyes were shy, and Mariella was thankful her midnight-blue gown was equally modest.

She complimented the girl on her dress and then held

her arms out to her son for a hug. Surprisingly, Josh didn't shun her. Maybe he didn't want to embarrass himself or her in front of his date. Whatever the cause, she wasn't complaining.

Principal Taylor grabbed the deejay's microphone. "Teachers. Chaperones. Places, everyone!"

"Josh, we better go," Emily said, taking his hand and pulling him toward the dance floor.

"See you later, Mom."

Mariella blinked back her tears. It was bittersweet to watch her son growing up and away from her. The painful loss of her son to adulthood was tempered by her love affair with Sam. She tried not to think about it ending, too.

As the night wore on, in between filling countless punch cups, she watched Sam interacting with the students. Though the gym was crowded, it wasn't hard to keep an eye on him. He was so easygoing and handsome, many of them hovered around him, and she saw smiles all around.

Mariella wondered if Sam wanted any kids of his own. It occurred to her she'd never even thought to ask him, which intrigued and frightened her. There was a lot she didn't know about him, and time was running out to discover.

Children meant commitment, and though she loved Josh dearly, she wasn't sure she wanted another child. Next year he would be out of the house, and she would start the next phase of her life. What that would entail, she didn't know, but she hoped and prayed that Sam would be a part of it.

The dance went off without a hitch, but when it was over, it was over. The overhead lights were flipped on, and the chaperones and teachers hustled the kids out of the gym as quickly as they could, so that the cleanup crew could get started.

Leslie left soon after Principal Taylor, but nobody had

expected her to stay. She always delegated the most mundane tasks to Mariella and other PTA moms.

Mariella lost sight of Sam as she helped the team get the gym back in tip-top shape, and assumed he'd gone home.

Empty punch cups and cookie trays were dumped into the garbage. The tables and chairs were stowed away. A couple of people were wielding large brooms, with others following behind with dustpans. The maintenance crew would take care of the streamers over the holiday break.

The lights, ornaments and bows were removed and packed up. The next day a crew of PTA dads would take the decorations, along with the Christmas trees, to a few local churches and a nursing home.

The whole process took over an hour. As chair of the cleanup crew, Mariella noted that everything was done to her satisfaction and dismissed the group with her thanks.

She folded the linen tablecloths, which she would launder and iron before returning them to Maisie.

She shut off the overhead lights and closed one of the doors. The other one she left open as a reminder to the janitors to remove the garbage and take down the streamers.

She picked up the linens but they were too heavy to carry all at once, so she placed them near the door. It only took her a few minutes to walk to the teachers' lounge to get the large paper shopping bag she'd left there, so that it wouldn't get thrown away by mistake.

When she returned to the gym, Sam stepped out of the shadows.

Startled, she let the bag tumble to the floor.

"What are you doing here, Sam?" Her hand went to her chest. "You scared me half to death. I thought you were gone."

He was still in his tux, but the tie was loosened from around his neck and the top two buttons of his shirt were undone.

A slant of light coming from the deserted hallway formed a perpendicular triangle on the gym floor. He stepped into it as if it was a stage, and she could see his face more clearly. Dark shadows in the planes and something wicked in his hooded eyes.

"I couldn't leave without saying goodbye one more time."

His voice sounded haggard with need, and tears sprang to her eyes.

"Oh, Sam," she whispered. "I'm going to miss you so much."

He lifted his chin. "Come over here."

Mariella stepped over the bag and jumped into his waiting arms.

Holding her by the waist, he lifted her up and buried his face in her bosom. Wrapping her legs around him, she bit her lip as Sam pressed his mouth into her skin, dipped his tongue into her cleavage.

She felt the hard nudge of his erection against her belly as he walked them over to the gym wall. The cold concrete on her back was a sharp contrast to the heat and desire that quickly enveloped her.

His lips ravished her skin, kissing the tops of her breasts over and over. His hands molded her curves, bringing her as close as two clothed bodies could be. Her loins pulsed with need as his mouth trailed up her neck, and finally closed on her lips.

Mariella went limp and her legs slipped from his waist. As their tongues swirled together, she nearly slid down the wall until he pressed his body tightly against hers, pinning her in place.

"Sam, I—"

Her words caught in her throat when the palm of his hand scraped lightly against her breast, arousing her through the confines of her dress.

"No talking in the gym," he whispered against her mouth.

Mariella wanted to tell him she loved him, but she cleaved against him instead. His grasp around her waist was a life preserver, a heart breaker. She wanted to possess him, but she couldn't, and knew her deep emotions for him might never have the chance to be fully expressed.

She held back tears as he claimed her lips as his again. In him, in his kisses, she found heat and comfort, and a profound sense of belonging.

He broke the kiss, put his cheek against hers and began to sway.

"What are you doing?"

"Dancing," he replied, his voice hot against her ear.

She planted a kiss in the concave at the base of his neck. "But there's no music."

"You know we can make our own, my love."

My love?

Her heart melted anew at his endearment. With those words, she pushed aside any fears that what they were doing was wrong. Before she could ask him what he meant, his lips hungrily sought hers again, sending shivers down her spine.

Her heart began to pound at the thought of being with Sam right here, right now. Her desire for him blinded her to the dangerous possibilities, and also made her feel free. She wiggled suggestively against him, trying to imprint the memory of his length on her abdomen.

She moaned softly, knowing just continuing these motions would drive them both crazy, but was too absorbed by her love and her lust for him to care.

She had the vague sense that something was wrong, when she heard the low crackle of the shopping bag.

He seemed as oblivious to his surroundings as she was as he pinned her back against the wall and deepened his kiss, arousing her even more. She croaked out his name and tried to push him away, but his hold on her was too tight.

Suddenly they were bathed in light and she knew her life would never be the same.

"Well, well, well." Leslie sneered. "This is most inappropriate."

Sam's grip loosened and she slipped out of his arms, tripping over his feet in the process.

Mariella and Sam glanced at one another, both squinting under the glare, and then at Leslie.

"What are you doing here?" Mariella blinked.

She wondered how long the woman had been there, and how much she'd heard, or seen.

Leslie crossed her arms and gave her a shocked, incredulous look. "I should ask you the same thing. But I'm not stupid. I *saw* what you both are doing here."

Mariella rushed forth to try to explain, but Leslie stepped back and her heels almost got caught in the shopping bag.

She reached for it, but Leslie snatched it up and crushed it between her hands into a tight ball.

"Don't bother. Just get out."

Mariella's heart pounded with fear. She glanced over at Sam. His face was impassive and he appeared unperturbed by Leslie's appearance.

"You're not being fair," he said.

"I'm not being fair?" Leslie narrowed her eyes. "You don't have the right to say that to me. Not anymore. I came back to get Dante's uniform so I could launder it during the break, and what do I find?"

She pointed her finger at him. "You won't get away with this. Neither of you will."

"It's not Sam's fault."

Sam took a step forward. "I'm sorry, Mrs. Watkins."

Leslie backed away, like he was poison. "Apology not accepted. It's clear that you're not fit to coach our kids. I tried to give you the benefit of the doubt, but it appears everything I've read and heard about you is true. You're nothing but an international playboy."

Mariella shook her head, even though she'd once accused Sam of the same thing.

"Leslie, don't. Please. Let's talk about this."

She whirled toward Mariella and pointed at her. "And you were stupid enough to fall for it, for someone like him."

"We weren't hurting anyone, Mrs. Watkins."

"Oh no? I disagree, Coach Kelly. And so will Principal Taylor."

Mariella wanted to run into Sam's arms and defend him further, but she didn't dare. She took a deep breath to calm her racing heart.

"What are you going to do?"

"You both should have thought about that before you brought your little affair onto school grounds."

Leslie threw the crumpled up shopping bag at their feet and marched out of the gym.

Chapter 10

Mariella dug into a large bowl and started mixing the dough inside with her hands, ignoring the white cloud billowing around her elbows. She was up to her arms in flour, and in trouble. Tomorrow was Christmas and she really needed a miracle.

Ever since Leslie caught her and Sam kissing in the gym, she'd been baking. It was the only thing she could do to keep her from going mad as she waited for the phone call from the principal, demanding she resign from the PTA.

The resulting scandal could even cause Sam to lose his job, and she could also lose hers.

Over the past three years she'd worked so hard to build a reputation as a good mother and a loyal employee to the mayor. Every time she thought about what Gregory would think about her when he found out, she wanted to faint.

If Josh found out, he'd be so embarrassed he'd probably never want to go to school or speak to her again.

She was even scared to pick up the *Bay Point Courier* from her front steps, worried the headlines she might find would reveal her relationship with Sam in big, bold print.

But there were no calls and no headlines, which worried her even more.

Mariella sprinkled flour on a sheet of wax paper, and then slapped the dough on top, intending to knead all her frustration away. She'd tried humming, but even her favorite holiday carols on the radio couldn't lift her spirits.

That night they'd hustled out of the gym. Sam carried half of Maisie's linens, and she carried the other half because Leslie had completely destroyed the shopping bag.

He'd tried to reassure her and told her to stop worrying, and she accused him of being flippant about the situation. He did not try to kiss her. They got into their cars and drove their separate ways. Since then, she'd refused to talk to him and ignored all his text messages.

Perhaps it was a good thing he had gone home for the holidays; maybe then he'd realize that their relationship was doomed from the start.

Getting caught by Leslie was serious business, even if he didn't think so. The threat of a scandal was something he dealt with all the time when he was playing pro. He was used to it, which is why he could take it in stride. Mariella kneaded the dough until her fingers hurt and placed it in a bowl to rise.

"Hi, Mom."

"Josh!" she exclaimed, turning around. "Why didn't you use the back door?"

Sam peeked his head in the room, and then stepped inside. "Can I come in, too?"

"We wanted to surprise you. Coach Kelly stayed in town."

Mariella put one hand against her head, forgetting it was full of flour.

"You did?"

He gave her a casual nod. "Change of plans."

When she shot him a questioning glance, he raised a brow as if to say "we'll talk about it later."

Mariella walked over to the sink and washed her hands.

"Nice apron," he said in a humorous tone. "I would have brought mine, but I left it at home."

Her red apron had brown reindeer made of felt, prancing on a snowy hillside. Each one had a sequined green collar and tiny jingle bells. It was a tradition to wear it while she was doing any baking during the holidays.

She glanced back at him and her face heated at the admiring smile on his face. Whatever tension was between them disappeared, and the pleasurable memories rushed back. Images of their night in his apartment danced in her head.

She turned toward the window, hid a smile and did a couple of little twists.

Ring-a-ding-ding. Ring-a-ding-ding.

"Mom, please," Josh groaned and clapped his hands over his ears. "Not the bells."

She turned and caught Sam's eyes watching her body as she removed the apron and hung it across one of the kitchen chairs.

"C'mon. Where's your Christmas spirit, Josh?"

She smoothed her hands on her blue jeans in an attempt to stop them from shaking under Sam's gaze.

"It is almost Christmas, you know."

Josh unzipped his hoodie. "Duh, Mom. I was shopping for your present and my ride bailed on me. I just happened to run into Sam, and he gave me a ride home."

"I was shopping, too," Sam said, and she detected a mysterious twinkle in his eyes.

"Both of you waited till the last minute?"

"Of course," Sam said. "We're men, right, Josh?"

"Right! Mom, where's the wrapping paper? I want to wrap Emily's gift."

She thought a moment. "Upstairs in my bedroom."

Josh went into the refrigerator and grabbed a bottle of water. While his back was turned, Mariella gave Sam a shy smile.

"Okay," Josh said after a large swig. "I'm going to go wrap it up so I can take it over to her house later. She wants to put it under her tree."

"If I don't see you, have a merry Christmas, Josh."

He nodded. "You, too, and thanks for the ride."

Mariella waited until she heard Josh shut his bedroom door, and then motioned Sam to join her near the sink.

He went to her side immediately. "Heard anything?"

"No, and it's killing me." She folded her arms across her chest. "What about your boss? Did he say anything to you?"

"Right now Brian thinks I'm back in England. But I suppose he'd text if he wanted to fire me, which he won't, and neither will Principal Taylor."

"How can you be so sure?"

"Because the Titans are winning. Now, if we were losing, then I'd be in trouble."

"How can you think about winning now?" She shook her head at the smugness in his tone. "You think this is all a joke, don't you?"

He tried to embrace her, but she pushed him away.

"Don't, Sam."

She grabbed a wet dishrag and waved it at him. It was an effective weapon, and he stepped back.

"Why didn't you go home like you'd planned?"

He was quiet as she furiously wiped away the flour from the countertop. Normally, she was very accurate and neat with measuring, but not this time.

"I couldn't leave with things so up in the air."

She paused her hand. "Between us or with Leslie?"

"Both," he said with no hesitation.

"Very charitable of you."

Mariella tossed the dishrag into the sink and washed her hands again, not sure why she was in such an irascible mood.

She wanted him to get out.

She wanted him to stay.

He let out a sigh as he sat down, and when she opened her mouth to protest, her heart resisted.

Sam looked so relaxed sitting in her kitchen, so warm and cozy in his black long-sleeved T-shirt and gray stonewashed jeans, it was as if he belonged there all along.

"What's going to happen to us, Sam?"

"Nothing, I hope." He shrugged. "Maybe Leslie had a change of heart."

She rolled her eyes. "Ha. The woman doesn't have one."

Sam got up and put his arms around her waist, and she collapsed against him, no longer able to resist. Being away from him for two hours, let alone two days, was torture.

"Mariella. We weren't doing anything wrong."

"No, we were just doing it in the wrong place."

"I know," he admitted, nuzzling the top of her head with his nose. "This is all my fault. I couldn't resist you. That's why I couldn't leave you right now."

But what about later?

Mariella snuggled her cheek against his chest. She was glad he'd decided to stay in town. His apology meant he was finally taking her concerns seriously, which was a sign he cared about her. Too bad it was a little too late.

"Thanks, Sam. I appreciate it. I've been so worried about everything."

"You needn't be. I told you I would take care of you. Why haven't you returned my calls or text messages?"

She pulled away again. "Because I'm confused. Because no matter whether we got caught or not, this is wrong."

"What? Us?" he asked.

She nodded, and he pulled her to him and drew his knuckle along her jaw.

"No way. This is right. *We're* right."

Mariella shook her head and refused to meet his eyes. "Not anymore."

Releasing her, he leaned back against the counter. "What are you saying, Mariella?"

Her heart pounded in fear, but she couldn't stop now.

"I'm saying we're finished. It's been fun, but we're done."

Sam's eyes widened, and she was willing to bet this was the first time a woman had ever broken up with him, instead of the other way around.

He put his hands on her shoulders. "No. This will blow over, Mariella. For all we know, it already has."

"Maybe it hasn't." She closed her eyes, not wanting to see the defeated look on his face, refusing to be persuaded. "Maybe it hasn't even begun."

"Look at me, Mariella." He cradled her face in his hands and she opened her eyes again.

"I came back because we have something special and I want to protect it."

She fought back tears as the meaning behind his words stirred her emotions. It was true that they had something special. So special she'd fallen in love with him.

How was she going to cope without him in her life?

But she'd thought it over and firmly believed that even though it would be painful, ending the relationship was the best course of action.

There was nothing she could do about her feelings, except try to stem the tide of their passion before it crashed into her heart, breaking it and her life into a thousand pieces.

She was rooted in California, while he had traveled the world. Their paths were divergent from the start, by thousands of miles, crossing continents and time zones. They were able to bridge the divide with their bodies, connecting in beautiful, sensual ways, but that would never be enough for her.

"You'd better go now, Sam."

"Don't you want my Christmas gift first?"

She stared up at him. "You didn't have to get me anything."

He left and retrieved a shopping bag from the front entrance to the kitchen where he and Josh had entered. With great flourish, he took from it a rectangular box, gift-wrapped in shiny gold paper and white sequin ribbon, with a card stuck on top.

"Before you cut me loose forever, I want you to open this box up tonight and then decide." He lifted her chin with the pad of his thumb. "Promise me?"

She stared at the beautifully wrapped gift, terrified and curious at the same time, and tears sprang into her eyes.

"What's the point, Sam? You didn't leave for Christmas. So what? We both know you'll be gone by Easter. And now with Leslie potentially telling the world, or at least everyone in Bay Point about us, I don't see how this can solve anything."

She tried to hand the box back to him, but he refused to take it. Finally, she set it on the counter, for fear of dropping it, as he approached her.

Sam's lips were inches away from hers, hovering close enough for her to turn away, and yet she couldn't.

"Let's be candid, shall we, Mariella? You've fallen in love with me."

She couldn't deny the truth of his words.

When had he first known?

It didn't matter now. He did know, and she was blissfully relieved. Tears of happiness welled in her eyes as he peppered her nose with sensual, butterfly kisses.

"Isn't it only fair to give me one last chance to prove that I've fallen in love with you?"

Sam brushed his lips against her mouth, tapped her tongue with his, and she was gone. As their embrace deepened, they became lost in one another and neither heard the wooden stairs creak.

Sam parked his car, locked it and saw Mr. Wexler walking down the stairs from his apartment.

"Good evening, Sam. Your mother emailed me. Wanted me to check in on you. She said you were supposed to be back in London for Christmas."

He jingled his keys in his hand. "Yes, I canceled my flight and decided to stay here."

"You might want to let her know. She sounded worried."

"I left her several messages, but she tends to want proof. Hence, her sending you on a reconnaissance mission."

Wexler chuckled. "I know. She's tough. Questions every piece of Staffordshire I find for her. I'm surprised she doesn't fly over and pick them up herself."

Sam gasped half jokingly. "Don't even suggest it because she would."

"If you're going to be around on Christmas Day, Lucy's serves a nice brunch. Most shops and restaurants are closed."

"Thanks. I may check it out."

"I'd invite you for dinner at my place, but I tend to put

on some holiday music, heat up a frozen dinner and kick back with a cigar in front of a fireplace. I'm not quite Scrooge, but close."

"I'll be fine. I may head down to San Francisco for the day," he said, in an effort to get him off his back. He had other plans in mind.

"Been quiet upstairs lately. Everything all right?"

He gave the man an odd look. "Sure, why?"

"I don't have Wi-Fi at home, just here. Makes it easier at tax time. Sometimes I stay late and scour the internet for my latest treasures. My computer is in an office at the back of the shop, right under your bedroom." He flashed a wicked grin. "If it was a woman who changed your mind to stay home for the holidays, it sounds to me like she's a keeper."

Sam felt his face get hot. Wexler must have heard some of his and Mariella's most intimate moments.

He managed a grin. "You may be right, Wexler."

"Did I hear right, Sam? You're not coming back?"

"For the holidays, Niles." Sam stretched out on the couch. "Don't I even get a merry Christmas?"

He'd taken a cold shower, and gotten into his long flannel pajama pants. He crossed his bare feet at the ankles.

"Don't change the subject," his agent scolded.

"Why aren't you wearing an ugly sweater and opening gifts today?"

"Because I have no children and no life. Listen to this… 'Independent sources have confirmed Sam Kelly will be back in Brent for the holidays, and for good.'"

Sam chuckled as he brought up the front page of a popular London newspaper on his phone.

"You're quite the story spinner."

"I didn't create this one, mate. The team is really missing you, Sam."

His phone was on speaker. Sam was tempted to hit the off button, in his boldest bah-humbug move yet.

"So say the headlines."

"This time it's true."

His agent's voice sounded as if he was sitting across the table from him, not halfway around the world.

"Oh, yeah? How come I never hear from them and only from you?"

"Because they don't want to persuade you into coming back. They know that's my job."

"Judging by the scores, Team Valor seems to be doing fine without me."

"They'd be doing better with you and you know it."

Sam shrugged. "I don't know much of anything anymore."

"What's this? You sound like you've lost your best friend."

"No, only the best woman I've ever known."

"Uh-oh. What gives?"

"Why should I tell you? You're part of the problem," Sam complained, even though Niles was the most sought-after sports agent in soccer.

"I only put those stories out there to boost your playboy image. It got you tons of press."

With only one or two months off, Niles knew Sam didn't have the time for a serious relationship. Traveling allowed him to meet, and sometimes bed, women all over the world. Sam never wanted those trysts to last, nor could they. Not with his schedule.

He frowned. "I guess it served a purpose. But now that I'm over here, none of that matters. In fact, it's only hurting me."

And the woman I love.

The thought gave him pause.

Was he really truly ready to love Mariella?

"I may have gotten myself into some hot water over here."

"Eh? What do you mean?"

"I got caught kissing the mom of one of my players, by another mom, in the school gym."

Sam could almost hear the man rubbing his hands together and plotting.

"Sounds like headline material here in the UK. We appreciate a juicy scandal, especially when it involves a handsome, still single footballer, like you."

Still single.

His agent's words entered Sam's brain and stuck there, taunting him with the possibilities.

"I'm told the same is true here in Bay Point, but the mom who caught us hasn't done anything about what she saw. Yet."

"Good news, right?"

"No. The woman I was kissing won't see *me* again."

"So? You don't need to get tangled up in a relationship for more than one night anyway. It will only make it harder to leave."

"And who says I'm leaving?" Sam demanded.

"I do. Your doctor says you're recovered enough to play," Niles replied in a mild tone. "It's only a matter of time, and dollar signs."

Sam was too angry to even speak for a moment. He didn't want to even think that he was capable of leaving Mariella now, but deep down, he knew that he was.

"Forget the woman, whomever she is, and come back to England, Sam. If you won't do it for me, will you do it for your country?"

"Way to turn up the guilt, Niles. You're starting to sound exactly like my mother."

Chapter 11

Mariella had some difficulty keeping a straight face as she walked through the revolving doors of the Horizon Intercontinental Hotel around noon on Christmas day. After all the worry and angst that she wouldn't be able to see Sam during the holidays, she was on her way to his room.

The luxury hotel wasn't scheduled to open to the public until New Year's Eve. Most of the furniture was covered in drop cloths, but she didn't have to see it to know it was expensive. She'd overheard a conversation with the owner of the hotel and Mayor Langston several weeks ago. Though Gregory had no stake in the property, he'd wanted to ensure that it was as opulent as possible because he knew it would be a huge draw for tourists and A-list clientele.

Her heels tapped on the white marble floors and echoed throughout the large lobby. She bit her lip and approached the front desk, hoping the attendant wouldn't recognize her.

"I'm here to see Sam Kelly."

The man smiled and she inwardly sighed with relief. She'd never seen him around town before, and figured he was new to the area. If he thought it was strange she was wearing a raincoat on a sunny day, it didn't show on his face.

Mariella waited while he typed something in his computer. "He's in the penthouse suite."

He gave her a pass card and directions to the private elevator, and then picked up a phone call.

She made her way to the farthest corner of the lobby. As the doors closed, she tightened the belt of her raincoat, and her excitement grew as the elevator rose to the penthouse level.

Yesterday she'd waited until Josh went to bed to open Sam's gift. The handwritten card with the invitation to the hotel was a surprise, but nothing prepared her for the shock of what was inside the box.

That morning, after opening their gifts and having breakfast, Josh wanted to go to Emily's house to spend the day with her family. She was meeting him there that evening for dinner.

She stepped out of the elevator, which opened up directly in the hotel room, and looked around, feeling like a mysterious vixen in a classic film.

The place was enormous, as large as an apartment, and the furniture was plush and modern. The teak floors were polished to such a high gloss she took off her kitten heels for fear of slipping.

A slight breeze lifted her hair from where it fell softly around her shoulders. From her vantage point she could see a large balcony. The air was circulated in the room by several rustic-style ceiling fans.

Mariella stood in one place in her bare feet, not sure how far to proceed.

"Sam?"

There was only the faint sound of the ocean and then

she remembered his note. He'd been very explicit in his instructions.

Before she lost her nerve, she unlooped the thick belt of her raincoat and undid the buttons. Just before she slipped out of it completely, Sam walked into the room from an unseen entrance with a bottle of champagne, wearing nothing but a pair of black silk boxers.

She momentarily forgot to speak or where she was as she openly admired him. She thought she knew every cut of every dark bronze muscle, but in the light of the mid-morning, it was clear she had a lot more to explore.

"Hello, Sam."

"I guess you read my note last night."

He bowed and it made her tremble more as the raincoat slipped from her shoulders.

Sam walked toward her, whistling low. "And you opened my gift. I need to see it from all sides."

He made a twirling motion with his fingers and she spun around.

"Baby, you look so sexy, I wish I could do backflips."

She laughed and tossed her hair. "Now, that would make for some interesting positions."

"Don't give me any wicked ideas." He grinned and held up the bottle. "I was just getting ready to open this. Want some?"

"It's never too early for bubbly."

"Let's have it out on the patio."

Her eyes widened and she crossed her arms over her chest. "But, Sam, somebody will see us."

He pulled her close for a slow, sweet kiss. "It's completely private. Just like this suite."

She bit her lip to taste him. "What about my raincoat?"

"You won't be needing it."

He grinned and led her outside. "This is the only penthouse suite at this hotel. It has two bedrooms, two baths and a full kitchen but the patio is my favorite."

Enclosed on three sides by white stucco, with its yellow-striped canvas canopy and terra-cotta tile floor, it had a very Mediterranean feel. There was a hot tub and a small pool with crystal-blue water.

"How did you get this place?" she asked, marveling at the magnificent view of the Pacific Ocean.

"I heard through the grapevine that there were a few rooms available before the official grand opening next week, so I snagged the best one. Do you like it?"

"Sam, it's gorgeous."

She crossed her arms and pointed to the small fireplace recessed into the wall.

"That could come in handy."

The temperatures were in the midsixties, under partly cloudy skies, and she was wearing next to nothing.

His gaze roamed her body. "Are you cold?"

Mariella cast her eyes downward to her black strapless leather bustier laced with grommets. She slid one of her fingers beneath her bikini underwear, the palest of pinks, in sheer chiffon. The contrast was striking and sensual.

"What do you think?" she asked with a saucy grin.

He set the bottle down on a small table next to a hammock built for two. Two glasses were already there.

"If you want me to warm you up, just say the word."

"First, pour me some champagne. I want to talk."

Mariella gingerly lay down on the hammock and accepted a glass. "We don't have much time. I'm due for an early dinner at Josh's girlfriend's house and I obviously can't go dressed in this."

"Uh-huh," he said. "That's for my eyes only."

She held a breath as Sam joined her. When she was sure the hammock could hold them both, she took a sip of champagne and rested her head back on the blue chintz pillow that stretched across the top.

"Two words. Why leather?"

He turned his head to face hers. "You look good in it. I loved that dress you wore to my apartment that night. I ordered it online and it looks like I was right about the size. Aren't you proud of me?"

Mariella gave him a kiss on the nose. "Very. I love it. This is something I never would have bought for myself."

"Get used to it. You deserve every good thing there is in this world."

His comment should have made her feel warm inside, but she only felt a sense of dread.

Sam frowned. "What's wrong?"

She drank the rest of her champagne, needing the temporary comfort it provided her.

"I'm not sure why I'm here, Sam. I was the one who wanted to end everything between us."

"Do you still?"

Mariella looked up and saw that the awning was one of those types that could be retracted into the wall. It was cozy underneath, but talking about her feelings made her feel raw and exposed.

"I don't know. I guess that's what I'm here to find out. You already know I've fallen in love with you."

"I've sensed that for a while. And I wanted to prove to you that I feel the same way, but even if I do, I'm guessing that's not enough."

She threw one arm over her eyes and peeked at him from under it. "You do realize that we don't know that much about each other, right?"

"Yes. We don't have to hide anything from each other." Sam picked up her arm and placed it on her chest. "Ask me anything."

She turned to face him. "Do you miss playing soccer professionally?"

"There are some parts I miss, others I don't."

"I want to hear all the juicy details."

He looked at her pointedly. "No, you don't."

She smiled, caught. "You're right, I don't."

"I got tired of the high expectations, the paparazzi and, believe it or not, the constant chase of women." He paused to take a sip of his drink. "I wanted a break, so I took it."

"Would you have stopped playing if you hadn't gotten injured?"

She waited while he considered the question.

"Honestly, probably not. My priorities would have stayed the same—money, fame and everything that comes with it. The injury was literally the kick that I needed to jolt my thinking and my lifestyle."

She paused, not sure if she should ask again a question they'd already hashed out. "And are you going back?"

"To England?" At her nod, he said, "Nothing has changed. I just haven't decided whether I'll continue to play professionally or just coach."

Mariella kept her face impassive, even though inside, she felt defeated at his decisive tone.

She watched the edges of the canopy snap in the ocean breeze. There was truly no chance for her and Sam to be together, but she didn't want to leave him. Not yet anyway.

He turned to face her. "I'm sorry if that upsets you."

She searched his eyes and got the sense that he wished things could be different. "It doesn't because I know it's the truth."

She took a deep breath. "I never wanted anything from you. Maybe you thought I did because of who you are, but I didn't."

Though she was careful to keep her tone light, he hitched in a breath as if he'd been punched.

"I never thought that about you."

"Regardless, it's something I've always worried about with any man. I married young, and my former husband died very young."

"I'm sorry," he frowned, stroking her arm. "I'm sure that was difficult."

She inhaled the salty air and adjusted her body more comfortably in the hammock.

"Sometimes I wonder if it was harder for me or for my son. Raising him by myself hasn't been easy."

He squeezed her hand. "You did a fine job."

"I'm not fishing for compliments, just like I'm not in the market for a dad for my son. Josh was crushed when the few relationships I have had didn't work out."

Mariella closed her eyes, remembering all the questions Josh asked her when a man she was seeing suddenly wasn't around anymore. She'd answered as honestly as his maturity at the time could withstand, but always felt bad she couldn't give him the whole picture.

"You missed having someone in your life, haven't you?"

She shook her head fiercely against what she knew was true in her heart. "A woman gets lonely, and when that happens, she can make unwise decisions. I can't let that happen again. Anyway, I think Josh has lost faith that I can ever find a man."

He laid his hand on one side of her face, and now his eyes were as tender as his touch.

"Tell him you've found one."

For now.

"Merry Christmas, Sam."

Her voice caught in her throat and she fought back tears, but not her desire, as he pulled her on top of him and kissed her.

Chapter 12

Sam jiggled his car keys in the pocket of his navy blue track pants, eager to end the day. When practice was over, he was heading straight for the gym. He glanced back at the bleachers, hoping to see Mariella, but she wasn't among the few parents who'd stopped by to watch their sons play soccer.

An old year had rolled into a new one. Today was the first day back to school and everyone seemed to have the post-holiday blues, including him.

After that day at the Horizon, he'd contacted her a few times over the holidays, but she never returned his calls.

He didn't believe in resolutions, but he'd made up his mind about one thing. If Mariella could let him go so easily, then he could do the same thing.

Or at least he could try.

He'd had plenty of practice over the years, of sleeping with a woman one night, and not calling her the next.

But he thought he and Mariella had something special together, besides mind-blowing sex. When they'd made love, she'd clung to him like a grape on a vine. He'd done the same to her.

His desire had blinded him to her fear. Normally, he wouldn't have a problem with that, but for the first time in a long time, he was in love.

Whether she was afraid of moving away from Bay Point, or moving on with him or something else, he didn't know, but she couldn't avoid him forever.

They had a meeting tomorrow with three vendors for the artificial turf project. Though he would have no part of the final selection, the athletic director and the principal wanted him there to view the presentation and ask questions. He agreed, and was glad for something to help keep his mind off Mariella and the disaster he'd made of their relationship.

Then Brian reminded him that because Mariella was working on the grant, she would be attending, too.

He checked his watch and blew his whistle three times. "That's all for today, guys. See you tomorrow."

Sam still hadn't heard anything from Leslie or anyone else at the school. He figured if he hadn't heard anything by now, he never would, so he let it pass. If he worried about every scandal he'd been involved in, real or imagined, he'd have an ongoing need for prescription anxiety pills and an attorney.

The past week he'd lain awake many nights thinking about Mariella and the trouble his lack of judgment may have caused her, and himself. He hadn't meant to be so insensitive about the situation. Mariella wasn't as thick-skinned as he was. He'd had to be, with the press and the paparazzi constantly circling around him like vultures.

Sam was beginning to wonder if he'd brought this bit of

trouble on himself as a way to get out of a relationship that was starting to mean more than anything else in his life.

A couple of the parents approached. They wanted to know if the Titans had a chance at winning the regional championship. He assured them he'd do everything possible to ensure the team maintained its current winning streak. He reminded them that much of the burden lay on the players, working together as one unit, instead of as individuals.

He thanked them for their concern and walked around the field, gathering practice balls. Here and there, he stopped in front of a clump of dirt and tapped it down with the toe of his cleats.

There was one more month of the regular season, then the playoffs, and possibly the regional championships.

Knowing he would only see Mariella in the bleachers would make every game even more bittersweet.

He spotted Josh hanging out by the goal, practicing his kicks. He was a terrific kid and he didn't want him to get hurt by their indiscretions.

It was near dinnertime. He thought about asking Josh if he wanted to join him for a slice of pizza, but quickly dismissed the idea. If the other kids or parents heard about it, he might be accused of showing favoritism.

It was better to stay clear. He would have a hard time not pressing the boy for more information about Mariella. He'd skirt around for a bit, asking him what he got for Christmas, what he did during his time off, but eventually, he'd get around to asking about his mother.

For all he knew, she was off in the arms of another man, though his heart told him she wasn't.

"Coach?"

The kid must have moved like a phantom across the field. He hadn't even heard him approach.

Sam zipped up his Titans windbreaker and whirled around.

"Josh! I saw you doing some extra practice." He gave him a thumbs-up. "Great job!"

In Sam's mind, he was one of the hardest working players on the team. By the time practice ended, he was usually the sweatiest and the dirtiest. Two tell-tale signs.

"Yeah. I was actually just hanging around until everyone was gone."

He raised a brow. "What for?"

"I saw you."

Sam felt like a rock had just dropped into his stomach. "What are you talking about?"

"You and my mother."

Josh's upper lip was trembling, even though his voice was calm.

"Where? How?"

"In the kitchen. On Christmas Eve. I'd come back downstairs to ask my mom if I could invite you to have Christmas dinner with us at my girlfriend's house. I didn't know you were still there. And I saw you kissing her."

He scratched at his jaw. "Josh. I—I'm sorry. We never meant to hurt you."

"Never mind about me," he replied, his voice suddenly protective. "What do you want from her?"

He stepped closer. "You don't think I know what you are? How many women you've dated and then dropped? And I admired you for it? How stupid of me."

Sam's mind was all jammed up. He hated being backed into a corner. Mariella had probably read the same articles. She knew about his past, but she cared for him anyway. He wasn't going to reveal his true feelings to anyone before he even had a chance to say the words to Mariella.

"Josh, you have the wrong idea about me. Don't believe everything you read."

"Do you really care about her?"

"I never meant to hurt your mother, and I never meant to hurt you."

Sam's eyes widened with alarm. The boy was near tears.

"I don't believe you. But if you really mean that, and if you're really not the liar I think you are, then stay out of our lives."

Sam watched as Josh grabbed his bag and ran off the field, choking back sobs. It occurred to him Mariella was probably in the parking lot, waiting to pick up her son. He debated running after him, and upon reaching her car, telling her all that had happened. Posing the question to her, right then and there.

Did she really want to never see him again?

But he turned away and continued tapping down clumps of grass, afraid of the answer.

Mariella reviewed the documents in her hands one last time, took a deep breath and then entered the mayor's office. She saw Gregory's trademark black fedora on his desk and a fresh flower arrangement, personally created by his wife, Vanessa.

"I have the report you'd asked for."

Gregory looked up. "Thanks for staying late to help me prepare for my meeting tomorrow."

She covered her nose and sneezed. "No problem. It was my pleasure."

There was concern in his hazel eyes. "Allergies?"

"No. Just a little cold."

Gregory shook his head, as he flipped through the pages. "I feel responsible. I know you've been working hard on this over the past several weeks."

"That's very kind, but this project was my idea."

"I hope you at least set it aside during your vacation."

She didn't want to think about the holiday because Sam was wrapped up in it.

"Let me take you through the document."

At the mayor's nod, she proceeded. "All the city projects you have in mind are listed, from the most expensive to the least. If there is a grant available that could be used to pay some or all of the costs, I've noted the name in the right-hand column."

Mariella waited patiently as he scanned the report. After a few minutes he got up and put his hat on, and then took his coat out of the closet.

"It appears to be time well spent. This is excellent work, Mariella. I'll give it a closer read tomorrow."

He slipped her report into his briefcase. "Whatever we can do to keep costs low and not raise taxes, we should do it. And this will give us a good start."

Mariella touched the collar of her navy turtleneck sweater and looked down briefly at her ivory pencil skirt.

"Mayor, I was wondering if I could set up some time to talk to you. It's about my job here."

His eyes narrowed. "You're doing wonderfully. What's the problem?"

She forced a smile. "As you know, I now have a degree in economics. I've enjoyed being your assistant, but I'm looking for something more."

"Understandable," he said. "Do you have a position in mind?"

"No. And that's the problem. I've been looking at the internal job listings and I don't see anything so far."

Gregory set his briefcase on the conference table. "What are you interested in doing?"

"I've found I really like grant writing, so I'm hoping to transition into a similar role."

"You're good at it, too. Congratulations on securing funding for another local playground."

She smiled. "Thank you. I'm now working on a grant application for artificial turf at the high school."

"I heard. No offense to Coach Lander, but Sam has really turned the team around."

And turned my world upside down.

Her relationship with Sam was over; she didn't want that to deter her from her goals. She had to focus on her future.

"Yes, Josh has really improved."

"All better from the injury?"

"He was a little wobbly in the beginning of the season, but he's done with physical therapy and scoring lots of goals. By the way, thanks for adding my idea to your list."

"Bay Point is a very walkable and rideable community. I want our residents to feel safe no matter how they choose to travel on our streets."

She nodded. "My research showed that dedicated bike lanes should help cut down on accidents. They're very popular now, so grants are competitive, but I think we have a good shot."

He adjusted his hat and walked out of his office. She followed him and closed the door.

"Though I'd hate to lose you to someone else, let me think about another role for you. I'll also check to see if there are job openings available that were not posted online."

"Thank you, Mayor," she said, exhaling with relief that she likely wouldn't have to move for a better job.

Mariella got her red peacoat and purse. It was after six o'clock at night, and she was late getting home.

They rode the elevator to the first floor of City Hall. Outside on the steps, Gregory turned to her.

"By the way, do you think Sam might consider staying in Bay Point?"

She tilted her head. "I'm not sure. Why?"

"I was thinking of starting a special recreation commission to help drive more participation in sports for boys and girls. I think he'd be a good leader for it, and I was hoping you could influence him to stay."

"I don't think I could," she replied.

He gave her a brief smile. "Really? I could have sworn I saw the two of you picnicking at Coquina Cove a couple of months ago."

"It wasn't me, Mayor," she said, with a firm shake of her head.

They said goodbye and Mariella walked over to Lucy's Bar and Grille. She picked up a couple of jerk chicken sandwiches, pasta salad and two sweet teas for dinner.

A part of her hoped she would run into Sam, but he wasn't there. She'd see him tomorrow at the vendor meeting for the artificial turf project.

As she drove past Relics and Rarities, she almost pulled around to the back to drop by his apartment. But what would she say when she got there?

Being in love was like being on high alert all the time. She didn't want to feel the constant butterflies in her stomach anymore, or feel her heart burst every time she heard someone say his name.

He knew that she loved him, but she would never say the words. Soccer season would be over in six weeks or so, and then he'd be back on a plane to the UK. And where did that leave her?

Same place she was now. Alone and hungry, and not for sandwiches.

She'd made a huge mistake in getting involved with Sam. Instead of putting aside her desires, like she had for years, she'd allowed Sam to flatter and pursue her.

His sexy body, his British accent and his out-of-this-world lovemaking skills were the kryptonite that doomed her. The reins on her heart had been broken and thrown aside. She'd gone galloping after him into the sunset, but had somehow missed the happy ending.

Mariella pulled into her driveway and by habit, steeled herself for an argument. Josh had been pretty quiet over the past two weeks and she was starting to worry.

When she walked through the back door, she raised a brow, surprised to see him doing his homework at the kitchen table. Since freshman year, he'd always done his homework up in his room.

"Hey, I've got your favorite."

She set the bag of food down on the counter and noticed he was still in his uniform.

They had a rule where he was supposed to change as soon as he got home. Then he was to put his grass- and mud-stained uniform to presoak in the washing machine.

But by the strained look on his face, she decided that now wasn't the time to remind him.

"How was practice today?"

"It was okay. Coach and I talked."

She feigned indifference. "Oh? About what?"

"You."

"Me? Why?" she asked without turning around.

"I told him I saw you kissing him on Christmas Eve."

The pit in her stomach deepened. She didn't need to ask how. It was enough that he saw.

"I asked him if he cared about you."

Mariella slowly faced him. "What did he say?"

"He wouldn't respond. And then I told him to stay away from you."

She frowned and her heart sank. "You shouldn't have done that, Josh. It's really none of your business."

"Why? He doesn't want you," he yelled. "Haven't you read any of the blogs and articles about him?"

"I have, but sometimes people can change."

Josh shook his head stubbornly. "Not someone like him. All he cares about is winning and keeping his player image. He doesn't care about you."

She flinched at his mean tone and said, "You're going off to college soon. You'll have your own life. And I need mine."

There was a long pause and she thought the conversation was over.

"Are you in love with him?"

Josh immediately looked embarrassed, and Mariella knew it was a hard question for him to ask.

He slumped back in his chair. "I care about you, Mom. I want you to be happy, but it won't happen with him."

"No comment. Besides, it doesn't matter, Josh. There's nothing going on between us."

"What about if I quit the team? Then you wouldn't have to see him again," he offered.

"No! You'll see the season through to the end. And so will I. End of discussion."

She unwrapped the sandwiches and set the sweet teas on the table. "Now, let's eat. Before the food gets cold."

Chapter 13

Sam woke with a start. Something was vibrating against his head. He leaned up on one elbow, shoved his hand under his pillow and brought out his phone. The glow of the screen was a shock to his eyes as was the time.

It was well after midnight. The tent between his legs slowly subsided, and he knew he must have been dreaming about Mariella.

He collapsed against the pillow and put the phone to his ear.

"This better be good, Niles."

"You're making the milk in my coffee turn sour. Don't sound so glum, mate."

He shut his eyes to ward off the grogginess and his annoyance. "I'm not glum, I'm exhausted, and you've interrupted what would have been a very nice dream."

"It's early here, too. Talk nice, I've got you on speakerphone."

The voice on the other end was a little too cheerful.

"Why are you so chipper at this hour in the morning?"

Sam heard the loud purr of Niles's Siamese cat, Angie, and he felt himself start to relax at the sound.

"Because I'm about to change your whole life."

His ears perked up even more. Right now he could use a bit of good news.

"Oh yeah, how?"

"I've just brokered a deal to make you the new head coach of the Emeralds. Since you're not sure you want to play soccer again, this will give you some time to think it over."

"What happened to the current coach?"

"Have you been hiding under a rock?"

Sam slid a hand behind his head and tried to get comfortable again. "I've been trying to, but you keep on finding me."

Niles snorted, and Sam knew he was not amused.

"The man was jailed three weeks ago on suspicion of supplying performance-enhancing drugs to his team members."

"Hmm...so that's why they've been winning matches."

"Well, they're losing now," he said, gleefully. "Half the team has been suspended."

Sam sat up against the headboard, leaned over and turned on the lamp. No way he could go to sleep now.

"Okay. Talk to me."

"You'll have the opportunity to recruit players. Be your own boss. Best of all, little chance for injury."

"Travel would be the same, right?"

"Sure, but you always liked that. More places to go, more women to meet."

"More scandals for you to hash up," Sam interrupted.

Niles laughed. "No need for those when you're a coach. In fact, you want your image to stay as boring as possible."

"Actually, I was thinking of staying in Bay Point."

"Why?"

Yesterday Brian told him Coach Lander had decided to retire. If he wanted the head coach position permanently, it was his for the taking, but he wasn't ready to share the details with his agent.

"I don't know. Sun always shines, rarely any rain."

"Is it the weather or that woman?"

That woman.

Sam chuckled. "You always were a shrewd man."

"And I've got the perfect solution. Just bring her along for the ride."

"It's more serious than that, Niles. I love her."

Niles grunted. "Wow. That's the first time I've heard you say you love anything other than soccer."

"Anyway," Sam continued. "I don't think it will work, dragging her with me. She's a package deal. She's got a teenage kid who will be going to college in September."

"Ever hear of a gap year? Bring him along, too. I'm sure he'd love to travel Europe on your dime."

Sam shook his head. "All I can say is I'll think about it."

"That's all I can ask of you at one o'clock in the morning. You talk to your girl. In the meantime, I'll continue to hammer out the details."

"All right, say good-night, Niles."

"Make me proud, Sam."

"So I can make you more money, right?"

"Isn't that what life is all about?"

Sam hung up. He wasn't sure what life was about, but his definitely had less meaning without Mariella in it.

Later that same day

Mariella crossed her legs at her ankles, settling back on a park bench to wait, holding a tissue to her nose. She hugged her arms against her red peacoat, trying to stay warm and ease her anxiety.

After the vendor meeting yesterday, she had asked Leslie to meet her at the town square. She was tired of not knowing what the woman would do with the damning information she had about her and Sam.

Leslie was not someone she considered a friend, but she was a fellow advocate for the kids of Bay Point High. She was hoping to appeal to her kinder, gentler nature, if she even had one, to let it go. Maybe she already had, but Mariella needed confirmation.

She sneezed and smoothed imaginary wrinkles from her beige pants. Over the past several days, her cold had gotten worse.

Though she didn't know it, Leslie was holding her back from truly getting over Sam. In a way, she had not only caused the distance between them, she was also standing in the way of closing it.

Heels tapped on the pavement and she looked up and raised a brow as Leslie approached, carrying two paper cups. She didn't automatically assume the beverage was for her, since Leslie's husband's office was close by.

She rubbed the tissue against her nose. "Ah-choo!"

"Bless you," Leslie said, handing her one. "Herbal green tea with lemon and honey. You sounded as if you could have used this yesterday."

Mariella took it from her, touched at the gesture, but also wary of it.

"You noticed, huh?"

"I think everyone in the meeting did."

She balled up the tissue and stuck it in her purse.

"Thank you. This is very kind." Her voice had a croaking sound to it, to match her raspy throat.

"I need it more today, but at least I haven't started coughing yet."

She pried off the plastic lid and took a tentative sip of the hot drink, wondering how to begin what could be a difficult conversation.

"I guess I've been worrying myself sick."

Leslie, dressed in black skinny jeans and a white turtleneck sweater, sat down.

"Over what?" she asked, turning toward her.

As if you didn't know, Mariella thought.

She reached into her purse and pulled out a folded piece of paper. "This."

Leslie met her eyes, took it from her and read it quickly. "It's a resignation letter. You're stepping down from your post as PTA vice president?"

"I thought it would be the best thing, before you kicked me out anyway."

Mariella had thought long and hard about the decision, having devoted so much time to the organization. When Josh was a freshman, she was simply a member of the PTA, but in subsequent years she rose through the ranks, serving as secretary, treasurer and finally, vice president.

Leslie folded the paper and laid it aside. "I can't deny I've thought about it. Sam is incredibly hot, but what you guys did and where you did it was incredibly stupid. You're actually lucky I was the one who discovered you."

"I know and I can promise you it will never happen again."

Leslie nudged her in the side with her elbow.

"At least on school grounds, right?"

"Maybe never again, anywhere. I broke it off with him."

She raised a brow. "You did what?"

"I broke up with him."

"Because of me?"

Mariella thought she saw a little smile cross Leslie's mouth, which put her on guard once again.

She debated telling her Josh had caught them, too. Her son no longer trusted Sam had her best interests in mind, and she was inclined to agree with him. Sam was just a sexual thrill-seeker, and she was just along for the ride.

"I admit I was very concerned about what you'd do. That night you hinted there would be consequences, but you left it open as to what they would be."

"I was shocked, Mariella. I mean, wouldn't you be, if the roles were reversed?" Leslie curled a finger on her chin. "Come to think of it, I wouldn't mind being in Sam's arms."

Mariella looked at her sideways. "You're married, remember?"

She grinned innocently. "A woman can still fantasize, can't she?"

"Of course, just not about my man."

Leslie laughed, and then her expression turned solemn, and her voice quieted. "In some respects, I'm jealous of you, Mariella."

Her eyes widened. "Jealous of me? Why? You have a wonderful husband who loves and adores you."

"Ha!" Leslie snorted. "Loves, yes. Adores? Not so much. I wish he would look at me the way Sam looked at you."

"You're wrong about Sam." She covered her nose with a clean tissue and sneezed.

"Maybe you couldn't tell, but I could."

Mariella shrugged her shoulders. "He was sitting in the back of the room. I was at the front."

"Right. And I was sitting next to him. I could tell he was having a hard time maintaining his focus on the vendor presentations. His eyes kept on floating over to you."

"And I was doing my best to ignore him."

Leslie pointed a finger at her and laughed. "See, you did notice."

"Did anyone else see, too?" she asked with a tentative smile.

It felt like she and Leslie were two teenagers discussing a crush.

"No. Principal Taylor and Brian didn't have a clue. They were too busy waiting for the cost portion of the Power-Point decks."

"Do you think there are some people in town who know about us?"

"Not sure. Maybe. Are you surprised?"

Mariella nodded her head. "Yes, I am, actually."

"I may like to talk about people, but I'm not evil."

"Then why do it?"

Leslie looked her straight in the eye. "Because I'm nosy, and because I like comparing other people's lives to my own. Isn't that awful?"

When Mariella did not reply, Leslie continued. "Can I give you some advice?"

She nodded, and mentally braced herself.

"If he's in love with you, don't let that go. If you do, you'll never know where it leads."

Mariella held the tea in both hands. "You're not going to tell anyone, are you?"

Leslie shook her head. "No, but only because I remember how it used to be with my husband and me. How we couldn't keep our hands to ourselves. I took that time for granted, and now I'm paying for it."

She felt like hugging Leslie, but didn't want to make her uncomfortable.

"Thanks. I'd better get to work."

Both women stood, and Mariella's resignation letter

slipped to the ground. Leslie picked it up, tore it in half and handed the pieces to her.

"Here. I can't accept this. You helped the PTA raise more money in the three years you've been involved than anybody else. Nobody stretches a dollar like you do."

Mariella stared at her. "Are you sure?"

"Yeah. Think of it as a belated Christmas gift. Now get out of here before I change my mind."

This time Mariella did hug her, and Leslie hugged her back.

Sam pushed through the revolving door of City Hall, and entered the rotunda. There was a small cart set up inside that sold sandwiches and beverages, and a line had already formed.

The elderly security guard manning the desk near a bank of elevators appeared to be half-asleep.

"Excuse me."

Sam pressed the small dome-shaped bell. The man roused to attention.

"I'm sorry, I didn't mean to startle you."

"At my age, sometimes I need a jump start to the heart. This little bell helps. What can I do for you?"

Sam saw the man's name badge: Prentice.

"I'm looking for the mayor's office."

Rather than wait for Mariella to approach him, he was going to talk to her.

She can't ignore me here.

He had to know if she loved him, and then he could figure everything else out later.

Following his conversation with Niles, he wasn't able to go back to sleep. He'd lain in bed, thinking of what he should do. Stay in Bay Point or take the coaching position back home in England?

There were pros and cons to both.

Here in Bay Point, he could live in relative anonymity. In time, his star status would dwindle and he'd be considered a permanent resident of the community. Maybe someday, he might even apply to become a United States citizen.

He could also focus on the game he loved, and continue the work of building the Titan soccer team into the powerhouse he knew it could be.

But what about the woman he loved? If she didn't feel the same way, he wasn't sure he'd be able to live here, knowing he wasn't the one for her. His pride would be hurt, but even worse, he wasn't too confident his heart would recover as quickly as he would need it to.

A gnarled finger pointed at him. "Sign the book."

Sam scrawled his name. Prentice noted the day and time, and gave him a wide-eyed look.

"Hey, I've heard about you. You're the guy who's putting Bay Point soccer on the map."

"Thanks, but the kids do all the work," he said, refusing to take all the credit.

With his thumb, Prentice pushed the brim of his cap farther up on his head. It was khaki-green, which, other than the white shirt, was the same color as the rest of his uniform.

"I've been to a few games. I wish my legs and feet could move as fast as theirs, then maybe Miss Maisie wouldn't be able to catch me."

Sam smiled. "Now if you could direct me to the mayor's office?"

"Oh, yeah." The guard scratched his head. "Elevators behind me to the second floor. Then go down the hall and to the right."

A thought occurred to him. "Is Mariella back from lunch?"

"Yes," Prentice said, nodding. "But come to think of it, the mayor just left twenty minutes ago. You may want to come back later."

"Thanks for the tip, but I think Mariella will be able to help me with what I need."

Prentice shrugged. "Suit yourself."

Sam stopped at the food cart and afterward, went to the elevator. Exiting on the second floor, his sneakers screeched on the polished tile.

He rounded the corner and saw Mariella emerging from an office he assumed was the mayor's.

She closed the door, and he heard her sharp intake of breath. "Sam, what are you doing here?"

There was a sandwich on her desk, unwrapped, and also a big bouquet of flowers. He assumed the sandwich came from the cart downstairs, but who had given her the flowers?

"Mariella, I hate to bother you on your lunch hour, but I had to see you. Is there someplace we can talk privately?"

Her expression was wary. "Sure, we can go into the conference room. What's in the bag?"

"Chicken soup. In the vendor meeting, I noticed you weren't feeling well." He gave her a slow grin. "Plus, you've been pretty cold to me for the past couple of weeks. Since you wouldn't let me see you, I had to do something to warm you up."

"Ha-ha. Lower your voice."

"But there's no one around."

"That's what we thought the first time." She held a tissue to her nose and took the paper sack. "Thanks. I'm feeling better now."

"Because of me, or because of those flowers on your desk?" he asked, encouraged by the hint of a smile on her lips.

"Maybe a little bit of both. Follow me. The conference room is right down the hall."

When they entered the room, he asked her to close the door. "What I need to tell you is private." She hesitated and he said, "I won't bite, though I know you like it."

Mariella gave him an exasperated look and shut the door.

He slid out of his black jacket and settled into a chair. It took his entire strength not to grab her by the arm and pull her onto his lap.

"It's quiet here. Is that normal?"

"No. The mayor and a few of his aides left for a meeting a little while ago. There's some vacant land that belongs to the city in the southeast corner of Bay Point where he is considering building affordable townhomes."

"Hmm…keep me posted. I may or may not be in the market for one."

She did not sit down, and leaned against the table next to him. "So you're considering staying in Bay Point?"

"That depends on a lot of things."

She tilted her head and seemed to consider his statement, but didn't press him further. "Actually, I'm glad you stopped by."

At her words, hope of a reconciliation raced through him. He touched her hand and kept his voice light. "You've missed me as much as I've missed you. Is that it?"

Sam was relieved when she nodded. "I have missed you. A lot. But that doesn't change the facts."

"Which are?"

She took a deep breath. "Josh knows about us."

"Yes. He told me to stay away from you."

"And I told him I would," she replied. "I can't break a promise to my son."

Sam got up, cupped his hand behind her neck and brought her face to his.

"Then how about I break it for you?" he whispered. "I still want to be with you."

She pushed him away. "It's not that simple, Sam. I don't want Josh to get hurt. I dated a few men when he was younger and he got emotionally attached to one or two. When things didn't work out, he was devastated because the men weren't sincere."

She turned her back on him, and his heart sank as she walked over to the office window.

"There is no you and me anymore."

"It doesn't have to be that way, Mariella."

Her words had squelched his courage and now he wasn't sure if he was ready to tell her he loved her. Not until he found out where he stood.

He went to where she sat on the windowsill, and sat next to her.

"It's Leslie, isn't it? You're still worried about what she might do."

"She's not going to tell. She's going to keep what she saw under wraps. I arranged to meet with her this morning, before work. I was afraid she wasn't going to show up, but she did."

"What did she say?"

Mariella seemed to consider her next words. "She understood why it had happened."

Sam folded his arms in disbelief. "She empathized with us? And what was her reasoning?"

"Past experience, I gather, but she didn't offer any specifics."

"That's good, right? Good for us?"

"It is good, but good for us? I'm not sure."

He touched her arm. "I'm thinking about going back to England, once the season is over."

"I understand and I hope you make a decision soon.

Quite frankly, I'm tired of your flip-flopping. One minute you want to stay in Bay Point, the next minute you don't. I don't want to start anything again we can't finish."

"Just calm down and listen to me, okay? My agent is negotiating a deal for me, where I would coach another team instead of play professionally. I want you to come back home with me."

Her eyes widened. "And leave Josh?"

"He can take a gap year and come with us. Or there are plenty of wonderful universities in the United Kingdom."

"When would you have to start?"

"Right after the season ends."

She bit her lip. "I don't think I'm ready to move, let alone take our relationship to the next step. Don't hinge your decision on me."

"I'm not, but you're important to me. Too important to leave without taking a chance to ask if you'll go with me."

"Do what is in your heart."

He took her hands in his, brought them to his lips.

"You're in my heart."

Her eyes filled with tears. "I can't go with you, Sam."

"But I thought you were bored with your job. You said you were looking for something new and challenging. If you didn't find it, you would leave."

She slipped away and sat down at the table.

"Right, but I spoke with the mayor. He's looking to see if there's anything available."

Sam stood and leaned against the wall with a tight smile. "That's wonderful."

"But not necessarily for us," Mariella said, and he noticed the sad tone in her voice.

"Everywhere we turn there seems to be a brick wall."

He joined her at the table, just to be near her.

"There must be some way for us to break through, and I'm not going to stop until I find it."

Mariella turned to him. "Why is this so important to you?"

"Don't you know?"

She shook her head and he touched his lips to hers, his heart about to burst with emotion.

"You and I have a future together."

"I'm sorry, Sam. My future is here. I'm not leaving Bay Point."

He frowned and was about to continue to try to change her mind when his phone rang. He dug it out of his pocket, saw who it was, and his stomach clenched.

"Excuse me," he said, turning slightly in his seat.

"Where are you?" he said, keeping his eye on Mariella, who didn't look happy at the interruption.

He listened again and stood. "I'll be there as soon as I can."

"Who was it?" she asked, dabbing at her eyes with a tissue as he zipped up his jacket.

He slipped his phone into his pocket. "My mother. She's in town and wants me to pick her up at the airport."

Chapter 14

His mother, Ida Kelly, was a year short of sixty, but could pass for forty. She kept her body trim with daily walks around their neighborhood, and occasional visits from her personal trainer. Her skin was smooth, wrinkle-free and untarnished, like a newly minted copper penny, which was apropos because she cherished money. And had plenty of it.

Sam's father was a prosperous banker and had been adored by local townspeople for his willingness to lend his financial advice, especially if they hadn't qualified for a loan. He had done well for himself and his family over the years, and when he passed away, he'd made good on his promise to take care of his wife forever.

Ida had never worked, and would never have to as long as she lived. Sam thought she had too much time on her hands. Maybe if she had a real job, she wouldn't butt into his personal life.

He brought in the last of his mother's suitcases and put them at the base of the stairwell.

"Mariella, I really appreciate you letting Ida stay in your home. As you know, my place is too small."

She raised a brow as she counted the luggage. "Only nine? Are you sure she's only visiting and not moving in?"

"Knowing my mother, it's anyone's guess. But I'm praying it's just a visit."

And a short one, he thought, *for both of our sakes.*

Ida claimed she'd decided on the spur of the moment to take a two-week mini vacation in the States. He hoped her travels included another destination besides Bay Point.

His mother was mum on her plans, and when Ida wanted to keep a secret, no one could coax it out of her.

A piece of gossip, however? All she needed was a willing ear.

"I'm sorry I couldn't convince her to stay at the Horizon, and Maisie's was booked."

"She wants to treat my home like a bed-and-breakfast. She offered me money for her stay."

"Take it," he advised her. "If you refuse, you'll never hear the end of it, and nor will I."

He suspected the only reason his mother left her beloved country was to convince him to come back with her. But it was one of those situations where if he asked her, it would start a conversation—or an argument—that he didn't want to have, so it was better to stay quiet.

"It's no problem. The guest room is available and I'm happy to help as long as I can."

He understood Mariella's reluctance to commit to a time frame. She had a busy life with her son. The last game of the regular season was tomorrow and the playoffs would begin. And after that, who knew where life would lead either of them?

Sam wiped his hands on his navy blue athletic pants.

"Do you want me to bring the bags up to her room? It's right next to your room, right?"

He had an ulterior motive besides helping his mother. He had never seen Mariella's bedroom, and probably never would, so was hoping to get a peek inside. He wanted to feel close to her, and getting a look at where she laid her head down at night and got dressed in the morning would help.

"No, while you were outside and I showed her to her room, she told me to not disturb her. Don't worry about her suitcases. Josh will get those when he gets home."

Sam shrugged his shoulders. "Okay. I guess tell her to call me when she gets up."

He followed Mariella to the back door, noting the graceful sway in her walk. Was she purposefully trying to entice him when she knew he couldn't do anything about it?

"Sam? I hope you don't mind me asking, but why is she here? You never mentioned she'd be visiting."

"Because I didn't know. But if I had to guess she's here to check out where I've been living for the past few months and who I've been hanging out with."

Mariella got quiet. "We were doing a lot more than hanging out."

Sam took her hand in his. "I miss those times very much."

"I do, too," she admitted. "But they brought us more trouble than we needed. Now that it's over, both of our lives will be calmer now."

He opened the door, turned and kissed her on the top of her forehead.

"You mean boring and unexciting, right?"

"I mean calm," she replied firmly. "Let's just keep it that way, okay?"

Mariella gave him a playful shove and shut the door.

"Keep dreaming, babe," Sam muttered under his breath as he pulled out of the driveway.

He knew he would never stop dreaming about her.

Mariella stood by the oven and glanced over at the woman who had stayed with her for the past two weeks. She felt as though she was being watched and evaluated on everything. From her housekeeping and cooking skills to the way she raised her son.

Not outwardly, or in any way that would be obvious to anyone but her. Ida had been nothing but polite, sometimes overly so, but expected to be waited on hand and foot.

"More tea, Mrs. Kelly? I can boil some more hot water, if you'd like."

Ida shook her head. "Even though your tea-making skills have improved since I got here, I must decline."

Mariella frowned inwardly. Ida had a way of saying no that made her feel guilty. She rinsed the breakfast dishes and placed them in the dishwasher. Josh had already left for school and she had to get to work.

Today she had a couple of interviews at City Hall so she was wearing her gray pantsuit. She purchased a new white silk tank to go under it and added a small string of pearls.

Ida eased her thin frame out of her chair and placed the teacup and saucer on the counter. Dressed in taupe wool pants, an ivory blouse and a red cardigan sweater, Ida appeared comfortable and elegant.

"Henry is picking me up soon. We're going to San Francisco for the day."

She gave her a sideways smile. "How nice. Another buying trip?"

Sam's mother had purchased a number of antiques during her stay, some of which were stored in her garage, leaving little room for her own car.

Ida laughed, unaware at the offhanded dig, or maybe she just didn't care, Mariella surmised.

"No, just sightseeing today. But you never know, the best finds are the unexpected ones."

"True," she replied as she put the orange juice back into the refrigerator.

But she wasn't talking about antiques.

Meeting Sam had been completely unexpected. She hadn't known he would walk into the gift shop, and she certainly hadn't expected to fall in love with him.

"Will you be back in time for dinner?"

"Doubtful," Ida said.

Mariella frowned. Sam had been eating dinner with them every night, so she had gotten used to spending time with him, even if it was only as a friend.

At first, it was difficult as she was so used to cooking for just her and Josh. But as the days went on, she got better at it. It helped that Sam and his mother were appreciative and noticed her efforts.

Sometimes Sam picked up Ida and took her to breakfast. On those occasions, she was lucky enough to see him twice.

But most days, he would arrive with Josh after soccer practice, and soon after they would all have dinner together. It was almost like they were a family. She would miss that feeling when Ida went home, and Sam had no reason to come around.

Only because I won't let him, she said to herself, knowing the reason she was keeping her distance was because she wanted to lessen the pain she would feel once he was gone for good.

"Josh forgot his jacket again," Ida commented, pointing to where it was slung over a kitchen chair.

Like her, Josh initially wasn't pleased with their sudden guest. It had just been the two of them in the house for years, so having to share it with someone else was difficult for the both of them.

Oddly, Ida had grown on the boy, and they seemed to enjoy each other's company. She was teaching him how to play chess and he liked to ask her questions about her travels throughout Europe and Asia. He seemed enthralled with her stories.

She hung the forgotten garment on the coatrack in the mudroom. "Don't worry, Ida. He always keeps a second one in his locker."

"Has he decided on what college he will attend?"

Mariella shook her head. "Since he decided against early decision, we won't hear until March which ones have accepted him." She sighed heavily. "It's going to be so hard to let him go."

Ida leaned against the counter. "I know, but you will. That's what mums like us have to do. I remember the day when I dropped Sam off at university. I cried all the way home, and the next day, too. But then I realized that in order for Sam to grow into a man, he had to fill his own larder and flap his own wings."

"Was he always as independent as he is now?"

"Yes, after my husband died, he had to be. I know he felt an obligation to take care of me, as any good son would, but I do hope he knows I'd never want to be a burden to him."

Mariella raised a brow, surprised she had something in common with Ida.

"Sometimes I'm afraid Josh will feel the same way."

She filled her travel mug with coffee. "Maybe that's why you and he get along so well. You understand him in a way most adults would not."

Ida nodded, watching her. "I've learned how to let go. Something I think you may need to get better at."

"What do you mean?" she asked, not believing Ida one bit. If she had no problem letting go of her son, then why was she here watching his every move?

"I see the way you look at Sam when he is here for dinner. And I see the way Sam looks at you. You're both crazy about each other. The question is what are you going to do about it?"

Was this a trick? Mariella thought, looping her purse over her shoulder. She hoped Ida would take the hint. If she didn't leave soon, she would be late for work.

"Sam and I have agreed that pursuing a relationship would not be in the best interest of either of us."

Ida *tsk-tsked*. "I know you don't want my opinion, but I think you're both being naive."

Mariella nearly dropped her coffee, not expecting that kind of remark. "You do? Why?"

"I admit, when I first arrived I was extremely skeptical of you. I thought you would detract from his career. Plus, I didn't want Sam to be involved with someone who already had a teenage son."

"Just because I'm over thirty doesn't mean I can't have any more children, Ida," she huffed. "Women are waiting longer and longer to have kids these days."

"I know, and I realize now how selfish I was being. Josh is a wonderful young man. You've done a great job with him," Ida added.

"And what about Sam?" Mariella asked, curious now about her opinion.

"I know my son. Sam is obviously very fond of you, and if you're both smart, you won't ruin a chance for love that you both might not ever find again."

Mariella jangled her keys in her hand. "It sounds like you've just given your blessing. I appreciate it, but unfortunately, this is not your decision to make."

She sighed heavily. "I know, but a mother should have some say in who her son should be with, and I'm just saying I hope Sam chooses you."

Mariella smiled and hugged her. "Does your son know you're trying to be a matchmaker?"

Ida put her finger to her lips. "Let's just keep it our little secret."

Sam pressed Mariella's front doorbell and waited, flowers in hand. With a grimace he realized that given what he'd learned in the past few hours, he wasn't sure if there was anything to celebrate. Still, he'd gone home and put on a clean, white shirt and blue jeans, no tie, rather than stay in his coaching outfit, so he'd look his best for her.

If Mariella was home, he knew she would be alone. Last night at dinner, he'd overheard Josh reminding her he would be at a friend's house today. His mother was off on another buying trip with Henry Wexler.

She opened the door, her face beaming. It was going to be hard to pretend he didn't know the reason why.

"Hi, beautiful. These are for you."

He handed her a beautiful bouquet of deep pink tulips and yellow daffodils, and then gathered her into his arms.

She lowered her nose into the flowers. "Hmm...smells like spring. What's the special occasion?"

Her hair was tied up, and she was casually dressed in a white T-shirt with a gold sunflower on it and mustard-colored jeans.

"Time alone with you," he said, kissing her tenderly.

It had been beyond wonderful to be able to spend every night with her over the past two weeks. Even though she wasn't in his bed at the time, at least she was in his presence. He'd been able to look at her, talk with her, over her delicious meals. It felt like they were a real couple, and he liked it.

"That is always something to celebrate," she murmured against his lips. "I've missed you."

"I'm here now," he said, but his last word hung in the air, like the last apple on a tree.

Mariella nudged him away with her shoulder, pulled him inside and shut the door.

"You'll never believe what happened."

"Try me," he said, playing along.

He took the flowers, and got what Mariella called her "everyday" vase, from the cupboard underneath the kitchen sink. She used the modest plastic as a holding vessel until she had time to transfer and arrange the stems into one of the other vases she had scattered throughout her house.

"I ran into Maisie Barnell, and she told me your mother actually paid her for a room, but declined to sleep in it. She's had a room available this entire time."

This was news to him, and he was appalled. He shook his head. "And I believed her when she told me the B & B was full. I'm sorry, Mariella."

He finished filling the vase with water, and she began to drop the stems into it.

"Don't be. I admit, I was mad at first. I felt like I'd been duped. But she and Josh are getting along so well, I don't feel it's necessary to mention I know."

Sam wiped his hands on a towel. "That's why I—"

He stopped short of saying the word *love*, even though he knew deep down that was what he felt. But his feelings didn't matter now.

"That's why I admire you," he finished. "You have the ability to overlook the imposition of others. My mother did a very dishonest thing."

"We both know she just wanted to learn more about me, and what better way than to board in my home?"

He stayed quiet until she had put the last stem in the vase. "At least one thing good came out of it. We got to be together more."

"Yeah, under your mother's watchful eye."

His heart clenched and they shared a brief embrace.

"I also have some good news," Mariella continued, motioning to him to follow her into the living room.

He chanced draping his arm around her on the couch, grateful when she let it remain on her shoulders, and snuggled closer.

"As you know, I've been interviewing, but haven't had much luck. Gregory hinted yesterday that he was going to create a new role just for me. It will be centered around grant writing, as well as managing any new citywide project initiatives."

Sam leaned his head back, not sure if he should ruin the moment, but the words slipped out before he could cinch them in.

"I know. I heard."

She turned and braced her left shoulder against the sofa. "You did? How?"

"Gregory was at the flower shop when I picked up the bouquet I had ordered from Vanessa. He told me about his conversation with you, and asked me to convince you to take the job."

Her tone sounded confused. "I never told him or anyone else about our relationship. I wonder why he felt he had to tell you?"

Sam patted her knee, knowing how much she valued her privacy. "Don't blame the mayor. It was my fault. He asked me who the flowers were for, and I told him they were for you. Maybe he thought you told me at soccer practice. I'm sorry."

"That makes sense. He knows I'm working on the artificial turf project and that you've been involved in some of the meetings."

She gave him a tentative smile, but he could tell she was eager to hear more of their conversation.

"Did he say anything else?"

He nodded. "You're the hardest worker he's ever known, the most qualified and you've had more input on the revitalization of Bay Point than most people knew."

Mariella dropped her chin, and he saw liquid swimming in her eyes.

"Hey," he said, lifting her chin with the tip of one finger. "I thought this would make you happy. Why the tears?"

She swiped at her eyes with the back of her hand. "It just feels so nice to be recognized. Even though there were some aspects of my job I really didn't like, I always gave one hundred percent."

"I told the mayor I would use all my persuasive powers to convince you to take the position."

He planted a trail of kisses down her neck behind her ear, enjoying her scent. "How am I doing so far?"

"I already decided I would take it, Sam."

She giggled, pushing him away again. "Before you started kissing me."

He wanted to laugh, but he couldn't.

"Gregory also let me know he got approval from city council to create a recreation board and he wants me to lead it."

He saw hope flare in her eyes. "And what did you say?"

"I turned him down."

"Why, Sam?"

"I've faced the fact that I'll never play professional soccer again, not because I can't, but I do need a change. I accepted the coaching job in England."

He took her hands in his and stared into her eyes, but the light he saw in them before was gone, and all that remained was pain.

"The contract is signed, Mariella."

She frowned, slipping her hands away. "But I thought you were thinking about staying here. You've said as much many times over dinner. Or was that just a ploy to keep your mother, and me, on our toes?"

He shook his head. "I actually spoke to my agent a day or two after our conversation in the conference room. When you told me you were dead-set against moving to England and that you were tired of my indecision."

Her hurt tone wrenched at his heart, but the accusation behind it angered him a little. They'd spent time together, not enough for either of them, but he thought she knew him better than to insinuate his words were less than genuine.

"I don't play games, Mariella. It's true I was thinking about staying in Bay Point permanently. But like you, I would be making a mistake if I didn't pursue this chance. We each have a great career opportunity in front of us."

She slumped against the couch, clearly upset. "You and Josh have gotten much closer over the past several weeks. He's going to be so disappointed you're not staying in Bay Point."

He sat up and put his elbows on his knees. "This isn't about Josh, Mariella. It's about you. What are you feeling right now?"

"Me? I care about you, Sam. But I was always ready to say goodbye."

He turned toward her, ready to protest, but the strength behind her words had taken his resolve away.

She took a deep breath. "Every time I talk to my own

mom, I don't complain how hard it is to be a single mother, but somehow she hears it in my voice. She asks me 'when are you going to put yourself first?'"

Mariella leaned forward and put her hands over his.

"I've been putting myself dead last for years. Now this is my chance to start a new chapter in my life. Can you understand that?"

No matter how hard he tried, Sam knew it would be difficult to get her to change her mind. Though he felt Mariella belonged with him in England, it was clear she wanted to stay in Bay Point.

"It's my chance, too, Mariella."

She nodded, and he didn't wipe away the tears falling down her cheeks.

He stood, and wished he could get rid of the entire painful conversation. "Since we've both made up our minds, I guess there's nothing else to say, is there?"

Without another word, Sam walked out, regretting he opened up his heart to Mariella in the first place.

Chapter 15

Sam watched his mother as she moved about his apartment. She was returning to Great Britain, and though he loved her, he couldn't wait until he could resume some semblance of normalcy.

If normal is even possible, he thought. Without Mariella, his life would be emptier than it ever was before.

"A man with your money and credentials shouldn't be living in such a tiny hovel. I bet you can't wait to get back to your flat at home."

"Don't worry, Mum. Niles is taking care of everything."

He rubbed his eyes and then drank some water, tired of feeling so sluggish all the time. Losing Mariella was taking a toll, but he had to keep it together for his team, who would soon play the biggest game of the season.

"He better," Ida warned, shaking a finger. "Or he'll have me to answer to."

"I wouldn't wish that on anyone," Sam said, forcing a laugh.

"I won't get a chance to say a final goodbye to Josh and Mariella, so will you give them both my regards tomorrow?"

"Of course, and I'm sorry you won't be here to see the Titans in the first game of the playoffs."

"Me, too, but London is calling. Did you remember to have my bags and other items shipped yesterday?"

Sam grinned. At least with his mother, he always knew where he stood. "Yes, and it cost me a fortune."

"Better than dealing with it at the airport."

She patted his cheek like she used to do when he was a kid. "Don't look so sad. I will tell you the same thing I told her. It's clear you two belong together."

He wondered why Mariella didn't mention their woman-to-woman conversation. Another sign she was completely done with him and their relationship.

"A little too late. She's staying here. The mayor is going to give her the job she always wanted."

"If she doesn't have the man she always wanted," Ida said, "it's not going to be the same."

"Try telling her."

"I think I'll leave that up to you."

She zipped up her black leisure jacket, topped over a pair of tailored black wool pants, both of which she deemed her traveling clothes. "Lord, it's chilly in here, but I'm glad I got a chance to visit with you before I catch my flight."

He gave her a curious look, wondering why she seemed so happy. "Is that the only reason?"

"Perhaps." She giggled, eyes flashing. "By the way, you really got home late yesterday."

"I went to the bar and watched soccer till three a.m. How did you know?" Sam asked, suddenly suspicious.

"We heard you coming up the stairs around that time."

"We heard me?" he repeated.

"Yes, Mr. Wexler and I."

Now he'd heard everything. "Explain."

"Well, we were arguing about the antiquarian merits of the Staffordshire cat versus the Staffordshire dog, and one thing led to another and—"

He held up his hand and she giggled again. "I don't need the details, but I'm happy for you, Mum." He checked his watch. "We better get going. I don't want you to miss your flight."

They went downstairs and Sam paused by the back door of the antiques store.

"What about your boyfriend?" he asked with a wry smile.

"Henry will be in London in a few weeks, so I don't need to say goodbye, and neither do you."

Sam gave her a placating smile, but he was no fool.

Whatever he and Mariella had was over. There would be no more good luck kisses, no more sex on the beach and no more chances to show his love for her.

Sometimes a goodbye was meant to be forever.

"Josh, hurry up. We don't want to be late."

Tonight was the first playoff game of the post-season, and the Titans were favored to win. It was a home game, so they didn't have to travel, but she wanted to get there early so she could see Sam before the game started.

After today she would never see him again, unless she turned on the television.

Ida had returned to England yesterday. The house was quiet again, at least when she didn't have to yell for her son.

Mariella stood at the base of the stairs, waiting for Josh to emerge from his room, and had a flashback. Not long ago there was a chance Josh would never play soccer again, but he'd made a complete recovery. Sam had played a part by encouraging his love for the game and patiently coaching him through the trouble spots.

She slumped against the wall not knowing what she would say when she saw Sam tonight. She couldn't let him leave Bay Point being hurt or angry with her. It was important to convince him that the time they'd spent together had meant something to her. He had changed her life in a good way.

Josh bounded down the stairs. She never mentioned her conversation with Sam because she didn't want to upset him.

They went outside and got into the car. The game forecast called for cloudy skies and temperatures in the low fifties. In her indigo-blue skinny jeans, red scoop neck T-shirt and quilted jacket, she knew she would be warm for the ninety minutes of play.

She backed out of the driveway and headed toward the high school.

Josh turned in his seat. "What's going to happen to Sam when the season is over?"

Mariella shrugged and watched his smile disappear.

"He won't be hanging around anymore, right?"

She shook her head. "No. He's returning to London to become head coach of Emerald Premier."

"I wonder why he hasn't told the team."

She stole a glance at him. "He's probably waiting until after the playoffs to announce it."

Josh slumped against the seat, a look of defeat on his face. "I was kind of getting used to him working with me on soccer one-on-one."

"I know, and I've seen how your playing has improved."

"Plus, you've been happier, Mom."

She braked for a red light. "What are you trying to say, Josh?"

"If he makes you happy, Mom, I think you should be together. Don't you?"

"What are you doing, trying to get rid of me?"

Mariella eased the car forward and gave him a sideways glance. "You know, there was a time when you didn't want us together."

"I'm a kid, what do I know?" he joked. Then a look of regret crossed his face. "Mom, I'm sorry, but I was wrong about Sam."

Her mind was in a whirl as she pulled into the school parking lot, but she knew Josh deserved to know the whole story.

"There's a second part to Sam's new job. He wants me to come to England with him. I'd have to give up our home, my new job, and I'm not sure I'm willing to do that right now. More important, I'd also miss you too much."

"But, Mom, when will you have another chance to travel the world with someone you care about?"

Mariella turned off the ignition and opened her mouth to protest, but deep down she knew Josh was right.

"I'm going away to college. It's time for me to grow up and get used to being on my own. I can fly out to see you on college breaks."

He grabbed his bag, signifying the conversation must end soon. "I have my whole life ahead of me, and so do you. Give him a chance, Mom. Do what makes you happy."

The door slammed and sounded like a wake-up call. This time, her heart listened.

The season was officially over.

Mariella took a deep breath as she watched Sam finalize their late-night meal. She could not imagine what was going through his mind. The Titans had lost the game when the opposing team made a goal in the final minutes, and they would not be advancing in the playoffs.

Josh was out with the rest of the team, consoling themselves with burgers and shakes, and she was with the man she loved.

A man who would soon be leaving her.

She walked up to Sam and tapped on his shoulder. He turned around, the expression on his face cloaked in the dimness of the candlelit room.

"Thanks again for coming over," he said. "Under the circumstances, I wasn't sure if you would."

"I'm sorry about the loss tonight. I couldn't let you be alone."

"Josh played a good game. They all did." He glanced up at the ceiling, and then shook his head. "We almost had them, until that hat trick at the end."

"Easy come, easy go, right?" she said, trying to invoke some cheer into her voice.

He lowered his chin. "It's never easy to lose, Mariella."

"Do you regret taking the job?"

"No. I don't regret anything. Not anymore."

Sam searched her eyes, and she felt herself succumbing to the tender emotion she saw in them.

"Mariella, we've both chosen the path we think will work best for us."

"Even though it will tear us apart?" she asked.

He cupped her face in his hands, but didn't kiss her.

"You may not believe this, but I wish things didn't have to be this way."

She smiled, held back tears. "Your agent is too good at his job."

Sam laughed. "Niles is a pain in my rear sometimes, but he does try to get the best deal for me."

"No heart, all bankroll?"

"And damn the consequences," he added, crushing her to his muscular chest. "I felt bad about the way we ended things the other night."

"I'm glad I'm here," she said, playing with his tie as she looked into his eyes. "I couldn't stay away, Sam."

After a few moments, though she didn't really want to, she stepped away from his embrace.

"I also wanted to tell you how much meeting you has meant to Josh. He has really bloomed as a player, and as a person, under your tutelage."

He reached out and pressed his thumb against her lips, stirring her desire.

"And what about you?"

"I still can't kick a soccer ball." She poked him in the chest. "Because you never taught me."

Sam gave her a sad, mischievous smile and slapped his own hand. "I didn't? Shame on me."

Tears smarted in her eyes and she brushed them away. "Don't worry. You may still get the chance."

Smiling brightly, she continued, "I know you probably don't want to hear this right now, but I do have some good news. I heard earlier today that we got the grant for the new field."

He clapped his hands, but he still looked forlorn. "That's terrific. The Titans and the entire district will benefit from a new field. Too bad I won't be here to see the construction of it."

"They can send us pictures," she blurted before she lost her nerve.

Sam cupped his hand behind his ear. "Say again?"

Mariella took a deep breath. "I want to go with you to England, Sam. If you'll still have me."

He whooped loudly, gathered her into his arms and

twirled her about the room. Afterward, he gave her a long, passionate kiss.

"What made you change your mind? Wait, don't tell me yet." He started to pepper her neck with more kisses and she giggled and squirmed with happiness.

"Okay, now tell me."

When she finally had a chance to speak, her tone was serious. "That a life without you is no life at all."

"I was thinking the very same thing. Losing a soccer game is no match to losing the love of your life. That's why I was so sad tonight. The thought that we were about to share one last meal, that I'd never see you again. It was too much to bear."

She felt a tingle go down her spine at his words and she laid her cheek against his chest. She felt his heart beating, and knew she would always cherish him.

"Now, we never have to be apart."

He traced a finger along her jaw and then stroked his hand through her long hair. "I do have a bit of bad news, though."

Mariella's heart plummeted and she broke away. "What is it? Tell me! Though I'm not sure I can take it."

Her eyes widened with surprise when he dug into his pants pocket and brought out a large, glittery diamond ring.

"Remember when I ran into Josh at the mall on Christmas Eve? I had just come out of the jewelry store. I'd bought this, not knowing exactly what I would do with it at the time, especially since I had to guess your size. I'm hoping I got it right, but the jeweler said I could come back and get it resized any time at no extra charge."

She felt her excitement growing as she watched him fumble with, and then hold up the ring. He really appeared to be nervous, but his eyes were full of emotion.

"Mariella, I'm great at soccer, but I've never been good with words, and I'm just really worried about what you'll say."

"Just ask me, Sam," she begged, tears running down her cheeks.

As he got down on his good knee before her, she put her hands over her open mouth.

"Mariella, I love you more than any other woman I've ever known. Will you marry me?"

"Yes!"

He slipped the ring on her finger and it fit perfectly.

Mariella fell to her knees and wrapped her hands around his neck.

"I love you, Sam. Oh, I love you so much."

She gave the man of her dreams a tender kiss, grateful for his love, and a second chance at happiness.

Epilogue

"This is for you, Mr. and Mrs. Kelly."

The flight attendant set a small box tied with a red bow on the table in front of them, and left the couple alone.

Sam had hired a private jet to take them from Bay Point to London.

"It's from Ruby's!" Mariella exclaimed, pointing at the sticker with the shop's logo.

He kissed his new bride on her neck. "Well, open it up and see what it is."

She pushed him away playfully and untied the ribbon.

Inside there was a miniature wedding cake with white frosting, adorned with two silver bells.

"Oh, it's so beautiful!" Mariella exclaimed as she carefully lifted it out of the box.

He snapped a photo with her phone.

"There's a card, too," Mariella continued, smiling for the picture. "It says 'Congratulations on your wedding day.

Enjoy this little slice of home on your journey to your new life. Love, Leslie and the entire Bay Point High PTA.'"

"So, she does have a heart," Sam joked.

"Of course she does, and I hope her husband sees that once again someday."

"What do you mean?"

"Oh, it's nothing. Just remembering some girl talk."

Mariella sprung out of her seat. "I have something for you."

She disappeared into the sleeping compartment and emerged with a small box in her hand. She presented it to him, palms up. He kissed one and took the gift out of the other.

When he opened it, he felt his face flush warm with love. It was the smallest whistle he'd ever seen, in 14-karat gold on a gold chain.

"It's my wedding gift to you, and a congratulations for your new job."

"Thank you, Mariella. Put it on for me, please?"

She hung it around his neck and fastened the tiny clasp. When she was finished, he pulled her into his lap.

"I love it, and I love you. I'm sorry I had to be away for so long."

A week after proposing to her, Sam left for London to join the Emeralds as coach. He'd been gone for two months, traveling around Europe for games.

"I love you, too." She gave him a quick kiss on the lips. "Don't worry about the time away. It gave me time to get the house ready for renting. Josh had his senior prom, and then the whirlwind of graduation. Plus, I had a wedding to plan."

"The wedding was beautiful, wasn't it?"

"It was perfect," Mariella agreed.

She admired the bouquet of flowers that were an exact replica of the ones she'd carried down the aisle.

"Small and elaborate at the same time. I can't wait to see the feature on our nuptials in *Bay Point Living* magazine."

Josh, Emily, Leslie and her husband, Ida and Mr. Wexler attended. Mariella's parents did, too. Niles, Sam's agent, and a few of Sam's former teammates had also flown in for the nuptials.

Josh was going to spend a few weeks in Mexico with Emily and her family, while Ida and Mr. Wexler were headed up to Alaska on a buying trip. Sam didn't know what antiques they would find there, but maybe his mother would finally find love, and would be as happy as he was. After all, she had caught Mariella's bouquet.

"You're so gorgeous. I would have married you anywhere, even naked on the beach."

She laughed.

"Are you blushing?" Sam teased.

Mariella nodded. "Yes. I'm wondering why you're staring at me."

He winked. "To be honest, I was trying to figure out how I'm going to run interference on all those pearl buttons running down your back."

"It's easy. All you have to do is close your eyes."

"With pleasure."

She stood up, reached her arm behind her back and slipped down the zipper.

Sam heard the gown fall to the ground and hardened instantly.

"You can open up your eyes now."

He'd hardly been able to keep his hands off her on the limousine ride to the airport. But now, seeing his wife in a white lacy corset and garters with silk hose was unbelievably exciting.

"Love the high heels," he muttered hoarsely.

She ran her hands down the hose he'd brought her from London. "Mind if I keep them on?"

"Only if you'll let me take them off eventually."

He followed her into the sleeping compartment, shut

the door and tore down his pants as Mariella undid her hair from its updo style. It flowed around her shoulders and breasts in the most tantalizing way. He reached out to touch her, and she batted his hand away and began to slowly unbutton his shirt.

She laughed. "You forgot something."

He looked down and his tuxedo pants were puddled around his ankles, his shoes still on.

He couldn't bear to be away from her, even for a moment, he'd waited so long. So anxious to be with his bride, to feel her skin against his, and finally be one in body and heart, as a married couple.

"I'm trying, I'm trying."

He gritted his teeth, refusing to sit down on the bed and take off his shoes normally.

She snapped one of her garters against her thigh.

"Try faster."

Finally, he was free of his clothing. "Ready to join the mile-high club?"

She pressed her body to his and nodded. "But first, give me a kiss for good luck?"

He gathered her in his arms. "I've got something better in mind. How about a kiss that lasts forever?"

Winning Mariella's heart was only the first step, and he was thankful that he had his whole life to prove how much he loved her.

She pursed her lips against his ear. "What are we waiting for?"

"Not a thing."

He cradled her in his arms and laid her on the bed, his voice choked with emotion. "Not anymore."

* * * * *

CHRISTMAS WITH HER MILLIONAIRE BOSS

BARBARA WALLACE

For Peter and Andrew,
who put up with a stressed-out writer trying
to juggle too many balls at one time. You two
are awesome, and I couldn't ask for a better
husband and son.

CHAPTER ONE

OH, WHAT FRESH hell was this?

A pair of ten-foot nutcrackers smiled down at him with giant white grins that looked capable of snapping an entire chestnut tree in half—let alone a single nut. Welcome to Fryberg's Trains and Toys read the red-and-gold banner clutched in their wooden hands. Where It's Christmas All Year Round.

James Hammond shuddered at the thought.

He was the only one though, as scores of children dragged their parents by the hand past the nutcracker guards and toward the Bavarian castle ahead, their shouts of delight echoing in the crisp Michigan air. One little girl, winter coat flapping in the wind, narrowly missed running into him, so distracted was she by the sight ahead of her.

"I see Santa's Castle," he heard her squeal.

Only if Santa lived in northern Germany and liked bratwurst. The towering stucco building, with its holly-draped ramparts and snow-covered turrets looked like something out of a Grimm's fairy tale. No one would ever accuse Ned Fryberg of pedaling a false reality, that's for sure. It was obvious that his fantasy was completely unattainable in real life. Unlike the nostalgic, homespun malarkey Hammond's Toys sold to the public.

The popularity of both went to show that people loved

their Christmas fantasies, and they were willing to shovel boatloads of money in order to keep them alive.

James didn't understand it, but he was more than glad to help them part with their cash. He was good at it too. Some men gardened and grew vegetables. James grew his family's net worth. And Fryberg's Toys, and its awful Christmas village—a town so named for the Fryberg family—was going to help him grow it even larger.

"Excuse me, sir, but the line for Santa's trolley starts back there." A man wearing a red toy soldier's jacket and black busby pointed behind James's shoulder. In an attempt to control traffic flow, the store provided transportation around the grounds via a garishly colored "toy" train. "Trains leave every five minutes. You won't have too long a wait.

"Or y-you could w-w-walk," he added.

People always tended to stammer whenever James looked them in the eye. Didn't matter if he was trying to be intimidating or not. They simply did. Maybe because, as his mother once told him, he had the same cold, dead eyes as his father. He'd spent much of his youth vainly trying to erase the similarity. Now that he was an adult, he'd grown not to accept his intimidating glower, but embrace it. Same way he embraced all his other unapproachable qualities.

"That depends," he replied. "Which mode is more efficient?"

"Th-that would depend upon on how fast a walker you are. The car makes a couple of stops beforehand, so someone with…with long legs…" The soldier, or whatever he was supposed to be, let the sentence trail off.

"Then walking it is. Thank you."

Adjusting his charcoal-gray scarf tighter around his neck, James turned and continued on his way, along the path to Fryberg's Christmas Castle. The faster he got to his meeting with Belinda Fryberg, the sooner he could lock in his sale and fly back to Boston. At least there, he only had to deal with Christmas one day of the year.

"What did you say?"

"I said, your Christmas Castle has a few years of viability in it, at best."

Noelle hated the new boss.

She'd decided he rubbed her the wrong way when he glided into Belinda's office like a cashmere-wearing shark. She disliked him when he started picking apart their operations. And she loathed him now that he'd insulted the Christmas Castle.

"We all know the future of retail is online," he continued. He uncrossed his long legs and shifted his weight. Uncharitable a thought as it might be, Noelle was glad he'd been forced to squeeze his long, lanky frame into Belinda's office furniture. "The only reason your brick-and-mortar store has survived is because it's basically a tourist attraction."

"What's wrong with being a tourist attraction?" she asked. Fryberg's had done very well thanks to that tourist attraction. Over the years, what had been a small hobby shop had become a cottage industry unto itself with the entire town embracing the Bavarian atmosphere. "You saw our balance sheet. Those tourists are contributing a very healthy portion of our revenue."

"I also saw that the biggest growth came from your online store. In fact, while it's true retail sales have remained constant, your electronic sales have risen over fifteen percent annually."

And were poised to take another leap this year. Noelle had heard the projections. E-retail was the wave of the future. Brick-and-mortar stores like Fryberg's would soon be obsolete.

"Don't get me wrong. I think your late husband did a fantastic job of capitalizing on people's nostalgia," he said to Belinda.

Noelle's mother-in-law smiled. She always smiled when speaking about her late husband. "Ned used to say that Christmas was a universal experience."

"Hammond's has certainly done well by it."

Well? Hammond's had their entire business on the holiday, as had Fryberg's. *Nothing Says Christmas Like Hammond's Toys.* The company motto, repeated at the end of every ad, sung in Noelle's head.

"That's because everyone loves Christmas," she replied.

"Hmm." From the lack of enthusiasm in his response, she might as well have been talking about weather patterns. Then again, his emotional range didn't seem to go beyond brusque and chilly, so maybe that was enthusiastic for him.

"I don't care if they love the holiday or not. It's their shopping patterns I'm interested in, and from the data I've been seeing, more and more people are doing part, if not most of their shopping over the internet. The retailers who survive will be the ones who shift their business models accordingly. I intend to make sure Hammond's is one of those businesses."

"Hammond's," Noelle couldn't help noting. "Not Fryberg's."

"I'm hoping that by the end of the day, the two stores will be on the way to becoming one and the same," he said.

"Wiping out sixty-five years of tradition just like that, are you?"

"Like I said, to survive, sometimes you have to embrace change."

Except they weren't embracing anything. Fryberg's was

being swallowed up and dismantled so that Hammond's could change.

"I think what my daughter-in-law is trying to say is that the Fryberg name carries a great deal of value round these parts," said Belinda. "People are very loyal to my late husband and what he worked to create here."

"Loyalty's a rare commodity these days. Especially in the business world."

"It certainly is. Ned, my husband, had a way of inspiring it."

"Impressive," Hammond replied.

"It's because the Frybergs—Ned and Belinda—have always believed in treating their employees like family," Noelle told him. "And they were always on-site, visible to everyone." Although things had changed over the last few years as Belinda had been spending more and more time in Palm Beach. "I'm not sure working for a faceless CEO in Boston will engender the same feelings."

"What do you expect me to do? Move my office here?"

He looked at her. His gaze, sharp and direct, didn't so much look through a person as cut into them. The flecks of brown in his irises darkened, transforming what had been soft hazel. Self-consciousness curled through Noelle's midsection. She folded her arms tighter to keep the reaction from spreading.

"No. Just keep Fryberg's as a separate entity," she replied.

His brows lifted. "Really? You want me to keep one store separate when all the other properties under our umbrella carry the name Hammond?"

"Why not?" Noelle's palms started to sweat. She was definitely overstepping her authority right now. Belinda had already accepted Hammond's offer. Today's meeting was a friendly dialogue between an outgoing owner and the new CEO, to ensure a successful transition. She couldn't help it. With Belinda stepping down, someone had to protect what Ned had created. James Hammond certainly wasn't. To hear him, Fryberg's Christmas Castle was one step ahead of landlines in terms of obsolescence. She gave him two years tops before he decided "Hammond's" Christmas Castle didn't fit the corporate brand and started downsizing in the name of change. Bet he wouldn't blink an eye doing it either.

Oh, but she really, really, *really* disliked him. Thank goodness the corporate headquarters were in Boston. With luck, he'd go home after this visit and she'd never have to deal with him again.

"Our name recognition and reputation are important elements to our success," she continued. "All those people who line up to see Hammond's displays every Christmas? Would they still remember to make the pilgrimage if Hammond's suddenly became Jones's Toys?"

He chuckled. "Hammond's is hardly the same as Jones."

"Around here it might as well be."

"She makes an interesting point," Belinda said. Noelle felt her mother-in-law's sideways gaze. When it came to giving a pointed look, Belinda Fryberg held her own. In fact, she could probably do it better than most since she always tossed in a dose of maternal reproach. "While you may think our physical store has a limited future, there's no need to hasten its demise prematurely. Maybe it would make more sense for Fryberg's to continue operating under its own name, at least for now."

Leaning back in his chair, Hammond steepled his fingertips together and tapped them against his lips. "I'm not averse to discussing the idea," he said finally.

I'm not averse... How big of him. Noelle bit her tongue. Her mother-in-law, meanwhile, folded her hands and smiled. "Then why don't we do just that over lunch? I made reservations at the Nutcracker Inn downtown."

"I don't usually have lunch..."

No surprise there. Noelle had read once that sharks only ate every few days.

"Perhaps you don't," Belinda replied, "but for a woman my age, skipping meals isn't the best idea. Besides, I find business always goes smoother when accompanied by a bowl of gingerbread soup. You haven't lived until you've tried it."

Either Hammond's cheek muscles twitched at the word *gingerbread* or else they weren't used to smiling. "Very well," he said. "I have some calls to make first though. Why don't I meet you at the elevator in, say, fifteen minutes?"

"I'll see you there."

Returning Belinda's nod, he unfolded his lanky self from the chair and strode from the room. If only he'd keep walking, Noelle thought as she watched his back slip through the door. Keep walking all the way back to Boston.

"Well, that was a surprise." Belinda spoke the second the door shut behind him. "I hadn't realized you'd joined the mergers and acquisitions team."

"I'm sorry," Noelle replied. "But the way he was talking...it sounded like he planned to wipe Fryberg's off the map."

"You know I would never allow that."

She hung her head. "I know, and I'm sorry. On the plus side, he did say he would consider keeping the Fryberg's name."

"Even so, you can't keep getting angry every time he says something that rubs you the wrong way. This is Hammond's company now. You're going to have to learn to bite your tongue."

She'd better hope Noelle's tongue was thick enough to survive the visit then, because there was going to be a lot of biting.

"I just..." Starting now. Gritting her teeth, she turned and looked out the window. Below her, a school tour was lining up in front of the reindeer petting zoo, the same as they did every year, the Wednesday before Thanksgiving. Later on, they would make wish lists for their parents and trek over to the Candy Cane Forest to meet Santa Claus.

Her attention zeroed in on a little girl wearing a grimy pink snow jacket, the dirt visible from yards away, and she smiled nostalgically at the girl's obvious excitement. That excitement was what people like James Hammond didn't understand. Fryberg's was so much more than a toy store or tourist attraction. When you passed through that nutcracker-flanked gate, you entered a different world. A place where, for a few hours, little girls in charity bin hand-me-downs could trade their loneliness and stark reality for a little Christmas magic.

A warm hand settled on her shoulder. "I wish things could stay the same too," Belinda said, "but time marches on no matter how hard we try to stop it. Ned's gone, Kevin's gone, and I just don't have the energy to run this place by myself anymore.

"Besides, a chain like Hammond's can invest capital in this place that I don't have."

Capital, sure, but what about heart? Compassion was part of the Fryberg DNA. Noelle still remembered that day in sixth grade when Kevin invited her to his house and she felt the family's infectious warmth for the very first time.

"I don't fault you for wanting to retire," she said, leaning ever so slightly into the older woman's touch. "I just wish you hadn't sold to such a Grinch."

"He is serious, isn't he?" Belinda chuckled. "Must be all that dour Yankee heritage."

"Dour? Try frozen. The guy has about as much Christmas spirit as a block of ice."

Her mother-in-law squeezed her shoulder. "Fortunately for us, you have enough Christmas spirit for a dozen people. You'll keep the spirit alive. Unless you decide to move on, that is."

Noelle tried for tongue biting again and failed. They'd had this conversation before. It was another one of the reasons Belinda sold the business instead of simply retiring. She insisted Noelle not be tied down by the family business. A reason Noelle found utterly silly.

"You know I have zero intention of ever leaving Fryberg," she said.

"Oh, I know you think that now. But you're young. You're smart. There's an entire world out there beyond Fryberg's Toys."

Noelle shook her head. Not for her there wasn't. The store was too big a part of her.

It was all of her, really.

Her mother-in-law squeezed her shoulder again. "Kevin and Ned wouldn't want you to shortchange your future any more than I do."

At the mention of her late husband's wishes, Noelle bit back a familiar swell of guilt.

"Besides," Belinda continued, heading toward her desk. "Who knows? Maybe you'll impress Mr. Hammond so much, he'll promote you up the corporate ladder."

"Him firing me is more likely," Noelle replied. She recalled how sharp Hammond's gaze had become when she dared to challenge him. Oh, yeah, she could picture him promoting her, all right.

"You never know" was all Belinda said. "I better go get

ready for lunch. Don't want to keep our Mr. Hammond waiting. Are you joining us?"

And continue bonding with Mr. Hammond over a bowl of gingerbread soup? Thanks, but no thanks. "I think Mr. Hammond and I have had enough contact for the day. Better I save my tongue and let you and Todd fill me in on the visit later."

"That reminds me. On your way out, can you stop by Todd's office and let his secretary know that if he calls in after the funeral, I'd like to talk with him?"

"Sure thing."

Her answer was buried by the sound of the phone ringing.

"Oh, dear," Belinda said upon answering. "This is Dick Greenwood. I'd better take it. Hopefully, he won't chat my ear off. Will you do me another favor and give Mr. Hammond a tour of the floor while I'm tied up?"

So much for being done with the man. "Of course." She'd donate a kidney if Belinda asked.

"And be nice."

"Yes, ma'am."

The kidney would have been easier.

"You're not going to have an insubordination problem, are you?"

On the other end of the line, Jackson Hammond's voice sounded far away. James might have blamed the overseas connection except he knew better. Jackson Hammond always sounded distant.

Struggling to keep the phone tucked under his ear, he reached for the paper towels. "Problem?" he repeated. "Hardly."

With her short black hair and red sweater dress, Noelle

Fryberg was more of an attack elf. Too small and precious to do any real damage.

"Only reason she was in the meeting was because the new general manager had to attend a funeral, and she's the assistant GM." And because she was family. Apparently, the concept mattered to some people.

He shrugged and tossed his wadded towel into the basket. "Her objections were more entertaining than anything."

He'd already come to the same conclusion regarding the Fryberg name, but it was fun seeing her try to stare him into capitulation. She had very large, very soulful eyes. Her glaring at him was like being glared at by a kitten. He had to admire the effort though. It was more than a lot of—hell, most—people.

"All in all, the transition is going smooth as silk. I'm going to tour the warehouse this afternoon." And then hightail it back to the airstrip as soon as possible. With any luck, he'd be in Boston by eight that evening. Noelle Fryberg's verve might be entertaining, but not so much that he wanted to stick around Christmas Land a moment longer than necessary.

"Christmas is only four weeks away. You're going to need that distribution center linked into ours as soon as possible."

"It'll get done," James replied. The reassurance was automatic. James learned a long time ago that his father preferred his world run as smoothly as possible. Complications and problems were things you dealt with on your own.

"If you need anything from my end, talk with Carli. I've asked her to be my point person while I'm in Vienna."

"Thank you." But James wouldn't need anything from his father's end. He'd been running the corporation for several years now while his father concentrated on over-seas and other pet projects—like his new protégé, Carli, for example.

Then again, he hadn't needed his father since his parents' divorce. About the time his father made it clear he didn't want James underfoot. Not wanting their eldest son around was the one thing Jackson Hammond and his ex-wife had in common.

"How is the trip going?" James asked, turning to other, less bitter topics.

"Well enough. I'm meeting with Herr Burns in the morning…" There was a muffled sound in the background. "Someone's knocking at the door. I have to go. We'll talk tomorrow, when you're back in the office."

The line disconnected before James had a chance to remind him tomorrow was Thanksgiving. Not that it mattered. He'd still be in the office.

He was always in the office. Wasn't like he had a family.

Belinda was nowhere in sight when James stepped into the hallway. Instead, he found the daughter-in-law waiting by the elevator, arms again hugging her chest. "Belinda had to take a call with Dick Greenwood," she told him.

"I'm sorry" was his automatic reply. Greenwood was a great vendor, but he was notorious for his chattiness. James made a point of avoiding direct conversations if he could.

Apparently, the daughter-in-law knew what he meant, because the corners of her mouth twitched. About as close to a smile as he'd seen out of her. "She said she'll join you as soon as she can. In the meantime, she thought you'd like a tour of the retail store."

"She did, did she?" More likely, she thought it would distract him while she was stuck on the phone.

Noelle shrugged. "She thought it would give you an idea of the foot traffic we handle on a day-to-day basis."

He'd seen the sales reports; he knew what kind of traffic they handled. Still, it couldn't hurt to check out the store. Hammond's was always on the lookout for new ways to engage their customers. "Are you going to be my guide?" he asked, reaching across to hit the elevator button.

"Yes, I am." If she thought he missed the soft sigh she let out before speaking, she was mistaken.

All the more reason to take the tour.

The doors opened, and James motioned for her to step in first. Partly to be a gentleman, but mostly because holding back gave him an opportunity to steal a surreptitious look at her figure. The woman might be tiny, but she was perfectly proportioned. Make that normally proportioned, he amended. Too many of the women he met had try-hard figures. Worked out and enhanced to artificial perfection. Noelle looked fit, but she still carried a little more below than she did on top, which he appreciated.

"We bill ourselves as the country's largest toy store," Noelle said once the elevator doors shut. "The claim is based on square footage. We are the largest retail space in the continental US. This weekend alone we'll attract thousands of customers."

"Black Friday weekend. The retailers' best friend," he replied. Then, because he couldn't resist poking the bee's nest a little, he added, "That is, until Cyber Monday came along. These days we move almost as much inventory online. Pretty soon people won't come out for Black Friday at all. They'll do their shopping Thanksgiving afternoon while watching TV."

"Hammond's customers might, but you can't visit a Christmas wonderland via a computer."

That again. He turned to look at her. "Do you really

think kids five or six years from now are going to care about visiting Santa Claus?"

"Of course they are. It's Santa."

"I hate to break it to you, but kids are a little more realistic these days. They grow fast. Our greeting card fantasy holiday is going to get harder and harder to sell."

"Especially if you insist on calling it a fantasy."

What should he call it? Fact? "Belinda wasn't kidding when she said you were loyal, was she?"

"The Frybergs are family. Of course I would be loyal."

Not necessarily, but James didn't feel like arguing the point.

"Even if I weren't—related that is—I'd respect what Ned and Belinda created." She crossed her arms. Again. "They understood that retail is about more than moving inventory."

Her implication was clear: she considered him a corporate autocrat who was concerned solely with the bottom line. While she might be correct, he didn't intend to let her get away with the comment unchallenged.

Mirroring her posture, he tilted his head and looked straight at her. "Is that so? What exactly is it about then?"

"People, of course."

"Of course." She was not only loyal, but naive. Retail was *all* about moving product. All the fancy window dressing she specialized in was to convince people to buy the latest and greatest, and then to buy the next latest and greatest the following year. And so on and so forth.

At that moment, the elevator opened and before them lay Fryberg's Toys in all its glory. Aisle upon aisle of toys, spread out like a multicolored promised land. There were giant stuffed animals arranged by environment, lions and tigers in the jungle, cows and horses by the farm. Construction toys were spread around a jobsite, around which cars zipped on a multilevel racetrack. There was even a wall of televisions blasting the latest video games. A special display for every interest, each one overflowing with products for sale.

"Oh, yeah," he murmured, "it's totally about the people."

A remote-control drone zipped past their heads as they walked toward the center aisle. A giant teddy bear made of plastic building bricks marked the entrance like the Colossus of Rhodes.

"It's like Christmas morning on steroids," he remarked as they passed under the bear's legs.

"This is the Christmas Castle, after all. Everything should look larger-than-life and magical. To stir the imagination."

Not to mention the desire for plastic bricks and stuffed animals, thought James.

"Santa's workshop and the Candy Cane Forest are located at the rear of the building," she said pointing to an archway bedecked with painted holly and poinsettia. "That's also where Ned's model train layout is located. It used to be a much larger section, but now it's limited to one room-size museum."

Yet something else lost to the march of time, James refrained from saying. The atmosphere was chilly enough. Looking around he noticed their aisle led straight toward the archway, and that the only way to avoid Santa was to go to the end, turn and head back up a different aisle.

He nodded at the arch. "What's on the other side?" he asked.

"Other side of what?"

"Santa's woods or whatever it is."

"Santa's workshop and Candy Cane Forest," she corrected. "There's a door that leads back into the store, or they can continue on to see the reindeer."

"Meaning they go home to purchase their child's wish item online from who-knows-what site."

"Or come back another day. Most people don't do their Christmas shopping with the kids in tow."

"How about in April, when they aren't Christmas shopping? They walk outside to see the reindeer and poof! There goes your potential sale."

That wouldn't do at all. "After the kids visit Santa, the traffic should be rerouted back into the store so the parents can buy whatever it is Little Susie or Johnny wished for."

"You want to close off access to the reindeer?"

She needn't look so horrified. It wasn't as though he'd suggested euthanizing the creatures. "I want customers to buy toys. And they aren't going to if they are busy looking at reindeer. What's that?"

He pointed to a giant Moose-like creature wearing a Santa's hat and wreath standing to the right of the archway. It took up most of the wall space, forcing the crowd to congregate toward the middle. As a result, customers looking to walk past the archway to another aisle had to battle a throng of children.

"Oh, that's Fryer Elk, the store mascot," Noelle replied. "Ned created him when he opened the store. Back in the day, he appeared in the ads. They retired him in the eighties and he's been here ever since."

"He's blocking the flow of traffic. He should be somewhere else."

For a third time, James got the folded arm treatment. "He's an institution," she replied, as if that was reason enough for his existence.

He could be Ned Fryberg standing there stuffed himself, and he would still be hindering traffic. Letting out a long breath, James reached into his breast pocket for his notebook. Once the sale was finalized, he would send his operations manager out here to evaluate the layout.

"You really don't have any respect for tradition, do you?" Noelle asked.

He peered over his pen at her. Just figuring this out, was she? That's what happened when you spent a fortune crafting a corporate image. People started believing the image was real.

"No," he replied. "I don't. In fact…" He put his notebook away. "We might as well get something straight right now. As far as I'm concerned, the only thing that matters is making sure Hammond's stays profitable for the next fifty years. Everything else can go to blazes."

"Everything," she repeated. Her eyes narrowed.

"Everything, and that includes elks, tradition and especially Chris—"

He never got a chance to finish.

CHAPTER TWO

FOUR STITCHES AND a concussion. That's what the emergency room doctor told Noelle. "He's fortunate. Those props can do far worse," she added. "Your associates really shouldn't be flying remote-control drones inside."

"So they've been told," Noelle replied. In no uncertain terms by James Hammond once he could speak.

The drone had slammed into the back of his head, knocking him face-first into a pile of model racecar kits. The sight of the man sprawled on the floor might have been funny if not for the blood running down the back of his skull. Until that minute, she'd been annoyed as hell at the man for his obvious lack of respect toward Fryberg tradition. Seeing the blood darkening his hair quickly checked her annoyance. As blood was wont to do.

That was until she turned him over and he started snarling about careless associates and customer safety. Then she went back to being annoyed. Only this time, it was because the man had a point. What if the drone had struck a customer—a child? Things could have been even worse. As it was, half of Miss Speroni's first grade class was probably going to have nightmares from witnessing the accident.

Then there was the damage to James Hammond himself. Much as she disliked the man, stitches and a concussion were nothing to sneeze at.

"How long before he's ready for discharge?" she asked.

"My nurse is bandaging the stitches right now," the doctor replied. "Soon as I get his paperwork written up, he'll be all yours."

Oh, goodie. Noelle didn't realize she'd gotten custody. She went back to the waiting room where Belinda was finishing up a phone call.

"Bob is working on a statement for the press," her mother-in-law told her. "And we're pulling the product off the shelves per advice from the lawyers. Thankfully, the incident didn't get caught on camera so we won't have to deal with that. I doubt Mr. Hammond would like being a social media sensation."

"I'm not sure Mr. Hammond likes much of anything," Noelle replied. She was thinking of the remark he made right before the drone struck him. "Did you know, he actually said he doesn't like Christmas? How can the man think that and run a store like Hammond's?" Or Fryberg's.

"Obviously, his disdain hasn't stopped him from doubling Hammond's profits over the past two years," Belinda replied. "What matters isn't that he like Christmas, but that he keeps the people in Fryberg employed, which he will."

"Hope they like working for Mr. Frosty. Did you know he wants to get rid of Fryer?"

"Well, some change is bound to happen," Belinda said.

"I know," Noelle grumbled. She bowed her head. She really did. Same way she understood that the retail industry was changing. She also knew she was acting irrational and childish about the entire situation. Ever since Belinda announced the sale, however, she'd been unable to catch her breath. It felt like there were fingers clawing inside her looking for purchase. A continual churning sensation. Like she was about to lose her grip.

James Hammond's arrival only made the feeling worse.

"Doesn't mean I have to like it though," she said referring to the prospect of change.

Belinda nudged her shoulder. "Sweetheart, you wouldn't be you if you did. Cheer up. Mr. Hammond will be out of your hair soon."

"Not soon enough," she replied.

"What wouldn't be soon enough?" Hammond's voice caused her to start in her chair. Turning, she saw a nurse pushing him toward her. He was slouched down in a wheelchair, a hand propping his head. Noelle caught a glimpse of a white bandage on the back of his scalp.

"The bandage can come off tomorrow," the nurse told them.

"How are you feeling, Mr. Hammond?" Belinda asked.

"Like someone split my head open. Who knew such a little device could pack such a wallop?"

"Lots of things pack a wallop when they're going thirty miles an hour. We pulled the toy from the shelves. Though I doubt it would have been popular anyway, once parents heard what happened."

"Don't blame them. Thing could slice an ear off." Groaning, he leaned forward and buried his face in both hands as though one was suddenly not enough to hold it up. "I'm going to have Hammond's pull them too as soon as I get back to Boston," he spoke through his fingers.

"That won't be anytime soon, I'm afraid. You heard what Dr. Nelson said," the nurse warned.

"What did she say?" Noelle asked. She didn't like the sound of the nurse's comment.

Hammond waved a hand before cradling his head again. "Nothing."

"Mr. Hammond has a slight concussion. He's been advised to rest for the next couple of days. That includes no air travel."

"You mean you're staying here?" No, no, no. Noelle's stomach started to twist. He was supposed to go away, not stick around for the weekend.

"The doctor merely recommended I rest," James replied. "No one said it was mandatory."

"Perhaps not, but it's generally a good idea to take doctors' advice," Belinda said.

"We're talking about a handful of stitches. Nothing I haven't had before. I'll be fine. Why don't we go have our lunch as planned and finish our conversation? I could use some food in my stomach. What kind of soup did you say they made?"

"Gingerbread," Noelle replied.

"The only place you should be going is to bed," the nurse said.

Much as Noelle hated to admit it, the nurse was right. He was looking paler by the minute. She remembered how unsteady he'd been right after the accident; he could barely sit up.

Funny, but he still looked formidable despite the pallor. A virile invalid. Noelle didn't think it possible. Must be the combination of square jaw and broad shoulders, she decided. And the dark suit. Black made everyone look intimidating.

Again, he waved off the nurse's advice. "Nonsense. I rested while waiting for the doctor. Why don't we go have our lunch as planned and finish our conversation? I could use some food in my stomach. What kind of soup did you say they made?"

"I just told you."

A crease deepened between his eyes. "You did?"

"Uh-huh. Two seconds ago."

"That only proves I'm hungry. I'm having trouble listening." He pushed himself to a standing position, squaring his shoulders proudly when he reached his feet. His upper body swayed back and forth unsteadily. "See?" he said. "Fine. Let's go."

Noelle looked over her shoulder at Belinda who shook her head in return. "I'm not going to negotiate anything while you're unsteady on your feet," her mother-in-law said. "I won't be accused of taking advantage when you're not thinking straight."

James laughed. "You're a smart businesswoman, Belinda, but I can assure you, no one ever takes advantage of me."

"That I can believe," Noelle murmured.

He looked at her and smiled. "I'll take that as a compliment, Mrs. Fryberg. Now how about we go get that lunch we missed…"

It took two steps for him to lose his balance. His eyes started to roll back in his head, and his knees started to buckle.

Noelle reached him first. "Okay, that's enough," she said, reaching around his waist. Thanks to the size difference, it took a minute to maneuver him, but eventually she managed to lower him into the wheelchair. Unfortunately, the downward momentum pulled her along as well. She landed with one hand pressed against his torso and knee wedged between his thighs. Man, but he was solid. A tall, lean block of granite.

She looked up to find herself nose to nose with him. Up close, his eyes were far more dappled than she realized, the green more of an accent color than true eye shade.

He had freckles too. A smattering across the bridge of his nose.

Cold-blooded businessmen weren't supposed to have freckles.

"Think you might listen to the nurse now?" she asked.

"I was lightheaded for a moment, that's all."

"Lightheaded, huh?" She pushed herself to her feet. To her embarrassment, the move required splaying her hand wider, so that the palm of her hand pressed over his heart. Fortunately, he was too dizzy or distracted to comment.

"Any more lightheaded and you would have hit the floor," she told him. "Are you trying to get more stitches?"

"I'm not…"

"Face it, Mr. Hammond, you're in no condition to do anything but rest," Belinda said. "We'll talk when you're feeling better. Monday."

"Monday?" He'd started to rest his head in his hands again, but when Belinda spoke, he jerked his head upward. The pain crossing his face made Noelle wince. "Why wait until then? I won't need that many days to recover."

"Maybe not, but that is the next time I'll be able to see you. Tomorrow is Thanksgiving. The only business I'll be discussing is whether the stuffing is too dry."

"What about Friday?"

Noelle answered for her. "Black Friday, remember? Around these parts, it's the kickoff for the annual Christmas festival, the biggest weekend of our year."

"I'll be much too busy to give you the proper time," Belinda added.

Noelle watched the muscle twitching in Hammond's jaw. Clearly, he preferred being the one who dictated the schedule, and not the other way around.

"Let me get this straight." Whether his voice was low by design or discomfort, Noelle couldn't guess. His tension came though nevertheless. "I'm not allowed to fly home for the next twenty-four hours…"

"At least," the nurse said.

The muscle twitched again. "*At least* twenty-four hours,"

he corrected. "Nor will you meet with me for the next five days?"

"That's correct," Belinda replied. "We can meet first thing Monday morning, and conclude our preliminary negotiations."

"I see." He nodded. Slowly. Anyone with two eyes could tell he didn't appreciate this change in plans at all. Noelle would be lying if she didn't say it gave her a tiny trill of satisfaction. Payback for his wanting to toss Fryer.

"Fine," he said, leaning back in his chair. "We'll talk Monday. Only because my head hurts too much to argue." Noelle had a feeling he wasn't kidding. "What was the name of that hotel?"

"The Nutcracker Inn," she replied.

"Right, that one. I'm going to need a room, and something to eat. What did you say that soup was?"

"Gingerbread." It was the third time he'd asked. She looked at the nurse who nodded.

"Temporary short-term memory loss can happen with concussions. It should recede soon enough. However, I think you might have a more pressing problem."

"I do?"

"He does?"

The two of them spoke at the same time. "I'm not sure the Nutcracker has any rooms," the nurse replied. "You know how booked it gets during the holidays."

"Wait a second." James tried to look up at the nurse, only to wince and close his eyes. "Please don't tell me there's no room at the inn."

"Wouldn't be the first time," the nurse replied. "Did you know that once we even had a baby born—"

"I doubt Mr. Hammond will have to do anything quite as dramatic," Noelle interjected. No need for the conversation to head down that particular road.

The nurse offered a tight-lipped smile. Apparently, she didn't appreciate being cut off. "Either way, you're going to need someone to look in on you. Doctor's orders."

"The concierge will love that request," Hammond muttered.

"We could arrange for a private duty nurse."

"Good grief," Belinda said. "That doesn't sound pleasant at all."

"Pleasant isn't exactly on the table right now." Hammond's eyes had grown heavy lidded and his words were slurred. It was obvious the entire conversation was exhausting him, and Noelle couldn't help but feel bad.

Although she doubted he'd appreciate the compassion. A man like Hammond, with his disregard for sentiment and tradition, would despise showing any hint of vulnerability.

"Of course pleasant is on the table," Belinda said. "This is Fryberg." The meaning behind her emphasis was obvious.

Hammond let out a low groan. Still feeling compassionate, Noelle decided the noise was coincidental.

Her mother-in-law continued as if the noise never happened. "We're not going to let you spend your weekend in some hotel room, eating room service and being attended to by a stranger. You'll spend the weekend with me. That way you can recuperate, and enjoy a proper Thanksgiving as well."

The strangest look crossed Hammond's face. Part surprise, part darkness as though her mother-in-law's suggestion unnerved him. Noelle didn't picture him as a man who got unnerved. Ever.

"I don't want to put you out," he said.

"You won't. I have plenty of room. I'll even make you

some…oh, shoot." A look crossed her features, not nearly as dark as Hammond's, but definitely distressed.

"What is it?" Noelle asked.

"The Orion House Dinner is this evening. I completely forgot."

In all the craziness, so had Noelle. Fryberg's was being honored for its fund-raising efforts on behalf of homeless veterans. "Would you mind?" her mother-in-law asked. "I don't want Orion House to think I don't appreciate the honor. The project meant so much to Ned."

"I know," replied Noelle. After Kevin's death, her father-in-law had channeled his grief into helping as many veteran programs as possible. Orion House had topped the list. "He was very passionate about wanting to help."

"That he was," Belinda said, getting the faraway look she always got when they discussed Ned. The family had been through a lot these past years, and yet they continued to channel their energy into the community. Their dedication in the face of grief made her proud to bear the Fryberg name.

"Would you mind stepping in instead?"

"Not at all," she told her. "I'd love to." It'd be an honor to accept an award for them.

"Thank goodness." The older woman let out a long sigh. "I was afraid that because of our words earlier… Never mind." Whatever her mother-in-law had been about to say she waved away. "Let me pull my car around. I'll help you get Mr. Hammond settled, and then go home to change."

Help her…? Wait… What exactly had she agreed to do?

Noelle opened her mouth, closed it, then opened it again. Nothing came out though. That's because she knew what she'd agreed to. As surely as the sickening feeling growing in her stomach.

Somehow, James Hammond had become *her* responsibility. She looked over to her mother-in-law, but Belinda was busy fishing through her purse. And here she thought she would be free of the man. Talk about your sick karmic jokes. If only she'd been the one hit in the head.

"Do you need an extra copy of the discharge instructions?" the nurse asked her.

"No," Noelle replied with a sigh. "I know what to expect."

There was only one consolation, if you could call it that. Hammond looked about as thrilled over this change of events as she was.

Goodie. They could be miserable together.

A few minutes later, James found himself being wheeled outside behind a tiny bundle of annoyance, who marched toward the waiting sedan with her arms yet again wrapped tightly across her chest. A voice behind his headache wondered if they were permanently attached to her body that way.

"Why don't you take the front seat?" Belinda opened the passenger door. "I've pulled it all the way back so you'll have plenty of leg room."

Front seat, back seat. Didn't make much difference. Neither were the cockpit of his private plane. His head felt split in two, the world was tipping on its axis and he wanted nothing more than to be in his bed back in Boston. Damn drone.

He pushed himself to his feet only to have the world rock back and forth like a seesaw. A second later, an arm wrapped around his biceps, steadying him, and he smelled the sweet scent of orange blossoms. The elf. He recognized the perfume from the confines of the elevator. Funny, but he expected her to smell Christmassy, not like Florida sunshine. Maybe they were out of sugar cookie perfume this week.

"Something wrong?"

Turning his head—barely—he saw her frowning at him and realized he'd snorted out loud at his joke. "Do you really need to ask?"

He was being an ass, he knew that, but with stitches in his scalp, surely he was entitled to a little churlishness?

The frown deepened. "Watch your head," she replied.

James did as he was told, and as his reward, the orange blossoms—as well as her grip—disappeared. In their absence, his headache intensified. He found himself slumped against a leather armrest with his fingers pressed against his temple to hold his head up.

"Fortunately, we don't have to drive too far," he heard Belinda say. "Noelle only lives a short distance from town."

"Great." What he really wanted to say was that two feet was too far what with the lights outside dipping and rocking as they passed by. Thankfully the sun had set. If those were buildings bobbing, he'd be lurching the contents of his stomach all over his Bostonians. He closed his eyes, and did his best to imagine orange blossoms.

"The nurse seemed to think the worst of the dizziness would pass by tomorrow," Noelle said from behind him.

"Thank God," he whispered. If true, then maybe he could snag a ride to the airport and fly home, doctor's orders be damned. He bet the elf would drive him. After all, she didn't want him at her house any more than he wanted to be there. He'd caught the look on the woman's face when Belinda foisted him on her.

Foisted. What a perfect word for the situation. Stuck

where he didn't want to be, dependent on people who didn't want him around.

Story of his life.

Great. He'd moved from churlish to pity party. Why not round out the trifecta and start whining too?

How he hated this. Hated having no choice. Hated being weak and needy. He hadn't needed anyone since he was twelve years old. Needing and foisting were incompatible concepts.

"It's too bad you can't look out the window," Belinda said. "The town looks beautiful all lit up."

James pried open one eye to see building after building decorated with Christmas lights. *Ugh.* One in particular had a giant evergreen dripping with red and green.

"That's the Nutcracker Inn. The Bavarian market is next door. It'll be packed on Friday for the festival."

"I doubt Mr. Hammond is very interested in a tour, Belinda."

"I'm merely pointing out a few of the landmarks since he's going to be here all weekend."

Not if he could help it, thought James.

"The man can't remember what kind of soup they serve—I doubt he'll remember what the place looks like."

"There's no need to be harsh, Noelle Fryberg."

"Yes, ma'am."

Actually, James rather liked the harshness. Beat being treated like a patient. "Pumpkin," he replied.

"Excuse me?" Belinda asked.

"The soup. It's pumpkin."

"You mean gingerbread," Noelle replied.

"Oh. Right." He knew it was some kind of seasonal flavor. His cheeks grew warm.

Belinda patted him on the knee. "Don't worry about

it, Mr. Hammond. I'm sure you'll be back to normal by tomorrow."

"Let's hope so," he heard the elf mutter.

James couldn't have agreed with her more.

CHAPTER THREE

THE NEXT MORNING James woke to what had to be the best-smelling candle in the universe—sweet with traces of allspice and cinnamon—which was odd since he didn't normally buy candles. Maybe the smell had something to do with the stinging sensation on the back of his head and the vague memories of dark hair and kitten eyes dancing on the edge of his brain.

And orange blossoms. For some reason, the first thought in his mind was that as delicious as the candle smelled, it wasn't orange blossoms.

Slowly, he pried open an eye. What the…?

This wasn't his Back Bay condo. He sprang up, only to have a sharp pain push him back down on the bed.

Sofa, he amended. He was lying facedown on a leather sofa, his cheek swallowed by a large memory foam pillow. Gingerly, he felt the back of his skull, his fingers meeting a patch of gauze and tape.

The drone. This must be Noelle Fryberg's living room. Last thing he remembered was leaning into her warm body as she led him through the front door. Explained why he had orange blossoms on the brain. The memory of the smell eased the tension between his shoulder blades.

Once the vertigo abated, he surveyed his surroundings. Given her slavish devotion to Fryberg's vision, he pictured his hostess living in a mirror image of the Christmas Castle, with baskets of sugarplums and boughs of holly. He'd been close. The house definitely had the same stucco and wood architecture as the rest of the town, although she'd thankfully forgone any year-round Christmas motif. Instead, the inside was pleasantly furnished with simple, sturdy furniture like the large pine cabinet lining the wall across the way. Brightly colored plates hung on the wall behind it. Homey. Rustic. With not a chandelier or trace of Italian marble to be found.

"You're awake."

A pair of shapely legs suddenly appeared in his line of vision, followed seconds later by a pair of big cornflower-colored eyes as the elf squatted down by his head. "I was coming in to check on you. I'm supposed to make sure you don't fall into a coma while sleeping," she said.

"I haven't."

"Obviously."

As obvious as her joy over having to play nursemaid.

She looked less elfish than yesterday. More girl next door. The red dress had been shucked in favor of a white-and-red University of Wisconsin sweatshirt and jeans, and her short hair was pulled away from her face with a bright red headband. James didn't think it was possible to pull back short hair, but she had. It made her eyes look like one of those paintings from the seventies. The ones where everyone had giant sad eyes. Only in this case, they weren't sad; they were antipathetic.

He tried sitting up again. Slowly this time, making sure to keep his head and neck as still as possible. He felt like an awkward idiot. How was it that people in movies bounced back from head wounds in minutes? Here he was sliding his legs to the floor like he was stepping onto ice.

"How did I end up here?" he asked.

Her mouth turned downward. "Do you mean the house or the sofa?"

"The sofa."

"Good. For a minute I was afraid you didn't remember anything." She stood up, taking her blue eyes from his vision unless he looked up, which didn't feel like the best idea. "You collapsed on it soon as we got through the door last night," she told him. "I tried to convince you to go upstairs to the bedroom, but you refused to budge."

That sounded vaguely familiar. "Stairs were too much work."

"That's what you said last night. Anyway, since you refused to move from the sofa, I gave you a pillow, threw an afghan over you and called it a night."

Out of the corner of his eye, James saw a flash of bright blue yarn piled on the floor near his feet. Tightness gripped his chest at the notion of someone tucking a blanket around his legs while he slept. Cradling his head while they placed a pillow underneath.

"Wait a second," he said as a realization struck him. "You checked on me every few hours?"

"I had to. Doctor's orders."

"What about sleep? Did you…"

"Don't worry—I didn't put myself out any more than necessary."

But more than she preferred. He was but an unwanted responsibility after all. The tightness eased, and the familiar numbness returned. "I'm glad. I'd hate to think you had to sacrifice too much."

"Bare minimum, I assure you. Belinda would have my head if you died on my watch. In case you hadn't guessed, she takes her responsibility to others very seriously. Especially those injured in her store."

His store now. James let the slip pass uncommented.

"Good policy. I'm sure your lawyers appreciate the extra effort."

"It's not policy," she quickly shot back. Her eyes simmered with contention. "It's compassion. The Frybergs have always believed in taking care of others. Belinda especially. I'll have you know that I've seen her literally give a stranger the coat off her back."

"I apologize," James replied. "I didn't mean to insinuate…"

She held up her hand. "Whatever. Just know that lawsuits are the last thing on Belinda's mind.

"You have no idea how special the Fryberg family is," she continued. Driving home the point. "Ned and Belinda were…are…the best people you'll ever meet. The whole town loves them."

"Duly noted," James replied. Must be nice, having a family member care so much they sprang to your defense at the slightest ill word. "I'll watch my language from now on."

"Thank you."

"You're welcome."

They both fell silent. James sat back on the sofa and rubbed his neck, an uncomfortable itch having suddenly danced across his collar. Normally silence didn't bother him; he didn't know why this lapse in conversation felt so awkward.

Probably because the entire situation was awkward. If they were in Boston, he would be the host. He would be offering to whip up a cappuccino and his signature scrambled eggs, the way he did for all his overnight guests. Instead, he was sitting on her sofa, feeling very much like the obligation that he was.

And here he'd thought he was done feeling that way ever again.

Noelle broke the silence first. Tugging on her sweatshirt

the way an officer might tug on his jacket, she cleared her throat. "I'm heading back into the kitchen. You might as well go back to sleep. It's still early. Not even seven-thirty."

"You're awake."

"I have cooking to do. You're supposed to rest."

"I'm rested out." Headache or not, his body was still on East Coast time, and according to it, he'd already slept several hours past his usual wake time. "I don't think I could sleep more if I wanted to."

"Suit yourself," she said with a shrug. "TV remote's on the end table if you want it. I'll be in the kitchen." The unspoken *Stay out of my way* came loud and clear.

She turned and padded out the door. Although James had never been one to ogle women, he found himself watching her jean-clad rear end. Some women were born to wear jeans, and the elf was one of them. With every step, her hips swayed from side to side like a well-toned bell. It was too bad the woman disliked his presence; her attractiveness was one of the few positive things about this debacle of a trip.

He needed to go back to Boston. It was where he belonged. Where he was…well, if not wanted, at least comfortable.

Slowly, he pushed himself to his feet. The room spun a little, but not nearly as badly as it had yesterday, or even fifteen minutes earlier, for that matter. If he managed to walk to the kitchen without problem, he was leaving. Grant him and Noelle a reprieve.

Plans settled, he made his way to the kitchen. Happily, the room only spun a little. He found his hostess in the center of the room pulling a bright yellow apron over her head. The delicious aroma from before hung heavy in the air. It wasn't a candle at all, but some kind of pie. Pumpkin, he realized, taking a deep breath.

His stomach rumbled. "I don't suppose I could get a cup of coffee," he said when she turned around.

She pointed to the rear cupboard where a full pot sat on the coffee maker burner. "Cups are in the cupboard above. There's cereal and toast if you want any breakfast. Do you need me to pour?" she added belatedly.

"No, thank you. I can manage." He made his way over to the cupboard. Like everything else in the house, the mugs were simple, yet sturdy. He was beginning to think she was the only delicate-looking thing in the house. "You have a nice place," he remarked as he poured.

"You sound surprised."

"Do I?" he replied. "I don't mean to."

"In that case, thank you. Kevin and his father came up with the design."

That explained the resemblance to the Christmas Castle.

"I'm curious," he said, leaning against the counter. She had bent over to look in the oven, giving him another look at her bottom. "Is there some kind of rule that the houses all have to look…"

"Look like what?" she asked, standing up.

"Alike." Like they'd all been plucked off a picture post-card.

"Well the idea *is* to resemble a European village. That's part of what makes us such a popular tourist attraction."

She was tossing around his words from yesterday. He'd insulted her again.

Which he knew before asking the question. Hell, it was why he'd asked it. Their exchange earlier reminded him how much he'd enjoyed her backbone yesterday. Next to her cute figure, pushing her buttons was the only other thing that made this trip enjoyable. "I'm sure it does," he replied.

"What is that supposed to mean?"

James shrugged. "Nothing. I was simply noting the town had a distinctive theme is all, and wondered if it was by design. Now I know."

"I'm sure you already knew from your research," she said, folding her arms. She had the closed-off pose down to a science. "You just felt like mocking the town."

"Actually..." What could he say? He doubted she'd enjoy knowing her anger entertained him. "Maybe I did."

She opened her mouth, and he waited for her to toss an insult in his direction. Instead she closed her lips again and spun around. Immediately, James regretted pushing too far. What did he expect? Surely, he knew she wouldn't find him as entertaining as he found her. Quite the opposite. She disliked him the same as everyone else. Pushing her buttons guaranteed the status quo.

There was one thing he could say that she might like.

"Your pie smells delicious, by the way. I'm sorry I won't get to taste it."

That got her attention. She turned back around. "Why not?"

Leaning against the counter, he took a long sip of his coffee. Damn, but she made a hearty cup. "Because as soon as I have my coffee and grab a shower, you're driving me to the airstrip so I can fly back to Boston."

Noelle almost dropped the pie she was taking out of the oven. Had she heard right? Not that she wouldn't be glad to see the back of him, but... "I thought the doctor said no flying."

"Doctors say a lot of things."

"Yeah, but in this case..." She flashed back to his falling into her at the hospital. "You could barely stand without getting dizzy."

"That was yesterday. Clearly, that's not the case today."

No, it wasn't. He appeared to be standing quite nicely against her counter, all wrinkled and fresh with sleep as he was.

The guy might be annoying, but he wore bedhead well.

Still, she couldn't believe he was serious about flying an airplane less than twenty-four hours after getting whacked in the head. What if he got dizzy again and crashed the plane? "It doesn't sound like the wisest of plans," she said.

From over his coffee mug, he looked at her with an arched brow. "You'd rather I stick around here with you all weekend?"

"No, but..."

"Then why do you care whether I fly home or not?"

Good question. Why did she care? She looked down at the golden-brown pie still in her hands. Setting it on the cooling rack, she took off her oven mitts, then nudged the oven door shut with her hip.

"I don't care," she said, turning back around. "I'm surprised is all. In my experience, doctors don't advise against things without reason.

"Why are you so eager to leave Fryberg anyway?" she asked. She could already guess the answer. It'd been clear from his arrival he didn't think much of their town.

Unless, that is, he had a different reason for returning to Boston. Something more personal. "If you have Thanksgiving plans with someone, wouldn't they prefer you play it safe?"

His coffee cup muffled the words, but she could swear he said "Hardly." It wasn't a word she'd expected him to use. *Hardly* was the same as saying *unlikely*, which couldn't be the case. A man as handsome as Hammond would have dozens of women interested in him. Just because he rubbed her the wrong way...

She must have misheard.

Still, it wasn't someone special calling him home. And she doubted it was because of Black Friday either. He could get sales reports via his phone; there was no need to physically be in Boston.

That left her original reason. "I'm sorry if our little town isn't comfortable enough for you to stick around."

"Did I say it wasn't comfortable?"

"You didn't have to," Noelle replied. "Your disdain has been obvious."

"As has yours," he shot back.

"I—"

"Let's face it, Mrs. Fryberg. You haven't exactly rolled out the welcome mat. Not that I mind," he said, taking a drink, "but let's not pretend the antipathy has been one-sided."

Maybe it wasn't, but he'd fired the first shot.

Noelle's coffee cup sat on the edge of the butcher-block island where she'd set it down earlier. Seeing the last quarter cup was ice-cold, she made her way to the coffee maker to top off the cup.

"What did you expect," she said, reaching past him, "coming in here and announcing you were phasing out the Christmas Castle?"

"No, I said the castle was near the end of its lifespan. You're the one who got all overprotective and jumped to conclusions."

"Because you called it a fading tourist attraction."

"I said no such thing."

"Okay, maybe not out loud, but you were definitely thinking it."

"Was I, now?" he replied with a snort. "I didn't realize you were a mind reader."

"Oh, please, I could hear it in your voice. I don't have

to be psychic to know you dislike the whole concept, even before you started making efficiency suggestions."

She set the pot back on the burner, so she could look him square in the eye. The two of them were wedged in the small spot, their shoulders abutting. "Or are you going to tell me that's not true?"

"No," he replied, in an even voice, "it's true. You shouldn't take it personally."

"Are you serious? Of course I'm going to take it personally. It's Fryberg's." The store represented everything good that had ever happened in her life since she was seven years old. "You didn't even want to keep the name!"

"I already conceded on that point, remember?"

"I remember." And considering how quickly he conceded, he'd probably already decided he didn't care. "That doesn't mitigate the other changes you want to make." The reindeer. Fryer. Those suggestions were the tip of the iceberg. Before anyone knew, her version of Fryberg's would be gone forever.

"Forgive me for wanting to improve the store's bottom line."

"Our bottom line is perfectly fine." As she glared into her coffee cup, she heard Hammond chuckle.

"So what you're saying is that you all would have been better off if I'd stayed in Boston."

"Exactly," she gritted.

"And you wonder why I don't want to stay in Fryberg."

Noelle's jaw muscles went slack. She looked back up in time to see Hammond tipping back the last of his drink. "I don't make a habit of staying where I'm not wanted," he said, setting the cup on the counter. "I'm certainly not about to start now. Would you mind if I grabbed that shower now? Then you can drop me off at the airstrip, and we'll both be free from an uncomfortable situation."

While he walked out of the kitchen, Noelle went back to contemplating the contents of her cup. She was waiting for a sense of relief to wash over her. After all, he was right; his leaving did free them both from an uncomfortable situation.

Why then wasn't she relieved?

Maybe because your behavior helped drive the man out of town? her conscience replied as she rubbed away a sudden chill from her right arm.

Perhaps she had been...prickly. Something about the man got under her skin. Everything he said felt like a direct assault on her life. Between the company being sold and Belinda moving to Florida, she felt cast adrift. Like a part of her had been cut away. The only things she had left were the castle, the town and its traditions. Without them, she'd go back to being...

Nothing. No, she'd be worse than nothing. She'd be the nameless little girl whose mother left her in the stable. She'd rather be nothing.

Still, regardless of how angry Hammond made her, she still had a responsibility as a host. Belinda would have never been as argumentative and...well, as bratty...as she'd been.

She found Hammond in the living room folding last night's cover. As he bowed his head to match one corner to another, he wobbled slightly, clearly off-balance. A stab of guilt passed through her. No way was he better.

"You're going to have to keep your head dry," she said, taking one end of the afghan for him. After making sure the folds were straight enough, she walked her end toward him. "That glue the doctor used to cover your stitches needs to stay dry until tomorrow. I could draw you a bath though." They met in the center, their fingers tangling slightly as he passed her his end.

"Anything that gets me clean works fine. Thank you."

Hammond's index finger ran along the inside of hers as he spoke. Coincidence, but Noelle got a tingle anyway. It had been a long time since a man's fingers touched her even accidentally. "It's the least I can do," she replied.

Tucking the afghan under her arm, she headed upstairs. The claw foot tub was going to be a tight fit for his long legs, she realized. Kevin had never been one for baths, and she'd never had any trouble, but Hammond was going to have to sit with his knees bent. Folded like a card table, as Belinda might say.

She felt another stab of guilt. Her mother-in-law would be mortified by Noelle's behavior this morning. In Belinda's world, everyone was welcome, no matter who they were. Hadn't she embraced Noelle that first afternoon? The Frybergs didn't pick fights like bratty children.

Or encourage men with concussions to fly home.

If he crashes, it's on your conscience.

He wasn't going to crash. He wouldn't take the risk if he didn't feel secure in his abilities. Right?

I don't make a habit of staying where I'm not wanted.

"That looks deep enough." Hammond's voice from behind her made her start. Looking at the water, Noelle saw the tub was three-quarters filled. Hammond's blurry reflection shimmered beside hers in the water. Tall and icy blue next to small bright red.

"The water?" he repeated.

Stupid her. "Spaced out for a moment, there," she said, reaching for the faucet handle. "I'll let some of the water out."

"No need. I think I can handle it. I didn't hit my head that hard."

"Right. Let me grab you a towel then and I..."

She sucked in her breath. Hammond had unbuttoned his shirt, revealing a white T-shirt beneath. Tucked tight in his waistband, the thin cotton emphasized the muscles in a way the dress shirt couldn't possibly. You could see the outline of his ribs. The bottom of the cage cut away to a narrow, trim waist. Above the ribs, a cluster of dark curls playing peekaboo at the V. It was to that spot that Noelle's gaze immediately zoned. Drawn by the contrast, of course, not by any memory of her hand splayed against the firmness.

Cheeks warming, she quickly yanked her gaze upward.

"There's blood on your collar," she said. It was the first thing that sprang to mind, and she needed something to explain her sudden loss of words. "Your shirt is ruined."

"Looks like the drone claims another victim." Hammond fingered the stiff corner. The red-brown stain covered most of the right side. "I'll toss it out when I get home. Who knew something so small could cause so much damage?"

"Consider yourself lucky it wasn't something bigger," Noelle replied. Her senses regained, she continued toward the linen closet. "Could have been a remote-control C-130."

"Or a crystal tumbler."

"What?"

"They can cause a lot of damage, is all."

"If you say so."

Was this knowledge from personal experience? Considering she'd thought about tossing a thing or two in his direction, she wouldn't be surprised. Taking a pair of towels from the cabinet, she piled them on a stool next to the tub along with a spare toothbrush.

"If you don't need anything else," she said, looking in his direction. Hammond had shed his dress shirt completely, and stood in his T-shirt studying the bloodied collar. Noelle struggled not to notice the way his biceps stretched his sleeves.

This sudden bout of awareness disturbed her. She'd never been one to check out other men. Of course, the fact that this was the first time a man had stood in her bathroom since Kevin probably heightened her sense of awareness. And while she didn't like Hammond, he was handsome. She had been struck by how much so when she'd checked on him during the night. He had been blessed with the most beautiful mouth she'd ever seen. Perfect Cupid's bow, full lower lip.

"What time do you have to be at Belinda's?"

His question jerked her back to the present. Dear God but she was having focus issues all of a sudden. "Not for a couple hours," she replied.

"Good. You'll have time to drive me to the airstrip."

Her stomach twisted a little. "So you're still planning to fly home today, then."

"What's the matter? Worried I changed my mind between the kitchen and here?" He grinned. Something else she'd noticed this morning. His mouth was capable of an annoyingly attractive smile.

Noelle scoffed. "Hardly. I doubt you ever change your mind."

"Only if I'm well and truly persuaded."

The intimate atmosphere made the comment sound dirtier than it was. Noelle fought to keep a flush from blossoming on her skin.

"That's what I thought," she said. He'd stick to his decision, even if the idea was a bad one. Nothing she could say would change his mind.

Oh, well. He was a grown man. If he wanted to risk his safety, it was his concern. She started to leave. "Do you need anything else?"

"No. I won't be long." From the corner of her eye, she saw him start to shake his head, then close his eyes.

He probably doesn't think I can see him.

Once again, Noelle's conscience twisted her stomach.

"You know…" she started. "Belinda isn't going to be happy with you. She was expecting you for Thanksgiving dinner."

"I'm sure she'll survive." There was an odd note to his words. Disbelief or doubt?

I don't make a habit of staying where I'm not wanted. His comment seemed intent on repeating itself in her brain.

"Survive? Sure," she replied. "That doesn't mean she won't be disappointed. Thanksgiving is a big deal to her. God knows she cooks enough for the entire state—and we're talking about a woman who gave up cooking when Ned made his first million. She'll hunt you down if you aren't around to try her sweet potato casserole."

"There's an image," he said with a soft laugh.

"But not far off. I'm willing to bet she was up early making something special for you."

"Something special?"

"That's the way the Frybergs do things. Seems to me the least you can do is stick around long enough to try whatever it is."

Noelle watched as his eyelashes swept downward and he glanced at the tile floor. He had pretty eyelashes too. When he raised his gaze, his eyes had an odd glint to them. The light looked right through her, and her argument.

"Is this your way of asking me not to fly?"

"I'm not asking you anything," she immediately replied. "I'm thinking of Belinda's feelings."

What was supposed to be nonchalance came out sounding way too affected, and they both knew it. Truth was, she didn't want to deal with a guilty conscience should something happen. "Belinda likes you."

The corners of Hammond's mouth twitched like they

wanted to smile. "Nice to know one member of the Fryberg family likes me."

"Don't get too flattered—Belinda likes everyone." Apparently, her conscience wasn't bothering her too much to stop being bratty.

To her surprise, he laughed. Not a chuckle, like previously, but a bark of a laugh that seemed to burst out of him unexpectedly. "Well played, Mrs. Fryberg. Tell me, are you always so upfront with your opinions?"

Honestly? Quite the opposite. She much preferred adaptation and assimilation to challenge. Hammond brought out an edge she hadn't known she had. "Not always," she replied.

"I'll take that as a compliment then." He crossed his arms, causing the T-shirt to stretch tighter. "There aren't a lot of people in this world who would say boo to me, let alone challenge me as much as you have these past twenty-four hours. It's been very entertaining."

Noelle wasn't sure if she should be flattered or feel condescended to. "I wasn't trying to entertain you," she said.

"I know, which makes me appreciate it even more. You've got backbone."

So, flattered it was. "You're complimenting me for being rude to you."

"Not rude. Honest. I like knowing where I stand with people. You may not like me, but at least you don't pretend, which is more than I can say for a lot of people."

He may have meant to be complimentary, but his words struck her uncomfortably. They pressed on her shoulders along with his comment from earlier. If he was trying to prick her conscience this morning, it worked. She took a long look at him. Tall, handsome, arrogant, and yet... Maybe it was the concussion misleading her, or maybe the injury shifted a mask, but she was seeing something in his expression she hadn't noticed before. It almost looked like...

Vulnerability.

The chip slipped a little off her shoulder. "I don't dislike you," she said, toeing the tile. "Not entirely. Like, I'd feel bad if you crashed your plane and died or something."

"Your kindness overwhelms."

"What can I say? I'm a giver." They smiled at one another, the air between them thawing a little more. The guy wasn't so bad when he wasn't talking about gutting tradition.

"Seriously," she said, "I wouldn't want to see anyone—you—do anything foolish."

"So now you're calling me foolish, are you?"

"I—"

"Relax, I'm joking. I know what you were trying to say. And I thank you."

"For what?" She hadn't done anything special.

His expression softened like she had, however, and she saw the man she'd watched sleep. "Caring about my safety," he replied. "Not many peop— That is, I appreciate it."

A tickle danced across the back of her neck at the gentleness in his voice. If he kept it up, they'd be friends before the bath water grew cold. "Does that mean you'll consider staying for dinner? I wasn't kidding about Belinda being disappointed."

"Well..." He ran his fingers across his mouth and along the back of his neck. "I'd hate to disappoint the woman who sold me her company. I suppose sticking around a few more hours wouldn't hurt."

"Good. Belinda will be glad."

"No one else?"

The cheeky question demanded a shrug in reply. "I

might be a little bit relieved. Lack of blood on my hands and all. Enjoy your bath, Mr. Hammond."

She closed the door before he could see in her eyes that she was way more than a little relieved.

Or that she was starting to like him.

CHAPTER FOUR

JAMES ADDED A LOG to the fireplace. The wood smoked and sputtered for a moment, before being hidden by the flames rising from the logs beneath. Warmth wrapped around his legs. Legs that were now clad in khakis, thanks to Noelle. She'd cajoled the Nutcracker's concierge into opening the hotel boutique so he could buy a fresh change of clothing. The casual pants and plaid sports shirt were more stylish than he'd expected, a fact Noelle took great pleasure in mocking once he'd completed his purchase. His rescue elf had a terrifically sharp sense of humor.

Then again, so did he. Tossing retorts back and forth in the car had him feeling as much like his old self as the bath and clean clothes.

Behind him, cheers erupted in the downstairs family room. Someone must have made a good play. A politer man would head down and join the other guests, lest he be labeled unsociable. Since James had stopped caring what people thought of him when he hit puberty, he stayed upstairs. He was content sitting in one of a pair of wingback chairs, studying the fire.

"People were wondering where you were." Noelle's heels click-clacked on the hard wooden floor until she drew up beside him. "Don't tell me you're not a football fan. Isn't that against the law in New England?"

"Only a misdemeanor," he replied. "I'll be down shortly. I was enjoying the fire. It's soothing."

"Hmm. Soothing, huh?" Perching on the arm of a wing-back chair, she looked up with a tilted glance. Before leaving the house, she'd swapped her sweatshirt for an angora sweater. The neon blue reflected in her eyes, giving them a gemlike glow. "Let me guess," she said, "you're not a fan of crowds either. Can't say I'm surprised."

"I don't dislike them," he replied. "But you're right, I prefer being by myself." It was easier that way. Less picking up on the negative vibes.

He shifted in his seat. The small space between the chairs caused their knees to knock. Laughing, they both pushed the seats back. "Let me guess," he said, "you love crowds."

"I don't love them, but they don't bother me either. I spent most of my childhood having to share my space, so I'm used to it."

An interesting choice of words. "You came from a big family then?"

"Not really."

Then with whom was she sharing space?

"Did you get enough to eat? There's more cornbread casserole if you'd like some."

"Dear God no," he replied. "Four servings is enough, thank you." Why such an abrupt change of subject? He was under the impression she was all about family. "I can't believe I ate as much as I did."

"That's what you get for sitting next to Belinda and her ever-moving serving spoon."

"Plus almost two days without eating." He literally had been the starving man at the buffet. The perfect match for Belinda's serving spoon.

Noelle wasn't joking when she said her mother-in-law cooked up a storm for the holiday. The woman must have served three times as much as the guests could eat. Granted, the turkey and side dishes were nothing like the five-star fare the family chef set out—on those rare occasions he and Jackson celebrated together—but James had enjoyed eating them ten times more. The food today came with wine and laughter and conversation. Real conversation. The kind where people debated, then joked the tension away. No stilted dialogues or pretend interest in each other's lives.

And not a single tumbler hurled across the room.

Funny how that memory had reappeared today, after twenty years of staying buried. Especially since it happened on Christmas Eve. Thanksgiving had been a Tiffany candlestick. Or had that been the dinner plate? The flying objects blended together after a while.

"You're frowning," Noelle said. "Is your head okay?"

"My head's fine." A faint headache at the base of his neck was all. The bulk of his dizziness had ebbed as well. Unless he whipped his head around quickly or hung upside down, he wouldn't have a problem.

"Guess that means you'll be able to fly home without a problem."

"Don't see why not," he replied. His original reason still stood. So long as he could control when and where he stayed, he would. "No sense overstaying my welcome, right?"

"Definitely not," Noelle replied. "Is it a long flight?"

"A few hours. One of the benefits of being the pilot, you save all that time waiting at the airport."

"No security pat down either. Is that why you fly? So you can avoid lines at the airport?" While she was talking, she slid backward off her perch and into the chair. The move left her sitting sideways with her calves balanced on the arm. "Wow, you really do hate people, don't you?"

Her smirk told him she was teasing. "Very funny," James replied. "I fly because it's more efficient. I don't like wasting time."

"Really? Who would have guessed?"

This time he smirked. Her sitting in such a cozy, casual position had made his muscles relax as well. He was at ease, he realized. An unusual experience outside the cockpit. The sky was the one place he felt truly at home. He would never tell that to anyone though. At thirty-nine-thousand feet, the sound of the engine roaring in your ears drowned out your thoughts. There was nothing to prove, nothing to forget.

"I was studying Belinda's mantel." He nodded toward the fireplace, and the collection of photographs and knick-knacks that lined the thick pine. Diverting the attention away from himself once more. "Couldn't help noticing you and she have a lot of the same pictures."

"No big surprise, considering I married into her family."

Family was definitely the theme. The largest photograph was a portrait of a man in a military uniform smiling from the passenger seat of a truck. Pushing himself to his feet, James walked over to take a closer look. A copy of the photo was on Noelle's mantel as well. "Kevin?" he asked. He already knew the answer. Who else could it be?

"He emailed the photo from Afghanistan a few months before the accident."

His jeep flipped over. James remembered from researching the sale. He'd been surprised to hear the Fryberg's heir had been in the military.

"He looks like he enjoyed being in the army."

"Guard," she corrected. "Signed up our senior year of high school." James heard a soft rustling noise, which he realized was Noelle shifting in her chair. A moment later, her heels tapped on the wood floor again. "He was so excited when his unit finally deployed. All he ever talked about was getting overseas. Ned and Belinda were crushed when they learned he'd been killed."

Was it his imagination or did all her answers go back to Ned and Belinda? "Must have been hard on you too."

"I was his wife. That goes without saying."

He supposed it did. It was odd is all, that she focused on her in-laws' grief instead of her own.

Then again, maybe it wasn't. Maybe that was how real families behaved.

The picture on the left of Kevin was from their wedding. The Fryberg quartet formally posed under a floral arbor. It too had a duplicate at Noelle's house. "How old were you when you got married anyway?" She looked about ten, the voluminous skirt of her wedding dress ready to swallow her.

"Twenty-one. Right after graduation. We were already living together, and since we knew Kevin was scheduled to leave after the first of the year..." She left the sentence hanging with a shrug.

No need to say more. "You didn't have a lot of time together."

"Actually, we had almost twelve years. We were middle school sweethearts," she added, in case that wasn't obvious. She smiled at the photograph. "I did a lot of growing up in this house."

"There you two are! Detroit's almost done letting everyone down." Belinda came strolling through the living room along with Todd Moreland, Fryberg's general manager. "I promised Todd here some pie for the road." When she saw he and Noelle were looking at her son's photo, she smiled. "I always liked how happy he looked in that photo."

"He was a real special kid," Todd added. "The whole company liked him. We always figured we'd be working for him one day. No offense, Mr. Hammond."

"None taken," James replied stiffly. "Everyone has their preferences." And it usually wasn't him.

"Noelle was filling me in on some of the family history," he said, turning to Belinda.

"You picked the right person for the job. She remembers more about the family history than I do at this point. In fact, she can tell you who those people in the portrait are. I forgot a long time ago."

"Ned's great-grandparents from Bamberg."

"See what I mean?" The older woman tugged at her companion's arm. "Come on, Todd. I'll get you that pie."

"So, keeper of the family history, huh?"

"Someone has to. Family's important."

"That, Mrs. Fryberg," he said, shuffling back to the chairs, "depends upon the family."

He shouldn't have said the words out loud; they invited a conversation he didn't want to have. Taking a seat, he steered the conversation back to her. "What about your family? Do you maintain your own history as diligently as your in-laws'?"

A shadow crossed her face. "Like you said," she replied. "Depends upon the family."

It appeared they had both dropped curious comments. In her case, she'd dropped two. Was it possible they had more in common than he'd thought?

Catching her gaze from across the space, he held it in his. Trying to tell her he understood. "What's that old saying about families? You can't live with them...you can't take them out and bury them in the woods."

"I don't think those are the words."

Her expression clouded again as she added, "Besides,

you can't bury something you don't have." The words came out low and hesitant. Her gaze broke from his and returned to the photographs on the mantel as though she was speaking more to them than James.

Normally when a woman made coy remarks, he ignored them, seeing how coy was nothing more than an attempt at attention. Something about Noelle's remark, however, cut through him. There was weight to her words that spoke to a piece inside him.

Maybe that's why he decided to ask. "You don't have a family?"

Her sigh rattled signs in Chicago. "What the hell. Not like it's a secret.

"I was raised by the state," she said. "My mother left me in the town crèche on Christmas Eve and disappeared never to be heard of again."

That wasn't necessarily a bad thing, he thought. Better that she disappear altogether than sell you a fantasy and then unceremoniously pop the bubble.

He stared at the crease in his new pants. No wonder her comment affected him the way it had.

The two of them had more in common than she realized.

"Anyway, I grew up in the foster system. The Frybergs were the first real family I ever had. If it weren't for them, people would still be calling me the Manger Baby."

"The what? Never mind." He figured it out as soon as he asked. She said she'd been left in the crèche.

Something else dawned on him as well. "Is that how you got your name? Because you were found at Christmas?"

Her cheeks turned crimson as she nodded. "Nothing like advertising your past, huh? I shudder to think what they'd have called me if I were a boy."

"Trust me, I can imagine."

They both chuckled. When they were finished, he sat

back in his chair and took a fresh look at the woman he'd spent the last twenty-four hours with. "It suits you," he said. "The name."

He wasn't surprised when she rolled her eyes. "So I've been told by half the town."

"Half the town would be right." There was a brightness about her that reminded him of a Christmas ornament. He could only imagine what she'd looked like as a kid. All eyes and luminosity.

No wonder Kevin Fryberg fell for her.

Knowing her story, a lot of things made sense now. Her loyalty. Her attachment to every tradition Ned Fryberg ever started.

He sat back in his chair. "You know, hearing all this, I've got to say I'm surprised Belinda sold to me when she had you around to take her place."

The muscle on her jaw twitched. He'd clipped a nerve. "I said the same thing. I suggested she retire, and let Todd run the place while he groomed me to be his replacement, but she said this was the best move for the store. Hammond's would give us the capital we needed to stay modern. Plus, she thought selling would give me more freedom to do other things. She didn't want me to feel trapped in Fryberg because I was tied to the business."

Interesting. Made sense. While Noelle professed loyalty now, she was also young, with a host of options in front of her. Better to sell the business while Belinda could control the deal. That's what he would do. His father as well. Hell, if James weren't so good at making money, Jackson probably would have sold the store years ago—and not because he wanted his son to have freedom.

Still, he could hear the disappointment in Noelle's answer. A part of her felt rejected. Cast aside. He knew that sting. It made him want to pull her into his arms for a hug, which was unsettling, since he didn't do comfort. And even if he did, she would deny the feelings.

Meaning they shared another trait in common as well: neither liked to show weakness.

"Look on the bright side," he said instead. "She could have fired you."

"You don't fire family."

"Speak for yourself, sweetheart. Not everyone is as family oriented as you are. There are as many people on the other side of the line who value profits over DNA."

She tilted her head. "I'm curious? Which side do you fall on?"

James didn't even have to pause and think. His answer was that reflexive. "The side that doesn't believe in family period."

Noelle stared at him. Unbelievable. No sooner did she catch a spark of warmth, then his inner Grinch came along to snuff out the flame.

"You do know how ironic that statement sounds, coming from the heir of Hammond's, right?"

Ask anyone in the industry and they'd tell you, Hammond's Toy Stores was the epitome of old-fashioned family values. Their history put Fryberg's hundred-year-old tradition to shame.

James's lashes cast shadows on his cheeks as he studied the palm of his hand. "Things aren't always what they seem," he said.

"They aren't? 'Cause I've studied Hammond's." And the last time she checked, Hammond's sure looked like a fifteen-decades-old success story. The Boston store dwelled in the same building where Benjamin Hammond originally opened it. Over the decades, the store had become a touchstone for people looking to recapture childhood innocence. Their window displays and decor was like walking into a magical piece of frozen history. And at Christmas time...

Noelle had seen the photos. It was the Christmas Castle, Santa's workshop and Rockefeller Center all rolled into one. "There's too much heart in your branding for it to have been pulled from a hat."

His reply was somewhere between a cough and a snort. "I'll let the marketing department know you appreciate their efforts. They put a great deal of effort into creating that 'heart.'"

She could feel the air quotations. There were exclamation points on the sarcasm.

"I hate to break it to you," he said, "but my family has made a small fortune selling a fantasy."

"For one hundred and fifty years? I don't think any company can fake their corporate culture for that long."

"Maybe once, a long time ago, someone believed in it," he said in a softer voice. "My grandfather or someone like that."

His fingers traced the plaid pattern on the chair arm. "Who knows? Maybe back then, life was different. But holidays are all manufactured now. There's no such thing as a 'family Christmas' except on TV. Divorce, dysfunction... most of the world's just trying to get through the day without killing each other."

Noelle didn't know what to say. She couldn't call him on his sarcasm, because he wasn't being sarcastic. He delivered his words in a flat, distant voice tinged with hopelessness. It took squeezing her fists by her sides to keep from hugging him. What was it he had said about glass tumblers?

"I'm sorry," she murmured.

"For what?"

Good question. She wasn't sure herself. "That you don't like Christmas."

Hammond shrugged before returning to his pattern tracing. "Don't have to like it to make money off it," he said.

"No," she said, "I don't suppose you do." And Hammond did make money. Lots of money. So, he was right. Who cared if he liked Christmas or not?

Except that the notion left her incredibly sad. Noelle didn't know if it was the cynicism of his words or something else, but this entire conversation left a pang in her stomach. She couldn't look at Hammond without wanting to perch on his chair and press him close.

To chase away his sadness. Talk about silly. Twenty-four hours ago she disliked the man and now here she was thinking about hugging him? As though a hug from her would solve the problem anyway. She didn't even know if he was sad, for crying out loud. Imagine what he would think if she suddenly nestled up against that hard torso.

That she was crazy, no doubt.

Still, possible personal demons aside, she wondered how long it would take before Hammond's cynicism bit him in the behind? She didn't care how good a marketing team he had, a store that didn't believe in its own brand couldn't last. Sooner or later the phoniness, as he put it, would seep through.

You can only bury the truth of your feelings for so long before the truth wins out.

The corner of her gaze caught the photo on the edge of the mantel. Noelle turned her head.

And thought of Fryberg's. Without sincerity at the helm, the castle would truly become a cheesy tourist destination. Wouldn't take long after that for Hammond to close the store down, in favor of his giant shipping warehouse.

The store was on borrowed time as it was. His cynicism shortened the timetable.

"Bet if you spent time here, you wouldn't be so negative."

"Excuse me?"

Oh, jeez. She'd spoken out loud, hadn't she? The point had merit though. "The magic of the place has a way of growing on you," she said.

"Is that so?"

Interesting that he hadn't said *no*. "Yeah, it's so. Do you think this cottage industry of a town sprang up because people wanted to live in Bavaria again?"

Her question made Hammond chuckle. "The thought crossed my mind."

It crossed a lot of people's. "The people here love the holidays. You want to see the Christmas spirit you need to see tomorrow's Christmas season kickoff. It'll convert the most frozen of hearts into holiday fans."

A light flickered in his eyes, along with an emotion Noelle couldn't quite recognize, but made her pulse quicken nonetheless. "Are you asking me to stick around, Mrs. Fryberg?"

"No. I mean, yes. Sort of." Articulating herself would be easier if he weren't chuckling. "So you could see how we do Christmas, is all."

"I've seen how you do Christmas. Part of the celebration struck me in the head yesterday, remember?"

"I meant how the town did Christmas. I thought, if you spent time with people who enjoy celebrating Christmas, it might make you less cynical."

"I see. Worried my cynicism will kill the Christmas Castle sooner rather than later?"

In a word? "Yes," she replied. Wasn't he already turning things upside down in the name of efficiency?

Damn if he didn't chuckle again. A throaty rumble that slid under a person's skin and brushed across her nerve endings. The sound left goose bumps on Noelle's skin. "No offense to your Christmas magic," he said, "but I highly doubt a few gingerbread cookies and a tree lighting will make me less cynical."

He had a point. She probably was giving the magic too much credit. "Once a Grinch, always a Grinch. Is that what you're saying?"

"Precisely. I always thought he was misunderstood."

"As misunderstood as a man with a tiny heart could be," Noelle replied.

This time, instead of chuckling, Hammond let out a full-on laugh. "I wasn't trying to be funny," she said when he finished.

"I know. I was laughing at how easily you're abrupt with me. It's so damn refreshing."

So he'd said this morning. "I'm not trying to be," she told him. "The words keep popping out before I have a chance to mentally edit."

"Making it all the more refreshing, knowing it's organic." He settled back in his chair and assessed her with, based on the tingling running up her arm, what had to be the longest look in the world.

"You know, I have half a mind to bring you along when I fly out of here so you could follow me around and make snarky comments."

"Excu—"

"Don't worry, I'm kidding." He wiped the words away with a wave of his hand. "I have no desire to move you from Fryberg. *Yet.*"

Noelle let out her breath.

"What's this about flying to Boston?" Todd asked. He and Belinda came around the corner from the kitchen. The general manager had on his coat and carried a plastic bag filled with Tupperware.

"You're not planning to fly back tonight are you, Jim? They showed Foxborough on TV and the rain looks miserable there."

Partially hidden behind the chair wings, Hammond winced at the nickname, leaving Noelle to fight back a smirk. If there was anyone who looked more unlike a Jim...

"I've flown in rain before," he said. "I doubt it'll be a problem."

"If you say so. All I can say is better you than me. That wind was blowing so strong the rain was sideways. Won't be much of a passing game, that's for sure."

"How strong is this wind?" Hammond asked, swiveling around to face the man. Noelle noticed he already had his phone in his hand. Checking the forecast, probably.

"No clue. They didn't say."

"Maybe you should stay like you planned," Belinda replied. "I would hate for you to be bounced around during a storm and hit your head again."

"I'm sure I'll be fine. We fly above the weather."

"What about you?" he asked Noelle, once the others had departed. "You want to ask me to stay again too?"

The sparkle in his eye caused a rash of awareness to break out along her skin. "I didn't ask you to stay. I *suggested* staying for tomorrow's Christmas Kickoff might change your mind about the holiday. There's a difference." One of semantics maybe, but she clung to the argument anyway. "Besides, you made it quite clear this morning that you make your own decisions. If you want to risk flying in the wind, that's your business."

She fought back a frown. That last sentence sounded a

little passive-aggressive. It was his business and she didn't care—not that much anyway.

"You're right. It is my business," he replied.

Noelle watched as he tapped the keys on his phone and pulled up the Boston weather. An odd feeling had gripped her stomach. A cross between nervousness and disappointment. Something about Hammond had her emotions skittering all over the place. One minute she detested him, the next she felt a kinship. The man had turned her into a collection of extremes. It wasn't like her, being this mass of shifting energy.

Rather than continue staring, she turned to the pictures on the mantel. Kevin smiled at her from the Humvee and her insides settled a little. Good old Kevin who she'd loved for nearly fifteen years.

Loved like a brother.

No sooner did the thought rise than she stuffed it back down. How she felt about Kevin was her secret and hers alone. No one need ever know the truth.

Besides, she *had* loved him. He was her best friend. Her shoulder. Her rock. He'd given her so much. A home. A family. When she became his girl, her world went from being cold to one full of love and meaning. Kevin turned her into someone special. Wasn't his fault she couldn't feel the passion toward him that he deserved.

"Looks like you got your wish." Hammond's voice sounded above her ear. Startled, Noelle stepped back only to have her shoulders bump against his muscled chest, causing her to start again.

"What wish?" she managed to say as she turned around.

"Todd was right. There's a high-wind warning up and down the New England coast. Logan's backed up until the nor'easter moves on."

"What does that mean?" she asked. Focused on putting distance between their bodies, the significance of his words failed to register.

"It means…" He reached out and cupped a hand on the curve of her neck. His thumb brushed the underside of her jaw, forcing her to look him in the eye. The sparkle she saw in his left her with goose bumps.

"It means," he repeated, "that you're stuck with me another day."

It was the perfect time for a sarcastic remark. Unfortunately, Noelle was too distracted by the fluttering in her stomach to think of one. The idea of his continuing to stay around didn't upset her nearly as much as it had yesterday.

In fact, heaven help her, it didn't upset her at all.

James was disappointed when the barbed comment he'd been expecting didn't come. Instead, he found himself standing by the fire while Noelle went to tell Belinda he'd changed his plans. Again. Oh, well, what good was flying your own plane if you couldn't control your flight schedule, right?

He twirled his smartphone between his fingers. Christmas Kickoff, he thought with a snort. He'd go, but there was no way he'd change his thoughts on the holiday. The Hammond dysfunction was far too ingrained.

Turning his attention from the now empty doorway and back to his phone, James tried to settle the disquiet that was suddenly rolling in his stomach. He wished he could blame the sensation on being stuck in Christmas Land, but his phone screen told the truth. The conditions weren't that bad in Boston; he'd flown in worse dozens of times.

He'd used the wind as an excuse. To hang around.

He didn't rearrange his schedule on a whim for anyone, let alone a woman, and yet here he was making up reasons to spend additional time with Noelle Fryberg, a woman he was sure wasn't one hundred percent happy about the decision. He was breaking his own number one rule and staying where he might not be wanted. All because she made him feel energized and connected in a way no one ever had.

No wonder his stomach felt like it was on a bungee.

CHAPTER FIVE

SOMEONE HAD SHOT OFF a Christmas bomb. How else could he explain it? Overnight, fall had disappeared and been replaced by poinsettias and tiny white lights. There were wreaths and red bows on doorways and evergreen garlands draped the fascia of every downtown building. It was even snowing, for crying out loud! Big, fluffy flakes straight out of central casting. An inch of the white stuff already coated the ground.

"What the heck?" he said as he looked out the passenger window of Noelle's SUV. "Did you drag a snow machine over from one of the ski resorts?"

"Nope. A happy coincidence is all," Noelle replied. "Makes a nice touch for the start of the Christmas season, doesn't it? Snow always puts people in the Christmas spirit."

"Keeps people off the roads too. People hate driving in snowstorms."

"Maybe back in Boston, but in this town, we deal perfectly fine with snowstorms."

"Residents maybe, but what about all those out-of-town shoppers?"

"Oh, I wouldn't worry about them," she replied.

They turned onto the main drag, where the bulk of the

shops and restaurants were located. First thing James noticed was the steady flow of people looking into windows.

"See? The town will do very well economically over the next few weeks, weather or no weather."

"Yeah, but will they drive from downtown to the toy store?" That was the real issue. No one minded walking a few blocks; it was risking the roads that made people balk. Today, Black Friday, was the day retailers counted on to jumpstart their yearly profits. A healthy turnout was vital. "Conditions like this are one of the reasons why I want to push the online business," he said. "Bad weather encourages people to stay inside and shop online." Where there was a lot more competition for their attention.

Not surprisingly, she ignored his comment. "I wouldn't worry too much. We've got things under control."

She pointed ahead to where a bus stop had been decorated with a big gold sign that read Trolley to Christmas Castle Every Fifteen Minutes. "Like I said, we're used to snow. There's already a line too. Everyone loves to visit Santa's workshop."

The smugness in her voice begged to be challenged. "Crowds don't necessarily equal sales. Half the people coming to see the foolish window displays at the Boston store never buy a thing. Not a very good return considering how much we spend on them every year."

She gave him a long look. "If that's how you feel, then why continue having them? Why not scale back?"

"Because..."

James frowned. Why did he continue doing the windows on such a grand scale? Not even his own father wanted to continue the tradition. Yet, every year, he saw the numbers, and then turned around and approved something equally lavish for the following December. It was the one budget item where he deviated from his own rules of business and he didn't have a decent explanation.

"People have come to expect them," he replied. That was the reason. He was preserving Hammonds' reputation with the public. "Those window displays are part of the Hammond brand."

"I'm surprised you haven't figured out a way to support the brand in a less expensive way. Building brand new, custom animatronic exhibits every year is expensive."

Tell me about it, he thought. "Cutting back would send a negative message to the public. They might equate it with financial difficulties that don't exist." James could imagine how the business press might speculate.

"In other words, it's not always a good idea to mess with tradition."

"Unfortunately, no."

"You mean like Fryer and the Santa's reindeer corral at the castle."

Damn. She'd boxed him in. Quite neatly too.

Shifting in his chair, he tipped an imaginary hat. "Well played, Mrs. Fryberg. I see your point."

"I thought you might, Mr. Hammond," she said, nodding her head in return.

Neatly playing him, however, did not mean she was getting all her own way. "You still can't have people leaving Santa's workshop, and not reentering the store. The idea is to keep them around the toys as long and as much as possible."

He waited for a response, half expecting another argument. Instead, she daintily flicked the turn signal handle with her fingers. "Fair enough. What about Fryer?"

"Fryer?" Parts of the other day were still a bit fuzzy. James had to think a moment about whom she was talking about. Finally, he remembered. "You're talking about the giant stuffed moose eating up space at the rear of the store."

"Elk," she corrected.

"What?"

"Fryer. He's an elk, and people love taking selfies with him. In fact, customers have been known to bring friends specifically to see him. Much like your window displays."

So it was the moo—elk she wanted to save. Strange item to draw a line over. Then again, she did mention something about Ned Fryberg using the creature in his early ads and as he'd learned yesterday, his hostess had a very strong attachment to Fryberg history.

"Fine," he said. "The elk can stay. But only until I get a good look at the profit per square foot. If we need to re-design the floor plan, I make no promises."

"But he stays for now?"

"Yes," James replied, his sigh sounding more exasper-ated than he truly felt. "He can stay."

She turned and smiled. "Thank you."

That made twice in three days that she'd managed to convince him to bend on a decision. Granted, neither were major sticking points. Still, she had a better record than most of the experienced negotiators he'd faced.

Beginner's luck, he told himself. It definitely didn't have anything to do with how her eyes got bluer when she smiled.

He continued studying her after she'd turned her eyes back to the road. Today she was dressed for the holidays in a red sweater and a brightly colored scarf. Candy cane stripes, naturally. A matching knit cap sat on her head. The outfit made her look like a tiny character from *Where's Waldo*, only she'd stand out in any crowd, regardless of her size.

A blush worked its way into her cheeks as she sensed

him studying her. "How's your head this morning?" she asked. "You never said."

"Better," he replied. Better than better actually. The spot around his stitches was still tender, but the dull ache had disappeared and he could bend and turn his head without the room spinning. "Being able to shower this morning helped." Nothing like being able to stick your head under a stream of water to erase the cobwebs. "Having a bed helped too. No offense to your sofa."

"I'm glad you were awake enough to climb the stairs this time," she replied. "I was thinking that considering how tired you were last night, it was a good thing you couldn't fly home after all."

"Yeah, a good thing." James forced his expression to stay blank. When they'd returned from Belinda's, he'd gone straight to the bedroom, telling Noelle he was too tired for conversation. In reality, he wanted the solitude so he could process his decision to stay. He wanted to say it boiled down to attraction. Noelle wasn't stereotypically beautiful—more cute really—but the more he studied her eyes, the more he found her gaze hypnotically compelling. If that was even a thing. And her curves…he did love those curves, no doubt about it.

Problem was, attraction didn't seem like a complete enough answer. It wasn't the challenge either, even though she clearly challenged him. He was drawn to her in a way that went beyond attraction. What that meant, he didn't have a clue, other than knowing he liked her in a way that was different from other women he'd known. Whatever the reason, he didn't like feeling this way. He didn't want someone getting under his skin. Didn't want the awkwardness when things inevitably blew up.

Why break his cardinal rule then by sticking around

last night? To spend time with a widow devoted to her late husband and his family, no less?

Hell. Maybe he did want the awkwardness. Maybe he had some subconscious desire to punish himself.

Certainly would explain a lot of things.

A flash of color caught his eye. They were passing an open-air market of some kind, the perimeter of which was marked off by a banner of rainbow-colored flags.

"That's the *Christkindlmarkt*," Noelle said. "It's German for Christmas market."

"Yes, I know. I've seen them in Europe."

"Really? Only other one I've seen is in Chicago. Ned and Belinda told me about the one they visited in Berlin. Sounded wonderful."

James watched as they passed a woman moving her collection of knit scarves out of the snow. "If you like flea markets," he said.

"It's a lot more than a flea market," Noelle replied. Even with his head turned to the window, he could feel her giving him the side-eye. It made his stitches tingle. "We hold the market every year. There are crafts, baked goods. Did you even spend time at the market in Europe? Or were you too busy studying the traffic patterns?"

"Contrary to what you might think, I don't analyze every retail establishment I visit. And no, I didn't have time to visit the market in Germany. My car drove past on the way to a meeting."

"No wonder you are being so derisive!" she said. "We'll visit this one on our way back from the store. Besides the castle, it's the linchpin of our Christmas Kickoff festival. One of the vendors, Heineman's Chocolatiers, has the most amazing hot chocolate you've ever tasted. Kevin and I made a point of visiting his stall first thing every festival. Mr. Heineman would never forgive me if I skipped it."

"God forbid you break tradition," James replied. The strangest flash of emotion passed through him when she mentioned Kevin. Not jealousy—he hadn't known Noelle long enough to feel possessive—but the sensation had the same sharp kind of pang. Like a tear in the center of his chest.

He'd been feeling a lot of odd things these past two days. Maybe that drone had jarred something loose when it struck him.

All he knew was the idea of Noelle and her beloved late husband strolling through the Christmas fair made his sternum ache.

"I owe you an apology. That was the most organized chaos I've ever seen."

Noelle's chest puffed with pride. Store management had spent years perfecting their Black Friday routine, so she knew James would be impressed. What she hadn't counted on was how his positive reaction would make her feel. She took his compliments as a personal victory. Unable to contain her smirk, she let the smile spread as she looked to the passenger seat. "I take it you no longer think of the castle as a fading tourist attraction then."

"I still think our retailing future lies online," he replied, "but I'll concede that you all know what you're doing here. Those handheld wish list scanners are genius."

"Thank you. Ned installed them shortly before he passed away."

Borrowed from the supermarket industry, the scanners let kids record items they fell in love with. The lists were downloaded to share with Santa as well as their parents. Moms and dads could purchase the items then and there and have them stored for pickup at a later date.

"We've boosted our Black Friday numbers by thirty

percent since installing them," she told him. "Of course, our numbers drop a little at the back end, but we prefer to start the season high rather then sweat it out at the end of the quarter."

"Don't blame you there." He smiled again, and this time Noelle got a little flutter in her stomach.

Her assessment of his smile hadn't changed in the last twenty-four hours; if anything, she was finding it more magnetic. Especially when he let the sparkle reach his eyes. That didn't always happen. Noelle found those smiles— the ones with shadows—intriguing too.

Despite the voice warning her the shadowy smiles were the more dangerous of the two.

"When I was a kid, the store made paper lists. Kids wrote down ten items and put the letter in a mailbox for Santa. Parents could come by and pick up their child's list at the front desk."

James had taken out his phone and was typing a note. "This is much more efficient," he said. "I'm sending a message to our logistics department about the scanners right now."

"I had a feeling the system would appeal to you. Although, I've got to admit…" She paused to back out of her parking space. "There was something special about folding up the letter and dropping it into that big red-and-white mailbox." Christmas always brought out the nostalgic in her. "Scanning bar codes doesn't feel the same."

"Even Santa's got to keep up with technology," James replied.

"Yes, he does. By the way, did you see how popular Fryer was with the crowd? I had a half dozen people ask me if we were bringing back our stuffed animal version."

"So you told me in the store. Twice," he replied, as he

tucked the phone back into his coat. "I take it this is your way of saying 'I told you so.'"

"You've got to admit. I did tell you." A chuckle bubbled out of her, cutting off the last word. Didn't matter. He got the point.

In the grand scheme of things, Fryer's continued existence was a small victory, but one that made her happy. She'd saved part of Fryberg's, which was like saving part of her family.

"Don't hurt yourself gloating," James said.

His comment only made her chuckle a second time. Heaven help her, but she was starting to enjoy their verbal jousts. "I'm trying, but it's hard when I was so right. People really love that elk. We should have taken your picture."

"Why? For you to hang in your office?"

"Uh-huh. With a piece of paper underneath that reads The Time I Told James Hammond So." She waved her hand over the wheel as though painting the words in the air.

"Oh, well. Guess my memory will have to do."

From the corners of her eyes, she saw him shifting his position until he faced her. "Anyone ever tell you that you're cute when you're being smug?"

"No," Noelle replied.

The feel of his eyes on her turned her skin warm. It had been a long time since a man had studied her, let alone one with eyes as intense as his. She'd be lying if she didn't admit she found his scrutiny flattering. All morning long, she'd sensed him stealing glances here and there, checking her out as she reached for an item from a shelf or adjusted her rearview mirror. The sensation left goose bumps on her skin, not to mention a warm awareness deep inside her.

It felt good, being noticed by a man. That was, a man like him. Someone smart and savvy. Who took charge of a space simply by entering it. His scrutiny left her feeling decidedly female.

Plus, it kept her from feeling guilty about her own stolen glances. She'd been looking his way since their conversation in front of the fire.

She was stealing a look now.

"Getting ready to gloat more?" James's eyes had slid in her direction, catching her. Try as she might to stop them, her cheeks started to burn.

"No," she said. "I'm done gloating."

"Glad to hear it. Why the look then? You looked like you were about to say something."

Had she? "I was looking at your shirt," she replied. "You…" Her cheeks burned hotter. "You wear plaid well."

"Thank you." The compliment clearly took him by surprise, which was okay, because she was surprised she'd said it out loud. "I'm glad you like it since it's going to be a wardrobe staple while I'm here."

Interestingly, he didn't say anything about leaving. But then, the snow probably made flying impossible.

More interesting was how relieved she felt about his staying.

Again.

And heaven help her, it wasn't only the banter she was enjoying. She was enjoying James's company. A lot. "We can stop at the boutique and grab you a new shirt if you'd like."

"Are you saying you don't like this shirt?" he asked.

"Not at all. I mean, I like the shirt," she corrected when his brows lifted. "I told you, you look good in plaid."

"Thank you. You look good in…red-and-white stripes."

Sensing that another blush was working its way to the surface, she quickly turned her face to scan the left lane. "Color of the day," she murmured.

"Shouldn't it be black? Being Black Friday and all."

"Technically, maybe, but red is far more festive." They were stuck behind a returning trolley. Flicking her turn signal, she eased into the left lane to pass. A little boy with his face pressed to the window saw the car and waved. "I'm not sure a bunch of people running around in black would inspire Christmas spirit," she continued.

"Good point. All that really matters is that the red color stays on the people and not on my balance sheet."

"Said every retailer everywhere today."

"No one said we weren't predictable," he observed with a laugh.

"You can say that again," Noelle replied. Bad Black Friday jokes were as much a tradition as Santa in her office. Hardly surprising that a man raised in the retail industry knew his share of them. "Although not every retailer was born into a retail dynasty."

On his side of the car, James made what sounded like a snort. "Lucky me," he replied.

"I'm sure some people would think so. Ned used to tell me about the early days, when his parents weren't sure the store would survive. He considered it a point of pride that Kevin would inherit a thriving business. I know we're not talking the same thing as a multimillion-dollar national chain…"

"Yeah," James said, reaching back to rub his neck, "if there's one thing my father knows how to do, it's make money."

"As do you. According to Belinda anyway. It's one of the reasons she chose to sell to Hammond's in the first place. Because she liked the idea that you would be stepping into your father's shoes. As she put it, the apple didn't fall far from the tree."

"That isn't necessarily a compliment," James replied.

No, thought Noelle. She supposed it wasn't. Especially if his father was like the man who'd arrived at their store two days ago. She thought him brusque and unsentimental. Absolutely hated the way he'd been focused solely on product and profit.

Oddly enough, James's comments today didn't upset her. Oh, sure, he was just as focused on profit and efficiency, but rather than annoy her, James's suggestions this time around had sounded incredibly astute. Probably because this time around, she liked him better.

Which might also explain why she detected a bitter edge to James's voice when she compared him to his father. "Don't you and your father get along?" she asked.

"Let's say my father does his thing, and I do mine," he said when she cast him a look. "It's a system that's worked quite well for us for a number of years."

Work or not, it sounded lacking. "I can't help but wonder," she said, "if some of these cynicisms of yours are exaggerated."

"I beg your pardon?"

"Well, you can't hate your family too much if you work for the family business."

He stiffened. "I work for the family business because I'm good at it. Like you said, the apple doesn't fall far from the tree. Not to mention that if I didn't, Hammond's wouldn't be a family business anymore," he added in a softer voice.

"There aren't any other family members?"

"None that are around," he said in a chilly voice. Clearly, it was a touchy subject.

Figuring it best to move on, Noelle focused on the rhythm of her windshield wipers going back and forth in the snow. Too bad the wipers couldn't swipe away the awkwardness that had overtaken the car.

As they got closer to downtown Fryberg, the road narrowed to one lane. Thanks to the snow, the already slower than normal traffic was reduced to a crawl. Only the castle trolley, which traveled in the bus lane, made any progress. Looking to the passenger seat, James was attempting to lean against the headrest without pressing on his stitches and not having much luck. His brow was furrowed and his mouth drawn into a tense line. Was he agitated because he was uncomfortable or from her uncomfortable question? Either way, it made Noelle anxious to see.

The sign for Bloomberg's Pharmacy caught her eye, giving her an idea. "Think your head can handle the snow?" she asked.

"It won't melt, if that's what you're asking," he replied.

"Good." With a flick of her directional handle, she eased the car to the right.

"From here until the central parking lot, traffic's going to be slower than molasses. I'll park at the drug store and we can walk."

James's frown deepened. "Walk where."

"To the Christmas market, remember?"

"Hot chocolate and gingerbread cookies. How could I forget?"

"You left out Christmas spirit," she said. "I thought maybe we could find you some. That way you don't have to rely on your marketing department to give your business heart."

"I told you yesterday, it's going to take a lot more than some midwestern Christmas craft fair."

Maybe, but a day at the market might make him smile. And for some reason, that was suddenly important to her.

Noelle swore the Christmas Kickoff got larger every year. At least the crowds did. Seemed to her that in middle school, she and Kevin darted from booth to booth without having to fight the flow of traffic.

James cut through the crowd like it was human butter. Hands in his coat pockets, he walked past the various stalls and vendors with such authority, the people naturally parted upon his approach. Noelle walked beside him and marveled.

Part of the deference had to be caused by his looks. He was, by far, the most handsome man there. The wind had burned his cheekbones pink while his hair and coat were dappled with snowy droplets. Dark and bright at the same time.

He looked over at her with eyes that refracted the light. "Where is this chocolate maker of yours?" he asked.

"I'm not quite sure." Rising on tiptoes, she tried to scan the aisle, but there were too many people taller than her. "In the past, Mr. Heineman liked to take a stall toward the rear."

"Then to the rear we go," he replied. "Like salmon heading upstream. This cocoa better be everything you claim it to be."

"Better. I promise, you'll be addicted." Mr. Heineman had a secret recipe that made the cocoa smooth and spicy at the same time.

"Addicted, huh? You're setting a pretty high bar, Mrs. Fryberg."

"It's not high if it's true," she told him with a grin.

And there it was. The start of a smile. Like a lot of his smiles, it didn't reach his eyes, but they had all afternoon. After the way he'd closed off in the car, she was determined to pull a bona fide grin out of him before they were finished.

She'd contemplate why the mission mattered so much later.

"Coming through!" Four teenage boys wearing matching school jackets were pushing their way through the crowd with the obnoxious aggression of teenage boys. The tallest of the four crashed his shoulder into Noelle. As she pitched sideways, an arm grabbed her waist. Instead of taking a face full of snow, she found herself pressed against cashmere-covered warmth.

"Looks like it's your turn to get knocked over," James said, his chest vibrating against her cheek as he spoke. "You all right?"

"Right as rain." His coat smelled faintly of expensive aftershave while his shirt smelled of her orange body wash. A subtle combination that tempted a woman to rest her head. Okay, tempted *her.* Instead, she pressed a palm to his shoulder to steady herself. "We do have a habit of falling around each other," she said. "Thank you for catching me. In this crowd, I might have gotten trampled."

"That would definitely kill your Christmas spirit." Among other things. "Maybe you should hold on in case you get jostled again."

Noelle stared at the arm he was holding out for a moment, then wrapped a hand around his biceps. The curve of his muscles was evident even through the coat, reminding her that his vulnerability over the past few days was an exception. All of a sudden she felt decidedly dainty and very female. Her insides quivered. To steady herself, she gripped his arm tighter.

"Hey? Everything all right?"

He was looking down at her with concern, his eyes again bending the light like a pair of brown-and-green prisms.

"F-f-fine," she replied, blinking the vision away.

"You sure? You seemed a little unsteady for a moment."

"Must be your imagination. I'm steady as can be," she told him. Or would be, so long as she didn't meet his gaze.

She met his gaze.

"Are you sure? Because we could…"

It had to be a trick of the light because his pupils looked very large all of a sudden.

"Could what?" she managed to ask.

"Go…" His gaze dropped to her lips.

Noelle's mouth ran dry.

CHAPTER SIX

"Go," JAMES REPEATED. "I mean... Back to the sidewalk. Where it's not as crowded." He shook the cotton from his brain. Was that what he meant? He'd lost his train of thought when she looked up at him, distracted by the sheen left by the snow on her dampened skin. Satiny smooth, it put tempting ideas in his head.

Like kissing her.

"Don't be silly," she replied. For a second, James thought she'd read his mind and meant the kiss, especially after she pulled her arm free from his. "It's a few inches of snow, not the frozen tundra. I think I can handle walking, crowd or no crowd. Now, I don't know about you, but I want my hot cocoa."

She marched toward the end of the aisle, the pom-pom on her hat bobbing in time with her steps. James stood and watched until the crowd threatened to swallow her up before following.

What the hell was wrong with him? Since when did he think about kissing the people he did business with? Worse, Noelle was an employee. Granted, a very attractive, enticing one, but there were a lot of beautiful women working in the Boston office and never once had he contemplated pulling one of them against him and kissing her senseless.

Then again, none of them ever challenged him either. Nor did they walk like the majorette in a fairy band.

It had to be the drone. He'd read that concussions could cause personality changes. Lord knows, he'd been acting out of character for days now, starting with agreeing to stay for Thanksgiving.

It certainly explained why he was standing in the middle of this oversize flea market when he could—should—be working. Honestly, did the people in this town ever do anything at a normal scale? Everywhere he looked, someone was pushing Christmas. Holiday sweaters. Gingerbread cookies. One vendor was literally making hand-blown Christmas ornaments on the spot. Further proof he wasn't himself, James almost paused because there was one particularly incandescent blue ornament that was a similar shade to Noelle's eyes.

The lady herself had stopped at a booth selling scented lotions and soaps wrapped in green-and-gold cellophane. "Smell this," she said, when he caught up with her. She held an open bottle of skin cream under his nose, and he caught the sweet smell of vanilla.

"It's supposed to smell like a Christmas cookie," she said. "What do you think?"

"I like the way your skin smells better." He spoke automatically. It wasn't until her eyes looked down and away that he realized how his answer sounded.

"I'm not a huge fan of vanilla," he quickly amended. "I prefer citrus smells."

"We have a holly berry scent which is fruity," the vendor said, reaching for a different sample. "Maybe you'll like this one better."

"I don't think…" Before Noelle could finish, the saleswoman grabbed her hand and squirted a circle of pale pink cream on her exposed wrist. "Scents smell different on than they do in the bottle," she said as she massaged the lotion into Noelle's skin. "That's why it's always best to try the sample out before you buy. What do you think? Fruity, eh?"

She started to lift Noelle's wrist, but James intercepted. Keeping his eyes on hers, he raised her wrist to his nose and inhaled. Traces of berry mingled with the orange blossom. "Better," he said.

Noelle was staring at him, her lower lip caught between her teeth, and he instantly thought about nibbling her lip himself. "But you don't need it," he finished. The scent and/or the nibbling.

He, on the other hand, was definitely going to see a neurologist when he got back to Boston.

For the second time, she slipped free of his touch. "I—I'll have to think about it," she told the saleswoman.

"Don't think too long," the woman replied. "I sell out every year."

"We'll keep that in mind," James replied. Noelle had already moved along.

"Sorry about that," he said when he caught up. He noticed she'd stuffed both her hands deep into her coat pockets. "I didn't realize she was going to make me smell your skin."

"The lady was definitely working for the sale."

"Vendors at these things always are."

They were conveniently ignoring that James was not a man who people made do anything, as well as the fact he could have sampled the scent without brushing the tip of his nose across her skin. "I hope my comment didn't stop you buying something."

"Of course not. I know what I like and don't like."

"I'm sure you do," he replied. In this case, as she'd twice

demonstrated, she didn't like sharing any more personal space with him than necessary.

Message received. Copying her, he stuffed his hands in his pockets.

"Heineman's Chocolatiers is straight ahead," she said, nodding toward the red-and-white-striped stall fifty yards away. "Doesn't look like there's too much of a line either."

Considering the crowds, that didn't bode too well for the chocolate. One would think the greatest cocoa in the world would have lines a mile long.

A burly man with gray bushy hair peeping out from beneath a Santa hat waved to them as they approached. "There's my Noelle! I wondered when I would see you!" Leaning over the table, he wrapped Noelle in a hug. His arms were so massive she nearly disappeared from view. "It's good to see you, child. Merry Christmas!"

Noelle replied something that sounded like "Murry Chrfmaf!" before breaking free. "It's good to see you too. I've been dreaming about your hot chocolate since last December."

"You say that every year."

"I mean it every year. You know it's not Christmas until I have my Heineman's Hot Chocolate fix."

James got a twinge in his stomach. Noelle wore a smile brighter than anything he'd seen on her face. Brighter than anyone had ever smiled around him actually.

"This is James Hammond," she said. "His company purchased the store."

"I read in the paper that Belinda had retired and sold the business. I'm surprised she lasted as long as she did after Ned's death. The store was always more his, and with Kevin gone…"

The man paused to wipe at a spot of dried chocolate with his hand. An impromptu moment of silence.

"I'm surprised she didn't have you take over," he said once the moment ended.

"I'm afraid I haven't worked long enough to have the experience," Noelle said. "I also didn't have the kind of money Mr. Hammond put up."

"I read that in the paper too. Nice to meet you, Mr. Hammond."

"Same here," James replied. "Noelle has been raving about your hot chocolate all day. She swears it has magical properties."

"I didn't say that," Noelle shot back. "I said it tasted magical."

"Auch! You and that man of yours were always saying that. Ever since you were in junior high.

"Did she tell you about her man?" he asked James.

"Some," he replied.

The old man nodded. "Kevin Fryberg. Belinda's son. Fine young man. A true hero."

"So I've been told."

"Left a hole in the town when he died," Mr. Heineman continued. "A huge hole. Can't imagine how Belinda coped. Or this one."

Noelle was looking down and fingering a tiny tear in the plastic tablecloth. Her cheeks had turned a darker shade of pink. "Mr. Heineman…"

But the vendor didn't get her hint. "Did she tell you how he died?" James shook his head, eager to learn details his research couldn't. "Truck rolled over and blew up while he was trying to pull one of his men free."

A true hero, like the man said. Bet he was a great guy through and through. The kind of guy who was easy to fall for. "Pretty amazing," James replied.

"The whole town loved him," Mr. Heineman repeated. "Isn't that so?"

Noelle, who still hadn't said anything beyond his name, nodded. "Everyone," she repeated softly.

"And this one… Joined at the hip, the two of them. Kevin Fryberg and the little Manger Baby. They made the perfect couple."

"Mr. Heineman…" This time, the words came out a little stronger, whether because of unwanted memories or the Manger Baby comment, James wasn't sure. Probably unwanted memories, considering how she started twitching the moment Kevin's name came up.

Personally, James wanted to hate the man—Kevin—but he couldn't. It was impossible to hate a saint. Instead he jammed his hands down deeper into his pockets.

"I don't mean to be rude, but I promised Mr. Hammond hot chocolate, not a trip down memory lane." Noelle did her best to smile brightly as she cut the older man off. "I need to prove to him that the drink's worth bragging about."

"Of course it's worth bragging about. Two cups of Heineman's Hot Chocolate coming right up."

"Prepare to be blown away," she said to James with an enthusiasm she no longer felt.

"My taste buds can hardly wait."

"Go ahead and joke. I will be vindicated."

Naturally, his responding smile didn't reach his eyes.

Dragging James to the market had been a bad idea. If she hadn't let his eyes get to her in the first place, they wouldn't have had to stand here listening to Mr. Heineman go on and on about Kevin. Normally, the man's effusiveness didn't bother her; people always talked about Kevin. Their marriage. His heroism. Being Kevin Fryberg's widow was part of who she was. This afternoon though, Mr. Heineman's reminiscing was too much like a spotlight. It left her feeling guilty and exposed.

Oh, who was she kidding? She was feeling guilty and exposed before they ever reached Mr. Heineman's booth.

It was all James's fault. Him and his stupid, sad, kaleidoscope eyes. Twice now, he'd looked at her in that intense way of his, and twice she'd had to move away before her knees buckled. Twice, she'd held her breath thinking he might kiss her. Which was stupid, because if a man like James wanted to kiss a woman, he would simply go ahead and kiss her.

And, since he hadn't kissed her, he obviously didn't want to. A point she should feel relieved over, but she didn't. She felt foolish. Mr. Heineman waxing on about her great love affair only made her feel worse.

James's voice pulled her from her thoughts. "Seems you and your late husband made quite an impression," he said.

"After a dozen years of buying hot chocolate, I should hope so." Her attempt at lightness failed, so she tried again. "That's the kind of person Kevin was. Everyone loved him. He didn't even have to try."

"Some people are naturally lovable," he replied.

"Only some?" Something about his comment struck her as odd. Looking over at him, she waited for his answer only to get a shrug.

"Not everyone is on that side of the bell curve," he said.

"Bell curve? What the heck's that supposed to mean?"

Mr. Heineman's arrival prevented him from answering. "Here you go. Two cups of Fryberg's finest hot chocolate. On the house," he added, when James reached for his wallet. "To celebrate you buying Belinda's company."

"That's very kind of you."

The old man waved off the compliment. "My pleasure. Besides, it's the least I can do for my longest and most vocal customer. You come back later in the season, okay?" he said to Noelle.

"Don't I always, Mr. Heineman?" There were customers waiting behind them. Leaning over the counter, she gave the chocolatier another hug and left him to his business.

"Moment of truth," she said to James. "What do you think?"

He took a long sip.

"Well…?" She was waiting to drink herself until she heard his verdict.

James smiled. "This is good. Like truly good."

"Told you." Her thrill at seeing his pleasure was ridiculously out of proportion. "And here you thought I was exaggerating."

"Yes, I did," he replied, taking another, longer sip, "and I take every thought back. This chocolate definitely qualifies as amazing. What's in it?"

"Beats me. Mr. Heineman won't share the recipe with anyone. Claims he'll take the secret to his grave." She took a sip and let the familiar delicious thrill wash over her. "That'll be a dark day for sure."

James was studying the contents. "I can't believe no one's suggested he bottle and sell it. A drink this good, sold in stores, would make him a fortune."

"He's been approached. So far as I know he's turned all the offers down. I think he feels it would lose what makes it special if you could have the drink all the time."

"Sort of like a store celebrating Christmas every day?" James replied.

"That's differ— Jerk."

He chuckled, forcing her to nudge him with her shoulder. It was like poking a boulder, and had as much effect, which made him chuckle again. Noelle hated to admit it, but the sound slid down her spine with a thrill similar to the cocoa. It was certainly as smooth and rich.

Quickly she raised her cup to her lips, before her reaction could show on her face. "You know exactly what I mean," she said.

"Yes," he replied, "I do. He's also a rare bird. Most people would willingly sell out for the sake of a fortune."

"Would you?" she asked.

His face had *Are you joking?* written all over it. "Weren't you listening yesterday? Hammond's already has."

Right. Their family fortune made by selling a fantasy.

Cocoa mission accomplished, the two of them began walking toward the market entrance. As their arms swung past one another, Noelle's muscles again tensed with a desire to make contact. She thought back to the lotion display and the way James's nose brushed her skin. Barely a wisp of contact, it nonetheless managed to send tingles up her arm. Now here she was having the same reaction from the memory.

Didn't it figure? All day, she'd been pulling away from his touch only to wish for it now, when the moments had passed.

But what if she touched him?

She snuck a glance through her lashes. Walking in the snow had left James's hair damp and shiny. At the back of his head, where the doctor had woven the stitches, there was a tuft sticking out at an odd angle. What would he do if she reached over and smoothed the unruliness with her fingers? Would his pupils darken the way they had before?

Would his eyes fall to her mouth?

She took a long swallow of cocoa. Thoughts like those were only asking for problems. Better to purge them from her brain.

"Before Mr. Heineman brought us our cocoa, you were talking about bell curves," she said. "You never explained what you meant."

He shrugged. "Ever take statistics?"

"In high school."

"Then you remember how results look when plotted for a spectrum, with the bulk of responses falling in the middle."

"The bell." Memories of mountain-shaped graphs popped into her head. "With the outliers on either end. I remember."

"Same thing works with personality traits, intelligence, etc. Most people are average and therefore fall in the middle. Every now and then, however, you meet someone who skews way over to one side. Like your late husband. He was clearly an outlier when it came to being well liked."

Noelle thought of how Kevin could charge a room with his presence. "He had a lot of personality. Like a big, enthusiastic teddy bear. It was easy to get caught up in his energy." So much so, a person could misread her own emotions. "All the Frybergs are like that."

"Having met Belinda, I know what you mean."

"I wonder where I would have fallen on the bell curve if I hadn't been with Kevin," she mused. "Probably in the middle." The poor little orphan girl dropped in the manger.

"Are you kidding?" They were passing a trash can, so he took their empty cups and tossed them away. "You are definitely an outlier."

"Don't be so sure. I'm talking about me without the Fryberg influence."

"So am I," he replied. "From where I'm standing, you'd be impressive, Frybergs or not."

Noelle was surprised the snow didn't melt from the blush spreading across her body. He'd looked her square in the eye as he spoke, with a seriousness to his gaze that matched his voice. The combination made her insides flutter. "Really? I mean, th-thank you." She cringed at the eagerness in her voice. Sounded like she was leaping at the approval.

Still, she'd been entwined with the Frybergs for so long. It was the first time anyone had ever suggested she was unique on her own. Well, Belinda had, but that was more maternal affection.

"You're welcome," he replied. "And..." He reached over and smoothed her scarf. Right before pulling away, his gloved fingers caught her chin. "Really."

Her insides fluttered again. Double the speed this time. "Wait a second."

They'd resumed their walk when the rest of his comment came back to her. "Didn't you say you were on the other side of the bell curve? That doesn't make sense."

"Why not?" Again, he shrugged. "We can't all be warm, huggable teddy bears. The world needs cool and efficient as well."

"True," Noelle replied. Why did his indifference sound forced, though? He was leaving something out of his comparison. Whatever that something was, its unspoken presence made her want to tell him he was wrong.

She settled for saying nothing. For his part, James seemed happy to see the subject dropped. "Traffic's eased up," he noted.

He was right. With the snow done and the bulk of the day over, there were fewer cars on the road. Most of the tourists were either on their way home or warming up before the evening festivities. "They'll start blocking streets for the Santa Light Parade soon." A few hardy souls were already setting up lawn chairs. "Santa will drive his sleigh down Main Street to light the town tree, and then Christmas season will be officially here."

"And you all do this every year?"

"Like clockwork," she told him. "I'm not the only one

who takes traditions seriously. You've got to admit it definitely kicks up the Christmas spirit."

"I'll admit the town has a certain marketable charm to it, but I still prefer Boston and its other three hundred and sixty-four days."

"Marketable charm? You spend a day surrounded by Christmas and that's the best you can come up with?" Worse, he still had those far away shadows in his eyes. "You really don't like Christmas, do you? I know…" She held up a hand. "We covered this last night."

They were coming up on the Nutcracker Inn. The hotel had been decorated to look like a real gingerbread house. "So much for my theory that Fryberg's enthusiasm could inspire anyone."

"Sorry." To her surprise, his apology sounded truly sincere. "You shouldn't take it personally. When it comes to Christmas…"

He paused to run a hand over his face. "Let's say my history with the holiday is complicated, and leave it at that."

In other words, sad. After all, people didn't hate the holidays because of happy memories.

"And here I thought I was the one with the juicy Christmas story," she said. "In fact, we're passing my birthplace now."

She pointed to the old nativity scene which had been relocated to the Nutcracker's front lawn. "Back when I was born, Mary and Joseph hung out in the park next to the Christmas tree. The Nutcracker took them in a few years ago."

"I'll refrain from pointing out the irony," James said.

"Thank you." Pointing to the baby in the center, she said, "That's where they found me. Bundled up next to the baby Jesus. I guess my mother thought he'd keep me warm."

They stopped in front of the display. "Anyway, a group of people walking by noticed there were two babies, alerted the authorities and a Fryberg legend was born."

"Manger Baby," James said.

"Exactly. And you say your Christmas history is complicated."

Noelle could make light of it now, but when she was a kid? Forget it. Being the odd man out, even at home. The foster families were decent enough and all, but she was never truly a part of them. Just the kid the state paid them to take care of. Whose mother abandoned her in a plaster nativity display.

Thing was, she could justify her mother giving her up, but why couldn't she have picked a fire station or somebody's doorstep? Why did she have to go with the cliché of all clichés on Christmas Eve, thus saddling her child with a nickname that wouldn't die?

"I hated that nickname," she said. "Every Christmas, without fail, someone would dredge up that story, and that's all I'd hear on the playground."

"I'm sorry."

"Don't be." Reaching across the gap separating them, she touched his arm. "I've gotten over it. People don't call me the name anymore, haven't since I was in high school." Or maybe they did, and she didn't notice because she'd had the Frybergs.

James looked down at her hand on his arm. Feeling her fingers begin to tingle with nerves, Noelle moved to break away only for him to cover her hand with his. "It's a wonder you don't hate Christmas as much as I do," he said. "Considering."

"Never even crossed my mind." She stared at the manger. "Christmas was never a bad holiday. I mean, yeah I got stuck with that nickname, but there was also all of this too."

With her free hand, she gestured at the decorations around them. "How can you dislike a holiday that makes an entire town decorated for your birthday?

"Besides," she added. "There was always Santa Claus. Every year, the school would take a field trip to Fryberg's and we'd tell him what we wanted. And every year, those very toys would show up under the tree.

"I found out when I was in high school that Ned Fryberg made a point of granting the low-income kids' wishes," she said. "But when I was six or seven, it felt like magic."

"At six or seven, everything seems like magic," James replied. Noelle could feel his thumb rubbing across the back of her hand. Unconsciously, probably, but the caress still comforted. "But then you grow up and stop believing."

"In Santa Claus maybe. Doesn't mean you have to stop believing in holiday magic. I believe that special things can happen at Christmas time. Like Ned making sure kids got their gifts. People come together during the holidays."

She waited for James to chuckle, and give her one of his cynical retorts. When none came, she looked up and saw him staring at the manger with sad, faraway eyes. "They also rip apart," he said in a low voice.

CHAPTER SEVEN

JAMES'S WORDS—or rather the way he said them—caught her in the midsection. Taking her free hand, she placed it on top of his, so that he was caught in her grasp. "Ripped apart how?" she asked.

"My parents broke up on Christmas," he replied. "Christmas Eve actually. I woke up on Christmas morning and my mother and my little brother were gone. Moved out."

"Just like that? Without a word?"

"Not to me."

Wow. Noelle couldn't imagine. At least she'd been a newborn when her mother dropped her off. Unable to notice the loss. "How old were you?"

"Twelve. Justin, my brother, was ten."

Definitely old enough to understand. She tried to picture James coming downstairs that Christmas morning and discovering his world had changed. "I'm sorry," she said, squeezing his hand. The words were inadequate, but she couldn't think of anything else.

"It wasn't a complete surprise. Whenever my parents got together it was a drunken screamfest. Mom liked her whiskey. Especially during the holidays," he said with a half smile. "And Justin had always been her favorite, so..." He shrugged. Noelle was beginning to realize it was his way of shaking it off whenever the moment got heavy. Or in this case, touched too close to a nerve.

"I'm sure she would have…" She stopped, realizing how foolish what she was going to say sounded. Mothers didn't always want their children; she of all people should know that. "Her loss," she said instead.

The right side of James's mouth curved upward. "From the woman who's only known me for seventy-two hours. And disliked me for at least twenty-four of them," he added, his smile stretching to both sides.

"Meaning I've warmed up to you for forty-eight. Besides," she added, giving a shrug of her own, "I don't have to know you for a long time to realize your mother missed out on knowing you. Same as my mother. Far as I'm concerned, they both didn't recognize what they had."

He squeezed her hand. Even trapped between her hands, his grip was sure and firm. Noelle felt it all the way up her arm and down to her toes. "Are you always this positive?" he asked.

"Me? Positive?" She laughed. "Only by necessity."

She let her gaze travel to the nativity set again. "For a long time, I dreamed about my mom coming back. She didn't have to take me away with her…"

"Just tell you why she left you behind."

Noelle nodded. He understood. "But she didn't. So, what else can I do but focus on being happy without her? Best revenge and all that, right?"

"You're right," James said. A chill struck her as he pulled his hand free from hers. Before the shiver could take true hold, however, gloved fingers were gripping her chin, and gently lifting her face skyward. James's eyes had a sheen to them as he smiled down at her. "Your mom lost out. Big time."

It might have been the nicest thing a man—anyone

really—had ever said to her. While the Frybergs—and Kevin, of course—complimented her, they always made a point of avoiding any mention of her mother. For as long as she'd known them, her past had been the great elephant in the room. Known but not spoken aloud.

She'd had no idea how good having her past acknowledged could feel. "Yours did too," she said, meaning it. "Your brother might be a modern-day saint for all I know, but your mom still missed out. On the plus side, though, at least your father didn't."

He dropped his hand away. "That, I'm afraid is debatable."

While he sounded self-deprecating, she'd clearly said the wrong thing. There was a cloud over his features that hadn't been there before. It made Noelle's stomach hurt. "I'm…"

"It's all right," James said, holding up a hand. "My father isn't the most lovable man himself.

"It's all right," he repeated. Noelle waited for the inevitable shrug to punctuate the sentence; she wasn't disappointed.

James was wrong though. It wasn't all right. The implication that he wasn't lovable wasn't right. Granted, she'd only known him a few days, but the man she was standing with right now seemed very lovable indeed.

She couldn't help herself. Rising on tiptoes, she wrapped her arms around his neck and pulled him into a hug. He stiffened, but only for a moment before sliding his arms around her waist.

"I think they're both idiots," Noelle whispered in his ear before laying her head on his shoulder. One of James's hands slid up her back to tangle in her hair.

They fit together well, thought Noelle.

Scarily so.

* * *

"What was I supposed to do? I mean, the guy's mother left him behind. On Christmas Eve, no less. I had to offer some kind of solace, didn't I?"

The photograph on the nightstand smiled knowingly. Kevin always did know when she was overjustifying. He would listen patiently, and when she finished talking, cock his head and say, "Who you trying to convince, Noelle? Me or you?"

"Me," she told the memory and flung herself face-first across the bed. Why else would she be in her bedroom talking to a picture?

Letting out a long breath, she splayed her fingers across her plaid duvet. The fresh air and snow had taken their toll. Fatigue spread through her body, causing her to sink deeper into the down filling. If she lay here long enough, she'd fall asleep.

James wouldn't care. He was locked in his own room, having retreated there as soon as they returned home. His head was bothering him, he claimed.

Could be true. Embarrassed was more like it though. Who wouldn't be when one of their new employees suddenly starts clinging to them in the middle of Main Street?

He'd hugged her back though. With warm, strong arms that made her feel safe all over. "Like the ones you used to give," she told Kevin.

Except for the way she'd flooded with awareness.

There had been a moment, when James slid his arm around her shoulder, that she swore the awareness was mutual. Apparently not. If James had wanted her, she thought, tracing the threading on her comforter, he would have kissed her. He wouldn't have retreated to his bedroom alone.

"Sorry," she said to Kevin. "S'not like I'm looking to

move on or anything. It's just I haven't been kissed in a long time—by a man, your mom doesn't count—and the idea is kind of nice."

Especially if the kiss came from a man with a mouth as beautiful as James's.

"You had a pretty mouth too, Kev," she said. Everyone in town used to say his smile was brighter than a Christmas tree. Once, when they were in high school, he'd taken her skiing, and face-planted in the snow getting off the ski lift. His laughter could be heard all over the mountain. God, but she missed that laugh.

She missed him. The private jokes. The Friday Old-Time Movie Nights.

"None of this would be a problem if you were here." She certainly wouldn't be drawn to her boss-slash-houseguest.

But, as her eyelids started to close, it was damp cashmere teasing her cheek, not brushed flannel, and the memory of warm arms cradling her close. Kevin's voice sounded in her ear. *Who you trying to convince, Noelle? Me or you?*

By all rights, James should have gone straight to bed, risen early and called a taxi to take him to the airport before Noelle was up for breakfast. Steps one and two went according to plan. Step three, on the other hand, had run into some difficulty. Instead of doing his preflight check, he was sitting on Noelle's leather sofa downing coffee number two and staring at her mantel.

She'd hugged him.

Flirting, kissing, sexual aggression, those he could handle. If Noelle had thrown herself at him, he would have gladly reciprocated, and the two of them would be waking up in tangled sheets.

But a hug? Hugs were tender. Caring. They reached into

vulnerable parts of you and offered compassion. How was he supposed to respond?

He'd hugged her back, that's how. Hugged her and took the comfort she was offering.

And when she put her head on his shoulder, it was like all the air had suddenly rushed to his throat. He'd nearly choked on the fullness. The last time anyone had bothered to comfort him was...

He couldn't remember. Certainly long before his mother left. God knows, she'd checked out on him long before that. His father even earlier. Was it any wonder he couldn't take the moment further?

Or were you afraid she'd say no?

The thought made his shoulders stiffen. Rejection had never been an issue before. Then again, a woman had never hugged him before either, or left him feeling so... so exposed. That made him want her even more, and he didn't mean sexually. He wanted to make her smile. Her eyes light up like a Christmas tree. To give her a dose of that magic she believed in so strongly.

Dear God. His mouth froze against his mug. He sounded like a sappy teenager. Could it be he was falling for Noelle?

"It can't be," he said.

"Can't be what?"

Noelle stood on the stairway in her Wisconsin sweatshirt and a pair of flannel sleep pants. Baggy plaid pants that obliterated her curves. He hated them.

"James? Everything okay?"

He blinked. "I was looking at your pajamas. They're very..." He sought for a decent adjective. "Plaid."

"Thank you," she replied, padding down the last couple steps. Barefoot, James noted. "I wasn't expecting you to be awake this early," she continued. "And you're dressed."

"You sound surprised. I didn't think you'd want me wandering around your kitchen in my briefs."

"Now that would have been a surprise. Is everything okay?"

"Huh?" James missed the question. He was too busy studying her bare feet. They were runner's feet—no painted toes for her—and to his horror he found them as attractive as the rest of her.

"I asked if you were feeling all right," she repeated.

"I'm fine. Why wouldn't I be?"

"Well, you didn't look good last night when you booked it to bed. I was worried you overdid it and made your headache return."

Dammit. Did she have to ask with concern increasing the vibrant blue of her eyes? It made his chest squeeze again, like yesterday.

"I'm fine," he said. "No headache. I got up to check the forecast."

"Oh." Was that disappointment darkening her eyes? "And what did you find out?"

"Actually..." He'd been too busy arguing with himself to look at his phone. It lay dormant on the coffee table.

"Is there coffee left?" Noelle asked.

He nodded, embarrassingly relieved that he didn't have to look quite yet. "I made a whole pot."

"Great. I'm going to grab a cup. Give me yours and I'll get you a refill." She held out her hand and waited while he finished the last swallow. "You can tell me about the weather when I get back."

Okay, the pajama bottoms weren't so bad after all, James decided as he watched her walk to the kitchen. Although, he would much prefer her bare legged.

The woman was definitely under his skin, big time.

Leaning forward, he picked up the phone and pressed

the weather app. As the radar loaded on his screen, he saw it was clear all the way to the coast. No excuse against flying home.

Fantastic, he thought, shoulders feeling heavy.

What a difference a few days made. Two days ago he couldn't wait to get out of the place. Now here he was dragging his feet.

Again.

"So, what's the verdict?" Noelle asked as she came around the corner.

Handing him one of the mugs, she took a seat in the opposite corner and waited.

"Smooth sailing," he replied. "Not a snowflake in sight. I'm back to thinking you had a hidden snow machine yesterday for ambience."

"Wouldn't surprise me if Ned considered it," she replied. "I know at one point he was looking for a way to make snow in July."

"Did he?"

"Apparently years ago he used soap flakes, but they got in the water and caused all sorts of problems. After that, Belinda put the kibosh on summer snow plans."

"Good thinking." He was beginning to think Ned Fryberg had been more than a little on the eccentric side. Envy twisted in his stomach. "Must have been fun, hanging out at their house as a kid."

"More like insane," she replied with a grin. "Ned was forever coming up with ideas. And they weren't all for the store. He went crazy at home too. You should have seen the to-do he made over Halloween. One year, he turned their living room into a haunted tableau. Kevin and his mom played haunted mannequins." James tried to picture the scene in his head. "What were you?" he asked.

"A flying monkey. Ned thought scary mannequins should be bigger than the fifth graders."

"I'm afraid he had a point there." Turning sideways, James rested his elbow on the back of the sofa, and propped his head with his hand. "I bet you made an adorable flying monkey."

"Scary! I was supposed to be scary!"

"Were you?" He waited while she sipped her coffee, noting her cheeks had grown the tiniest bit pink.

"No," she replied. Leaning in, she set the mug on the coffee table. The action brought along the orange blossom scent James had come to associate only with her. He breathed in deep through his nostrils. "I'm not surprised," he said once she'd left his senses. "I can't picture you as anything but adorable."

"Explains why we decided to decorate only outside the following year," she said, the blush James had been trying to deepen coming through. "Anyway, Ned was always coming up with something different. The neighborhood kids loved coming to the house to get candy."

"They sound like a fun family," he said. A true Rockwell painting. "My parents had the housekeeper pass out the candy." Bags of Hammond's brand goodies assembled by employees and doled out from a silver tray.

A hand suddenly covered his. Noelle's eyes were incandescent with unreadable emotion. "I'm sorry—I didn't mean to send us down that road again," she said.

"Road?"

"You know, our collective lousy childhoods."

James knew. But he wanted to hear how she framed the conversation.

"Bad enough we opened up all those wounds last night." She paused, reached for her coffee then changed her mind and pulled back. "I hope I didn't make you feel uncomfortable when I hugged you."

A loaded question. Depended upon her definition of uncomfortable.

"No," he lied. "Not at all."

"Good." He could hear her relief. "Because the moment seemed to call for one, you know? I didn't mean to overreach."

"You didn't," he told her. *You were the first person I'd ever shared my childhood with.*

Her eyes widened, and for a brief second, James wondered if he'd spoken his thoughts aloud. "So, you didn't go to bed early because you were avoiding me?"

Yes, I did. "Don't be silly. I had work to do, and I was tired."

"That's a relief. I... That is, we were..." A frown marred her features as she stared at their joined hands. "I wanted yesterday to jumpstart your Christmas spirit, not make things all awkward between us."

"They didn't make anything awkward," he told her. "As for the hug...it was nice. I liked it."

Soon as the words were out, his insides relaxed with a vengeance, as if they'd been gripped by tension for weeks, not a few days. He played with the fingers holding his. "I enjoyed spending time with you," he added.

"Me too," she said softly. "Even if we did get off on the wrong foot."

"More like wrong feet," James said, smiling. He took a good long look at her.

With one leg tucked under her body, she looked small and delicate against the dark leather. Only she wasn't delicate, was she? She was as resilient a person as he'd ever known. Strong, smart, loyal, gorgeous. A rare package.

Suddenly it struck him. Why he couldn't leave.

"What are you doing tonight?" he asked her.

As he suspected, her eyes got wide again. "Nothing. Why?"

"Because," he said, "I'd like to take you to dinner." And he knew the perfect place too.

"Dinner? You mean, like on a date?" From the look on her face, the question caught her by surprise. A good surprise, he hoped.

"Exactly like a date. Two minutes ago, we both said we enjoyed each other's company. I don't know about you…" Lifting his hand, he risked brushing the hair from her face. "But I'd like to continue enjoying it a little longer."

Wow. Noelle didn't know what to say. She'd gone to bed last night convinced she'd embarrassed both of them by hugging him, that this morning he would be flying back to Boston as soon as possible. Instead, he was asking her out. "But you're my boss," she blurted out. "Isn't that against some kind of rule?"

James chuckled. Noelle hated when he chuckled because the rumbling sound tripped through her every time. "I promise, where we're going, we won't run into a single coworker."

"Is that so?" Goodness, when did her voice grow husky? She sounded breathless.

"Absolutely. What do you say? Spend a few more hours with me? We can call it a thank-you for taking me in during my time of need."

His fingers were brushing her cheek again. Feathery light touches that made her mouth dry and turned her insides warm and liquid. Who exactly was supposed to be thanking whom in this proposal?

"All right," she said, fighting to keep from closing her

eyes and purring. His touch felt that good. "I'd love to have dinner with you."

"Fantastic. You have my word you won't regret a single second. This is going to make your Christmas Kickoff look like a roadside yard sale."

She laughed. Good to know his audacity was alive and well. "I'll have you know I happen to like yard sales."

"You'll like this better. Now…" To her dismay, he took both his touch and the hand beneath hers away. "Why don't you go get dressed while I make the arrangements? If we hurry, we'll have time to walk around before the show."

Show? There weren't any shows going on in Fryberg. The closest performances she knew of were at least a two hours' drive away.

"Are we going to Chicago?" she asked.

James was on his feet and taking her coffee cup. A man in command. "Not Chicago. I'm taking you to Radio City Music Hall."

"Radio what?" She'd heard wrong. "Isn't that in New York City?"

"Yes, it is," he replied. "Which is why you'd better hurry and get dressed."

CHAPTER EIGHT

SIX HOURS LATER found Noelle sitting in the back of an airport town car on her way to Manhattan, and wondering when—or if—her head would stop spinning. New York City for dinner? That was the sort of thing they did in movies. Yet there was the Empire State Building on the skyline ahead. And the Statue of Liberty alone on her island.

James's hand brushed her knee. "You haven't said much since we left the airfield. Everything okay?"

"I can't believe I'm actually in New York City for dinner" was all she could manage to say. "It's…"

"Amazing?"

"Yes. And overwhelming. When you said dinner, I never dreamed you meant—is that the Freedom Tower?" She pointed to a gigantic building with a large antenna, on top of which waved an American flag. She'd seen pictures of the structure built to replace the Twin Towers, but they were nothing compared to the real thing. "It's huge. Even from this far away."

"That was the idea," he replied before shifting a little closer. "To make a statement to the rest of the world about our resilience."

"They won't keep New York down."

"Precisely. New York Strong, as we'd say in Boston," he replied. He shifted again and unbuttoned the top of his coat. Noelle caught a glimpse of pearl gray. Before leaving Fryberg, they'd stopped at the boutique so he could purchase another set of clothes, the plaid, he'd said, having worn out its welcome. The soft color was a toned-down version of the executive she'd met three days ago. That man, she thought with a smile, would never have flown her to New York.

His hand slid along hers, breaking her train of thought. "Would you like to see it up close?" he asked.

"Careful how often you ask the question. I want to see everything up close."

Now that she'd accepted the ginormousness of where they were, excitement was quickly replacing disbelief. "I've always dreamed of going to New York ever since I was a little girl, but never got the chance."

"Never?"

"I almost went. Once. Right after Kevin and I got engaged. There was a merchandising conference I thought of attending."

"What happened?"

"The conference conflicted with an awards banquet Kevin had to attend. People expected me to be there too, so I cancelled. I could always go to Manhattan another time. Wasn't like the city was going to go anywhere."

"At least not last time I looked," James replied. "And now you're here."

"Now I'm here." She sat back against the leather seat and watched the traffic. Despite being the middle of the afternoon on a Saturday, the streets were lined bumper to bumper, with more cars than ten Fryberg Christmas Kickoffs. Everywhere she looked, buildings reached toward the sky. Big, square buildings jammed with people. She could feel the city's energy pulsing through the limousine's windows. It was fantastical.

Next to her, James was watching the window as well, his long fingers tapping on the armrest. He looked quite at home with the traffic passing by them. Same way he'd looked at home in the cockpit of his plane. Noelle had watched him the entire flight, his deftness at the controls far more interesting than the ground below. Surely he knew how gracefully he moved. If he didn't, the universe really should hold up a mirror for him to see.

"What?" He turned his face to hers. "Why are you staring at me?"

"Thank you," she replied, the words bubbling out of her. "For today."

"You haven't seen anything worth thanking me for yet."

Was he kidding? They were passing the biggest Christmas billboard she'd ever seen that very minute. "I don't have to see anything," she told him. "Being here is already amazing."

His eyes really did turn into sparkling hazel diamonds when he smiled. "You ain't seen nothing yet. You, Noelle Fryberg, are going to get the full New York Christmas experience."

"I can't wait."

It wasn't until she felt his squeeze that she realized they were still holding hands. Their fingers were entwined like puzzle pieces. Yet again they fit together with unnerving perfection.

James instructed the driver to pull over at the corner of Fifth and West Thirty-Third. Looking at the block of office buildings, Noelle frowned. "I might be a New York City virgin, but even I know this isn't Radio City Music Hall."

"There's no moss growing on you, is there?" James replied. Opening the door, he stepped outside and offered her a hand. "Since we have time before the show, I figured you'd enjoy a bird's-eye view of the city. Watch your step."

A blast of cold east coast air struck Noelle as she stepped onto the sidewalk. If not for James's warm hand holding hers, she might have shivered. His grip, however, left her impervious to the wind. "Bird's-eye view?" she said. "I don't under... *Ohhhh!*" Spying the crowd ahead, it clicked where they were. The Empire State Building.

"Precisely. Best view in the city, if you don't mind getting cold."

What a silly comment. "I'm from the Midwest, remember?" she replied. "We invented cold. Or have you already forgotten what it was like walking around yesterday?"

Despite James's warnings of cold, the outside observation deck was lined with tourists. The two of them had to wait before finding a space near the rail. When they finally made their way to a viewing spot, Noelle leaned as close to the barricade as possible. Below, the city spread for miles. She squinted past the rooftops and spotted Lady Liberty. From up there, the majestic statue looked no bigger than an action figure. "It's like standing at the top of the world," she said, only to cringe a little afterward. "Not that I'm being clichéd or anything."

"Hey, phrases become cliché for a reason." A pair of arms came around to grip the rail on either side of her, blocking the wind and securing her in a cashmere cocoon.

Noelle's fingers tightened their grip. She could feel the buttons on his coat pressing through hers, letting her know how close he was. So close that she need only relax her spine to find herself propped against his body. Did she dare? If she did, would he wrap his arms tighter? Her stomach quivered at the thought.

"I wonder if you can see the Christmas tree from the other side," she said.

"The one at Rockefeller Center? I haven't a clue."

Turned out she didn't need to slouch, because James stepped in closer. "Want to know a secret?" he whispered in her ear. His breath was extra warm against her cold skin. "I've been to Manhattan dozens of times over the years and this is my first visit to the top of the Empire State Building."

"Really?" The sheepish nod she caught over her shoulder made her smile. "You're a virgin too?"

Several heads turned in their direction, earning her a playful shoulder nudge. "Say it a little louder," James replied. "There are a couple of people below that didn't hear you."

"Okay. James Hammond is a—"

The rest of her sentence died in a giggle as he grabbed her by the waist and pulled her to him. Her head leaned back against his collarbone. "I'm glad we could experience this together," she told him.

For a second there was silence, then his voice was back at her ear. "Me too," he murmured. Noelle swore he brushed the shell of her ear with his lips.

Like a kiss.

They took their time on the deck, making sure they saw all four views. Each was spectacular in its own right, and Noelle decided that if her tour ended then and there, it would still be an unforgettable day. "You really need to stop thanking me," James said as they left the observation deck. "I'm feeling self-conscious."

"Then you shouldn't have sprung for such a marvelous day," she told him. "Isn't the whole point of a day like today to make a woman feel grateful?"

She meant it as a tease, but he took her seriously, looking down at her with eyes filled with sincerity. "Not this time," he said. "Not you."

If they weren't trapped in a line of tourists, Noelle would have kissed him then and there.

The crowd herded itself downstairs and into the gift shop. "I see they've got the traffic flow issue managed," she remarked, hoping shop talk would distract the fluttering in her stomach. It didn't help that James's hair was windblown. The bonded strands around his stitches stuck out at an angle. "Considering all their years of practice, I'd be disappointed if they didn't," he replied.

Noelle only half listened. She was too distracted by those errant strands. Her fingers itched to run through them. Because those mussed-up strands looked all wrong, she argued. If she were him, she'd want someone to adjust his appearance, right?

"Hold on a second." Grabbing his arm, she stopped him from heading toward the doorway. "Let me..." As gently as possible, she combed his hair smooth, making sure her fingers barely grazed the bump on the back of his head. "Much better."

Did she just purr? Wouldn't surprise her. Stroking his hair was nearly as soothing as being petted herself.

"You realize the wind is going to mess up my hair again the second we step outside."

"Then I'll simply have to fix it again." She smoothed a patch around his ear, which was really an excuse to continue touching him.

Her reward was a smile, and a brush of his fingers against her temple. "Well, if that isn't incentive to spend the day stepping in and out of the wind, I don't know what is. Now, what do you say? Should we continue exploring?"

Noelle shivered. Explore could mean so many things. Whatever the meaning, she had the same answer. "Absolutely," she said. "Lead the way."

* * *

They were walking out of Radio City Music Hall when James's phone buzzed. "Maybe you should answer," Noelle said. "That's what? The fourth call today?"

While she was flattered he considered her to be the higher priority, she knew from experience that not all calls could be ignored. "Generally speaking, people only bother the boss on weekends if there's an emergency."

"And what makes you so sure these calls are from the office?" he asked. "How do you know I don't have an expansive social life?"

Like a girlfriend back in Boston? The thought passed as quickly as it popped into her head. James wasn't the type to play around. He was, however, the type to work all hours. "Okay, Mr. Social Life," she challenged, "what would you be doing right now if you hadn't been stuck with me all weekend?"

"A person can be dedicated to his job and have a social life, I'll have you know. And I'm not stuck with you."

Still, her point had been made and he pulled out his phone. "I was right. Nothing that can't wait," he said. He rejected the call. Not, however, before Noelle caught the name on the call screen—Jackson Hammond—and the frown that accompanied it.

Curiosity got the best of her. "You don't want to talk to your father?"

"Not particularly," he replied. "I'm sure all he's looking for is a trip update. I can fill him in when I get home."

Ignoring the unexpected pang that accompanied the words *get home*, Noelle instead focused on the rest of his comment. "I'm sure he wants to hear how you're feeling as much as he cares about the trip."

The sideways glance he sent her said otherwise. She thought about what he said yesterday, about his father and he doing their own thing. "He does know about your accident, doesn't he?" she asked.

James shrugged. "Word's gotten to him by now, I'm sure. I left a message with his 'protégé' that I was detained by a drone attack. She makes sure he's kept abreast of things."

"So you haven't spoken to him at all since your accident?"

"No." He stepped aside to let her exit the building first. "I told you," he continued, once he joined her, "my father and I aren't close. We don't do the family thing. In fact, I think I've made it pretty clear that the Hammonds are the anti-Frybergs."

Selling the world a clichéd myth. So he'd told her. Ad nauseum. "Still, your father is trying to reach you. You don't know it's all about business."

"I know my father, Noelle. When I was a kid and broke my leg, he didn't come home for two days because he was in Los Angeles meeting with a distributor."

Poor James. "How old were you?" Not that it mattered. A child would feel second-best at any age.

"Twelve and a half."

Right after his mother left. A time when he needed to feel wanted and special. Her heart clenched on preteen James's behalf. Being abandoned by her parents sucked. Still, James had something she didn't, and she needed to point that out. "He came eventually. I know it doesn't sound like much," she said when he snorted, "but I would have killed for even that much parental attention."

"Don't take this the wrong way, but you got the better end of the deal. At least you knew where you stood from the start."

"More like where I didn't stand. My parents were out

of my life from day one. So long as your father is around, you still have hope for a relationship."

Up until then, the two of them had been strolling the sidewalk. Now James stopped to look at her and for a moment, Noelle saw the twelve-year-old boy who'd been struggling to keep his hurt at bay. "Why hope for something that won't happen?"

And yet he did hope. She saw how his eyes flashed when she'd suggested his father might be worried.

"Never say never," she replied. "You can call me naive, but there's always hope. Look at me. For years, I burnt my Christmas wish on wanting a family, and then the Frybergs came into my life and poof! My wish came true."

"What do you wish for now?"

"I—" She resumed walking. "We're talking about you, remember?"

"We're also talking about hopes and dreams. You said you used to wish for a family. Since your wish was granted, you must hope for something else. What is it?"

"Peace on earth."

"I'm serious," he said.

"So am I." Every year, she, like every Fryberg's employee, filled out her Christmas wish list, and asked for large, conceptual things like peace or good health for all. There was no need for her to hope for anything personal. After all, hadn't she'd gotten everything she wanted when she'd become Noelle Fryberg? What more could she want?

James took her hand.

"This conversation is getting way too serious," he said. "Today is supposed to be about you getting the New York Christmas Experience. What did you think of the show?"

Noelle shook off her somberness with a laugh. "I loved it." She loved how he described the day with capital letters more. "If I were six inches taller, I'd start practicing my high kicks so I could audition."

"That's something I'd pay to see—you kicking your leg past your ears. I had no idea you were that limber," he added, leaning in to her ear.

Noelle's knees nearly buckled. It wasn't fair, the way he could lower his voice to the exact timbre to zap her insides. "Who said anything about ears? Waist-high is more like it.

"S'all a moot point anyway," she added. "With my size, I'd be more likely to get cast as one of the elves."

"And a right adorable one at that."

Noelle tried to shove him with her shoulder. Unfortunately, the impact had no effect. Instead, she found herself trapped against his side when he snaked his hand around her waist. The position left her arm no choice but to respond in kind and slip her arm around his waist as well.

"I mean it," he said, adding a side hug for good measure. "First thing I thought when I saw you was that you were Belinda's attack elf. So much feistiness in such a tiny package."

"I'm not sure if I should be flattered or actually try to attack you," she replied. With her luck, she'd end up wrapped in both his arms.

"Definitely flattered," he told her. "My second thought was I didn't know elves could be so beautiful. Are your knees all right?"

They wouldn't be if he kept purring compliments in her ear. "Careful," she purred back. "Keep up the sweet talk, and I'll get a big head."

"You deserve one. I've never met a woman like you, Noelle."

"You must not get out much."

Once more, he stopped, this time to wrap a second arm around her. Noelle found herself in his embrace. Heavy-lidded heat warmed her face as his eyes travelled to her mouth. "I'm not joking," he said. "You're an original."

If this were Fryberg, his features would have been hidden by the early darkness, but being the city that never slept, she could see his dilating pupils beneath his lashes. Their blackness sucked the breath from her lungs. She parted her lips, but couldn't take more than a shallow breath. Her racing heart blocked the air from going farther.

"I want to kiss you," she heard him say. "Right here, on this sidewalk. I don't care if people stare or make rude comments. I need to kiss you. I've wanted to since I—"

"Shut up, James." She didn't need to hear any more.

Standing on tiptoes, she met him halfway.

Kissing was something James thought he had a handle on. He'd kissed dozens of women in his lifetime, so why would kissing Noelle be any different?

Only it was different. With other women, his kisses had stemmed from attraction. He'd kissed them to stoke his sexual desire—and theirs. But he'd never *needed* to kiss a woman. Never had a bone-deep ache to feel their mouths on his.

The second his lips met Noelle's, a feeling he'd never felt before ballooned in his chest. Need times ten. It was the blasted hug all over again. Talking about his father and hope, she'd ripped open a hole inside him and now he couldn't get enough, couldn't get *close* enough.

Which was why he surprised himself by breaking the kiss first. Resting his head against her forehead, he cradled her face in his hands as they came down to earth.

"Wow," Noelle whispered.

Wow indeed. *Wow* didn't come close. "I think…" He inhaled deeply, to catch his breath. "I think we should get some dinner."

Noelle looked up her lashes. Her brilliant blue eyes were blown black with desire. "Is that what you want?" she asked. "Dinner?"

No.

And yes.

Some things were meant to simmer. "We've got all night," he said, fanning her cheek with his thumbs. The way her lips parted, he almost changed his mind, but inner strength prevailed. "Dinner first," he said with a smile. "Then dessert."

She nodded. Slowly. "All right. Dinner first."

"Wow. That might be one of the first times this weekend that you haven't disagreed with one of my suggestions." Maybe miracles could happen.

"What can I say?" she replied. "I'm hungry. Although…" The smile on her face turned cheeky as she backed out of his embrace. "Since you decided to postpone dessert, I'm going to make you work for it."

Her words went straight below his belt. Snagging a finger in the gap between her coat buttons, he tugged her back into his orbit. He leaned in, feeling incredibly wolfish as he growled in her ear. "Challenge accepted."

As seemed to be the theme of the past few days, James was completely wrong about the restaurant. He made their reservation based on an internet article about New York's top holiday-themed restaurants and wrote off the writer's ebullience over the decor as a marketing spin. For once, though, spin matched reality.

"Oh. My." Noelle gave a small gasp as they stepped inside. The place was completely done in white and gold to resemble an enchanted winter forest. Birch branches trimmed with tiny white lights formed a wall around the central dining room, making it look as though the tables were set up on the forest floor. There were Christmas ornaments and stockings strung about, as well as fluffy cottony-white snow on the window edges.

"Talk about a winter wonderland," Noelle said.

Indeed. Silly as it was, he actually felt the need to hold her hand tighter, in case some woodland creature tried to whisk her away. This was what she'd call magical. "I'm glad you like it," he said.

"Like it? It's unreal." She had her phone out and was snapping away at the various objects. Suddenly, she paused. "I'm not embarrassing you, am I?"

"Not at all." She was enchanting. "Take as many photos as you want. We'll be eating in a different room."

She frowned, and James almost felt bad for disappointing her. *Almost*. "You mean we're not eating in the forest?"

"Mr. Hammond requested a table in our crystal terrace," the maître d' informed her. He gestured to the elevator on the other side of the birch barricade. "Upstairs."

"We're eating on the roof," Noelle said a few moments later. He smiled at her disbelief as she stated the obvious.

Actually a glass atrium, the famed Crystal Terrace was decorated similarly to downstairs, only instead of recessed lighting, patrons ate under the night sky.

"I figured since this was our only meal in the Big Apple you should eat it with a view of the skyline," he told her. "By the way, this time you can see the Rockefeller Christmas tree. *And* the Empire State Building."

"Amazing."

Letting go of his hand, she moved toward the window while he and the maître d' exchanged amused glances.

"I had a feeling you'd like the view," James replied. He waited until the maître d' had disappeared behind the elevator doors before joining her at the glass. Noelle stood like a child pressed to a window display with her hands clutching the brass guardrail. Her lower lip was caught between her teeth in wonder. James stood behind her and captured her between his arms, the same way he had on the observation deck. "As good as the Fryberg town tree?" he asked.

"The Empire State Building really is red and green. I've read about how they projected the colors, but I had no idea they would be so vivid. The building looks like a giant cement Christmas tree."

"I'm not quite sure that's the analogy the city was going for, but…"

"I love it. Thank you for bringing me here."

Still trapped in his arms, she whirled around to face him. Up close, her smile knocked the wind out of him. He had to swallow before he could find his voice.

"I thought we agreed this afternoon that you could stop thanking me."

"We did, but a place like this deserves a special thank-you." She slipped her arms around his neck. "Makes sense now, why you wanted to have dinner. I'd have been disappointed if I'd learned… Are we the only people here?"

He was wondering when she'd notice. "No. There's a waiter and a bartender on the other side of the room."

"I don't mean the staff. I mean dinner guests. The other tables are empty."

"Are they, now?" He pretended to look over his shoulder. The Terrace only housed seven tables; the limited seating was part of how the place got its exclusive reputation. All seven tables were unoccupied.

"Well, what do you know. So they are empty," he said before turning back to her. "Must be because I booked them."

"You what?" Noelle's expression was worth every cent he'd paid too. Her eyes widened, and her lips formed an

O. She looked so charming; he had no choice but to press a kiss to her nose.

"You know how I like efficiency," he told her. "Service is so much better when you don't have to compete with other patrons for the server's attention. Besides, I wanted to give you something special since you took me in these last few days."

"I was under the impression flying me to New York was the something special," she replied. "This is…"

Shaking her head, she slipped from his arms. "Do you do this sort of thing often? Buy out restaurants?"

James wasn't sure of the right answer. Had he gone too far? The impulse had popped into his head when he'd read the internet article. Yes, it was over the top—this whole day was over the top—but he'd wanted to make it memorable.

Face it: he'd wanted to impress her. Because he liked her. And how else was he supposed to compete with a dead war hero who gave her the family she'd always dreamed of?

"I didn't mean to make you uncomfortable," he replied. "If you want, I can tell the maître d' to open the other tables…"

"No." She shook her head again. "You went to a lot of trouble, and I'm sounding ungrateful. It's just that you didn't have to do all this. Any of this. I would have been perfectly happy having dinner with you at the Nutcracker."

"I know. I told you, I wanted to do something special. To make you feel special. Because I kind of think you're worth it. Hell, after kissing you, I know you're worth it."

He scuffed the ground with his foot. Stumbling for words wasn't like him. But once again, she had him feeling and thinking uncharacteristically.

"Thank you," Noelle replied. Unlike the other times,

she spoke in a gentle, tender voice that hung in the air. "No one has ever put so much effort into trying to impress me. Ever. You've made me feel very special. I think you're crazy. But you make me feel special."

James smiled. So what if he was crazy? The satisfaction he was feeling right now far surpassed that of any deal or successful investment. "So does this mean you'll stick around for dinner?"

"What do you think?" she replied.

Turning to the first table within reach, James pulled out a chair. "After you."

CHAPTER NINE

"HERE'S WHAT I THINK." It was an hour later, and the wine had loosened Noelle's tongue. "I think that you're not as anti-holiday as you claim."

"I'm not?"

"Nope." Giving an extra pop to the *p*, she leaned forward across the table. Shadows cast by the flame in the hurricane lamp danced on the planes of James's cheek, giving his handsome features a dark and mysterious vibe. She'd been thinking about this for a while, analyzing the clues he'd dropped. Tonight's rooftop surprise sealed her theory. "I think you're sentimental and I think you're a romantic," she told him.

He rolled his eyes. "Why? Because I bought out a restaurant? Hate to break it to you, honeybunch, but that doesn't mean I'm romantic—it means I'm rich and trying to seduce you."

And he was succeeding. Not even the wine and duck with truffles could wash the kiss they'd shared off her lips. James kissed like a man in charge. She might have met him halfway, but there was no doubt who dominated whom once the kiss began, and frankly, so caught up was she in the moment, that she didn't care. She liked being overwhelmed.

Right now, however, she didn't like him distracting her.

"Why are you so quick to paint yourself negatively?" she asked, getting back on track. "Last time I checked, a person could be rich and seductive and a sentimental romantic. This restaurant is only one example. The entire day..."

"Again rich and..."

"Trying to seduce me. I know," she replied.

James reached for the bottled water to pour himself a glass. "So far, I've got to say that your argument isn't too compelling."

"I have other examples."

"Such as?"

"You were tapping your toe during the show."

"It was a catchy tune!"

And the enthusiastic smile he wore at the end of the performance? He'd probably say he was rewarding a job well done. "What made you pick that particular show in the first place, huh? Why not that hot hip-hop musical everyone's gushing about, if you were simply out to impress me? Don't tell me you couldn't have scored tickets to that if you'd wanted them. Instead, you picked a Christmas show, and not just any show. The Christmas Spectacular. Heck, even your choice of restaurant," she said, gesturing at the winter wonderland around them, "is Christmassy."

"I didn't exactly pluck the theme out of thin air. Since I arrived in Fryberg, you've made your attachment to Christmas quite clear. For crying out loud, your in-laws celebrate Christmas year-round."

"All the more reason for a person who hates holidays to show me something different," she replied. "But you didn't. You went full-on Christmas. What's more, you enjoyed everything as much as I did. And not—" she wagged her finger "—not simply because I was having fun."

James raised his glass to his lips. "How could I not have a good time with such amazing company?"

Noelle blushed at the compliment. There was more though. She'd stolen enough looks during the day when he thought she wasn't looking. Saw the enjoyment on his face. Their adventure today had touched something inside him. The same sensitive part that was inspired to rent out the dining room.

She still couldn't believe he'd rented an entire rooftop for her. Talk about intimidating. She'd never been the focus of attention before, not by herself. Not without a Fryberg attached. The notion unsettled her.

Her thoughts were getting off track. "You're trying to distract me with compliments," she said, shaking her index finger. "No fair."

"*Au contraire*. I'm pretty sure all's fair," he replied.

"This isn't love or war."

"Yet."

He was joking. It was one date and, possibly, a few hours of intimacy. Neither of them expected anything more. Nevertheless, her stomach fluttered anyway. She reached for her wine, changed her mind, picked up her water and took a long drink to drown the sensation.

"Do you have any good memories of Christmas?" she asked, changing the subject.

He made a noise in his throat that sounded like an unformed groan. "We're back to talking about Christmas, are we?"

"We never left," she said. In spite of his efforts to dissuade her. "Surely, you must have some decent memories before your parents' marriage went sour." She was curious. There was a different James Hammond behind the cynicism, one that believed in moonlight dinners and making a woman feel like a princess, not for seduction purposes, but because he thought that's what a woman deserved. She wanted to get to know that James.

If she could coax him to talk.

He sat back and let out a long breath. "Easier asking for the Holy Grail. My parents never got along. Even before they separated, as soon as they spent extended time together, they would end up screaming and tossing dishes."

"Glass tumblers." She remembered.

"Exactly. Honestly, it's amazing they managed to have two kids." Frowning, he pushed his plate toward the center of the table. "There was this one Christmas. I was four. Maybe five. Hammond's was having some kind of event, for charity I think—I'm not sure. All I know is Santa was supposed to be there so my parents took Justin and me into Boston to see him. We had these matching wool coats and hats with flaps on them."

"Stylish," she said.

"Best-dressed kindergartener in the city."

His frown eased into a nostalgic-looking smile. "It was the first time I'd ever seen the Hammond's window displays. First time I remember seeing them anyway. We stood outside and watched them for hours. Although now that I say it out loud, it was probably more like ten minutes."

"Time has a way of slowing down when you're a kid."

"That it does," he said. "I read somewhere the passage of time changes based on how much of your lifetime you've lived. The author was very scientific. All I know is, on that afternoon, I could have watched those window displays forever."

He chuckled. "In one of the windows, a bunch of animals had broken into Santa's workshop. There was this squirrel inside a pot on one of the shelves that kept popping up. Every time he did, Justin would squeal and start laughing. Every time," he repeated. "Like it was the first time." And he rolled his eyes the way Noelle imagined his four-year-old self had. The image made her heart turn over.

"But you knew better," she teased.

"Totally. Who cared about some stupid squirrel when there was a polar bear looking in the window? At least the squirrel was inside the workshop. The bear was obviously in the store. What if he ate Santa Claus?"

"Obviously."

"Hey, don't laugh. Polar bears can be ruthless creatures."

"I'm not laughing." Not much anyway. His exaggerated earnestness made staying completely serious impossible. She could picture the moment in her head. Little James, his eyes wide and serious, worried about Santa's safety. "What did you do?"

"I thought we should call the police so they could tranquilize him, but my father assured me that all the polar bears at the North Pole were Santa's friends, and if there was one in the store, he was probably Santa's pet. Like a puppy."

"And that worked?"

His gaze dropped to the table. "Yeah, it did. If my father said the polar bear was a pet, then I believed him. Funny how at that age, you believe everything your parents tell you."

"The voice of definitive authority," Noelle said.

"I guess," he replied. "Anyway, we saw Santa, he told me the bear was taking a nap when I asked, and that Christmas I found a stuffed polar bear in my stocking. Damn thing sat on my bureau until junior high school."

When his world fell apart.

Afraid he'd come to the same conclusion, she reached

across the table and took his hand. He responded with a smile and a fan of his thumb across her skin.

"I bet you were an adorable little boy. Protecting Santa Claus from danger."

"More like worried I wouldn't get presents. I'd have gladly sacrificed Justin if it meant finding a race car set under the tree."

"Did you?"

"You know, I don't remember."

But he remembered the window displays, and the polar bear toy, and his childhood wonder.

"You know," she said, "they say Christmas brings out the child in people. That's why adults go so gung ho for the holiday."

"Oh, really?" He entwined their fingers. "In your case, I'd say that's definitely true."

"It is for you as well. Seriously," she said when he rolled his eyes. "You can talk about hating Christmas all you like, but today's little adventure proves that little boy who watched the window displays is in there, way down deep."

"That little boy also pulled off Santa's beard."

He was so determined to pretend he didn't have a soft side. "Fine, be that way," she told him. "I know better. Thou protest too much."

"I beg your pardon?"

"You heard me," she said, reaching for her glass. "You may act all cynical and talk about greeting card fantasies, but you don't one hundred percent believe it. If you did, you'd convince your father to redo the Boston store, tourist attraction or no. We both know you could do so successfully." Instead, he doubled down on the Christmas fantasy every year. The reason hadn't hit her until tonight, as she looked around the winter wonderland he'd rented.

He may never have had a greeting card family Christmas, but he wanted one. Over the years, whenever she'd looked at photos of the Boston store, she had sensed a secondary emotion hovering behind the nostalgia and charm, but she could never give the feeling a name. Until tonight. Like a completed jigsaw, now that the pieces had fallen in place, she could recognize the emotion clear as day. It was longing.

Hope.

That was why James authorized the window displays every year, and why he kept the Boston store unchanged despite his insistence they focus on the future. The Boston store wasn't selling a greeting card fantasy to tourists. It represented *his* Christmas fantasy.

How on earth had she missed it? If anyone knew what it was like to hope on Christmas… She'd bet he didn't even realize what he was doing.

"You're staring," James said.

"Am I?" Lost in thought, she hadn't realized. "I didn't mean to stare. I was thinking how stubborn you are."

"Me, stubborn? Says the woman who refused to move a moose?"

"Elk, and that's different. Fryer is part of our great tradition. And at least I fought to protect something the town has had for years. You're going out of your way to avoid looking sensitive."

As expected, he rolled his eyes again. At least, there was a blush accompanying it this time. She was making progress. "You know," she said, sitting back in her chair. "There's nothing wrong in admitting a vulnerable side. Some people might even be impressed."

He laughed. "Some people being you."

"Maybe." She shrugged. Truthfully, she was already impressed. Probably too impressed, if she stopped to think about it.

She waited while he studied their hands, a smile playing on his lips. "I never should have told you I enjoy it when you challenge me," he said.

"Yeah, well, hindsight is always twenty-twenty," she teased before sobering. "What I'm trying to say—very badly, apparently—is that it's okay for you to let your guard down around me. That is, you don't have to feel awkward about showing…"

Thinking of all the ways he'd already opened up, she realized how foolish she sounded. Psychoanalyzing and advising him on his feelings. "Never mind. You don't need my encouragement."

Slipping her hand from his, she pushed her chair away from the table and started folding her napkin. "I wonder what time it is? We probably won't get back to Fryberg until after midnight."

"Once," James said.

"Once what?" She set her napkin on the table and waited. James hadn't moved. His eyes remained on the spot where their hands had been.

"You wanted to know how often I bought out restaurants to impress women. The answer is once." He lifted his eyes. "Tonight."

Holy cow.

His answer rolling around her brain, Noelle stood up and walked to the window where, a few blocks away, the lights of Rockefeller Center created a glowing white canyon amid the buildings. "I was pretty sure you were joking about the whole rich-and-trying-to-seduce-you thing, but at the same time, I thought for sure you'd done stuff like this before."

She heard his chair scraping against the wood floor. A moment later, her back warmed with his presence. "Stuff?"

"You know… Sweeping a girl off her feet. Making her feel like Cinderella at the ball."

"Nope," he replied, mimicking the way she'd said the word earlier. "Only you."

She pressed a hand to her stomach to keep the quivers from spreading. "What makes me so special? If you don't mind my asking."

Silence greeted her question. The warmth disappeared from behind her, and then James was by her side, leaning against the chair rail. "I've been trying to answer that same question for two days," he said, "and damned if I know. All I know is you've had me acting out of character since Thanksgiving.

"Damn disconcerting too," he added under his breath.

"Most men would have answered a little more romantically," she said.

"I thought you knew by now that I'm not most men. Besides, you wanted me to drop my guard and be honest."

"Yes, I did," she replied, and James did not disappoint. What she hadn't expected was how enticing his honesty would be. Romantic words could be laughed off or discounted, but truth? Truth went right to your heart. Noelle liked that he didn't know why. Liked that his behavior frustrated him. That made her feel more special than any word ever could.

Suddenly, James wasn't close enough.

She moved left until they stood face-to-face, hip to hip. "I can't explain why you get to me either."

There was heat in his eyes as he wrapped her in his arms. "Then we'll just have to be confused together."

CHAPTER TEN

"I KNOW WHAT'S topping my Christmas list this year."

Beneath Noelle's cheek, James's chest rumbled with his husky voice. She tucked herself tighter against his ribcage and let her fingertips ghost across his bare chest. "What's that?" she asked.

"A couple hundred more nights like this."

Sounded perfect. "You think Santa can fit them all in his sleigh?"

"He'll have to make them fit, because I won't settle for anything less. Wouldn't want to have to give him a bad online review. You know how he is about naughty and nice and all that."

"Sounds like someone gets silly when they're tired," she said, before planting a kiss on his skin. She liked silly. It was a side of him, she imagined, very few people got to see.

James rolled over and surrounded her in his embrace. They lay together like opposing spoons, with her head on his shoulder. "I'm not that tired," he said.

A yawn belied his words.

"All right, maybe a little. That was…"

"Amazing?" The word washed warm over her, causing her already boneless body to melt a little more.

"Mmm."

Noelle hadn't known. Sex with Kevin had been fine—she hadn't known anything else—but this… Her skin still hummed from being stroked. It was as if in touching her, James marked her inside and out, each caress and kiss seared into her skin like a brand.

The sensations went beyond physical though. She felt she'd woken from a long, unproductive sleep. When James sent her over the edge, he sent her to a place beyond her body. A place so high and bright, she swore she saw white. She'd wanted to float there forever.

And very nearly did.

James's fingers were tracing patterns along her arm. In her mind, she imagined them painting lines along her skin. To match the other marks he'd made.

"How about we fly to Boston in the morning, and lock ourselves in my apartment?" he suggested. "We can stay in bed until next year."

"We'd have to move though." Physical separation didn't seem possible at the moment. "Wouldn't it be easier to stay right here?"

"Nuh-uh. Boston's better." Sleep was turning his voice into a slur.

"Better than New York?"

"Better than anywhere. You'll see."

"I wouldn't say anywhere," she replied. "Fryberg's pretty special too, you know."

A soft snore stopped her from saying anything more.

So much for pillow talk. Shifting onto her elbow, Noelle used her new position to steal an uninterrupted look at the man beside her. Like she had on his first night in Fryberg, she marveled at James's beauty. The way all his features worked together to create the perfect face. Not perfect as in perfection, but perfect as in captivating. His cheekbones. His lashes. His parted lips. Leave it to him to make snoring seem attractive.

Awake, he looked older. There was a weight of the world behind his hazel eyes. When he slept, that weight faded, and hints of the boy he must have been leaked through. She would have liked to have known James as a boy. She would have told him he wasn't alone. She would have made him feel like he belonged, same way the Frybergs did her.

The Frybergs.

Her heart started to race. What had she done? She'd slept with another man. No, not slept with, *connected* with. What happened between her and James went beyond sex. Her entire love life with Kevin paled in comparison.

She felt awful just thinking the words. But they were the truth. She didn't feel guilty for sleeping with James; if anything, she felt guilty for enjoying the experience. She wanted to curl up in his arms and when James woke up, make love with him again. For crying out loud, she couldn't even use the word *sex*, because it was too inadequate a word.

"Damn you," she whispered. Why couldn't he remain the annoyingly dislikable boss she'd met on Wednesday morning? Why'd he have to get all romantic and vulnerable? Someone she could fall for?

If she hadn't fallen for him already.

She sat up, causing James's arm to slip away. He grumbled softly before rearranging himself, his head coming to rest on her hip while his arm wrapped around her thigh.

Reflexively, her fingers started combing his hair. The bump under his stitches was beginning to recede, she noticed. That was a good sign. She combed around the unruly patch where the hair and stitches met and tried to ignore the way her heart was expanding.

She *was* falling for him. Hard. And he was falling for

her—there was no way that tonight had been one-sided. No, they might be at the very beginning, but the emotions in this bed had the potential to become something very real and special. It was the last thing she'd expected, but there it was.

The air in the room was suddenly getting close. Her lungs wouldn't fill. She tried breathing in as hard as she could, but it was as if the air wouldn't flow past her lips.

Fresh air. That's what she needed. To clear her head so she could think.

Slipping out from beneath the covers, she padded toward the window only to find it couldn't open. Apparently New Yorkers didn't believe in throwing up the sash like they did in Fryberg. Very well, she'd risk a walk. A couple of moments of fumbling in the dark later, she was dressed and slipping out the door.

The brightness caught her off guard. She was used to seeing stars after midnight, not soft drink billboards and scrolling news feeds. After the soft lighting of their hotel room, the contrast hurt her eyes. Noelle leaned against the icy marble, and inhaled. The air was cold and sour smelling. A mixture of body odor and exhaust. A few blocks away, a trio of young women giggled their way toward her. They looked cold with their short jackets and exposed legs. Just looking at them made Noelle stuff her hands deeper into her pockets. If she were smart, she'd turn around and head back inside.

Back to James. No sooner did she think his name than her heart started racing again.

She was scared. She didn't want to be falling in love.

Was that what was happening? James certainly was someone she *could* love. Being with him these past two days, she'd felt like a different person. Not Kevin Fryberg's widow or the infamous Manger Baby, but like *herself*. For the first time that she could remember, she hadn't felt grateful for the attention. Maybe it was because they shared similar pasts, but when she was with James, she felt worthy. As though she was the gift.

She should be thrilled by the feeling. Why then was she standing panicked and shivering on a New York sidewalk?

"Like I would even be interested in the loser... Not that desperate... She's such a skank!" The female trio was crossing the street, talking simultaneously. They had their arms linked. Holding each other up, no doubt, since they swayed back and forth as they walked. A blonde on the far end looked to be swaying more than the others, and as they got closer, Noelle realized it was because she was bouncing to a song she was singing. Her movement caused the middle one to pitch forward and stumble.

"What are you looking at?" she slurred as they stumbled past.

Noelle blinked. "Nothing," she replied, but the trio had already passed on, the blonde turning the air blue as she heaved a string of crude obscenities in her direction. Half the words, Noelle had never heard a person actually say out loud. Feeling like she'd been punched, she tried to flatten herself farther against the building.

Something fuzzy brushed her ankle.

Oh, God, a rat! Noelle shrieked and jumped forward. City rats were rabid, weren't they? She whipped her head back and forth to see which direction the horrid creature went.

Except it wasn't a rat at all. It was a hand. A rattily gloved hand that had slipped free of a dark lump. In her distraction, she hadn't noticed the body rolled up tight against the building. The person moaned and rolled over to reveal a weathered dirty face partially covered by a winter hat. White eyes stared out at her in the darkness as he moaned again. Despite the late hour, there was enough light to see his lips moving. He was trying to tell her something.

Swallowing in nerves, she moved closer and crouched down so she could hear. As she did, she realized he was the source of the sour smell from earlier. Body odor and alcohol swamped her nostrils.

"Do you need something?" she asked, opening her pocketbook. She only had a few dollars on her, but if it would help…

The vulgar name he called her brought her up short.

Her head snapped back. "Wh-What?"

"You ain't takin' my vent. Get your own fraking spot. I ain't sharin' my heat with nobody."

The rant pushed her backward. Stumbling, she sat down hard. Tears sprang to her eyes from the impact, but she ignored them as she pushed herself to her feet. The homeless man was waving her off now as well, his voice growing loud and angry.

"I'm—I'm…sorry. I'm leaving right now." Dropping a handful of bills by his hand—which he snatched while continuing to swear at her—she scurried backward, afraid to turn around until she'd put a safe distance between them. She traveled no more than a yard or two when her foot slipped off the curb. A horn blared. A taxicab had stopped in the intersection.

"Hey, lady. Watch where you're going!"

Nodding, she hurried across the street, and didn't stop until she reached a sign indicating an all-night coffee shop. There was a waitress behind the counter playing with her phone. She looked up when Noelle entered, and pointed to an empty stool.

"Counter service only," she said, before going back to her phone.

Noelle took a seat between two bulky customers, both of whom glared at her desire for space. "Sorry," she heard herself murmur again.

"Coffee?" the waitress asked.

Not really, but Noelle was too shy to ask for anything else. "Yes, please," she replied.

The waitress slapped down a mug and a bowl of plastic creamers. Noelle shivered and wrapped her hands around the cup. Everything was so cold all of a sudden. Cold and angry. This was nothing like the New York James had shown her. But then, he'd gone out of his way to show her only the magical parts. What she was seeing now was the other New York, the part that dwelt beneath the twinkling lights and Christmas trees.

The realistic part, James would say. She'd been trying to keep this part of the world at bay since foster care.

What if falling in love with James was like that?

Sure, everything seemed wonderful now, but what if being with him was like New York and what looked beautiful at the beginning turned out to be filled with garish lights and cold, burnt coffee? It had happened before with Kevin. Hadn't she convinced herself he was the love of her life? What if she woke up one morning and discovered she'd made another mistake? Where would she be then? *Who* would she be then? She wouldn't be a Fryberg, not after betraying Kevin's memory, and they were the only family she'd ever had.

She'd be alone again. Back to the days when she was an outsider at the dinner table. Present but not truly belonging.

Manger Baby.

Suddenly, she felt very small and alone. Add in a few

schoolyard taunts and she'd be ten years old again. Lost
and longing for a family to call her own.

"You want anything else?" a voice asked.

Noelle looked up to find the waitress looking in her direction. *Yeah*, she thought, *I could use a hug.* "No thanks.
I'm good."

If she were home, Belinda would hug her. Like her son,
she hugged fiercely. When a Fryberg encircled you in their
arms, nothing in the world could harm you.

*You come visit us anytime you want, Noelle. Any friend
of Kevin's is a friend of ours.*

Tears sprang to her eyes as Noelle remembered that
wonderful first afternoon at Kevin's house. Had Mr. Low-
estein known what he was giving her when he assigned
Kevin as her lab partner? One step over the threshold and
she had the family she'd always wanted.

And now, Kevin and Ned were dead. Belinda was moving. The store had changed hands. Everything she cared
about and deemed important was slipping out of her fingers. If she lost Belinda's love along with everything else…

She couldn't lose it. She couldn't go back to being alone.
She needed…

Needed…

"I need to go home."

Her announcement fell on deaf ears, but it didn't matter. Noelle knew what she had to do. With any luck, James
would understand.

Slapping a five-dollar bill on the counter, she headed
outside.

James woke up to the sound of his cell phone buzzing. At
first he tried ignoring the noise by putting the pillow over
his head, but no sooner did the call stop, than the phone
started buzzing again.

"Whoever it is, they're fired," he groaned. Leaning over the side of the bed, he groped along the floor until he found his jacket and dug the phone from the breast pocket. The name on the call screen made his shoulders stiffen.

"It's the crack of dawn," he said. "Is something wrong?"

"It's early afternoon here," his father replied. "You're usually up this hour."

"I slept in." Sort of. Raising himself on his elbows, he looked to the other side of the bed, only to frown at the empty sheets. Noelle must have slipped into the bathroom. "Is everything all right?" he asked. "You don't usually call on Sunday mornings."

"Shouldn't I be asking you that question?" Jackson said in return. "Carli said there was an…" He cleared his throat. "An issue at the Fryberg store the other day."

How like Jackson to call his being struck in the head an "issue." "I had a minor accident is all," he said.

"So everything is all right there?"

"Everything is fine." He told his father he had the Fryberg deal under control. A bump on the head wouldn't change anything.

Jackson cleared his throat again. "I'm glad to hear it. Carli didn't have too many details so I wanted to make certain myself. When I had trouble connecting with you, I thought perhaps there had been a problem."

"No," James said. "No problems. I've just been very busy here, and with the time change and all…"

"Right. Right. I'm glad…things…are going smoothly." There was a pause on the other end of the line, like his father was reading something. Multitasking and distraction were par for the course with Jackson. "When do you think you'll be back in Boston?"

"I'm not sure." The irony of his answer made him smile.

Three days ago, he'd been champing at the bit to leave. "There are some...developments I want to look into."

"Developments?"

"Nothing problematic, I assure you."

On the contrary. If last night was any indication, he was on the cusp of something very significant. Noelle made him feel... He couldn't think of how to articulate his feelings. Special? Important? Neither word fit. How did he describe his heart suddenly feeling a hundred times larger?

"You'll keep me advised though, won't you? I want to know if there are any complications," his father said. "Doesn't matter if they are big or small. I'd prefer you not go silent again."

"Of course. I didn't mean to give you cause for concern."

"James, I'm always..." There was another pause. A longer one this time.

James couldn't help the way his breath caught. If he didn't know better, he'd say his father had been worried. "You're what?" he asked.

"I've decided to stop in Copenhagen before I head home."

"Oh." That wasn't what he was going to say. He looked down at the wrinkles on the sheets beneath him. Like tiny white rivers leading to Noelle's side.

Maybe it isn't all about business, she'd said. *You still have hope.*

What the hell. It was worth a try. "Hey, Dad?" The word felt odd on his tongue from lack of use. "Do you remember going into Boston to see the window displays?"

"I'm afraid you're going to have to be more specific. I examine the window displays every year."

"This was with me and Justin and…and Mom. Back when we were…" A family. "We went to see Santa Claus."

"I remember your mother hated those trips. She only went because Justin insisted. Why?"

So much for his wonderful family memory. "I was thinking about repeating one of the designs next year. Vintage is very trendy right now."

"But will it be in fashion next year, that's the question," his father replied. "Trends fall out of favor quickly these days."

As did memories. "It was just a thought."

"Well, you know my position on those displays. They outlived their expenditure long ago. I'll be back by the middle of the week. Why don't we connect then? Over dinner, perhaps."

"Okay," James said. With any luck he would have to cancel to take a certain sexy little elf sightseeing in Boston. "Have a safe trip."

"You too, James."

He let the phone drop to the floor. Stupid, his feeling kicked in the gut over one comment. Wasn't like his father was revealing some kind of family secret. At least Noelle wanted him. The way he felt with her trumped anything—everything—else. Simply thinking her name chased his dark thoughts away.

Damn, but he was falling hard for her.

He stretched his arm to pull her close, only to remember when he struck bare sheets that she was still in the bathroom. "You can come out of hiding! I'm off the phone," he called with a smile. It was sweet that she wanted to give him privacy.

When she didn't respond, he flipped over on his back. "Noelle? Babe? You okay?"

The bathroom door was wide open.

What the hell? Jumping from the bed, he rushed across the room and slapped on the bathroom light. The room was empty. He knew it would be empty. He'd just hoped…

That was the problem with hope. It always ended with a sucker punch.

Noelle was gone. While he'd been dreaming of waking up beside her, she'd gotten dressed and left.

Maybe she went to get coffee, a small, desperate voice in his head said. He angrily shoved the idea away before it could take hold. He didn't want to entertain possibilities, didn't want *hope*. His fingers squeezed the towel rod, his body trembling with the desire to rip it from the wall. He could still see the way she looked at him in the restaurant. Like she cared.

Dammit. He smashed a fist on the marble vanity, roaring through gritted teeth at the pain. Dammit, dammit, dammit! Why couldn't she have stayed a mildly attractive employee? No, she had to crawl under his skin and make him start to believe the damn greeting card was possible? He thought yesterday had been as mind-blowing for her as it had for him. He thought they were starting something here. He thought…

He thought she cared.

Joke was on him, wasn't it? Like he could compete with her dead war hero of a husband. For crying out loud, his own parents didn't want him; what made him think Noelle would?

If only she hadn't been so damn special.

Forget it. Taking a deep breath, James pushed the rage down as deep as possible. He tucked it away along with the crazy dream he'd had of sharing the holidays with Noelle.

Turned out, he'd been right all along. Things like family and holiday cheer, hope, love—they were pipe dreams.

Marketing concepts designed to manipulate emotions and sell products. They didn't really exist. At least not for him.

Lesson learned.

CHAPTER ELEVEN

IF NOELLE HEARD the guy on the sound system sing about Santa coming to town one more time, she was going to scream. The song, part of a continual loop in the store, had been playing for the past three days. Usually, she embraced Christmas carols, but she hadn't slept well since returning from New York, and the lack of sleep had left her with a throbbing knot at the back of her head. Like she'd been smacked in the head by a drone.

If only she could be so lucky. A smack to the head and temporary amnesia sounded pretty good about now. Anything would, if it meant whipping out Saturday's memories. She had her own continual loop of sounds and images tormenting her. Every night when she tried to sleep, they repeated in her head. James smiling. James propped on his elbows above her. James raining kisses on her skin. Over and over, the memories repeated until she ended up clutching a pillow to her aching insides while she waited for the clock to signal morning.

Not that daytime was all that much better. If she drove past the Christmas market, she thought of James. If she visited Santa's workshop, she thought of James. If she walked past her living room sofa…

For goodness' sake, they'd known each other four days!

Their relationship didn't warrant this kind of obsession. Yet, here she was obsessing.

Her guilty conscience didn't help. She should have gone back to the hotel and explained in person, but she'd been so freaked out by what she was feeling that she was halfway home before she'd thought things through. By then, embarrassment had kicked in, and the best she could do was a text reading *I'm sorry.* As far as regrets went, it was the stupidest, most immature thing she'd ever done.

Her gaze drifted to her telephone. It wasn't too late. She could still call and explain. What would she say? *Sorry I ran out on you, but I liked you so much I freaked?* While true, she doubted it would make a difference. When push came to shove, it was still only one night—one fantastical, mind-blowing, life-altering night—but one night all the same. And there was still the chance she'd read the situation wrong. After all, she was assuming he felt the same way. For all she knew, the way she felt after they'd made love was commonplace for James and his talk of showing her Boston was nothing more than pillow-talk promises. It had only been a few days, but he might have already moved on, and calling would simply make her look foolish.

A knock sounded on her door. Looking up, she saw Todd standing in the doorway. His arms were folded, and he wore a frown. "You okay?" he asked.

"Fine," she replied, pretending to shuffle some papers. "What can I do for you?"

"I was wondering if you've read the email from the Boston office yet."

Boston office meaning James. Her stomach did a little bounce. "No. What did it say?"

"Hammond sent a list of recommendations for how we can streamline operations and improve traffic flow in the store. Looks like he took a lot of mental notes during his tour last week. Pretty impressive for a guy with stitches in his head."

"Streamlining is his thing," she replied. Along with renting out restaurants and nipping at shoulders, she thought, fighting a blush.

Either she succeeded or Todd was too polite to say anything. "Some of his changes we won't be able to implement until after the holidays, but a few we can put in place now. Why don't you read the list and then you and I can talk?"

"Sure thing." Reaching for her mouse, she clicked on the email icon and brought up her inbox on the screen. "Has Belinda seen the list? What did she say?"

"Nothing. She officially stepped away from operations on Monday afternoon, remember?"

"Sorry. I forgot." This time, Noelle did blush.

"Totally understand," Todd replied. "It's going to take some getting used to, not thinking of her as being in charge."

Or being around, thought Noelle. The first thing her mother-in-law mentioned after Noelle's return on Sunday was that she planned to leave for Florida right after Christmas and not return until mid-April. So in the end, Noelle didn't have James or her family.

Todd cleared his throat. "You sure you're okay? You seem a little spacey."

"Sorry," she apologized again. "I was scanning the memo."

He nodded, even though the expression on his face said he didn't believe her for a second. "Soon as you've gone through it, come find me. I'm looking forward to hearing your thoughts. Especially about point number five."

Point number five, huh? She clicked open the email. Turned out, it wasn't from James after all, but rather a Carli Tynan. The suggestions were all James, however. She recognized the first two as ones he'd made during the tour. Quickly she scanned down to point five.

Remove the Elk statue from the rear of the store. In addition to taking up a large amount of space, the crowd that gathers around it impacts other shoppers' ability to maneuver in the aisles. Recommend statue be placed either outside on the grounds or in storage.

That rat! He'd promised Fryer would stay.

This was clearly revenge for her walking out. Completely unacceptable. It was one thing for him to be angry with her, but he had no business taking his anger out on a poor innocent elk. Fryer hadn't done a thing except uphold tradition.

Retrieving the Boston number from the bottom of the email, she picked up her phone and dialed.

"I want to talk to James Hammond," she snapped when the receptionist answered. There'd be plenty of time to regret her rudeness later. "Tell him Noelle Fryberg is on the phone, and that it's important."

Apparently, there was a part of her that didn't expect him to answer, because she nearly dropped the phone when James's voice drawled in her ear. "I'm in the middle of a meeting."

Nevertheless, he took her call. She might have taken that as a hopeful sign, if not for his chillingly business-like voice.

She got straight to the point. "Fryer," she said.

"Carli sent out the memo."

"She sent it out, all right. What are you doing removing Fryer? We agreed he was a popular attraction, and deserved to stay."

"I changed my mind," James replied. "I had some time to think on my flight alone back to Boston and decided it wasn't a good idea. There's enough chaos in that store without teenagers blocking the aisles and taking selfies."

"On Friday you called that chaos organized."

"My perspective changed."

Noelle didn't think she'd ever heard his voice so emotionless, not even on his first day in Fryberg. He sounded like the warmth had been sucked out of him and it was her fault.

She grew sick to her stomach. "I'm sorry about the other night."

"I know. I received your text."

She winced. "I know I shouldn't have run out the way I did."

"Forget it, Noelle. I already have."

"You—you have?" Of course he had. Hadn't he said at the restaurant that he was a rich man trying to seduce her? She was the one who'd gone and attached deeper meaning to his behavior. Maybe all the importance had been in her head. "But Fryer…"

"Business, Noelle. The store is a Hammond's property now. It seemed silly to wax nostalgic about the previous ownership." She could hear him shifting in his chair and pictured him sitting straight and stiff behind his desk. "Besides, I'm taking the chain in a different direction after the first of the year. Your elk clashes with the new brand."

"But we agreed," Noelle said. The protest came out a whine. Worst of all, it wasn't Fryer she cared about. It was the chill in his voice. So cold and detached. She wanted the voice that scorched her skin.

"Disappointment's part of life."

Ouch. Then again, what did she expect his attitude would be? Relief? He was angry, and Noelle deserved every ounce of wrath thrown her way.

"James—" *I'm sorry.*

Too late. He'd hung up.

Noelle let the receiver slip from her fingers. What had she done? Handled the whole situation like a child, that's what. One-night stand or not, James deserved a proper goodbye.

Everything was messed up.

"Argh!" Squeezing her eyes shut, she ground the heels of her palms into her lids. "What a freaking idiot."

"Little harsh, don't you think?" she heard Belinda ask. "I'm sure whoever you're talking about isn't that stupid."

The blurry image of her mother-in-law carrying a newspaper walked into the office. She was dressed in her off-duty clothes—jeans and a soft hand-knit sweater—and looked so much like the day they first met, that Noelle immediately jumped up and ran into her arms. Immediately, Belinda's arms went around her in a bear grip more comforting than she deserved. Noelle's shoulders started to shake.

"Whoa, what's this all about?" Belinda asked. "Are you crying?"

"I c-can't help it." Noelle gulped between sobs. The safer she felt, the more she cried.

"Come now, I'm sure it's not that bad."

Did she want to bet? Sniffing back her tears, Noelle let herself catch her breath before speaking. "Fryer's gone," she said, sniffing again. "The Boston office wants him put in storage." And it was all her fault because she'd been a childish coward.

"Don't tell me all these tears are because of a battered old elk," Belinda said.

She stepped back and looked Noelle in the eye. "I know you're fond of tradition, sweetheart, but he's only an old statue. I tried to convince Ned to get rid of him for years. Thing takes up way too much space on the floor."

Great. In addition to dashing out on James, she'd been protecting a tradition no one else wanted.

How fitting.

"Then I guess you've finally gotten your wish." Backing out of her mother-in-law's embrace, Noelle turned back to her desk. "If I'd known you didn't care, I wouldn't have put up a fight."

"Don't be silly," Belinda said. "Of course you would have. You'll fight for every tradition. It's who you are. But something tells me all these tears aren't for our soon-to-be-departed mascot. Something's been bothering you all week."

"That obvious, is it?"

"Thirty seconds ago you were sobbing on my sweater. A billboard would be less obvious. What's wrong?"

Where to start? "It's complicated."

"Is it my retiring? I know my leaving for Florida is happening quickly."

"The business is only part of the problem," Noelle replied.

"I see." She wore Kevin's same skeptical expression as she folded her arms. "What's the other part?"

Shame burned in Noelle's stomach. Thinking her mistakes were bad enough, but speaking them aloud?

"I messed up," she said. "I did something really, really stupid."

"Oh, sweetheart." The older woman stepped up and rested a hand on Noelle's shoulder. "I'm sure you're exaggerating. Todd would have told me if it was super serious."

"Todd doesn't know, and worse, it's too late to fix things."

"You don't know that, sweetheart. Nothing is so horrible it can't be repaired."

"Not this time," Noelle replied, turning around. Taking a deep breath, she relayed what had happened in New York.

"Well," Belinda said when she finished, "that explains why James mysteriously cancelled our Monday meeting *and* why you were acting so strangely when you came by the house on Sunday afternoon. Why on earth would you run off and leave him like that?"

"Because I freaked out." She rubbed her forehead, the pain from the back of her head having decided to relocate there. "The way he made me feel. The emotions. They were too overwhelming. I've never felt like that before."

"Not even with Kevin?"

Noelle froze. Here she thought she couldn't mess up any further. "Kevin was… That is, I loved Kevin…"

"It's all right," Belinda said. "I know what you meant."

"Y-you do?"

"You and Kevin were practically babies when you started dating. Only natural the grown-up you would feel things a little differently.

"Maybe…" Her mother-in-law's smile was indulgent as she cupped Noelle's cheek. "Maybe even a little stronger."

How did she earn such a wonderful person in her life?

"You have to know, I loved Kevin," Noelle replied. "I wanted to spend the rest of my life with him." Who knows how things would have worked out between them if he'd returned? They'd already had a strong foundation. Passion might have blossomed eventually as well.

"No matter what, he'll always own a big piece of my heart."

Belinda smiled down at her. "I know, sweetheart. Now, the question is—does James Hammond own any of that heart? Are you in love with him?"

Was she? Noelle shook her head. "We've only known each other four days." Far too soon to fall head over heels.

"But…" She thought about how her heart felt fuller when he walked into a room.

"But you could see yourself falling in love with him someday," Belinda finished for her.

"Yes." Very much so, Noelle thought as she looked to the ground. She had the sinking feeling she was halfway in love now. Not that it mattered given her foolish behavior. "I'm sorry."

"Don't be ridiculous," Belinda replied. She forced Noelle to look up. "You never have to apologize for falling in love with someone else."

"But Kevin…"

"Kevin would want you to move on. So would Ned and I. You're much too young to spend your life alone."

Right, because Belinda was leaving. The reminder she would soon be alone in Fryberg only made the hollow feeling in Noelle's chest grow larger. "What if I'm wrong?" she asked. "What if James isn't as awesome as I think?"

"Then you try again," Belinda told her. "Relationships don't come with guarantees. Some work. Some don't."

"Yeah, but if I choose him, and we don't make it, then I'll be alone again." Her eyes had lost the battle and teared up again. One dripped down her cheek onto Belinda's fingers. "You're the only family I've ever had. I don't know what I'd do without you."

"My goodness, is that what you're scared of? Losing your family?"

She didn't see how she could move on and keep them. "I'm only family because I married Kevin. If I move on, I won't belong anymore."

"What are you talking about? Of course you'll belong. Don't you realize that with Kevin gone, I need you more than ever?"

Before she could say another word, Noelle found herself

back in Belinda's embrace. Her mother-in-law squeezed her tight. "You, Noelle Fryberg, have always been more than Kevin's wife," she said. "I love you like a daughter, and that's never going to change, whether you fall in love with James Hammond or a hundred different men. Family is forever, and you..."

She kissed Noelle's forehead. "You are my family. Got that?"

Noelle tried to keep her jaw from trembling as she nodded. What a fool she was. So busy being grateful for Belinda and Ned's affections, she couldn't see that when it came to Belinda, family wasn't an either-or proposition. Her heart was large enough to accommodate everyone. Take Thanksgiving and the mishmash of characters who joined every year. Todd, Jake from the mail room, Nadifa from sales. None of them blood related and yet all of them embraced like they were.

When she thought about it, Belinda had pulled Noelle into that welcoming web the day Kevin brought her home. She didn't inherit a family *because* she dated Kevin; dating Kevin was an added bonus. Chances are she would have been enfolded into the Thanksgiving Day group regardless. After all, the only qualification was being alone at the holidays.

"Your family was—is—the greatest gift I could ever ask for," she told Belinda. "Being a Fryberg was a dream come true. It was all I ever wanted."

By now Belinda's eyes were shining too. "Oh, sweetheart, you're my dream come true too. Don't get me wrong, I loved Kevin, but I always wanted a daughter to keep the family traditions alive."

Offering a smile, the older woman bent down and kissed Noelle on the forehead. "I never imagined I'd end up with a daughter who's more Fryberg than anyone with actual Fryberg blood."

They both laughed. "Does that mean I can still have Grandma Fryberg's recipe book?" Noelle asked, wiping her eyes.

"Absolutely. I'll even laminate the pages so you can pass the book along to your daughter.

"And you will have a daughter. Or daughter-in-law," Belinda added. Her smile faded and once again, her expression grew serious. "There's a whole world out there beyond this store and our family name. I fully expect you to build a happy life beyond Fryberg's. You deserve one."

"But I wouldn't have a life without Fryberg's," Noelle replied. Breaking out of her mother-in-law's grasp, she reached for the box of tissues on her desk. Her eyes and nose were runny with tears. "I can't imagine anything else."

"Really? Then why are you crying over James Hammond?"

All right, maybe Noelle could imagine a little more. The other night, in James's arms, she'd imagined all types of future. "Doesn't matter whether I'm crying over him or not," she said, blowing her nose. "He and I are finished."

"Are you certain?"

"Man said so himself."

Forget it, Noelle. I already have.

She blew her nose. "You should have heard his voice, Belinda." Remembering sent a chill down her spine. "I called him to discuss his email, and I might as well have been talking to a stranger."

A feeling of hopelessness washed over her. "I thought... That is, the whole reason I freaked out was because I thought we had some kind of special connection. Now I wonder if maybe I wasn't simply confusing good sex with affection and blew the weekend out of proportion."

Thankfully, Belinda chose to let the good sex comment slide. Hearing her thoughts out loud, however, made Noelle even more certain she was right, and had let the romanticism of Saturday night get the best of her. "Other than being angry with the way I took off, I wonder if James has even given me a second thought."

"I'm sure he has. He didn't strike me as someone who took…those kinds of encounters…lightly."

"Me either," Noelle replied. "He certainly sounded businesslike enough today though. Talking about the company's new direction and all."

"New direction?"

"Uh-huh. Based on the points in his email, I'd say he's back to focusing on streamlining and internet sales." She could see it now. Today Fryer. Tomorrow the Christmas Castle.

"Hmm."

Noelle frowned. "What?"

"I'm not sure," Belinda replied. "Did you see today's business headlines?"

"No."

"I think you should. There's something very interesting in it." Her mother-in-law retrieved the newspaper she'd dropped on the desk during their talk. It was folded in thirds, to highlight the headline on the weekly marketing column. Noelle's heart sank as she read.

Hammond's to discontinue iconic window displays.

The article below quoted James as saying he wanted to take the chain in a "new direction" and build a store for the next generation.

"'It's time Hammond's let go of the past,'" she read. "'We can't bring the past back, no matter how badly we may want to.'" It was a harsh-sounding quote, one she imagined marketing hadn't wanted to use.

"When I read the article this morning, something didn't hit me as right. Still doesn't, although I can't put my finger on what."

Noelle stared at the headline.

All week she'd been downplaying Saturday night to ease the giant ache in her chest, but her efforts hadn't worked. There were too many reminders in the Christmas music and lights. She wanted the holiday to go away so she could breathe again. She who held Christmas in her heart fifty-two weeks a year.

But ending the window displays? They represented the one decent family memory he had. It was why he kept them going year after year, regardless of the cost. Because there was a part of him, the ghost of that little boy, that wanted to believe family meant something. That he meant something to his family. Before his mother's midnight departure convinced him otherwise.

No. Noelle's heart seized. Dropping the newspaper, she stumbled toward a chair. The room had become a tunnel, a narrow dark tube with black all around.

"Are you all right?" she heard Belinda ask from far away. "Is something wrong? What is it?"

No. Yes. Everything. The answers flew through her head as her realization became clear.

She'd disappeared in the middle of the night without a word just like his mother. He'd spent the day revealing himself, at her urging, and she'd let her cowardice trample that vulnerability. In doing so, she solidified all of James's fears.

That was why he was closing the window displays. Not because he wanted to take the chain in a new direction—though he would and do so brilliantly—but because that little boy no longer believed in his own memory. James had retreated, quit, waved the white flag in defeat.

He had given up hope, and it was her fault.

It wasn't right. Someone needed to tell him he had too much sweetness and light inside him to hide behind profits and modern retail. Someone had to show him he was special.

Lovable.

Not someone. Her. Noelle needed to fix the horrible wrong she had done to him. And not by text or by phone either. In person.

"I need to go to Boston," she told Belinda. "As soon as possible."

She may have thrown away her chance to be with him, but Noelle would be damned if she cost him Christmas.

"Why are you still wearing your coat?" Jackson asked, as he slipped into his seat. As usual, he was dressed impeccably in a suit from his London tailor.

"I'm cold," James replied. "This table picks up a draft from the front door."

He and his father were meeting for a business lunch in the bistro across from Hammond's. Outside, Copley Square bustled with Christmas shoppers, many of who stopped to watch the Hammond's displays. In fact, there was a crowd of preschoolers clumped in front of them that very moment, watching the elves make mischief in Santa's kitchen. Why they were standing out in such blasted cold was beyond him. A shiver passed through him, and he looked away.

"If you're uncomfortable, we can move," Jackson said.

"That won't be necessary. I'll warm up soon enough." He hoped. He'd been chilled to the bone for days. At home, he'd cranked both his gas fireplace and the thermostat, and slept with an extra comforter. It was going to be a long winter, at this rate.

Maybe if he found someone to warm him up? He dismissed the idea as quickly as it appeared. Female company didn't appeal to him right now.

Meanwhile, for some reason, his father refused to let the subject drop. After the waiter took their orders, he laid his napkin on his lap and leaned forward. "Are you sure it's temperature-related and not something to do with the 'issue' you had in Fryberg?"

"I'm sure." Other than a minor case of temporary insanity, his "issue" had been side-effect-free. "A cup of hot coffee and I'll be fine."

Jackson stared at him for a beat or two. "If you say so," he said finally, before reaching for his water glass. "I saw the article in the *Business Journal* today about the window displays. I have to say I didn't think you would ever agree to eliminate them."

"What can I say? Even I couldn't ignore the numbers."

"I'm glad you finally came around. Although it would have been nice if you'd alerted me to your decision. I realize you handle these kinds of day-to-day operations, but..."

"You were in Copenhagen," James interrupted. "And I wanted to make the announcement early enough to take advantage of the entire Christmas season. I didn't mean to blindside you."

"*Surprise* is a better word."

James returned his father's flat smile and sipped his coffee. "Marketing tells me we're getting quite a bit of local press attention from the announcement. This could turn into a public relations bonus for us."

"That reminds me," Jackson said, "you need to talk to whoever wrote the press release. They should have drafted a less caustic quote."

James had written the quote himself. Molly, their communications assistant, had clearly wanted something else, but she hadn't argued.

Noelle would have. He suppressed a shiver. "Actually, I thought the quote went straight to the point."

"'We can't bring the past back, no matter how badly we may want to'?" Jackson quoted. "I would have preferred something a little less cynical."

"Why? It's true, isn't it?"

"Yes, but we're not in the business of selling truth, James—we sell toys."

"Don't worry. I've no intention of letting sales slide." Amazing how unaffected he was about the whole thing. Not too long ago, he would have argued the window displays brought in customers. But when he'd visited the store on Sunday afternoon and saw this year's intricate displays, he'd suddenly thought *Why bother?* All that money spent and what did it matter?

"The rest of the chain does quite well without window displays," James said, reaching for his coffee again. "Boston will too. A month from now, people won't remember what the display looked like."

"I could have told you that," Jackson replied.

The waiter arrived with their food. While he waited for the man to serve his soup, James let his eyes travel back to the crowd across the street. The preschoolers had been joined by several mothers with strollers. For a moment, he thought he saw a red-and-white knit hat mixed in the crowd and his pulse stuttered. His eyes were playing tricks on him. He hadn't thought about Noelle since he left New York—prolonged thought anyway—and he wasn't about to start.

Although yesterday's phone call nearly killed him. When the receptionist said her name, a tearing sensation had gripped his chest. The first intense feeling he'd had in days, it nearly knocked him to his knees. Then there was the way she'd lowered her voice to apologize. It took all his reserves, but thankfully he kept himself from breaking and asking why she left. No need to hear her excuse. He already knew.

The sound of his father clearing his throat drew back his attention.

"Are you certain you feel all right?" Jackson asked. "Perhaps you should see a specialist."

"I'm *fine*," he insisted.

"You say you're all right, but you're clearly not acting like yourself. You're difficult to reach. You're making sudden changes in company policy."

James let out a long sigh. "So this is about my not discussing the announcement with you beforehand." He knew this sudden interest in his health had to mean something.

"This has nothing to do with the announcement," Jackson said, killing that theory immediately. "I'm simply concerned about you."

"Why? You've never been before." The words came flying out before James realized what he was saying. They landed between them, causing his father to sit back, his features frozen in shock.

"You don't think I care?" Jackson said. He actually sounded stung.

What did he do now?

Aww, heck. Might as well put this bit of the past to rest too. "I'm not making an accusation," James said, holding up a hand. "I understand that you were stuck with me when Mom left and that put you in an awkward position."

His father stared at him. A long look similar to the ones he'd given James as a teenager. And like then, James had to fight the urge to tug at his collar.

Finally, Jackson put down his fork. "Are you suggesting that I was unhappy when your mother left you behind?"

Wasn't he? "I remember the look on your face when I came downstairs that morning and you definitely weren't expecting to see me. If anything," he added, looking down at his chowder, "you looked disappointed."

"That's because I was," Jackson replied. "For you." He let out a sigh. "Your mother was a very unpredictable woman. Doing one thing one day, and something else the next. She insisted that I encouraged your analytical side to spite her, and that I didn't understand what it took to raise a child. I had no idea she'd left you behind until you came downstairs that morning.

"She was right," he said, smoothing a wrinkle from the tablecloth. "I was completely unprepared."

Silence filled the table while his father paused to sip his water and James struggled for what to say next. It was true; his mother had been high-strung. Hence the flying crystal. He remembered preferring the quiet of his father's study to being around her whirling dervish personality.

"I'm not..." Jackson took another drink. "I'm not a naturally affectionate person. Your mother complained all the time that I was too detached. Too stiff. It's how I am. Looking back, I can see how an impressionable teenager might misconstrue my behavior.

"I can assure you, though," he added, "that at no time did I ever consider myself 'stuck' with you."

Slowly stirring his soup, James digested his father's confession. So he had been wanted after all. As far as family reconciliations went, the moment wouldn't win any prizes, but he got a tightness in his chest nonetheless. "Thank you," he said. "I appreciate you telling me."

For the first time in James's life, Jackson Hammond looked bashful. "You're welcome. Son."

By unspoken agreement, they spent the rest of the luncheon discussing business, a far more comfortable subject. When they were finished, Jackson suggested they meet for lunch again the next week. "Or you could come by for dinner," he offered.

"Sure," James replied. If his father could try, then so could he. "Dinner would be great."

Jackson responded with the most awkward shoulder pat in history. Still it was a start.

Not that he would ever say so, but his father had terrible timing. Short as it was, their heart-to-heart killed the numbness he'd so carefully cultivated when Noelle left. Granted, he'd been cold, but with one or two exceptions, he'd been able to function without thinking about what a fool he'd been.

But then, Jackson decided to pat his shoulder, and the first thought that popped into his head was *Noelle was right*. Suddenly, the entire weekend was replaying in his head.

Telling his father he had an errand, James hung back on the sidewalk as Jackson entered the building. He needed to clear his head of the frustration his father's apology had unleashed. It felt like a giant fist shoving upward in his chest. If he didn't push it back down, he was liable to scream out loud.

Why was he letting one tiny woman get to him so badly?

Dammit! He'd had one-night stands before. Some of them even told him to go to hell after they discovered they were nothing more than one-night stands. None of those experiences had ever turned into an existential crisis. His weekend with Noelle shouldn't have either, late-night escape or otherwise. Yet here he was, making long overdue peace with his father and wishing it was Noelle reaching out to him instead.

He never should have let her past his defenses. From the start, he knew nothing *real* could happen between them. Relationships didn't happen on his end of the bell curve. But then she'd hugged him, shifting around his insides and allowing things like hope and longing to rise to the surface. She'd made him believe their night together went deeper than sex. He hadn't just taken her in his arms; he'd shared his soul with her. Every touch, every kiss was his way of expressing the feelings she unlocked in him. Fool that he was, he'd actually started believing in Hammond's marketing pitch.

And now, thanks to his father's apology, those feelings threatened to return, this time to mock him. He didn't want to feel. He didn't want to hope anymore.

From here on in, it was about business. Profit and efficiency.

"Ooh, look, Andre! There's a monkey swinging in the lights. Do you see him?"

Lost in his thoughts, James didn't realize he'd joined the crowd in front of the window displays. Next to him, a young mother in a leather jacket stood holding a toddler. She had a second baby, bundled in pink bunting in a stroller beside her.

The woman pointed a manicured finger toward the window. "Look at him," she said. "He's trying to steal Santa's cookies."

The toddler, Andre presumably, had a frown on his pudgy puce-colored face. "Bad monkey," he said. "No cookies."

"You don't think he should take the cookies?" the mother asked, laughing as the toddler shook his head.

"Someone's taken the naughty list concept to heart," James caught himself saying.

"Let's hope he feels that way when he's ten," she replied. "You ready to see the next window, Dre?"

Watching the trio walk away, a pang struck James in the midsection as he realized Dre and his little sister wouldn't see the displays next year. Oh, well, at their age, they wouldn't even realize the loss. Most kids wouldn't. It was just James holding on to the memory.

Did his brother ever think about the window displays? Last time he saw Justin... When was the last time he'd seen him? The boat races maybe? Jackson had said something about his brother going to business school out west somewhere. James didn't even know what college his brother had attended. Or where he did his undergrad, for that matter. Like mother, like son, Justin had had little to do with them once he left. He'd apparently built quite a nice Hammond-free life and wasn't looking back.

James needed to do the same. It helped that at least Jackson had confessed he wasn't completely unwanted.

Just unwanted by his mother.

And by Noelle. Out of the corner of his eye, he saw another flash of red and white, causing the frustration to rise anew.

Four more weeks. Come January first, Christmas would be done, they would pack away the decorations, and he would be rid of any and all reminders of Fryberg. No more thoughts of blue eyes or snow-dotted lashes.

In the meantime, James had a business to run. The numbers at their Cape Cod store were especially troublesome and needed to be addressed.

Feeling his control return, he marched into the store.

His renewed focus lasted until he reached the top floor.

There, he barely managed to round the corner to his office when a red-and-white cap stopped him in his tracks.

So much for blaming his imagination.

Noelle rose from her seat. "I need to talk with you," she said.

CHAPTER TWELVE

SHE LOOKED...BEAUTIFUL. The image of her lying in his arms flashed before him, and his body moved to take her in his arms. Catching himself, James clasped his hands behind his back.

"If you're here about that blasted elk there's nothing more to talk about," he said.

"I'm not here about Fryer," she said.

"Good. Then we have even less to talk about. If you'll excuse me..."

He tried to brush past her and head into his office, but she stepped in front of him. A five-foot-two roadblock. "I read about you canceling the window displays."

"And let me guess, you're worried how the new direction will affect your Christmas Castle." Why else would she fly halfway across the country instead of emailing? All roads led to Fryberg, didn't they?

"You could have saved yourself the airfare. Our plans for the castle haven't changed. Your family business will live to bring another year of Christmas cheer."

Again, he moved to his office and again, she blocked his path. "I'm not here about the castle either."

"Then why are you here?" he asked. It was taking all his effort to keep his voice crisp and businesslike. What he wanted was to growl through clenched teeth.

"Because I owe you an apology."

Seriously? James ignored how her answer made his heart give a little jump. Not again, he reminded himself. No more being fooled into believing emotions existed when they didn't.

"You wasted your airfare. I told you on the phone, the matter has already been forgotten."

This time, he managed to pass her and reach his office door.

"I know what you're doing." Noelle's voice rang through the waiting area.

Don't take the bait. Don't turn around.

"Is that so?" he replied, turning. "And what is that, exactly?"

"You're trying to kill Christmas."

Someone dropped a stapler. Out of the corner of his eye he saw his administrative assistant picking up several sheets of paper from the floor.

"You're being ridiculous." He couldn't kill Christmas if he tried. Damn holiday insisted on existing whether he wanted it to or not.

"Am I? I know what those displays meant to you. How much you loved them…"

His assistant dropped her stapler again.

He closed his eyes. "Noelle, this is neither the time nor the place for us to have this conversation."

"Fine," she replied. "When and where would you like to have it?"

"How about nowhere and never?"

"Nice try, but I flew across five states to talk to you so I can say what I have to say now or I can say it later, but I'm not leaving until I speak my piece."

He expected her to fold her arms after her speech, but instead, she looked up at him through her lashes, and added, "Please?" Her plea totally threw him a curveball. No way he could resist those cornflower eyes.

"Fine. We'll talk." Opening his office door, he motioned for her to step in first. "But take off that hat." No way was he rehashing Saturday night with her looking adorable.

Unfortunately, she looked more adorable with tousled hat hair. He went back to clasping his hands to keep from combing his fingers through it.

Nodding to one of the chairs, he walked around to the other side of his desk and sat down figuring a three-foot cherrywood barrier would keep him from doing something stupid.

"Okay, you've got the floor," he said. "What was so important that you had to fly all the way to Boston to say?"

"Aren't you going to take off your coat?"

"No. I'm cold." Although that status was rapidly changing, thanks to his heart rate. It had started racing the second he saw her. "Now what is it you wanted?"

"Why are you closing down the window displays?"

"Because they're a financial drain on the company."

"Funny how you didn't think so before," she replied coming toward the desk.

"Well, I saw them with a new perspective. I realized we were spending a lot of money trying to sell a concept that no longer resonated." Was she coming around to his side of the desk? "My decision shouldn't be a surprise," he said. "My feelings about this kind of kitschy Christmas marketing were hardly a secret."

She stopped at the desk corner. "You didn't think them so kitschy on Saturday night when you told me about the polar bear."

"That's because I was trying to charm you into bed. And it worked. At least for a little while," he added. If she was going to stand so close, he was going to wield sarcasm.

God, but he wished she'd back away. It was easier to be furious with her when he couldn't smell orange blossoms.

"It was wrong of me to run out like that," she said. "It was stupid and childish."

The earnestness in her eyes left him aching. With his hands gripping the chair arm, he pushed himself closer to the desk. "Congratulations. We agree."

He didn't have to look to know his words hit their mark. "I don't suppose you'd let me explain," she said.

"Would it make any difference?"

"Maybe. No. I don't know."

"Thank you for summarizing everything so clearly." He didn't want to hear any more. Didn't want her orange blossom scent interfering with his anger. "I think you should go," he told her.

Noelle twisted her hat in her hands. This wasn't going at all the way she'd envisioned. Seeing him again reminded her how intimidating a presence he could have when he wanted. It also reminded her how much vulnerability there was beneath the surface. Icy as he sounded, she could see the flashes of pain in his eyes. She wanted to hug him and tell him how amazingly special he was. Only he wouldn't believe her. Not until she cleared the air.

Which was why she stood her ground. She came to explain and make amends for hurting him, and she would.

"I freaked out," she told him. "Saturday was…it felt like a fairy tale with me as Cinderella. You had me feeling all these emotions and suddenly they were too much. I felt scared and guilty and so many things. I needed to get some air."

"All the way back in Michigan? What, New York air not good enough?"

She deserved that. "At first, I only meant to stand outside for a little bit, maybe get a cup of coffee. But then there was this homeless man and these women and… It doesn't matter. Bottom line is, I got scared and ran home where I knew I'd be safe."

"I would have thought you'd find me safe, considering."

"You were. You made me feel incredibly safe. That was part of what freaked me out."

"How reassuring," James replied.

Yeah, listening to what she was saying, Noelle wouldn't buy it either. "I made a mistake," she said.

"No kidding." He shoved the chair away from his desk, causing her to jump. "I told you things I've never shared with anyone," he said, as he stood up. "I opened up to you—and you were the one who pushed me."

Shame at her behavior welled up inside her. "I know," she replied.

"You made me think…" The rest of his sentence died when he ran his hand over his face. "I should have known. When I saw that mantel full of photos, I should have known I couldn't compete with Kevin."

"What?" No, he had it all wrong. "That's not true."

"Noelle, listen to yourself. Thirty seconds ago, you said you felt guilty."

"Yes, but not because of my feelings for Kevin. I felt guilty because I realized Kevin couldn't measure up to you."

Confusion marked his features. "What?"

Noelle took a deep breath. After all his openness, he deserved to know her deepest secret. "Kevin was a special person," she said. "Every girl in school wanted to date him, so I couldn't believe how lucky I was that he wanted to be with me. Being Kevin Fryberg's girl was the best thing that ever happened to me. Being part of the Frybergs was the biggest dream come true."

"So you've told me," James replied.

"But what I didn't tell you was that Kevin was…he was like the big, wonderful brother I never had."

The confusion deepened. "I don't understand."

"That's the reason I felt so guilty," Noelle said, moving to look out the window herself. "I loved Kevin. I loved our life together, especially when his parents were around. But we never had that phase where we couldn't keep our hands off each other, and I just figured that was because we'd been together for so long. It wasn't until shortly after the wedding that I realized I didn't love him the way a wife should. But by that time, we were committed."

Her fingers ran along the blinds lining the window. "And I had the family I'd always wanted. If he and I ended… So I stuck it out, figuring I'd eventually fall more in love with him. Then Kevin deployed."

And then he died, leaving her the widow of the town hero and forced to keep pretending lest she hurt her surrogate family. She turned so she could study James with her damp gaze. "I didn't know," she whispered.

"Know what?"

"What it felt like to be truly attracted to someone. To have this continual ache in the pit of your stomach because you desperately want them to touch you. Until this past weekend. You made me feel out of control and off-balance and it scared the hell out of me."

"You could have told me," he said. "I would have understood."

"How was I supposed to tell you I could see myself falling for you, when it was those feelings that terrified me?" she replied. "Don't you get it? I was afraid my feelings would blow up in my face and cost me the only family I've ever known."

She waited, watched, while her confession settled over

him. After a moment, he ran his hand over his face again and sighed. "If it frightened you, why are you telling me now?"

"Because you deserved to know," she replied. "And because I've realized that family isn't an either-or proposition. Nor is it about being related. It's about love, pure and simple. So long as you have love, you have family."

Risking his rejection, she walked toward him. When she got close enough, she took his hand. "And maybe all that greeting card stuff you despise is a myth, but Christmas can still be wonderful if you're with someone special. Please don't close off the part of you that believes that too."

But James only looked down at their hands. Noelle could take a hint. Foolish of her to think an apology would change much. At least she'd tried. "Anyway, that's what I came to tell you. That you're on the lovable side of the bell curve, and that I wish I hadn't messed up, because there's nothing I would like more than to have been your someone special this Christmas."

"Are you still scared?"

A spark lit in her heart. There was hope in his voice. He was trying to fight it, but it was there. "Terrified," she replied.

His grip tightened around her fingers. "Me too." Slowly, he lifted his gaze and she saw brightness sparkling in his eyes. "I've never had anyone think I'm special before," he told her.

"I've never been anyone's princess," she told him back. "So maybe…"

She held her breath and waited.

"Be a shame for you not to see Boston since you flew all the way here," he said.

A hundred-pound weight lifted from her shoulders. She

felt like she had the day she met the Frybergs, times ten. "What about my flight home?"

Letting go of her hand, James wrapped an arm around her waist and leaned in until their foreheads touched. "Don't worry," he said. "I know a pilot."

EPILOGUE

Three weeks later

FOR THE LIFE of him, James was never going to get used to those nutcrackers. They were the stuff kids' nightmares were made of. Whistling to himself, he passed under them and headed for the conductor's shack.

"Good afternoon, Ed," he greeted. "How's the train business?"

The conductor blanched. "M-M-Mr. Hammond. We weren't expecting you today. I'm afraid the castle closed early."

"Are you telling me everyone has gone home?" James asked in his sternest voice. "It's only two o'clock."

"Well, it...it is Christmas Eve..."

"James Hammond, stop scaring the employees." Noelle came bouncing out of the conductor's shack wearing a Santa Claus hat and carrying a gold-and-white gift bag. Like it always did when he saw her, James's breath caught in his throat.

"Don't mind him, Ed," she said. "He's not nearly as Grinchy as he'd like people to believe." Rising on tiptoes, she flung her arms around his neck and kissed him soundly. Completely confirming her charge, James kissed her back with equal enthusiasm. Her gift bag crinkled as she wrapped her arms tighter.

"Merry Christmas," she said, smiling. "Nice sweater. You look very festive." He was wearing a red-and-white reindeer jumper purchased at the hotel on his last visit a few days before. One of the advantages of having his own plane was that it made long-distance relationships a lot easier.

"So do you," he replied. "Careful though. If Santa finds out you stole his hat, he'll put you on the naughty list."

"Then we'd better not tell him." Giving him one more kiss, she untangled herself and held out the gift bag. "This is for you. Merry Christmas Eve."

James fingered the red polka-dotted tissue paper peering out from the top of the bag. He might as well have been five again, for the thrill that passed through him.

No, he corrected, a five-year-old wouldn't get this choked up over a simple gift bag. "I thought we agreed to wait and exchange presents tomorrow night when we were alone."

Back in Boston, there was a stack of boxes with Noelle's name on them. More than necessary, probably, but he hadn't been able to help himself. Finally, he understood the joy that came from giving to the people for whom you cared.

"I know," she replied. "This is more of a pre-Christmas present."

Meaning she'd cared enough in return to shop for him. His throat constricted a little more. As far as he was concerned, he already had the best Christmas present in the world standing in front of him.

Her hand came down to rest on his forearm. Shaking off his thoughts, he focused on her shimmering blue gaze instead. "Consider it a small thank-you for asking me if

I'd help with next year's window displays," she said. "A very small thank-you. I'm poor from all my Christmas shopping."

"You didn't have to buy anything. Asking for your assistance was a no-brainer. No one is better suited to work on our chain-wide window display extravaganza than you, my little elf." It was true. Hammond's "new direction" involved rolling out Boston's iconic displays on a nationwide basis. The new displays would be more modern and inclusive to reflect the current consumer public, and focus on the message that Christmas was a time for spreading love and goodwill. James was excited for the new project, and for Noelle's involvement since she'd be making frequent trips to Boston. He didn't want to get too ahead of himself, but if things went well he hoped Noelle might someday consider spending even more time in Boston.

Seemed hope had become a habit for him these days.

"Aren't you going to open it?" Noelle asked.

"What?" The gift. He pretended to study the bag. "Considering the size, I'll go out on a limb and say you didn't buy me a drone."

Noelle stuck out her tongue. "Ha-ha-ha. You should be sending that drone a thank-you present. If you hadn't stood in the way, we might never have gotten past the dislike stage."

"True enough."

He shook the bag, only to hear the useless rustling of paper. "It's one of those stuffed Fryer collectibles, isn't it?" After he and Noelle made up, they'd compromised— sort of. Fryer was to be given one last season and then retired with an official ceremony after the first of the year.

"How about you stop guessing and open the package?" Noelle replied. "And don't forget to read the note. It's important."

James did as he was told and discovered a bag full of gingerbread cookies. Two dozen of them.

"I baked them last night," Noelle told him. "In case we get hungry on the way to Belinda's," she said. "Or on the flight tomorrow." They were spending Christmas Eve with Noelle's mother-in-law before flying to Boston for Christmas dinner.

"If you look," she said, "I gave them all little business suits."

Sure enough, she had. "So you can literally bite my head off?"

"Or lick your tummy."

"Sweetheart, you don't need a cookie to do that."

She slapped his arm, and he laughed. Like hope, laughter had also become a regular part of his life.

Funny how quickly things changed. A month ago he'd been utterly alone, and convinced he liked life that way. Now, for the first time in years, he was having a true family Christmas. He was making tentative strides with his father, and with the reappearance of his brother within the family business, it even looked like he and Justin might regain some of the bond they'd lost.

His brother had undergone his own collection of changes this past month. As a result, the two of them had discovered the Hammond family dysfunction had left a mark on both of them. Fortunately, they—and their father—were getting a second chance.

At the end of the day, though, the only person he really needed in his life was the woman in front of him. How right she'd been that day in his office when she said Christmas was wonderful when you had someone special.

And she was special. No longer were the two of them standing on the cusp of something extraordinary; they were over-their-heads deep in the middle. And with each passing day, he fell a little deeper. As soon as the timing was right, he planned to let Noelle know he'd fallen in love with her.

"The note," Noelle said prodding him.

Pretending to roll his eyes at her eagerness, he fished out the folded piece of paper. "For our first Christmas together. Made with all my love."

Damn, if he couldn't feel his heart bursting through his chest. "All your love?" he asked.

"Every ounce," she told him. "I love you, James Hammond."

Never had five words filled him with such hope and happiness. They were Christmas, Easter and every holiday in between. "I love you too," he said, pulling her close.

It was going to be a perfect Christmas.

* * * * *

OUT NOW!

3 BOOKS IN ONE

Ami WEAVER

Janice MAYNARD

Yvonne LINDSAY

CHRISTMAS NIGHTS with the Ex

Available at
millsandboon.co.uk

MILLS & BOON

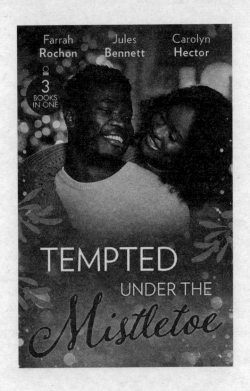

OUT NOW!

Available at
millsandboon.co.uk

LET'S TALK
Romance

For exclusive extracts, competitions and special offers, find us online:

f MillsandBoon

𝕏 @MillsandBoon

◉ @MillsandBoonUK

♪ @MillsandBoonUK

Get in touch on 01413 063 232